Living Nightmare

Others were emerging from the darkened burrows that ringed the chamber—slouched figures only dimly glimpsed and vaguely human. And a figure in a tattered cloak came toward him from the shadow—stretched out a claw-like hand to seize his wrist and draw him toward the sacrificial table . . .

ENTER, IF YOU DARE . . .

. . . the shadowy domain of today's top horror talents. Robert Bloch. Karl Edward Wagner. Fritz Leiber. Ramsey Campbell. Dennis Etchison. And more masters of the macabre. They will show you the dark heart of naked fear—and deliver you unto sleepless nights of dread. So come along. Enter the world of . . .

WHISPERS

WHISPERS

EDITED BY
STUART DAVID SCHIFF

A JOVE BOOK

This Jove book contains the complete
text of the original hardcover edition.
It has been completely reset in a typeface
designed for easy reading and was printed
from new film.

WHISPERS

A Jove Book / published by arrangement with
Doubleday & Company, Inc.

PRINTING HISTORY
Doubleday edition published 1977
Jove / HBJ edition / February 1979
Jove edition / February 1987

ISBN: 0-515-08881-1

Jove Books are published by The Berkley Publishing Group,
200 Madison Avenue, New York, NY 10016.
The words ''A JOVE BOOK'' and the ''J'' with sunburst
are trademarks belonging to Jove Publications, Inc.

PRINTED IN THE UNITED STATES OF AMERICA

For my Parents, who nurtured my love for the weird and fantastic, and my wife Susan, who puts up with it

ACKNOWLEDGMENTS

"STICKS," copyright © 1974 by Stuart David Schiff for *Whispers* #3, reprinted by permission of the author.

"THE BARROW TROLL," copyright © 1975 by Stuart David Schiff for *Whispers* #8, reprinted by permission of the author.

"THE GLOVE," copyright © 1975 by Stuart David Schiff for *Whispers* #6–7, reprinted by permission of the author.

"DARK WINNER," copyright © 1976 by Stuart David Schiff for *Whispers* #9, reprinted by permission of the author.

"LADIES IN WAITING," copyright © 1975 by Stuart David Schiff for *Whispers* #6–7, reprinted by permission of the author.

"GRADUATION," copyright © 1977 by Stuart David Schiff for *Whispers* #10–11, reprinted by permission of the author.

"MIRROR, MIRROR," appears here for the first time, copyright © 1977 by Ray Russell.

"THE HOUSE OF CTHULHU," copyright © 1973 by Stuart David Schiff for *Whispers* #1, reprinted by permission of the author's agent, Kirby McCauley.

"A WEATHER REPORT FROM THE TOP OF THE STAIRS," copyright © 1973 by Stuart David Schiff for *Whispers* #2, reprinted by permission of the authors.

"THE INGLORIOUS RISE OF THE CATSMEAT MAN," copyright © 1971 by Sphere Books, copyright © 1974 by Stuart David Schiff for *Whispers* #4, reprinted by permission of the author.

"LE MIROIR," copyright © 1977 by Stuart David Schiff for *Whispers* #10–11, reprinted by permission of the author's American agent, Kirby McCauley.

"THE WILLOW PLATFORM," copyright © 1973 by Stuart David Schiff for *Whispers* #1, reprinted by permission of the author's agent, Kirby McCauley.

"GOAT," copyright © 1971 by Sphere Books, copyright © 1975 by Stuart David Schiff for *Whispers* #8, reprinted by permission of the author.

CONTENTS

INTRODUCTION   xiii
  Stuart David Schiff

STICKS   1
  Karl Edward Wagner

THE BARROW TROLL   24
  David Drake

THE GLOVE   36
  Fritz Leiber

THE CLOSER OF THE WAY   49
  Robert Bloch

DARK WINNER   62
  William F. Nolan

LADIES IN WAITING   70
  Hugh B. Cave

WHITE MOON RISING   80
  Dennis Etchison

GRADUATION 97
　　Richard Christian Matheson

MIRROR, MIRROR 112
　　Ray Russell

THE HOUSE OF CTHULHU 117
　　Brian Lumley

ANTIQUITIES 130
　　John Crowley

A WEATHER REPORT FROM THE 139
　　TOP OF THE STAIRS
　　James Sallis and David Lundē

THE SCALLION STONE 147
　　Basil A. Smith

THE INGLORIOUS RISE OF THE 165
　　CATSMEAT MAN
　　Robin Smyth

THE PAWNSHOP 173
　　Charles E. Fritch

LE MIROIR 181
　　Robert Aickman

THE WILLOW PLATFORM 191
　　Joseph Payne Brennan

THE DAKWA 208
　　Manly Wade Wellman

GOAT   224
David Campton

THE CHIMNEY   236
Ramsey Campbell

INTRODUCTION

This anthology is both a best of my *Whispers* magazine *and* an original anthology. I welcome the opportunity to place between covers the choicest tales that *Whispers* has produced and, additionally, create another *new* outlet for fantasy and horror material. This was my reason for concocting my journal in the first place, and I have succeeded far beyond the dreams any little magazine editor is entitled to have.

People refer to me as the editor of *Whispers* magazine, but I like to think of myself as an alchemist, selecting from my unwholesome stores the proper ingredients to conjure up an irresistible volume of fantasy, terror, and horror. *Whispers* is a true little magazine, dedicated to the task of stimulating new and quality additions to the art and literature of our genre. I would like to think that the World Fantasy Award I recently won told me the recipe for the publication has borne fruit. It seemed quite appropriate that the trophy signifying that achievement was a bust of Howard Phillips Lovecraft whose story "The Unnameable" created a fictitious horror magazine titled *Whispers,* an entity I magicked to unholy life. But even an alchemist must start from somewhere and early 1973 saw my witches' brew begin to bubble . . .

Whispers began with the premise that the fantasy and horror field lacked adequate outlets to induce talented writers and artists to make efforts toward the field. I came to the conclusion that offering money for material was the best way to draw qualified people's attention to the genre and, thankfully, this spell was the proper one. By the time the first issue of the magazine appeared in July 1973, I had purchased original material by Brian Lumley, Joseph Payne Brennan,

L. Sprague de Camp, Henry Hasse, Tim Kirk, Steve Fabian, Lee Brown Coye, and others, all of them noted talents who had created *new* gems for the field. *Whispers* was off to a great start.

Just as scary, though, as the terrors and horrors in the tales I published, were the incredible logistics of editing, publishing, and distributing a little magazine. Until one is actually forced to do it, it is difficult to comprehend the entire process of producing a "simple" magazine; it includes soliciting material, evaluating submissions, perfect typing for offset reproduction, paste-up, composition, proofreading, and the very careful packing of the irreplaceable manuscript for shipment to the printer. When that is accomplished, your immediate problem is selling the journal. There are many long hours of producing ads, addressing envelopes for direct mailings, and trying to sell your magazine to the seemingly uninterested dealers. When these tasks are accomplished and the magazine arrives back from the printer, it is time to mail out everything and perform all the physical tasks that entails. When I exhaustedly finished the first issue of *Whispers,* I paused briefly to rest, but then realized I was already behind on the next issue and began anew. Since that time, a dozen issues of *Whispers* have seen print, and I have yet to pause again.

While the magazine is basically a one-man operation, the eventual brew is the result of the efforts and talents of many people. Above all others, Dave Drake towers high. His professional expertise as a writer has made him invaluable as my assistant editor. Without his aid, the magazine just would not be as good. Other major ingredients in the *Whispers* concoction include: Don Grant, Lee Brown Coye, Willis Conover, Tim Kirk, Karl Edward Wagner, Fritz Leiber, Steve Fabian, Kirby McCauley, Manly Wade Wellman, and Dave Sutton. And let us not forget Dave Hartwell, Gahan Wilson, Jim Pitts, Alan Hunter, Hugh B. Cave, Robert Bloch, Henry Hasse, David Campton, John Linton, Charles Collins, Jon Lellenberg, William Nolan, Vincent Di Fate, and Frank Utpatel. All of these gentlemen made vital contributions to the magazine that were above and beyond their duty as a contributor or supporter. I would like to personally thank them all for adding their individual spells to the *Whispers* magic. They certainly made this alchemist's job an easier one.

Stuart David Schiff

Of all the fiction that has appeared in Whispers, *I am most proud of Karl Edward Wagner's ''Sticks,'' which took a real-life experience of artist Lee Brown Coye and created from it a most exceptional tale. The British Fantasy Society awarded it an August Derleth Award for 1974 as the best short fiction of that year. Karl is also known as today's best writer of heroic fantasy, his four (at last count) volumes relating the adventures of his Kane plus his excellent continuation of Robert E. Howard's Bran Mak Morn saga bear this out. He is also editor of Carcosa, a small press that won a World Fantasy Award in 1976 for its* Worse Things Waiting *(by Manly Wade Wellman) and* Far Lands, Other Days *(by E. Hoffmann Price). In his spare time Karl is a licensed physician taking a residency in psychiatry.*

STICKS

by Karl Edward Wagner

1

The lashed together framework of sticks jutted from a small cairn alongside the stream. Colin Leverett studied it in perplexment—half a dozen odd lengths of branch, wired to-

1

gether at cross angles for no fathomable purpose. It reminded him unpleasantly of some bizarre crucifix, and he wondered what might lie beneath the cairn.

It was the spring of 1942—the kind of day to make the War seem distant and unreal, although the draft notice waited on his desk. In a few days Leverett would lock his rural studio, wonder if he would see it again—be able to use its pens and brushes and carving tools when he did return. It was goodby to the woods and streams of upstate New York, too. No fly rods, no tramps through the countryside in Hitler's Europe. No point in putting off fishing that troutstream he had driven past once, exploring back roads of the Otselic Valley.

Mann Brook—so it was marked on the old Geological Survey map—ran southeast of DeRuyter. The unfrequented country road crossed over a stone bridge old before the first horseless carriage, but Leverett's Ford eased across and onto the shoulder. Taking fly rod and tackle, he included pocket flask and tied an iron skillet to his belt. He'd work his way downstream a few miles. By afternoon he'd lunch on fresh trout, maybe some bullfrog legs.

It was a fine clear stream, though difficult to fish as dense bushes hung out from the bank, broken with stretches of open water hard to work without being seen. But the trout rose boldly to his fly, and Leverett was in fine spirits.

From the bridge the valley along Mann Brook began as fairly open pasture, but half a mile downstream the land had fallen into disuse and was thick with second growth evergreens and scrub-apple trees. Another mile, and the scrub merged with dense forest, which continued unbroken. The land here, he had learned, had been taken over by the state many years back.

As Leverett followed the stream he noted the remains of an old railroad embankment. No vestige of tracks or ties—only the embankment itself, overgrown with large trees. The artist rejoiced in the beautiful dry-wall culverts spanning the stream as it wound through the valley. To his mind it seemed eerie, this forgotten railroad running straight and true through virtual wilderness.

He could imagine an old wood-burner with its conical stack, steaming along through the valley dragging two or three wooden coaches. It must be a branch of the old Oswego Midland Rail Road, he decided, abandoned rather suddenly in the 1870s. Leverett, who had a memory for detail, knew of it from a story his grandfather told of riding the line in 1871 from Otselic to DeRuyter on his honeymoon. The engine had so labored up the steep grade over Crumb Hill that he got off to walk alongside. Probably that sharp grade was the reason for the line's abandonment.

When he came across a scrap of board nailed to several sticks set into a stone wall, his darkest thought was that it might read "No Trespassing." Curiously, though the board was weathered featureless, the nails seemed quite new. Leverett scarcely gave it much thought, until a short distance beyond he came upon another such contrivance. And another.

Now he scratched at the day's stubble on his long jaw. This didn't make sense. A prank? But on whom? A child's game? No, the arrangement was far too sophisticated. As an artist, Leverett appreciated the craftsmanship of the work—the calculated angles and lengths, the designed intricacy of the maddeningly inexplicable devices. There was something distinctly uncomfortable about their effect.

Leverett reminded himself that he had come here to fish and continued downstream. But as he worked around a thicket he again stopped in puzzlement.

Here was a small open space with more of the stick lattices and an arrangement of flat stones laid out on the ground. The stones—likely taken from one of the many dry-wall culverts—made a pattern maybe twenty by fifteen feet, that at first glance resembled a ground plan for a house. Intrigued, Leverett quickly saw that this was not so. If the ground plan for anything, it would have to be for a small maze.

The bizarre lattice structures were all around. Sticks from trees and bits of board nailed together in fantastic array. They defied description; no two seemed alike. Some were only one or two sticks lashed together in parallel or at angles. Others were worked into complicated lattices of dozens of sticks and boards. One could have been a child's tree house—it was built in three planes, but was so abstract and useless that it could be nothing more than an insane conglomeration of sticks and wire. Sometimes the contrivances were stuck in a pile of stones or a wall, maybe thrust into the railroad embankment or nailed to a tree.

It should have been ridiculous. It wasn't. Instead it seemed somehow sinister—these utterly inexplicable, meticulously con-

structed stick lattices spread through a wilderness where only
a tree-grown embankment or a forgotten stone wall gave
evidence that man had ever passed through. Leverett forgot
about trout and frog legs, instead dug into his pockets for a
notebook and stub of pencil. Busily he began to sketch the
more intricate structures. Perhaps someone could explain them;
perhaps there was something to their insane complexity that
warranted closer study for his own work.

Leverett was roughly two miles from the bridge when he
came upon the ruins of a house. It was an unlovely colonial
farmhouse, box-shaped and gambrel-roofed, fast falling into
the ground. Windows were dark and empty; the chimneys on
either end looked ready to topple. Rafters showed through
open spaces in the roof, and the weathered boards of the walls
had in places rotted away to reveal hewn timber beams. The
foundation was stone and disproportionately massive. From
the size of the unmortared stone blocks, its builder had intended the foundation to stand forever.

The house was nearly swallowed up by undergrowth and
rampant lilac bushes, but Leverett could distinguish what had
been a lawn with imposing shade trees. Farther back were
gnarled and sickly apple trees and an overgrown garden where
a few lost flowers still bloomed—wan and serpentine from
years in the wild. The stick lattices were everywhere—the
lawn, the trees, even the house were covered with the uncanny structures. They reminded Leverett of a hundred misshapen spider webs—grouped so closely together as to almost
ensnare the entire house and clearing. Wondering, he sketched
page on page of them, as he cautiously approached the abandoned house.

He wasn't certain just what he expected to find inside. The
aspect of the farmhouse was frankly menacing, standing as it
did in gloomy desolation where the forest had devoured the
works of man—where the only sign that man had been here in
this century were these insanely wrought latticeworks of sticks
and board. Some might have turned back at this point. Leverett,
whose fascination for the macabre was evident in his art,
instead was intrigued. He drew a rough sketch of the farmhouse and the grounds, overrun with the enigmatic devices,
with thickets of hedges and distorted flowers. He regretted
that it might be years before he could capture the eeriness of
this place on scratchboard or canvas.

The door was off its hinges, and Leverett gingerly stepped within, hoping that the flooring remained sound enough to bear even his sparse frame. The afternoon sun pierced the empty windows, mottling the decaying floorboards with great blotches of light. Dust drifted in the sunlight. The house was empty—stripped of furnishings other than indistinct tangles of rubble mounded over with decay and the drifted leaves of many seasons.

Someone had been here, and recently. Someone who had literally covered the mildewed walls with diagrams of the mysterious lattice structures. The drawings were applied directly to the walls, crisscrossing the rotting wallpaper and crumbling plaster in bold black lines. Some of vertiginous complexity covered an entire wall like a mad mural. Others were small, only a few crossed lines, and reminded Leverett of cuneiform glyphics.

His pencil hurried over the pages of his notebook. Leverett noted with fascination that a number of the drawings were recognizable as schematics of lattices he had earlier sketched. Was this then the planning room for the madman or educated idiot who had built these structures? The gouges etched by the charcoal into the soft plaster appeared fresh—done days or months ago, perhaps.

A darkened doorway opened into the cellar. Were there drawings there as well? And what else? Leverett wondered if he should dare it. Except for streamers of light that crept through cracks in the flooring, the cellar was in darkness.

"Hello?" he called. "Anyone here?" It didn't seem silly just then. These stick lattices hardly seemed the work of a rational mind. Leverett wasn't enthusiastic with the prospect of encountering such a person in this dark cellar. It occurred to him that virtually anything might transpire here, and no one in the world of 1942 would ever know.

And that in itself was too great a fascination for one of Leverett's temperament. Carefully he started down the cellar stairs. They were stone and thus solid, but treacherous with moss and debris.

The cellar was enormous—even more so in the darkness. Leverett reached the foot of the steps and paused for his eyes to adjust to the damp gloom. An earlier impression recurred to him. The cellar was too big for the house. Had another dwelling stood here originally—perhaps destroyed and rebuilt by one of lesser fortune? He examined the stonework. Here were great blocks of gneiss that might support a castle. On closer look they reminded him of a fortress—for the dry-wall technique was startlingly Mycenaean.

Like the house above, the cellar appeared to be empty, although without light Leverett could not be certain what the shadows hid. There seemed to be darker areas of shadow along sections of the foundation wall, suggesting openings to chambers beyond. Leverett began to feel uneasy in spite of himself.

There was something here—a large table-like bulk in the center of the cellar. Where a few ghosts of sunlight drifted down to touch its edges, it seemed to be of stone. Cautiously he crossed the stone paving to where it loomed—waist-high, maybe eight feet long and less wide. A roughly shaped slab of gneiss, he judged, and supported by pillars of unmortared stone. In the darkness he could only get a vague conception of the object. He ran his hand along the slab. It seemed to have a groove along its edge.

His groping fingers encountered fabric, something cold and leathery and yielding. Mildewed harness, he guessed in distaste.

Something closed on his wrist, set icy nails into his flesh.

Leverett screamed and lunged away with frantic strength. He was held fast, but the object on the stone slab pulled upward.

A sickly beam of sunlight came down to touch one end of the slab. It was enough. As Leverett struggled backward and the thing that held him heaved up from the stone table, its face passed through the beam of light.

It was a lich's face—desiccated flesh tight over its skull. Filthy strands of hair were matted over its scalp, tattered lips were drawn away from broken yellowed teeth, and, sunken in their sockets, eyes that should be dead were bright with hideous life.

Leverett screamed again, desperate with fear. His free hand clawed the iron skillet tied to his belt. Ripping it loose, he smashed at the nightmarish face with all his strength.

For one frozen instant of horror the sunlight let him see the skillet crush through the mould-eaten forehead like an axe-cleaving the dry flesh and brittle bone. The grip on his wrist failed. The cadaverous face fell away, and the sight of its caved-in forehead and unblinking eyes from between which thick blood had begun to ooze would awaken Leverett from nightmare on countless nights.

But now Leverett tore free and fled. And when his aching legs faltered as he plunged headlong through the scrub-growth, he was spurred to desperate energy by the memory of the footsteps that had stumbled up the cellar stairs behind him.

2

When Colin Leverett returned from the War, his friends marked him a changed man. He had aged. There were streaks of gray in his hair; his springy step had slowed. The athletic leanness of his body had withered to an unhealthy gauntness. There were indelible lines to his face, and his eyes were haunted.

More disturbing was an alteration of temperament. A mordant cynicism had eroded his earlier air of whimsical asceticism. His fascination with the macabre had assumed a darker mood, a morbid obsession that his old acquaintances found disquieting. But it had been that kind of a war, especially for those who had fought through the Apennines.

Leverett might have told them otherwise, had he cared to discuss his nightmarish experience on Mann Brook. But Leverett kept his own counsel, and when he grimly recalled that creature he had struggled with in the abandoned cellar, he usually convinced himself it had only been a derelict—a crazy hermit whose appearance had been distorted by the poor light and his own imagination. Nor had his blow more than glanced off the man's forehead, he reasoned, since the other had recovered quickly enough to give chase. It was best not to dwell upon such matters, and this rational explanation helped restore sanity when he awoke from nightmares of that face.

Thus Colin Leverett returned to his studio, and once more plied his pens and brushes and carving knives. The pulp magazines, where fans had acclaimed his work before the War, welcomed him back with long lists of assignments. There were commissions from galleries and collectors, unfinished sculptures and wooden models. Leverett busied himself.

There were problems now. *Short Stories* returned a cover painting as "too grotesque." The publishers of a new anthology of horror stories sent back a pair of his interior drawings—

"too gruesome, especially the rotted, bloated faces of those hanged men." A customer returned a silver figurine, complaining that the martyred saint was too thoroughly martyred. Even *Weird Tales,* after heralding his return to its ghoul-haunted pages, began returning illustrations they considered "too strong, even for our readers."

Leverett tried half-heartedly to tone things down, found the results vapid and uninspired. Eventually the assignments stopped trickling in. Leverett, becoming more the recluse as years went by, dismissed the pulp days from his mind. Working quietly in his isolated studio, he found a living doing occasional commissioned pieces of gallery work, from time to time selling a painting or sculpture to major museums. Critics had much praise for his bizarre abstract sculptures.

3

The War was twenty-five years history when Colin Leverett received a letter from a good friend of the pulp days—Prescott Brandon, now editor-publisher of Gothic House, a small press that specialized in books of the weird-fantasy genre. Despite a lapse in correspondence of many years, Brandon's letter began in his typical direct style:

"The Eyrie/Salem, Mass./Aug. 2
To the Macabre Hermit of the Midlands:
Colin, I'm putting together a deluxe 3-volume collection of H. Kenneth Allard's horror stories. I well recall that Kent's stories were personal favorites of yours. How about shambling forth from retirement and illustrating these for me? Will need 2-color jackets and a dozen line interiors each. Would hope that you can startle fandom with some especially ghastly drawings for these—something different from the hackneyed skulls and bats and werewolves carting off half-dressed ladies.
Interested? I'll send you the materials and details, and you can have a free hand. Let us hear—Scotty"

Leverett was delighted. He felt some nostalgia for the pulp days, and he had always admired Allard's genius in transforming visions of cosmic horror into convincing prose. He wrote Brandon an enthusiastic reply.

He spent hours rereading the stories for inclusion, making notes and preliminary sketches. No squeamish sub-editors to offend here; Scotty meant what he said. Leverett bent to his task with maniacal relish.

Something different, Scotty had asked. A free hand. Leverett studied his pencil sketches critically. The figures seemed headed in the right direction, but the drawings needed something more—something that would inject the mood of sinister evil that pervaded Allard's work. Grinning skulls and leathery bats? Trite. Allard demanded more.

The idea had inexorably taken hold of him. Perhaps because Allard's tales evoked that same sense of horror; perhaps because Allard's visions of crumbling Yankee farmhouses and their depraved secrets so reminded him of that spring afternoon at Mann Brook . . .

Although he had refused to look at it since the day he had staggered in, half-dead from terror and exhaustion, Leverett perfectly recalled where he had flung his notebook. He retrieved it from the back of a seldom used file, thumbed through the wrinkled pages thoughtfully. These hasty sketches reawakened the sense of foreboding evil, the charnel horror of that day. Studying the bizarre lattice patterns, it seemed impossible to Leverett that others would not share his feeling of horror that the stick structures evoked in him.

He began to sketch bits of stick latticework into his pencil roughs. The sneering faces of Allard's degenerate creatures took on an added shadow of menace. Leverett nodded, pleased with the effect.

4

Some months afterward a letter from Brandon informed Leverett that he had received the last of the Allard drawings and was enormously pleased with the work. Brandon added a postscript:

"For God's sake Colin—*What is it* with these insane sticks you've got poking up everywhere in the illos! The damn things get really creepy after awhile. How on earth did you get onto this?"

Leverett supposed he owed Brandon some explanation.
Dutifully he wrote a lengthy letter, setting down the circumstances of his experience at Mann Brook—omitting only
the horror that had seized his wrist in the cellar. Let Brandon
think him eccentric, but not madman and murderer.

Brandon's reply was immediate:

Colin—Your account of the Mann Brook episode is
fascinating—and incredible! It reads like the start of one
of Allard's stories! I have taken the liberty of forwarding
your letter to Alexander Stefroi in Pelham. Dr. Stefroi is
an earnest scholar of this region's history—as you may
already know. I'm certain your account will interest
him, and he may have some light to shed on the uncanny
affair.

Expect 1st volume, *Voices from the Shadow*, to be
ready from the binder next month. The proofs looked
great. Best—Scotty"

The following week brought a letter postmarked Pelham,
Massachusetts:

"A mutual friend, Prescott Brandon, forwarded your
fascinating account of discovering curious sticks and
stone artifacts on an abandoned farm in upstate New
York. I found this most intriguing, and wonder if you
recall further details? Can you relocate the exact site
after 30 years? If possible, I'd like to examine the
foundations this spring, as they call to mind similar
megalithic sites of this region. Several of us are interested in locating what we believe are remains of megalithic construction dating back to the Bronze Age, and to
determine their possible use in rituals of black magic in
colonial days.

Present archeological evidence indicates that ca.
1700–2000 BC there was an influx of Bronze Age peo-
ples into the Northeast from Europe. We know that the
Bronze Age saw the rise of an extremely advanced
culture, and that as seafarers they were to have no peers
until the Vikings. Remains of a megalithic culture origi-
nating in the Mediterranean can be seen in the Lion Gate
in Mycenae, in the Stonehenge, and in dolmens, passage

graves and barrow mounds throughout Europe. Moreover, this seems to have represented far more than a style of architecture peculiar to the era. Rather, it appears to have been a religious cult whose adherents worshipped a sort of earth-mother, served her with fertility rituals and sacrifices, and believed that immortality of the soul could be secured through interment in megalithic tombs.

That this culture came to America cannot be doubted from the hundreds of megalithic remnants found—and now recognized—in our region. The most important site to date is Mystery Hill in N.H., comprising a great many walls and dolmens of megalithic construction— most notably the Y Cavern barrow mound and the Sacrificial Table (see postcard). Less spectacular megalithic sites include the group of cairns and carved stones at Mineral Mt., subterranean chambers with stone passageways such as at Petersham and Shutesbury, and uncounted shaped megaliths and buried "monk's cells" throughout this region.

Of further interest, these sites seem to have retained their mystic aura for the early colonials, and numerous megalithic sites show evidence of having been used for sinister purposes by colonial sorcerers and alchemists. This became particularly true after the witchcraft persecutions drove many practitioners into the western wilderness—explaining why upstate New York and western Mass. have seen the emergence of so many cultist groups in later years.

Of particular interest here is Shadrach Ireland's "Brethren of the New Light," who believed that the world was soon to be destroyed by sinister "Powers from Outside" and that they, the elect, would then attain physical immortality. The elect who died beforehand were to have their bodies preserved on tables of stone until the "Old Ones" came forth to return them to life. We have definitely linked the megalithic sites at Shutesbury to later unwholesome practices of the New Light cult. They were absorbed in 1781 by Mother Ann Lee's Shakers, and Ireland's putrescent corpse was hauled from the stone table in his cellar and buried.

Thus I think it probable that your farmhouse may have

figured in similar hidden practices. At Mystery Hill a
farmhouse was built in 1826 that incorporated one dol-
men in its foundations. The house burned down ca.
1848–55, and there were some unsavory local stories as
to what took place there. My guess is that your farmhouse had been built over or incorporated a similar
megalithic site—and that your "sticks" indicate some
unknown cult still survived there. I can recall certain
vague references to lattice devices figuring in secret
ceremonies, but can pin-point nothing definite. Possibly
they represent a development of occult symbols to be
used in certain conjurations, but this is just a guess. I
suggest you consult Waite's *Ceremonial Magic* or such
to see if you can recognize similar magical symbols.

Hope this is of some use to you. Please let me hear
back.

Sincerely, Alexander Stefroi"

There was a postcard enclosed—a photograph of a 4½-ton
granite slab, ringed by a deep groove with a spout, identified
as the Sacrificial Table at Mystery Hill. On the back Stefroi
had written:

"You must have found something similar to this.
They are not rare—we have one in Pelham removed
from a site now beneath Quabbin Reservoir. They were
used for sacrifice—animal and human—and the groove
is to channel blood into a bowl, presumably."

Leverett dropped the card and shuddered. Stefroi's letter
reawakened the old horror, and he wished now he had let the
matter lie forgotten in his files. Of course, it couldn't be
forgotten—even after thirty years.

He wrote Stefroi a careful letter, thanking him for his
information and adding a few minor details to his account.
This spring, he promised, wondering if he would keep that
promise, he would try to relocate the farmhouse on Mann
Brook.

5

Spring was late that year, and it was not until early June that Colin Leverett found time to return to Mann Brook. On the surface, very little had changed in three decades. The ancient stone bridge yet stood, nor had the country lane been paved. Leverett wondered whether anyone had driven past since his terror-sped flight.

He found the old railroad grade easily as he started downstream. Thirty years, he told himself—but the chill inside him only tightened. The going was far more difficult than before. The day was unbearably hot and humid. Wading through the rank underbrush raised clouds of black flies that savagely bit him.

Evidently the stream had seen severe flooding in the past years, judging from piled logs and debris that blocked his path. Stretches were scooped out to barren rocks and gravel. Elsewhere gigantic barriers of uprooted trees and debris looked like ancient and mouldering fortifications. As he worked his way down the valley, he realized that his search would yield nothing. So intense had been the force of the long ago flood that even the course of the stream had changed. Many of the drywall culverts no longer spanned the brook, but sat lost and alone far back from its present banks. Others had been knocked flat and swept away, or were buried beneath tons of rotting logs.

At one point Leverett found remnants of an apple orchard groping through weeds and bushes. He thought that the house must be close by, but here the flooding had been particularly severe, and evidently even those ponderous stone foundations had been toppled over and buried beneath debris.

Leverett finally turned back to his car. His step was lighter.

A few weeks later he received a response from Stefroi to his reported failure:

"Forgive my tardy reply to your letter of 13 June. I have recently been pursuing inquiries which may, I hope, lead to the discovery of a previously unreported megalithic site of major significance. Naturally I am disappointed that no traces remained of the Mann Brook site. While I tried not to get my hopes up, it did seem likely that the foundations would have survived. In searching through regional data, I note that there were particularly severe flashfloods in the Otselic area in July 1942 and again in May 1946. Very probably your old farmhouse with its enigmatic devices was utterly destroyed not very long after your discovery of the site. This is weird and wild country, and doubtless there is much we shall never know.

I write this with a profound sense of personal loss over the death two nights ago of Prescott Brandon. This was a severe blow to me—as I am sure it was to you and to all who knew him. I only hope the police will catch the vicious killers who did this senseless act—evidently thieves surprised while ransacking his office. Police believe the killers were high on drugs from the mindless brutality of their crime.

I had just received a copy of the third Allard volume, *Unhallowed Places*. A superbly designed book, and this tragedy becomes all the more insuperable with the realization that Scotty will give the world no more such treasures. In Sorrow, Alexander Stefroi''

Leverett stared at the letter in shock. He had not received news of Brandon's death—had only a few days before opened a parcel from the publisher containing a first copy of *Unhallowed Places*. A line in Brandon's last letter recurred to him—a line that seemed amusing to him at the time:

"Your sticks have bewildered a good many fans, Colin, and I've worn out a ribbon answering inquiries. One fellow in particular—a Major George Leonard—has pressed me for details, and I'm afraid that I told him too much. He has written several times for your address, but knowing how you value your privacy I told him simply to permit me to forward any correspondence. He wants to see your original sketches, I gather, but these overbearing occult-types give me a pain. Frankly, I wouldn't care to meet the man myself.''

6

"Mr. Colin Leverett?"

Leverett studied the tall lean man who stood smiling at the doorway of his studio. The sports car he had driven up in was black and looked expensive. The same held for the turtleneck and leather slacks he wore, and the sleek briefcase he carried. The blackness made his thin face deathly pale. Leverett guessed his age to be late 40 by the thinning of his hair. Dark glasses hid his eyes, black driving gloves his hands.

"Scotty Brandon told me where to find you," the stranger said.

"Scotty?" Leverett's voice was wary.

"Yes, we lost a mutual friend, I regret to say. I'd been talking with him just before . . . But I see by your expression that Scotty never had time to write."

He fumbled awkwardly. "I'm Dana Allard."

"Allard?"

His visitor seemed embarrassed. "Yes—H. Kenneth Allard was my uncle."

"I hadn't realized Allard left a family," mused Leverett, shaking the extended hand. He had never met the writer personally, but there was a strong resemblance to the few photographs he had seen. And Scotty had been paying royalty checks to an estate of some sort, he recalled.

"My father was Kent's half-brother. He later took his father's name, but there was no marriage, if you follow."

"Of course," Leverett was abashed. "Please find a place to sit down. And what brings you here?"

Dana Allard tapped his briefcase. "Something I'd been discussing with Scotty. Just recently I turned up a stack of my uncle's unpublished manuscripts." He unlatched the briefcase and handed Leverett a sheaf of yellowed paper. "Father collected Kent's personal effects from the state hospital as next-of-kin. He never thought much of my uncle, or his writing. He stuffed this away in our attic and forgot about it. Scotty was quite excited when I told him of my discovery."

Leverett was glancing through the manuscript—page on page of cramped handwriting, with revisions pieced throughout like an indecipherable puzzle. He had seen photographs of Allard manuscripts. There was no mistaking this.

Or the prose. Leverett read a few passages with rapt absorption. It was authentic—and brilliant.

"Uncle's mind seems to have taken an especially morbid turn as his illness drew on," Dana hazarded. "I admire his work very greatly but I find these last few pieces . . . Well, a bit *too* horrible. Especially his translation of his mythical *Book of Elders*."

It appealed to Leverett perfectly. He barely noticed his guest as he pored over the brittle pages. Allard was describing a megalithic structure his doomed narrator had encountered in the crypts beneath an ancient churchyard. There were references to "elder glyphics" that resembled his lattice devices.

"Look here," pointed Dana. "These incantations he records here from Alorri-Zrokros's forbidden tome: 'Yogth-Yugth-Sut-Hyrath-Yogng'—Hell, I can't pronounce them. And he has pages of them."

"This is incredible!" Leverett protested. He tried to mouth the alien syllables. It could be done. He even detected a rhythm.

"Well, I'm relieved that you approve. I'd feared these last few stories and fragments might prove a little too much for Kent's fans."

"Then you're going to have them published?"

Dana nodded. "Scotty was going to. I just hope those thieves weren't searching for this—a collector would pay a fortune. But Scotty said he was going to keep this secret until he was ready for announcement." His thin face was sad.

"So now I'm going to publish it myself—in a deluxe edition. And I want you to illustrate it."

"I'd feel honored!" vowed Leverett, unable to believe it.

"I really liked those drawings you did for the trilogy. I'd like to see more like those—as many as you feel like doing. I mean to spare no expense in publishing this. And those stick things . . ."

"Yes?"

"Scotty told me the story on those. Fascinating! And you have a whole notebook of them? May I see it?"

Leverett hurriedly dug the notebook from his file, returned to the manuscript.

Dana paged through the book in awe. "These things are totally bizarre—and there are references to such things in the manuscript, to make it even more fantastic. Can you reproduce them all for the book?''

''All I can remember,'' Leverett assured him. ''And I have a good memory. But won't that be overdoing it?''

''Not at all! They fit into the book. And they're utterly unique. No, put everything you've got into this book. I'm going to entitle it *Dwellers in the Earth,* after the longest piece. I've already arranged for its printing, so we begin as soon as you can have the art ready. And I know you'll give it your all.''

7

He was floating in space. Objects drifted past him. Stars, he first thought. The objects drifted closer.

Sticks. Stick lattices of all configurations. And then he was drifting among them, and he saw that they were not sticks—not of wood. The lattice designs were of dead-pale substance, like streaks of frozen starlight. They reminded him of glyphics of some unearthly alphabet—complex, enigmatic symbols arranged to spell . . . what? And there *was* an arrangement—a three dimensional pattern. A maze of utterly baffling intricacy . . .

Then somehow he was in a tunnel. A cramped, stone-lined tunnel through which he must crawl on his belly. The dank, moss-slimed stones pressed close about his wriggling form, evoking shrill whispers of claustrophobic dread.

And after an indefinite space of crawling through this and other stone-lined burrows, and sometimes through passages whose angles hurt his eyes, he would creep forth into a subterranean chamber. Great slabs of granite a dozen feet across formed the walls and ceiling of this buried chamber, and between the slabs other burrows pierced the earth. Altarlike, a gigantic slab of gneiss waited in the center of the chamber. A spring welled darkly between the stone pillars that supported the table. Its outer edge was encircled by a groove, sickeningly stained by the substance that clotted in the stone bowl beneath its collecting spout.

Others were emerging from the darkened burrows that ringed the chamber—slouched figures only dimly glimpsed and vaguely human. And a figure in a tattered cloak came

toward him from the shadow—stretched out a claw-like hand
to seize his wrist and draw him toward the sacrificial table.
He followed unresistingly, knowing that something was expected of him.

They reached the altar and in the glow from the cuneiform
lattices chiselled into the gneiss slab he could see the guide's
face. A mouldering corpse-face, the rotted bone of its forehead smashed inward upon the foulness that oozed forth . . .

And Leverett would awaken to the echo of his screams . . .

He'd been working too hard, he told himself, stumbling
about in the darkness, getting dressed because he was too
shaken to return to sleep. The nightmares had been coming
every night. No wonder he was exhausted.

But in his studio his work awaited him. Almost fifty drawings finished now, and he planned another score. No wonder
the nightmares.

It was a grueling pace, but Dana Allard was ecstatic with
the work he had done. And *Dwellers in the Earth* was waiting. Despite problems with typesetting, with getting the special paper Dana wanted—the book only waited on him.

Though his bones ached with fatigue, Leverett determinedly
trudged through the graying night. Certain features of the
nightmare would be interesting to portray.

8

The last of the drawings had gone off to Dana Allard in
Petersham, and Leverett, fifteen pounds lighter and gut-weary,
converted part of the bonus check into a case of good whiskey. Dana had the offset presses rolling as soon as the plates
were shot from the drawings. Despite his precise planning,
presses had broken down, one printer quit for reasons not
stated, there had been a bad accident at the new printer—
seemingly innumerable problems, and Dana had been furious
at each delay. But the production pushed along quickly for all
that. Leverett wrote that the book was cursed, but Dana
responded that a week would see it ready.

Leverett amused himself in his studio constructing stick
lattices and trying to catch up on his sleep. He was expecting
a copy of the book when he received a letter from Stefroi:

"Have tried to reach you by phone last few days, but no answer at your house. I'm pushed for time just now, so must be brief. I have indeed uncovered an unsuspected megalithic site of enormous importance. It's located on the estate of a long-prominent Mass. family—and as I cannot receive authorization to visit it, I will not say where. Have investigated secretly (and quite illegally) for a short time one night and was nearly caught. Came across reference to the place in collection of 17th century letters and papers in a divinity school library. Writer denouncing the family as a brood of sorcerers and witches, references to alchemical activities and other less savory rumors—and describes underground stone chambers, megalithic artifacts, etc. which are put to 'foul usage and diabolic praktise.' Just got a quick glimpse but his description was not exaggerated. And Colin—in creeping through the woods to get to the site, I came across dozens of your mysterious 'sticks!' Brought a small one back and have it here to show you. Recently constructed and exactly like your drawings. With luck, I'll gain admittance and find out their significance—undoubtedly they have significance—though these cultists can be stubborn about sharing their secrets. Will explain my interest is scientific, no exposure to ridicule—and see what they say. Will get a closer look one way or another. And so—I'm off! Sincerely, Alexander Stefroi''

Leverett's bushy brows rose. Allard had intimated certain dark rituals in which the stick lattices figured. But Allard had written over thirty years ago, and Leverett assumed the writer had stumbled onto something similar to the Mann Brook site. Stefroi was writing about something current.

He rather hoped Stefroi would discover nothing more than an inane hoax.

The nightmares haunted him still—familiar now, for all that its scenes and phantasms were visited by him only in dream. Familiar. The terror that they evoked was undiminished.

Now he was walking through forest—a section of hills that seemed to be close by. A huge slab of granite had been dragged aside, and a pit yawned where it had lain. He entered the pit without hesitation, and the rounded steps that led downward were known to his tread. A buried stone chamber, and leading from it stone-lined burrows. He knew which one to crawl into.

And again the underground room with its sacrificial altar and its dark spring beneath, and the gathering circle of poorly glimpsed figures. A knot of them clustered about the stone table, and as he stepped toward them he saw they pinned a frantically writhing man.

It was a stoutly built man, white hair disheveled, flesh gouged and filthy. Recognition seemed to burst over the contorted features, and he wondered if he should know the man. But now the lich with the caved-in skull was whispering in his ear, and tried not to think of the unclean things that peered from that cloven brow, and instead took the bronze knife from the skeletal hand, and raised the knife high, and because he could not scream and awaken, did with the knife as the tattered priest had whispered . . .

And when after an interval of unholy madness, he at last did awaken, the stickiness that covered him was not cold sweat, nor was it nightmare the half-devoured heart he clutched in one fist.

9

Leverett somehow found sanity enough to dispose of the shredded lump of flesh. He stood under the shower all morning, scrubbing his skin raw. He wished he could vomit.

There was a news item on the radio. The crushed body of noted archeologist, Dr. Alexander Stefroi, had been discovered beneath a fallen granite slab near Whately. Police speculated the gigantic slab had shifted with the scientist's excavations at its base. Identification was made through personal effects.

When his hands stopped shaking enough to drive, Leverett fled to Petersham—reaching Dana Allard's old stone house about dark. Allard was slow to answer his frantic knock.

"Why, good evening, Colin! What a coincidence your coming here just now! The books are ready. The bindery just delivered them."

Leverett brushed past him. "We've got to destroy them!" he blurted. He'd thought a lot since morning.

"Destroy them?"

"There's something none of us figured on. Those stick lattices—there's a cult, some damnable cult. The lattices have some significance in their rituals. Stefroi hinted once they might be glyphics of some sort, I don't know. But the cult is still alive. They killed Scotty . . . they killed Stefroi. They're onto me—and I don't know what they intend. They'll kill you to stop you from releasing this book!"

Dana's frown was worried, but Leverett knew he hadn't impressed him the right way. "Colin, this sounds insane. You really have been overextending yourself, you know. Look, I'll show you the books. They're in the cellar."

Leverett let his host lead him downstairs. The cellar was quite large, flagstoned and dry. A mountain of brown-wrapped bundles awaited them.

"Put them down here where they wouldn't knock the floor out," Dana explained. "They start going out to distributors tomorrow. Here, I'll sign your copy."

Distractedly Leverett opened a copy of *Dwellers in the Earth*. He gazed at his lovingly rendered drawings of rotting creatures and buried stone chambers and stained altars—and everywhere the enigmatic latticework structures. He shuddered.

"Here." Dana Allard handed Leverett the book he had signed. "And to answer your question, they *are* elder glyphics."

But Leverett was staring at the inscription in its unmistakable handwriting: "For Colin Leverett, Without whom this work could not have seen completion—H. Kenneth Allard."

Allard was speaking. Leverett saw places where the hastily applied flesh-toned makeup didn't quite conceal what lay beneath. "Glyphics symbolic of alien dimensions—inexplicable to the human mind, but essential fragments of an evocation so unthinkably vast that the 'pentagram' (if you will) is miles across. Once before we tried—but your iron weapon destroyed part of Althol's brain. He erred at the last instant—almost annihilating us all. Althol had been formulating the evocation since he fled the advance of iron four millennia past.

"Then you reappeared, Colin Leverett—you with your artist's knowledge and diagrams of Althol's symbols. And now a thousand new minds will read the evocation you have returned to us, unite with our minds as we stand in the Hidden Places. And the Great Old Ones will come forth from the earth, and we, the dead who have steadfastly served them, shall be masters of the living."

Leverett turned to run, but now they were creeping forth from the shadows of the cellar, as massive flagstones slid back to reveal the tunnels beyond. He began to scream as Althol came to lead him away, but he could not awaken, could only follow.

AFTERWORD

Some readers may note certain similarities between characters and events in this story and the careers of real-life figures, well known to fans of this genre. This was unavoidable, and no disrespect is intended. For much of this story *did* happen, though I suppose you've heard that one before.

In working with Lee Brown Coye on Wellman's *Worse Things Waiting*, I finally asked him why his drawings so frequently included sticks in their design. Lee's work is well known to me, but I had noticed that the "sticks" only began to appear in his work for Ziff-Davis in the early '60s. Lee finally sent me a folder of clippings and letters, far more eerie than this story—and factual.

In 1938 Coye *did* come across a stick-ridden farmhouse in the desolate Mann Brook region. He kept this to himself until fall of 1962, when John Vetter passed the account to August Derleth and to antiquarian-archaeologist Andrew E. Rothovius. Derleth intended to write Coye's adventure as a Lovecraft novelette, but never did so. Rothovius discussed the site's possible megalithic significance with Coye in a series of letters and journal articles on which I have barely touched. In June 1963 Coye returned to the Mann Brook site and found it obliterated. It is a strange region, as HPL knew.

Coye's fascinating presentation of their letters appeared in five weekly installments of his "Chips and Shavings" column in the *Mid-York Weekly* from August 22 to September 26, 1963. Rothovius, whose research into the New England megaliths has been published in many journals, wrote an excellent and disquieting summary of his research in Arkham House's *The Dark Brotherhood*, to which the reader is referred.

David Drake is both the assistant editor of Whispers *and the assistant Town Attorney of Chapel Hill, North Carolina. I know I could not do without him and figure that Chapel Hill would also be in dire straits if he decided to strike out on his own. Besides occasionally allowing me to purchase a story of his, he has offered and sold fiction to* Analog, Galaxy *(his Hammer series has been a cover feature), and the* Magazine of Fantasy and Science Fiction. *His heroic fantasy is strong stuff that is extensively researched for accuracy, and one feels the reality of the worlds he creates. "The Barrow Troll" was one of only four stories to be nominated for a World Fantasy Award in 1976. It is a brutal and shocking piece.*

THE BARROW TROLL

by David Drake

Playfully, Ulf Womanslayer twitched the cord bound to his saddlehorn. "Awake, priest? Soon you can get to work."

"My work is saving souls, not being dragged into the wilderness by madmen," Johann muttered under his breath. The other end of the cord was around his neck, not that of his horse. A trickle of blood oozed into his cassock from the reopened scab, but he was afraid to open the knot. Ulf might

24

look back. Johann had already seen his captor go into berserk rage. Over the Northerner's right shoulder rode his axe, a heavy hooked blade on a four-foot shaft. Ulf had swung it like a willow-wand when three Christian traders in Schleswig had seen the priest and tried to free him. The memory of the last man in three pieces as head and sword arm sprang from his spouting torso was still enough to roil Johann's stomach.

"We'll have a clear night with a moon, priest; a good night for our business." Ulf stretched and laughed aloud, setting a raven on a fir knot to squawking back at him. The berserker was following a ridge line that divided wooded slopes with a spine too thin-soiled to bear trees. The flanking forest still loomed above the riders. In three days, now, Johann had seen no man but his captor, nor even a tendril of smoke from a lone cabin. Even the route they were taking to Parmavale was no mantrack but an accident of nature.

"So lonely," the priest said aloud.

Ulf hunched hugely to his bearskin and replied, "You soft folk in the south, you live too close anyway. Is it your Christgod, do you think?"

"Hedeby's a city," the German priest protested, his fingers toying with his torn robe, "and my brother trades to Uppsala . . . But why bring me to this manless waste?"

"Oh, there were men once, so the tale goes," Ulf said. Here in the empty forest he was more willing for conversation than he had been the first few days of their ride north. "Few enough, and long enough ago. But there were farms in Parmavale, and a lordling of sorts who went a-viking against the Irish. But then the troll came and the men went, and there was nothing left to draw others. So they thought."

"You Northerners believe in trolls, so my brother tells me," said the priest.

"Aye, long before the gold I'd heard of the Parma troll," the berserker agreed. "Ox broad and stronger than ten men, shaggy as a denned bear."

"Like you," Johann said, in a voice more normal than caution would have dictated.

Bloody fury glared in Ulf's eyes and he gave a savage jerk on the cord. "You'll think me a troll, priestling, if you don't do just as I say. I'll drink your blood hot if you cross me."

Johann, gagging, could not speak nor wished to.

With the miles the sky became a darker blue, the trees a

blacker green. Ulf again broke the hoof-pummeled silence, saying. "No, I knew nothing of the gold until Thora told me."

The priest coughed to clear his throat. "Thora is your wife?" he asked.

"Wife? Ho!" Ulf brayed, his raucous laughter ringing like a demon's. "Wife? She was Hallstein's wife, and I killed her with all her house about her! But before that, she told me of the troll's horde, indeed she did. Would you hear that story?"

Johann nodded, his smile fixed. He was learning to recognize death as it bantered under the axehead.

"So," the huge Northerner began. "There was a bonder, Hallstein Kari's son, who followed the king to war but left his wife, that was Thora, behind to manage the stead. The first day I came by and took a sheep from the herdsman. I told him if he misliked it to send his master to me."

"Why did you do that?" the fat priest asked in surprise.

"Why? Because I'm Ulf, because I wanted the sheep. A woman acting a man's part, it's unnatural anyway.

"The next day I went back to Hallstein's stead, and the flocks had already been driven in. I went into the garth around the buildings and called for the master to come out and fetch me a sheep." The berserker's teeth ground audibly as he remembered. Johann saw his knuckles whiten on the axe helve and stiffened in terror.

"Ho!" Ulf shouted, bringing his left hand down on the shield slung at his horse's flank. The copper boss rang like thunder in the clouds. "She came out," Ulf grated, "and her hair was red. 'All our sheep are penned,' says she, 'but you're in good time for the butchering.' And from out the hall came her three brothers and the men of the stead, ten in all. They were in full armor and their swords were in their hands. And they would have slain me, Ulf Otgeir's son, *me*, at a woman's word. Forced me to run from a woman!"

The berserker was snarling his words to the forest. Johann knew he watched a scene that had been played a score of times with only the trees to witness. The rage of disgrace burned in Ulf like pitch in a pine faggot, and his mind was lost to everything except the past.

"But I came back," he continued, "in the darkness, when all feasted within the hall and drank their ale to victory. Behind the hall burned a log fire to roast a sheep. I killed the two there, and I thrust one of the logs half-burnt up under the eaves. Then at the door I waited until those within noticed the heat and Thora looked outside.

" 'Greetings, Thora,' I said. 'You would not give me mutton, so I must roast men tonight.' She asked me for speech. I knew she was fey, so I listened to her. And she told me of the Parma lord and the treasure he brought back from Ireland, gold and gems. And she said it was cursed that a troll should guard it, and that I must have a mass priest, for the troll could not cross a Christian's fire and I should slay him then."

"Didn't you spare her for that?" Johann quavered, more fearful of silence than he was of misspeaking.

"Spare her? No, nor any of her house," Ulf thundered back. "She might better have asked the flames for mercy, as she knew. The fire was at her hair. I struck her, and never was a woman better made for an axe to bite—she cleft like a waxen doll, and I threw the pieces back. Her brothers came then, but one and one and one through the doorway, and I killed each in his turn. No more came. When the roof fell, I left them with the ash for a headstone and went my way to find a mass priest—to find you, priestling." Ulf, restored to good humor by the climax of his own tale, tweaked the lead core again.

Johann choked onto his horse's neck, nauseated as much by the story as by the noose. At last he said, thick-voiced, "Why do you trust her tale if she knew you would kill her with it or not?"

"She was fey," Ulf chuckled, as if that explained everything. "Who knows what a man will do when his death is upon him? Or a woman," he added more thoughtfully.

They rode on in growing darkness. With no breath of wind to stir them, the trees stood as dead as the rocks underfoot.

"Will you know the place?" the German asked suddenly. "Shouldn't we camp now and go on in the morning?"

"I'll know it," Ulf grunted. "We're not far now—we're going downhill, can't you feel?" He tossed his bare haystack of hair, silvered into a false sheen of age by the moon. He continued, "The Parma lord sacked a dozen churches, so they say, and then one more with more of gold than the twelve besides, but also the curse. And he brought it back with him to Parma, and there it rests in his barrow, the troll guarding it. That I have on Thora's word.''

''But she hated you!''

''She was fey.''

They were into the trees, and looking to either side Johann could see hill slopes rising away from them. They were in a valley, Parma or another. Scraps of wattle and daub, the remains of a house or garth fence, thrust up to the right. The firs that had grown through it were generations old. Johann's stubbled tonsure crawled in the night air.

''She said there was a clearing,'' the berserker muttered, more to himself than his companion. Johann's horse stumbled. The priest clutched the cord reflexively as it tightened. When he looked up at his captor, he saw the huge Northerner fumbling at his shield's fastenings. For the first time that evening, a breeze stirred. It stank of death.

''Others have been here before us,'' said Ulf needlessly.

A row of skulls, at least a score of them, stared blank-eyed from atop stakes rammed through their spinal openings. To one, dried sinew still held the lower jaw in a ghastly rictus; the others had fallen away into the general scatter of bones whitening the ground. All of them were human or could have been. They were mixed with occasional glimmers of buttons and rust smears. The freshest of the grisly trophies was very old, perhaps decades old. Too old to explain the reek of decay.

Ulf wrapped his left fist around the twin handles of his shield. It was a heavy circle of linden wood, faced with leather. Its rim and central boss were of copper, and rivets of bronze and copper decorated the face in a serpent pattern.

''Good that the moon is full,'' Ulf said, glancing at the bright orb still tangled in the fir branches. ''I fight best in the moonlight. We'll let her rise the rest of the way, I think.''

Johann was trembling. He joined his hands about his saddle horn to keep from falling off the horse. He knew Ulf might let him jerk and strangle there, even after dragging him across half the northlands. The humor of the idea might strike him. Johann's rosary, his crucifix—everything he brought from Germany or purchased in Schleswig save his robe—had been left behind in Hedeby when the berserker awakened him in his bed. Ulf had jerked a noose to near-lethal tautness and whispered that he needed a priest, that this one would do, but that there were others should this one prefer to feed crows. The disinterested bloodlust in Ulf's tone had been more terrifying than the threat itself. Johann had followed in silence to the waiting horses. In despair, he wondered again if a quick death would not have been better than his lingering one that had ridden for weeks a mood away from him.

"It looks like a palisade for a house," the priest said aloud in what he pretended was a normal voice.

"That's right," Ulf replied, giving his axe an exploratory heft that sent shivers of moonlight across the blade. "There was a hall here, a big one. Did it burn, do you think?" His knees sent his roan gelding forward in a shambling walk past the line of skulls. Johann followed of necessity.

"No, rotted away," the berserker said, bending over to study the post holes.

"You said it had been deserted a long time," the priest commented. His eyes were fixed straight forward. One of the skulls was level with his waist and close enough to bite him, could it turn on its stake.

"There was time for the house to fall in, the ground is damp," Ulf agreed. "But the stakes, then, have been replaced. Our troll keeps his front fence new, priestling."

Johann swallowed, said nothing.

Ulf gestured briefly. "Come on, you have to get your fire ready. I want it really holy."

"But we don't sacrifice with fires. I don't know how—"

"Then learn!" the berserker snarled with a vicious yank that drew blood and a gasp from the German. "I've seen how you Christ-shouters love to bless things. You'll bless me a fire, that's all. And if anything goes wrong and the troll spares you—I won't, priestling. I'll rive you apart if I have to come off a stake to do it."

The horses walked slowly forward through brush and soggy rubble that had been a hall. The odor of decay grew stronger. The priest himself tried to ignore it, but his horse began to balk. The second time he was too slow with a heel to its ribs, and the cord nearly decapitated him. "Wait!" he wheezed. "Let me get down."

Ulf looked back at him, flat-eyed. At last he gave a brief crow-peck nod and swung himself out of the saddle. He looped both sets of reins on a small fir. Then, while Johann dismounted clumsily, he loosed the cord from his saddle and took it in his axe hand. The men walked forward without speaking.

"There . . ." Ulf breathed.

The barrow was only a black-mouthed swell in the ground, its size denied by its lack of features. Such trees as had tried to grow on it had been broken off short over a period of years. Some of the stumps had wasted into crumbling depressions, while from others the wood fibers still twisted raggedly. Only when Johann matched the trees on the other side of the tomb to those beside him did he realize the scale on which the barrow was built: its entrance tunnel would pass a man walking upright, even a man Ulf's height.

"Lay your fire at the tunnel mouth," the berserker said, his voice subdued. "He'll be inside."

"You'll have to let me go—"

"I'll have to nothing!" Ulf was breathing hard. "We'll go closer, you and I, and you'll make a fire of the dead trees from the ground. Yes . . ."

The Northerner slid forward in a pace that was cat soft and never left the ground a finger's breadth. Strewn about them as if flung idly from the barrow mouth were scraps and gobbets of animals, the source of the fetid reek that filled the clearing. As his captor paused for a moment, Johann toed one of the bits over with his sandal. It was the hide and paws of something chisel-toothed, whether rabbit or other was impossible to say in the moonlight and state of decay. The skin was in tendrils, and the skull had been opened to empty the brains. Most of the other bits seemed of the same sort, little beasts, although a rank blotch on the mound's slope could have been a wolf hide. Whatever killed and feasted here was not fastidious.

"He stays close to hunt," Ulf rumbled. Then he added, "The long bones by the fence; they were cracked."

"Umm?"

"For marrow."

Quivering, the priest began gathering broken-off trees, none of them over a few feet high. They had been twisted off near the ground, save for a few whose roots lay bare in wizened fists. The crisp scales cut Johann's hands. He did not mind the pain. Under his breath he was praying that God would punish him, would torture him, but at least would save him free of this horrid demon that had snatched him away.

"Pile it here," Ulf directed, his axe head nodding toward

the stone lip of the barrow. The entrance was corbelled out of heavy stones, then covered over with dirt and sods. Like the beast fragments around it, the opening was dead and stinking. Biting his tongue, Johann dumped his pile of brush and scurried back.

"There's light back down there," he whispered.

"Fire?"

"No, look—it's pale, it's moonlight. There's a hole in the roof of the tomb."

"Light for me to kill by," Ulf said with a stark grin. He looked over the low fireset, then knelt. His steel sparked into a nest of dry moss. When the tinder was properly alight, he touched a pitchy faggot to it. He dropped his end of the cord. The torchlight glinted from his face, white and coarse-pored where the tangles of hair and beard did not cover it. "Bless the fire, mass-priest," the berserker ordered in a quiet, terrible voice.

Stiff-featured and unblinking, Johann crossed the brushwood and said, "In nomine Patris, et Filii, et Spiritus Sancti, Amen."

"Don't light it yet," Ulf said. He handed Johann the torch. "It may be," the berserker added, "that you think to run if you get the chance. There is no Hell so deep that I will not come to get you from it."

The priest nodded, white-lipped.

Ulf shrugged his shoulders to loosen his muscles and the bear hide that clothed them. Axe and shield rose and dipped like ships in a high sea.

"Ho! Troll! Barrow fouler! Corpse licker! Come and fight me, troll!"

There was no sound from the tomb.

Ulf's eyes began to glaze. He slashed his axe twice across the empty air and shouted again, "Troll! I'll spit on your corpse, I'll lay with your dog mother. Come and fight me, troll, or I'll wall you up like a rat with your filth!"

Johann stood frozen, oblivious even to the drop of pitch that sizzled on the web of his hand. The berserker bellowed again, wordlessly, gnashing at the rim of his shield so that the sound bubbled and boomed into the night.

And the tomb roared back to the challenge, a thunderous BAR BAR BAR even deeper than Ulf's.

Berserk, the Northerner leaped the brush pile and ran down

the tunnel, his axe thrust out in front of him to clear the stone arches.

The tunnel sloped for a dozen paces into a timber-vaulted chamber too broad to leap across. Moonlight spilled through a circular opening onto flags slimy with damp and liquescence. Ulf, maddened, chopped high at the light. The axe burred inanely beneath the timbers.

Swinging a pair of swords, the troll leapt at Ulf. It was the size of a bear, grizzled in the moonlight. Its eyes burned red. "Hi!" shouted Ulf and blocked the first sword in a shower of sparks on his axehead. The second blade bit into the shield rim, shaving a hand's length of copper and a curl of yellow linden from beneath it. Ulf thrust straight-armed, a blow that would have smashed like a battering ram had the troll not darted back. Both the combatants were shouting; their voices were dreadful in the circular chamber.

The troll jumped backward again. Ulf sprang toward him and only the song of the blades scissoring from either side warned him. The berserker threw himself down. The troll had leaped onto a rotting chest along the wall of the tomb and cut unexpectedly from above Ulf's shield. The big man's boots flew out from under him and he struck the floor on his back. His shield still covered his body.

The troll hurtled down splay-legged with a cry of triumph. Both bare feet slammed on Ulf's shield. The troll was even heavier than Ulf. Shrieking, the berserker pistoned his shield arm upward. The monster flew off, smashing against the timbered ceiling and caroming down into another of the chests. The rotted wood exploded under the weight in a flash of shimmering gold. The berserker rolled to his feet and struck overarm in the same motion. His lunge carried the axehead too far, into the rock wall in a flower of blue sparks.

The troll was up. The two killers eyed each other, edging sideways in the dimness. Ulf's right arm was numb to the shoulder. He did not realize it. The shaggy monster leaped with another double flashing and the axe moved too slowly to counter. Both edges spat chunks of linden as they withdrew. Ulf frowned, backed a step. His boot trod on a ewer that spun away from him. As he cried out, the troll grinned and hacked again like Death the Reaper. The shield-orb flattened as the top third of it split away. Ulf snarled and chopped at the troll's knees. It leaped above the steel and cut left-handed, its blade knocking the shaft an inch from Ulf's hand.

The berserker flung the useless remainder of his shield in the troll's face and ran. Johann's torch was an orange pulse in the triangular opening. Behind Ulf, a swordedge went *sring!* as it danced on the corbels. Ulf jumped the brush and whirled. "Now!" he cried to the priest, and Johann hurled his torch into the resin-jeweled wood.

The needles crackled up in the troll's face like a net of orange silk. The flames bellied out at the creature's rush but licked back caressingly over its mats of hair. The troll's swords cut at the fire. A shower of coals spit and crackled and made the beast howl.

"Burn, dog-spew!" Ulf shouted. "Burn, fish-guts!"

The troll's blades rang together, once and again. For a moment it stood, a hillock of stained gray, as broad as the tunnel arches. Then it strode forward into the white heart of the blaze. The fire bloomed up, its roar leaping over the troll's shriek of agony. Ulf stepped forward. He held his axe with both hands. The flames sucked down from the motionless troll, and as they did the shimmering arc of the axehead chopped into the beast's collarbone. One sword dropped and the left arm slumped loose.

The berserker's axe was buried to the helve in the troll's shoulder. The faggots were scattered, but the troll's hair was burning all over its body. Ulf pulled at his axe. The troll staggered, moaning. Its remaining sword pointed down at the ground. Ulf yanked again at his weapon and it slurped free. A thick velvet curtain of blood followed it. Ulf raised his dripping axe for another blow, but the troll tilted toward the withdrawn weapon, leaning forward, a smouldering rock. The body hit the ground, then flopped so that it lay on its back. The right arm was flung out at an angle.

"It was a man," Johann was whispering. He caught up a brand and held it close to the troll's face. "Look, look!" he demanded excitedly. "It's just an old man in a bearskin. Just a man."

Ulf sagged over his axe as if it were a stake impaling him. His frame shuddered as he dragged air into it. Neither of the troll's swords had touched him, but reaction had left him weak as one death-wounded. "Go in," he wheezed. "Get a torch and lead me in."

"But . . . why—" the priest said in sudden fear. His eyes met the berserker's and he swallowed back the rest of the protest. The torch threw highlights on the walls and flags as he trotted down the tunnel. Ulf's boots were ominous behind him.

The central chamber was austerely simple and furnished only with the six chests lining the back of it. There was no corpse, nor even a slab for one. The floor was gelatinous with decades' accumulation of foulness. The skidding tracks left by the recent combat marked pavement long undisturbed. Only from the entrance to the chests was a path, black against the slime of decay, worn. It was toward the broken container and the objects which had spilled from it that the priest's eyes had narrowed.

"Gold," he murmured. Then, "Gold! There must—the others—in God's name, there are five more and perhaps all of them—"

"Gold," Ulf grated terribly.

Johann ran to the nearest chest and opened it one-handed. The lid sagged wetly, but frequent use had kept it from swelling tight to the side panels. "Look at this crucifix!" the priest marvelled. "And the torque, it must weigh pounds. And Lord in heaven, this—"

"Gold," the berserker repeated.

Johann saw the axe as it started to swing. He was turning with a chalice ornamented in enamel and pink gold. It hung in the air as he darted for safety. His scream and the dull belling of the cup as the axe divided it were simultaneous, but the priest was clear and Ulf was off balance. The berserker backhanded with force enough to drive the peen of his axehead through a sapling. His strength was too great for his footing. His feet skidded and this time his head rang on the wall of the tomb.

Groggy, the huge berserker staggered upright. The priest was a scurrying blur against the tunnel entrance. "Priest!" Ulf shouted at the empty moonlight. He thudded up the flags of the tunnel. "Priest!" he shouted again.

The clearing was empty except for the corpse. Nearby, Ulf heard his roan whicker. He started for it, then paused. The priest—he could still be hiding in the darkness. While Ulf searched for him, he could be rifling the barrow, carrying off the gold behind his back. "Gold," Ulf said again. No one must take the gold. No one must ever find it unguarded.

"I'll kill you!" he screamed into the night. "I'll kill you all!"

He turned back to his barrow. At the entrance, still smoking, waited the body of what had been the troll.

Fritz Leiber has won Hugos, Nebulas, and World Fantasy Awards. He is undoubtedly the most-honored author in the fantasy and science-fiction field, and Whispers Press has published a Tim Kirk-illustrated, hardcover volume featuring his famous fantasy heroes, Fafhrd and the Gray Mouser. Here, though, Mr. Leiber turns from heroic fantasy or science fiction to show that he can write a supernatural horror story with the best of them. "The Glove" was the featured story in the special Weird Tales *issue of* Whispers *and was a fitting tribute to that revered magazine which was the spawning ground for Howard Phillips Lovecraft, Robert Erwin Howard, Clark Ashton Smith, Robert Bloch, and, of course, Fritz Leiber.*

THE GLOVE

by Fritz Leiber

My most literally tangible brush with the supernatural (something I can get incredibly infatuated with yet forever distrust profoundly, like a very beautiful and adroit call girl) occurred in connection with the rape by a masked intruder of the woman who lived in the next apartment to mine during my San Francisco years. I knew Evelyn Mayne only as a neighbor and I slept through the whole incident, including the arrival and departure of the police, though there came a point in the case when the police doubted both these assertions of mine.

36

The phrase "victim of rape" calls up certain stereotyped images: an attractive young woman going home alone late at night, enters a dark street, is grabbed . . . or, a beautiful young suburban matron, mother of three, wakes after midnight, feels a nameless dread, is grabbed . . . The truth is apt to be less romantic. Evelyn Mayne was 65, long divorced, neglected and thoroughly detested by her two daughters-in-law and only to a lesser degree by their husbands, lived on various programs of old age, medical and psychiatric assistance, was scrawny, gloomy, alcoholic, waspish, believed life was futile, and either overdosed on sleeping pills or else lightly cut her wrists three or four times a year.

Her assailant at least was somewhat more glamorous, in a sick way. The rapist was dressed all in rather close-fitting gray, hands covered by gray gloves, face obscured by a long shock of straight silver hair falling over it. And in the left hand, at first, a long knife that gleamed silver in the dimness.

And she wasn't grabbed either, at first, but only commanded in a harsh whisper coming through the hair to lie quietly or be cut up.

When she was alone again at last, she silently waited something like the ten minutes she'd been warned to, thinking that at least she hadn't been cut up, or else (who knows?) wishing she had been. Then she went next door (in the opposite direction to mine) and roused Marcia Everly, who was a buyer for a department store and about half her age. After the victim had been given a drink, they called the police and Evelyn Mayne's psychiatrist and also her social worker, who knew her current doctor's number (which she didn't), but they couldn't get hold of either of the last two. Marcia suggested waking me and Evelyn Mayne countered by suggesting they wake Mr. Helpful, who has the next room beyond Marcia's down the hall. Mr. Helpful (otherwise nicknamed Baldy, I never remembered his real name) was someone I loathed because he was always prissily dancing around being neighborly and asking if there was something he could do—and because he was six foot four tall, while I am rather under average height.

Marcia Everly is also very tall, at least for a woman, but as it happens I do not loathe her in the least. Quite the opposite in fact.

But Evelyn Mayne said I wasn't sympathetic, while Marcia

(thank goodness!) loathed Mr. Helpful as much as I do—she thought him a weirdo, along with half the other tenants in the building.

So they compromised by waking neither of us, and until the police came Evelyn Mayne simply kept telling the story of her rape over and over, rather mechanically, while Marcia listened dutifully and occupied her mind as to which of our crazy fellow-tenants was the best suspect—granting it hadn't been done by an outsider, although that seemed likeliest. The three most colorful were the statuesque platinum-blonde drag queen on the third floor, the long-haired old weirdo on six who wore a cape and was supposed to be into witchcraft, and the tall, silver-haired, Nazi-looking lesbian on seven (assuming she wore a dildo for the occasion and was nuttier than a five-dollar fruit cake).

Ours really is a weird building, you see, and not just because its occupants, who sometimes seem as if they were all referred here by mental hospitals. No, it's eerie in its own right. You see, several decades ago it was a hotel with all the rich, warm inner life that once implied: bevies of maids, who actually used the linen closets (empty now) on each floor and the round snap-capped outlets in the baseboards for a vacuum system (that hadn't been operated for a generation) and the two dumb-waiters (their doors forever shut and painted over). In the old days there had been bellboys and an elevator operator and two night porters who'd carry up drinks and midnight snacks from a restaurant that never closed.

But they're gone now, every last one of them, leaving the halls empty-feeling and very gloomy, and the stairwell an echoing void, and the lobby funereal, so that the mostly solitary tenants of today are apt to seem like ghosts, especially when you meet one coming silently around a turn in the corridor where the ceiling light's burnt out.

Sometimes I think that, what with the smaller and smaller families and more and more people living alone, our whole modern world is getting like that.

The police finally arrived, two grave and solicitous young men making a good impression—especially a tall and stalwart (Marcia told me) Officer Hart. But when they first heard Evelyn Mayne's story, they were quite skeptical (Marcia could tell, or thought she could, she told me). But they searched Evelyn's room and poked around the fire escapes and listened to her story again, and then they radioed for a medical policewoman, who arrived with admirable speed and who decided after an examination that in all probability there'd been recent sex, which would be confirmed by analysis of some smears she'd taken from the victim and the sheets.

Officer Hart did two great things, Marcia said. He got hold of Evelyn Mayne's social worker and told him he'd better get on over quick. And he got from him the phone number of her son who lived in the city and called him up and threw a scare into his wife and him about how they were the nearest of kin, God damn it, and had better start taking care of the abused and neglected lady.

Meanwhile the other cop had been listening to Evelyn Mayne, who was still telling it, and he asked her innocent questions, and had got her to admit that earlier that night she'd gone alone to a bar down the street (a rather rough place) and had one drink, or maybe three. Which made him wonder (Marcia said she could tell) whether Evelyn hadn't brought the whole thing on herself, maybe by inviting some man home with her, and then inventing the rape, at least in part, when things went wrong. (Though I couldn't see her inventing the silver hair.)

Anyhow the police got her statement and got it signed and then took off, even more solemnly sympathetic than when they'd arrived, Officer Hart in particular.

Of course, I didn't know anything about all this when I knocked on Marcia's door before going to work that morning, to confirm a tentative movie date we'd made for that evening. Though I was surprised when the door opened and Mr. Helpful came out looking down at me very thoughtfully, his bald head gleaming, and saying to Marcia in the voice adults use when children are listening, "I'll keep in touch with you about the matter. If there is anything I can do, don't hesitate . . ."

Marcia, looking at him very solemnly, nodded.

And then my feeling of discomfiture was completed when Evelyn Mayne, empty glass in hand and bathrobe clutched around her, edged past me as if I were contagious, giving me a peculiarly hostile look and calling back to Marcia over my head, "I'll come back, my dear, when I've repaired my appearance, so that people can't say you're entertaining bedraggled old hags."

I was relieved when Marcia gave me a grin as soon as the door was closed and said, "Actually she's gone to get herself another drink, after finishing off my supply. But really, Jeff, she has a reason to this morning—and for hating any man she runs into." And her face grew grave and troubled (and a little frightened too) as she quickly clued me in on the night's nasty events. Mr. Helpful, she explained, had dropped by to remind them about a tenants' meeting that evening and, when he got the grisly news, to go into a song and dance about how shocked he was and how guilty at having slept through it all, and what could he do?

Once she broke off to ask, almost worriedly, "What I can't understand, Jeff, is why any man would want to rape someone like Evelyn."

I shrugged. "Kinky some way, I suppose. It does happen, you know. To old women, I mean. Maybe a mother thing."

"Maybe he *hates* women," she speculated. "Wants to punish them."

I nodded.

She had finished by the time Evelyn Mayne came back, very listless now, looking like a woebegone ghost, dropped into a chair. She hadn't got dressed or even combed her hair. In one hand she had her glass, full and dark, and in the other a large, pale gray leather glove, which she carried oddly, dangling it by one finger.

Marcia started to ask her about it, but she just began to recite once more all that had happened to her that night, in an unemotional, mechanical voice that sounded as if it would go on forever.

Look, I didn't like the woman—she was a particularly useless, venomous sort of nuisance (those wearisome suicide attempts!)—but that recital got to me. I found myself hating the person who would deliberately put someone into the state she was in. I realized, perhaps for the first time, just what a vicious and sick crime rape is and how cheap are all the easy jokes about it.

Eventually the glove came into the narrative naturally: ". . . and in order to do that he had to take off his glove. He was particularly excited just then, and it must have got shoved behind the couch and forgotten, where I found it just now."

Marcia pounced on the glove at once then, saying it was important evidence they must tell the police about. So she called them and after a bit she managed to get Officer Hart himself, and he told her to tell Evelyn Mayne to hold onto the glove and he'd send someone over for it eventually.

It was more than time for me to get on to work, but I stayed until she finished her call, because I wanted to remind her about our date that evening.

She begged off, saying she'd be too tired from the sleep she'd lost and anyway she'd decided to go to the tenants' meeting tonight. She told me, "This has made me realize that I've got to begin to take some responsibility for what happens around me. We may make fun of such people—the good neighbors—but they've got something solid about them."

I was pretty miffed at that, though I don't think I let it show. Oh, I didn't so much mind her turning me down—there were reasons enough—but she didn't have to make such a production of it and drag in "good neighbors." (Mr. Helpful, who else?) Besides, Evelyn Mayne came out of her sad apathy long enough to give me a big smile when Marcia said "No."

So I didn't go to the tenants' meeting that night, as I might otherwise have done. Instead I had dinner out and went to the movie—it was lousy—and then had a few drinks, so that it was late when I got back (no signs of life in the lobby or lift or corridor) and gratefully piled into bed.

I was dragged out of the depths of sleep—that first blissful plunge—by a persistent knocking. I shouted something angry but unintelligible and when there was no reply made myself get up, feeling furious.

It was Marcia. With a really remarkable effort I kept my mouth shut and even smoothed out whatever expression was contorting my face. The words one utters on being suddenly awakened, especially from that matchless first sleep that is never recaptured, can be as disastrous as speaking in drink. Our relationship had progressed to the critical stage and I sure didn't want to blow it, especially when treasures I'd hoped to win were spread out in front of my face, as it were, under a semi-transparent nightgown and hastily-thrown-on negligee.

I looked up, a little, at her face. Her eyes were wide.

She said in a sort of frightened little-girl voice that didn't seem at all put on, "I'm awfully sorry to wake you up at three o'clock in the morning, Jeff, but would you keep this 'spooky' for me? I can't get to sleep with it in my room."

It is a testimony to the very high quality of Marcia's treasures that I didn't until then notice what she was carrying in front of her—in a fold of toilet paper—the pale gray leather glove Evelyn Mayne had found behind her couch.

"Huh?" I said, not at all brilliantly. "Didn't Officer Hart come back, or send someone over to pick it up?"

She shook her head. "Evelyn had it, of course, while I was at my job—her social worker did come over right after you left. But then at supper time her son and daughter-in-law came (Officer Hart did scare them!) and bundled her off to the hospital, and she left the glove with me. I called the police, but Officer Hart was off duty and Officer Halstead, whom I talked to, told me they'd be over to pick it up early in the morning. Please take it, Jeff. Whenever I look at it, I think of that crazy sneaking around with the silver hair down his face and waving the knife. It keeps giving me the shivers."

I looked again at her "spooky" in its fold of tissue (so that she wouldn't have to touch it, what other reason?) and, you know, it began to give *me* the shivers. Just an old glove, but now it had an invisible gray aura radiating from it.

"Okay," I said, closing my hand on it with an effort, and went on ungraciously, really without thinking. "Though I wonder you didn't ask Mr. Helpful first, what with all his offers and seeing him at the meeting."

"Well, I asked *you*," she said a little angrily. Then her features relaxed into a warm smile. "Thanks, Jeff."

Only then did it occur to me that here I was passing up in my sleep-soddenness what might be a priceless opportunity. Well, that could be corrected. But before I could invite her in, there came this sharp little cough, or clearing of the throat. We both turned and there was Mr. Helpful in front of his open door, dressed in pyjamas and a belted maroon dressing gown. He came smiling and dancing toward us (he didn't really dance, but he gave that impression in spite of being six foot four) and saying, "Could I be of any assistance, Miss Everly? Did something alarm you? Is there . . . er? . . . ." He hesitated, as if there might be something he should be embarrassed at.

Marcia shook her head curtly and said to me quite coolly, "No thank you, I needn't come in, Mr. Winter. That will be fine. Good night."

I realized Baldy *had* managed to embarrass her and that she was making it clear that we weren't parting after a rendez-vous, or about to have one. (But to use my last name!)

As she passed him, she gave him a formal nod. He hurried back to his own door, a highlight dancing on the back of his head. (Marcia says he shaves it; I, that he doesn't have to.)

I waited until I heard her double-lock her door and slide the bolt across. Then I looked grimly at Baldy until he'd gone inside and closed his—I had that pleasure. Then I retired myself, tossed the glove down on some sheets of paper on the table in front of the open window, threw myself into bed and switched out the light.

I fully expected to spend considerable time being furious at my hulking, mincing, officious neighbor, and maybe at Marcia too, before I could get to sleep, but somehow my mind took off on a fantasy about the building around me as it might have been a half century ago. Ghostly bellboys sped silently with little notes inviting or accepting rendezvous. Ghostly waiters wheeled noiseless carts of silver-covered suppers for two. Pert, ghostly maids whirled ghostly sheets through the dark air as they made the bed, their smiles suggesting they might substitute for non-arriving sweethearts. The soft darkness whirlpooled. Somewhere was wind.

I woke with a start as if someone or something had touched me, and I sat up in bed. And then I realized that something *was* touching me high on my neck, just below my ear. Something long, like a finger laid flat or—oh God!—a centipede. I remembered how centipedes were supposed to cling with their scores of tiny feet—and *this* was clinging. As a child I'd been terrified by a tropical centipede that had come weaving out of a stalk of new-bought bananas in the kitchen, and the memory still returned full force once in a great while. Now it galvanized me into whirling my hand behind my head and striking my neck a great brushing swipe, making my jaw and ear sting. I instantly turned on the light and rapidly looked all around me without seeing anything close to me that might have brushed off my neck. I thought I'd felt something with my hand when I'd done that, but I couldn't be sure.

And then I looked at the table by the window and saw that the glove was gone.

Almost at once I got the vision of it lifting up and floating through the air at me, fingers first, or else dropping off the table and inching across the floor and up the bed. I don't know which was worse. The thing on my neck *had* felt leathery.

My immediate impulse was to check if my door was still shut. I couldn't tell from where I sat. A very tall clothes cabinet abuts the door, shutting the view of it off from the head of the bed. So I pushed my way down the bed, putting my feet on the floor after looking down to make sure there was nothing in the immediate vicinity.

And then a sharp gust of wind came in the window and blew the last sheet of paper off the table and deposited it on the floor near the other sheets of paper *and the glove* and the tissue now disentangled from it.

I was so relieved I almost laughed. I went over and picked up the glove, feeling a certain revulsion, but only at the thought of who had worn it and what it had been involved in. I examined it closely, which I hadn't done earlier. It was rather thin gray kid, a fairly big glove and stretched still further as if a pretty big hand had worn it, but quite light enough to have blown off the table with the papers.

There were grimy streaks on it and a slightly stiff part where some fluid had dried and a faintly reddish streak that might have been lipstick. And it looked old—decades old.

I put it back on the table and set a heavy ashtray on top of it and got back in bed, feeling suddenly secure again.

It occurred to me how the empty finger of the gray leather glove is really very much like a centipede, some of the larger of which are the same size, flat and yellowish gray (though the one that had come out of the banana stalk had been bright red), but these thoughts were no longer frightening.

I looked a last time across the room at the glove, pinioned under the heavy ashtray, and I confidently turned off the light.

Sleep was longer in coming this time, however. I got my fantasy of hotel ghosts going again, but gloves kept coming into it. The lissom maids wore work ones as they rhythmically polished piles of ghostly silver. The bellboys' hands holding the ghostly notes were gloved in pale gray cotton. And there were opera gloves, almost armpit length, that looked like spectral white cobras, especially when they were drawn inside-out off the sinuous, snake-slender arms of wealthy guesting ladies. And other ghostly gloves, not all hotel ones, came floating and weaving into my fantasy: the black gloves of morticians, the white gloves of policemen, the bulky fur-lined ones of polar explorers, the trim dark gauntlets of chauffeurs, the gloves of hunters with separate stalls only for thumb and trigger finger, the mittens of ice-skaters and sleigh riders, old ladies' mitts without any fingers at all, the thin, translucent elastic gloves of surgeons, wielding flashing scalpels of silver-bright steel—a veritable whirlpool of gloves that finally led me down, down, down to darkness.

Once again I woke with a start, as if I'd been touched, and shot up. Once again I felt something about four inches long clinging high on my neck, only this time under the other ear. Once again I frantically slashed at my neck and jaw, stinging them painfully, only this time I struck upward and away. I *thought* I felt something go.

I got the light on and checked the door at once. It was securely shut. Then I looked at the table by the open window.

The heavy ashtray still sat in the center of it, rock firm.

But the rapist's glove that had been under it was gone.

I must have stood there a couple of minutes, telling myself this could not be. Then I went over and lifted the ashtray and carefully inspected its underside, as if the glove had somehow managed to shrink and was clinging there.

And all the while I was having this vision of the glove painfully humping itself from under the ashtray and inching to the table's edge and dropping to the floor and then crawling off . . . almost anywhere.

Believe me, I searched my place then, especially the floor. I even opened the doors to the closet and the clothes cabinet, though they had been tightly shut, and searched the floor there. And of course I searched under and behind the bed. And more than once while I searched, I'd suddenly jerk around thinking I'd seen something gray approaching my shoulder from behind.

There wasn't a sign of the glove.

It was dawn by now—had been for some time. I made coffee and tried to think rationally about it.

It seemed to boil down to three explanations that weren't wildly farfetched.

First, that I'd gone out of my mind. Could be, I suppose. But from what I'd read and seen, most people who go crazy know damn well ahead of time that something frightening is happening to their minds, except maybe paranoiacs. Still, it remained a possibility.

Second, that someone with a duplicate or master key had quietly taken the glove away while I was asleep. The apartment manager and janitor had such keys. I'd briefly given my duplicate to various people. Why, once before she got down on me, I'd given it to Evelyn Mayne—matter of letting someone in while I was at work. I *thought* I'd got it back from her, though I remember once having a second duplicate made—I'd forgotten why. The main difficulty about this explanation was motive. Who'd want to get the glove?—except the rapist, maybe.

Third, of course, there was the supernatural. Gloves are ghostly to start with, envelopes for hands—and if there isn't a medieval superstition about wearing the flayed skin of another's hand to work magic, there ought to be. (Of course, there was the Hand of Glory, its fingers flaming like candles, guaranteed to make people sleep while being burgled, but there the skin is still on the dried chopped-off hand.) And there are tales of spectral hands a-plenty—pointing out buried treasure or hidden graves, or at guilty murderers, or carrying candles or daggers—so why not gloves? And could there be a kind of telekinesis in which a hand controls at a distance the movements and actions of a glove it has worn? Of course that would be psionics or whatnot, but to me the parapsychological is supernatural. (And in that case what had the glove been trying to do probing at my neck?—strangle me, I'd think.) And somewhere I'd read of an aristocratic Brazilian murderess of the last century who wore gloves woven of spider silk, and of a knight blinded at a crucial moment in a tourney by a lady's silken glove worn as a favor. Yes, they were eerie envelopes, I thought, gloves were, but I was just concerned with one of them, a vanishing glove.

I started with a jerk as there came a measured *knock-knock*. I opened the door and looked up at the poker faces of two young policemen. Over their shoulders Mr. Helpful was peering down eagerly at me, his lips rapidly quirking in little smiles with what I'd call questioning pouts in between. Back and a little to one side was Marcia, looking shocked and staring intently at me through the narrow space between the second policeman and the door jamb.

"Jeff Winters," the first policeman said to me, as if it were a fact that he was putting into place. It occurred to me that young policemen look very *blocky* around their narrow hips with all that equipment they carry snugly nested and cased in black leather.

"Officer Hart—" Marcia began anxiously.

The second policeman's eyes flickered towards her, but just then the first policeman continued, "Your neighbor Miss Everly says she handed you a glove earlier this morning," and he stepped forward into the private space (I think it's sometimes called) around my body, and I automatically stepped back.

"We want it," he went on, continuing to step forward, and I back.

I hesitated. What was I to say? That the glove had started to spook me and then disappeared? Officer Hart followed the first policeman in. Mr. Helpful followed *him* in and stopped just inside my door, Marcia still beyond him and looking frantic. Officer Hart turned, as if about to tell Mr. Helpful to get out, but just then Officer Halstead (that was the other name Marcia had mentioned) said, "Well, you've still got it, haven't you? She gave it to you, didn't she?"

I shook and then nodded my head, which must have made me look rattled. He came closer still and said harshly and with a note of eagerness, "Well, where is it, then?"

I had to look up quite sharply at him to see his face. Beyond it, just to one side of it, diagonally upward across the room, was the top of the tall clothes cabinet, and on the edge of that there balanced that damned gray glove, flat fingers dripping over.

I froze. I could have sworn I'd glanced up there more than once when I was hunting the thing, and seen nothing. Yet there it was, as if it had flown up there or else been flicked there by me the second time I'd violently brushed something from my face.

Officer Halstead must have misread my look of terror, for he ducked his head toward mine and rasped, "Your neighbor Mr. Angus says that it's *your* glove, that he saw you wearing gray gloves night before last! What do you say?"

But I didn't say anything, for at that moment the glove slid off its precarious perch and dropped straight down and landed on Mr. Helpful's (Angus's) shoulder close to his neck, just like the hand of an arresting cop.

Now it may have been that in ducking his head to look at it, he trapped it between his chin and collarbone, or it may have been (as it looked to me) that the glove actively clung to his neck and shoulder, resisting all his frantic efforts to peel it off, while he reiterated, his voice mounting in screams, "It's not my glove!"

He took his hands away for a moment and the glove dropped to the floor.

He looked back and forth and saw the dawning expressions on the faces of the two policemen, and then with a sort of despairing sob he whipped a long knife from under his coat.

Considerably to my surprise I started toward him, but just then Officer Hart endeared himself to us all forever by wrapping his arms around Mr. Angus like a bear, one hand closing on the wrist of the hand holding the knife.

I veered past him (I vividly recall changing the length of one of my strides so as not to step on the glove) and reached Marcia just in time to steady her as, turned quite white, she swayed, her eyelids fluttering.

I heard the knife clatter to the floor. I turned, my arms around Marcia, and we both saw Mr. Angus seem to shrink and collapse in Officer Hart's ursine embrace, his face going gray as if he were an empty glove himself.

That was it. They found the other glove and the long silver wig in a locked suitcase in his room. Marcia stayed frightened long enough, off and on, for us to become better acquainted and cement our friendship.

Officer (now Detective) Hart tells us that Mr. Angus is a model prisoner at the hospital for the criminally insane and has gone very religious, but never smiles. And he—Hart—now had the glove in a sort of Black Museum down at the station, where it has never again been seen to move under its own power. If it ever did.

One interesting thing. The gloves had belonged to Mr. Angus's father, now deceased, who had been a judge.

I would like to think Robert Bloch is most noted as the man whose novel Psycho *made Alfred Hitchcock famous; I know it made Hitchcock money. Bloch's fiction first appeared in* Weird Tales *during the 1930s and his work was greatly influenced by his literary mentor, Howard Phillips Lovecraft. He was the first recipient of the World Fantasy Award for life work, an honor he richly deserved. Recent years have seen a paucity of short stories from his pen as a result of his many commitments to novels, movies, and television, but Bob, ever generous with his time, kindly wrote the following story specifically for this book. The main character is one Robert Bloch, a man who—well, read on . . .*

THE CLOSER OF THE WAY

by Robert Bloch

To this day I don't know how they got me to the asylum.

The events leading up to my committal constitute a mystery which defies the probe of memory, and so it shall remain.

Family and friends spoke, at the time, of a "nervous condition," but that is undoubtedly a polite euphemism. They preferred to call the asylum a "private sanatorium" and my incarceration was referred to as "convalescence."

But now that I have no family—and no friends—I can at least speak freely and frankly of my situation.

I was insane.

God, what hypocrites we've become! The higher the incidence of insanity in our society, the more the word itself has been tabooed. In a world gone mad it is no longer possible to speak freely of madmen; in this era of lunacy there are supposedly no lunatics; the craziness compounds because we refuse to admit that anyone is crazy.

"Mentally ill." That's the phrase which Dr. Connors used. "Paranoid schizophrenia" was another and more highly clinical description. Neither of which really conveys an accurate impression of the horror inherent in the reality—or the unreality.

Insanity is a long nightmare from which some never awaken. Others, like myself, eventually open their eyes to greet the dawn of a new day, rejoicing in renewed awareness. It's a wonderful feeling to realize that the nightmare has ended. Makes you want to sing, as I did.

"Yes, we have no bananas—"

Dr. Connors eyed me dispassionately. "What's that supposed to mean?" he said.

"That I'm all right again," I smiled. "Bananas—the current slang for insanity. It's a kind of a joke."

"I see."

But Dr. Connors didn't really see anything.

When I assured him that I was no longer disoriented, no longer hostile or afraid, he merely nodded. And when I told him I was ready to go home, he shook his head.

"There are some problems we must work through first," he said.

"Work—that's my only problem," I told him. "I've got to get back to work! Do you realize what staying here has cost me?"

Dr. Connors shrugged. "Your work is one of the problems we're going to be talking about. I think it may help us to find the cause of your difficulties." He opened a desk drawer and took out a book. "I've been reading some of the things you've written, and there are a number of questions—"

"Okay," I said. "If you want to play games, suppose you let me have the first guess. The book you have there, the one you've been reading—it's *Psycho*, isn't it?"

"Yes."

"Don't look so surprised. Everybody seems to start out by reading *Psycho*. And reading things *into* it. I've been through this sort of inquisition so many times that you don't even need to ask the questions. We can both save valuable time if I just give you the answers."

"I'm listening."

"First of all, I don't hate my mother. And she never dominated me. My family background was perfectly normal—I had no hangups as far as my parents or my sister are concerned. My mother was a social worker and teacher, a very intelligent woman who encouraged me to write. I loved her dearly, but there was no oedipal fixation involved.

"Secondly, I have never been conscious of any homosexual tendencies, never felt a desire to experiment in transvestism. Or taxidermy, for that matter. I know nothing about motel operation, or hiding cars and bodies in swamps.

"So you can see I'm not Norman Bates. And as for identifying with other characters in the book—I never embezzled any money from an employer, never ran away, never conducted a long-term clandestine liaison. For that matter, I've always preferred a tub bath instead of a shower."

I smiled at Dr. Connors. "The idea for the book came to me after reading about an actual murder case. I didn't use any of the real-life participants as characters, nor the real-life situation. What set me off was wondering how a man living in a small town all his life, under constant scrutiny of his neighbors, could manage to conceal his crimes of violence. What I did—call it the case entry, if you will—was to construct a psychological profile of such a man, just as you do in your work. Once I felt I understood the character and his motivations, the rest was simple."

Dr. Connors nodded. "Thank you for your cooperation. You've anticipated and answered all of my questions except one."

"And that is—?"

"Let me put it this way. I imagine you read up on quite a few murder cases as a matter of course; it would be the natural thing to do, in your line of work."

"That's true."

"And some of them are pretty sensational, aren't they? Mass murders, bizarre slayings, ritual killings, weird deaths occurring under strange circumstances?"

"Also true."

"Some of them, I'm sure, are far more shocking and violent than the particular crime which, in your words, set you off?"

"Right."

"Then my question is simply this. *Why* did this one murder intrigue you? Why did you choose it rather than another?"

"But I've already explained—it was wondering how the killer managed to conceal his activities and get away with it—how he was able to avoid suspicion, lead a double life."

"That's interesting. The problem of concealment, avoiding suspicion." Dr. Connors leaned forward. "Do *you* lead a double life?"

I stared at him for a long moment before answering. "Forgive me for saying so, but you're out of your mind."

"Perhaps. But being out of my mind doesn't matter. It's getting into your mind that's important."

He stood up. "That's enough for now, I think. We'll talk again tomorrow."

"More questions?"

"Hopefully, more answers." He gave a little chuckle. "It appears I'm going to have to do some further reading tonight."

"Well, good luck to you. And pleasant dreams."

"That's the title of one of your books, isn't it—*Pleasant Dreams*?"

"I've written a lot of books," I said. "And a lot of stories."

"I know." He walked me to the office door. "Oh, one final thought. Did it ever occur to you that all fiction writing is a form of lying? And that the only major difference between an author and a psychotic is that the former puts down his fantasies on paper? You might think that over."

"I will," I told him.

And I did, all that day and during the night which followed. In the end I arrived at one firm conclusion.

I disliked Dr. Connors intensely.

It was late in the afternoon next day before Miss Frobisher came to my room and said that Dr. Connors was ready to see me. The long wait hadn't been easy on the nerves, and I'm sure she noticed how uptight I was. Miss Frobisher was a good nurse, I suppose, and treating patients like naughty children was just a part of her job. The fact that she was a little on the butch side probably contributed to her kindly authoritarianism, but I found her manner irritating.

"And how are we today?" she greeted me. "Are we ready for our therapy session?"

"Speaking for myself, I've no objection," I said. "But I happen to be alone. If you insist on addressing me in the plural, perhaps you need therapy more than I do."

Miss Frobisher laughed professionally (never show anger, never let them get to you, that's the secret) and guided me down the hall.

"Doctor's waiting for you in surgery," she said.

"Don't tell me I'm going to have a prefrontal lobotomy," I murmured. "This I need like a hole in the head."

Miss Frobisher laughed again. "Nothing of the sort! But the painters are doing his office and won't be finished until sometime tomorrow. So if you don't mind—"

"Fine with me."

She led me into the elevator and we got off on the third floor. I'd never been up there before, and was a little surprised to discover that Dr. Connors had a very efficient and compact medical unit installed. I knew, of course, that he was a neurosurgeon as well as a practicing psychiatrist, but I found myself quite impressed by the completely equipped modern surgery which I glimpsed beyond the glass wall of the outer room where Dr. Connors waited for me.

I smiled at him as Miss Frobisher left. "We've got to stop meeting this way," I said.

"Sit down."

One look convinced me he wasn't in the mood for fun and games. I seated myself and faced him across a small table on which rested a note-pad and a book.

"Aha!" I murmured, glancing at the book. "So you *did* read *Pleasant Dreams*."

"All last evening."

"I see you made some notes," I told him. "Since when did you become a critic?"

"I'm not here to criticize, only to discuss."

"Go ahead. We writers like to hear people talk about our work."

"I was hoping you might do the talking."

"What's to say? It's all in the book."

"Is it?"

"Look," I said, "is it really necessary to talk like a shrink?"

"Not if you're willing to stop talking like a patient." Dr. Connors smiled and glanced at the note-pad.

"But I am a patient," I said. "According to you."

"According to *Pleasant Dreams* you're quite a number of things. For instance, a collaborator of Edgar Allan Poe's."

" 'The Light House.' " I nodded. "A Poe scholar back East found the unfinished story and suggested that I complete it."

"Do you frequently get plots or ideas from other people?"

"None that I can use. Most of my stuff comes from my own background or interests. I wrote 'The Dream-Makers' because I was always a silent-movie fan, and 'Mr. Steinway' represents a similar preoccupation with music. I like to use locales I've visited or lived in. Milwaukee, in 'The Cheaters,' New Orleans in 'The Sleeping Beauty,' upstate Wisconsin in 'Sweet Sixteen,' 'That Hellbound Train,' and 'Hungarian Rhapsody.' " I grinned at Dr. Connors. "But that's the bottom line. I've never owned a pair of magic eyeglasses, slept with a skeleton, ridden a motorcycle, made a bargain with the Devil, or had an affair with a vampire."

"Granted." Dr. Connors squinted at his notes. "So far we've talked about things you like—now, let's get on to what you dislike."

"That's easy," I told him. "Formal dinner parties inspired 'The Proper Spirit.' And I suppose 'The Hungry House' represents an aversion to mirrors. In fact, if you really want to probe, it means I've always been self-consciously displeased with my own looks. Is that candid enough for you, Doc?"

"Not quite." He stared at me. "Why don't you want to discuss the real problems?"

"Such as?"

"Your attitude toward children."

"I've got nothing against children."

"That's not what your stories say." He tapped the note-pad with his pen. "In 'Sweets to the Sweet,' a little girl is a witch. 'The Sorcerer's Apprentice' deals with a mentally retarded youth whose delusions lead to murder. 'Catnip' is a thoroughly vindictive portrait of adolescence. 'Sweet Sixteen' is an indictment of an entire generation—you were writing about Satanist motorcycle gangs almost a decade before others picked up the notion for films. Even in a comparatively gentle story like 'That Hellbound Train,' your protagonist starts life as a runaway, a drifter who steals hubcaps and gets stoned on canned heat. And in 'Enoch,' your central character is a psychotic teenager who becomes a mass murderer.''

"Kids aren't my hangup," I said. "Don't forget, I write horror stories. And in a youth-oriented society, people are most apt to be shocked by having children depicted as monsters. The trick lies in violating the taboos we hold sacred—that's what I did to the mother image in *Psycho*.''

"Trick," said Dr. Connors softly. "Lies.''

I grinned again. "So now we're playing word games, right? In that case, let's just call it a Freudian slip.''

He shrugged. "That reminds me of another element in your work—not just in this collection, but in literally dozens of your stories. The hostility toward psychiatrists.''

"I don't hate psychiatrists.''

"Your characters seem to. There are disparaging references to psychotherapists in 'The Sorcerer's Apprentice,' 'I Kiss Your Shadow,' and other titles in the book. And in 'Enoch,' your Dr. Silversmith is a caricature, a gross libel of the profession.''

"But that's just another way of shocking people," I said. "Psychiatrists have become the high priests in a society that worships science. Showing them as incompetent or powerless to prevail against the forces of evil is an effective gimmick.''

Dr. Connors stared at me. "Effective gimmicks—that's what you look for. Meaning things that induce fear in the reader. Your entire career has been spent in finding ways to shock people, horrify them.''

"It's a living.''

"Which you yourself chose. Nobody spends a lifetime frightening those he loves. Why do you hate people?''

"I don't.''

"Think about it. Think about it seriously. I intend to." He glanced at his watch. "Until tomorrow, then.''

"Sorry if it sounds like I'm stonewalling," I said, "but I really don't hate people.''

Which was true. I didn't hate my readers, or kids, or shrinks per se.

But I was beginning to hate Dr. Connors.

It was a bad night. I didn't get any sleep, because I was too busy planning my own defense. Perhaps that sounds a trifle melodramatic, but there really was no other word for it. I had to defend myself when Dr. Connors attacked me by using my own words, my own work. It was unfair, unjust, unspeakable—only an idiot would equate make-believe with reality. Actors who played villains weren't monsters in real life: Boris Karloff and Christopher Lee were two of the nicest persons I've ever known. My own literary mentor, H. P. Lovecraft, was a kind and gentle man. If Dr. Connors thought otherwise, he was only displaying his own ignorance.

Or his own cleverness.

He was searching for something; something which escaped me. Something connected with my own condition, no doubt, something blocked and obscured by an amnesic reaction. If I could only recall what happened—

But that wasn't important now. The important thing was to be prepared for tomorrow's attack. Attack through my own books.

Which title would he select?

I tried to anticipate his choice in my own mind. *American Gothic, Night-World, Firebug, The Dead Beat, The Kidnapper, The Will to Kill, The Scarf*—all were possible selections. But all of these novels possessed a common theme: the ease with which a psychopath could operate within our supposedly sane society. Surely such a premise is a legitimate subject for examination. And if Dr. Connors planned to play devil's advocate and ask why I was so preoccupied with psychopaths, I'd tell him the truth. *I'm afraid of them, Doctor. Aren't we all?*

That was it. Just tell the truth. *The truth shall make ye free—*

I had plenty of time to consider the matter, because Miss Frobisher didn't come for me until after dinner the following evening.

Dr. Connors, she said, had been called away on personal business during the afternoon. But he'd returned now and was waiting for me again in the anteroom to the surgery unit.

"Sorry about that," he told me, as Miss Frobisher departed. "The painters finished my office, but I haven't had time to get things straightened out yet. So if you don't mind—"

"Not at all."

Dr. Connors was seated at the table, note-pad resting on top of a book. I glanced at the book as I spoke, trying to see the title. Which one had he chosen?

There was no need to play guessing games. He was already lifting the pad, exposing the volume beneath.

It was *The Opener of the Way*.

He nodded at me. "As you can see, I've done my homework. You expected that, didn't you?"

"Yes. But not your choice. Why this, instead of a novel?"

"Because it's your first book, your first published story collection. And because of the title."

"If you read it, you know that 'The Opener of the Way' is one of the stories."

"But that's not why you selected that title, is it? You were making a statement of intention—this book was opening the way to your writing career."

"Very perceptive. What else did you notice?"

"That certain constant elements in your work go back almost to the beginning. Mass murders, for example, in 'Waxworks,' 'House of the Hatchet,' 'Yours Truly, Jack the Ripper.' The invasion or desecration of the human body— 'Beetles,' 'The Dark Demon,' 'The Shambler from the Stars,' 'The Fiddler's Fee,' and 'The Opener' itself. Plus the theme of possession by evil forces or an alter ego, in 'The Cloak,' 'The Mannikin,' 'The Dark Demon,' 'The Eyes of the Mummy.' You must admit, it all seems to add up."

"To what?"

"To the recurrent image of a man possessed by a demon, mutilating his victims in a series of multiple murders."

I shrugged. "As I told you, it's a living. And as you told me, all fiction is a form of lying. These particular lies happen to be the ones I live by. They worked for me when I started writing, and they still work for me today."

"But you don't lie all the time, do you?" Dr. Connors opened the book. "What about the introduction you wrote for this collection? You start out by asking the very same question I've been asking you. *Where do you get the ideas for your stories?''*

"I've already told you that."

Dr. Connors flipped a page. "You give a different answer here. You say that a fantasy author is cast in the dual role of Jekyll and Hyde."

"Just a figure of speech."

"Is it?" He glanced down at the text. "Let me read you your own words. 'Dr. Jekyll attempts to deny the very existence of Mr. Hyde. But . . . Mr. Hyde exists. I know, for he is a part of me. He has been my literary mentor now for more than a decade.' And now, the last paragraph of your introduction. 'And when anyone inquires as to where I get the ideas for my stories, I can only shrug and answer, *From my collaborator—Mr. Hyde.*' That's an exact quote."

I stared at him. Yesterday I'd told myself that I was beginning to hate this man. Today—

"Something wrong?"

"Only with your conclusions."

"Not mine. Yours."

"Cut the double-talk. Are you saying I'm a multiple personality?"

"You're saying it, in your introduction here. And in your work. That's double-talk with a vengeance."

"I'm not interested in vengeance." I shook my head. "And I don't hate people."

"So says Dr. Jekyll. But Mr. Hyde tells a different story. Over and over and over again."

"It's just a story."

"Are you sure?" Dr. Connors shook his head. "Then why are you here?"

"I don't know."

"Don't know, or don't remember?"

"Both."

"Exactly. In multiple-personality disorders, there's always this element of amnesia, of disassociation. My job is to help you recall. I was hoping that analyzing your work would lead you to find clues to reality. Once you face the truth—"

"What is the truth?"

"There are many truths. Consider them. You're in a private sanatorium—and you wouldn't be here unless there was a reason. You're under tight security—and that should suggest the reason is a serious one. You can't remember what happened prior to your arrival; surely this implies a personality split protected by an amnesic reaction."

I took a deep breath. "What you're saying is that I flipped out and killed somebody?"

"No." Dr. Connors smiled. "Consider the facts. If you'd killed somebody, you'd be downtown, at the county jail."

"But I did flip, didn't I?"

"Yes." He smiled again. "Before we continue, perhaps I'd better remind you of another truth. I'm here because I'm interested in your welfare. I'm not your enemy."

Locking me up. Playing cat-and-mouse games with me. Prying into my stories, my secrets. And then, expecting me to believe he wasn't my enemy? Maybe I was crazy, but I wasn't stupid.

"Of course not." I returned his smile. "Shall we get on with it?"

Dr. Connors consulted his note-pad. "There's another thread weaving itself through your fiction. Not just the fantasies but the mystery-suspense stories I've read—so many of them deal with variations on a single *dénouement*."

"What's that?"

"Decapitation."

"Is that so unusual? It's a common enough device for shocking the reader. Even the Queen in *Alice in Wonderland* kept saying—"

"Let's stick to your own work, and what *you* say. About the collector of heads in 'Man with a Hobby,' and the collector of skulls in 'The Skull of the Marquis de Sade.' And that other collector called Enoch. What motivated you to write 'The Cure,' 'The Head-Hunter,' or 'See How They Run'? There's a head lopped off in *Psycho*, and the final scene in *Night-World* speaks for itself. Heads roll in 'The Hound of Pedro' and 'That Old College Try.'" Dr. Connors picked up the book. "You did it here, in 'Waxworks.' And in your very first published story, 'The Feast in the Abbey.'"

"And a damned good thing," I said. "That's what made an impression on the readers. Not just the idea of cannibalism. But when the narrator finds out what he's been eating—when he lifts the lid of the small silver platter and sees the head of his brother—"

"Quite effective, I agree." Dr. Connors looked up at me. "I notice you wrote in the first person."

"That's part of the impact."

"But where did the idea come from? A newspaper story? Something you heard or read about?"

"I don't remember. After all, that was so long ago—"

"Odd, isn't it, that this should be one of your earliest efforts? And that you continued the same theme over the years?" He kept staring at me. "You've told me the source of so many of your stories. Surely there's a point of origin for this one and those which follow the pattern."

"I told you, I can't recall!"

"Nothing in your personal background?"

"I'm not a cannibal, if that's what you're hinting. I *do* have a younger sister, but no brother, so I could hardly cut off his head—"

It was hard to speak quietly because I hated him so. And it was hard to hear him now, because of the way my heart was pounding, pounding, pounding—

"Look," said Dr. Connors. "I'm going to tell you something that will help you to remember. It may shock you, but sometimes shock therapy is the most effective method."

"Go ahead," I said. *Ahead. Head. It was the head of my brother—*

Dr. Connors was watching my face, but I'm positive he couldn't hear the voice inside my head. *My head. His head. Their heads.*

I forced myself to look at him, forced myself to smile. "Don't tell me I cut off somebody's head," I said.

"No. But you tried."

"That's a lie!" I stood up, and I wasn't smiling now. "That's a lie!"

"You mean you can't remember. But you did, and they stopped you just in time. It's all there in the record."

"But why—why?"

"Because the person you attempted to kill apparently reminded you of someone else. Someone long ago." Dr. Connors leaned forward, speaking very softly, so that I had to strain to hear him.

I *did* hear him, though—I must have—because the hate kept building, building as he spoke.

Only I still can't recall what he said. It was about something that happened when I was very young. Something I did to someone and Mama found out about it and the doctor came and then they sent me away for a long time and when I came home again I forgot all about everything. I was just a kid, I didn't know, I didn't mean it, I hated him, but I forgot and nobody ever even talked about it, nobody ever even knew about it. Except now, Dr. Connors knew—he'd gone away today and looked up the information and now he was telling me about it and he'd tell everybody and I hated him because I still couldn't remember.

But I *do* remember what I did when he told me. It was all luck, really—being in that room next to the surgery, and then later finding the backstairs exit and getting over the wall.

It was even luck that there was one of those silver things with a lid on top, right next to the knife cabinet in the surgery.

I keep thinking of that now—thinking of how Miss Frobisher must have come back, and what she saw when she lifted up the lid . . .

It was the head of my psychiatrist.

William Nolan is the co-author of Logan's Run, *a $9,000,000 motion picture as well as the co-author of the "Burnt Offerings" screenplay. His short fiction has appeared in over seventy-three anthologies, but he now spends most of his time scripting for the more lucrative fields of film and television. Science fiction, fantasy, and horror are not his only short-fiction fortes, and he has won an Edgar Award from the Mystery Writers of America. In this tale, Mr. Nolan has taken the classic "return to childhood" theme and handled it in a most unique way. We never encounter the main character and the mood of horror is created from "sterile" nondescriptive transcripts. It is quite successful.*

DARK WINNER
by *William F. Nolan*

NOTE: The following is an edited transcript of a taped conversation between Mrs. Franklin Evans, resident of Woodland Hills, California, and Lieutenant Harry W. Lyle of the Kansas City Police Department.
Transcript is dated July 12, 1975, K.C., Missouri.

LYLE: . . . and if you want us to help you, we'll have to know everything. When did you arrive here, Mrs. Evans?

MRS. EVANS: We just got in this morning. A stopover on our trip from New York back to California. We were at the airport when Frank suddenly got this idea about his past.

LYLE: What idea?

MRS. E: About visiting his old neighborhood . . . the school he went to . . . the house where he grew up . . . He hadn't been back here in twenty-five years.

LYLE: So you and your husband planned this . . . nostalgic tour?

MRS. E: Not *planned*. It was very abrupt . . . Frank seemed . . . suddenly . . . *possessed* by the idea.

LYLE: So what happened?

MRS. E: We took a cab out to Flora Avenue . . . to Thirty-first . . . and we visited his old grade school. St. Vincent's Academy. The neighborhood is . . . well, I guess you know it's a slum area now . . . and the school is closed down, locked. But Frank found an open window . . . climbed inside . . .

LYLE: While you waited?

MRS. E: Yes—in the cab. When Frank came out he was all . . . upset . . . Said that he . . . Well, this sounds . . .

LYLE: Go on, please.

MRS. E: He said he felt . . . very *close* to his childhood while he was in there. He was ashen-faced. His hands were trembling.

LYLE: What did you do then?

MRS. E: We had the cab take us up Thirty-first to the Isis Theater. The movie house at Thirty-first and Troost where Frank used to attend those Saturday horror shows they had for kids. Each week a new one . . . Frankenstein . . . Dracula . . . you know the kind I mean.

LYLE: I know.

MRS. E: It's a porno place now . . . but Frank bought a ticket anyway . . . went inside alone. Said he wanted to go into the balcony, find his old seat . . . see if things had changed . . .

LYLE: And?

MRS. E: He came out looking very shaken . . . saying it had happened again.

LYLE: *What* had happened again?

MRS. E: The feeling about being close to his past . . . to his childhood . . . As if he could—

LYLE: Could what, Mrs. Evans?

MRS. E: . . . step over the line dividing past and present . . . step back into his childhood. That's the feeling he said he had.

LYLE: Where did you go from the Isis?

MRS. E: Frank paid off the cab . . . said he wanted to walk to his old block . . . the one he grew up on . . . Thirty-third and Forest. So we walked down Troost to Thirty-third . . . past strip joints and hamburger stands . . . I was nervous . . . we didn't . . . belong here . . . Anyway, we got to Thirty-third and walked down the hill from Troost to Forest . . . and on the way Frank told me how much he'd hated being small, being a child . . . that he could hardly wait to grow up . . . that, to him, childhood was a nightmare . . .

LYLE: Then why all the nostalgia?

MRS. E: It wasn't that . . . it was . . . like an *exorcism* . . . Frank said he'd been haunted by his childhood all the years we'd lived in California . . . This was an attempt to get *rid* of it . . . by facing it . . . seeing that it was really gone . . . that it no longer had any reality . . .

LYLE: What happened on Forest?

MRS. E: We walked down the street to his old address . . . which was just past the middle of the block . . . 3337 it was . . . a small, sagging wooden house . . . in terrible condition . . . but then, *all* the houses were . . . their screens full of holes . . . windows broken, trash in the yards . . . Frank stood in front of his house staring at it for a long time . . . and then he began repeating something . . . over and over.

LYLE: And what was that?

MRS. E: He said it . . . like a litany . . . over and over . . . ''I hate you! . . . I hate you! . . . I hate you!''

LYLE: You mean, he was saying that to *you?*

MRS. E: Oh, no. Not to *me* . . . I asked him what he meant . . . and . . . he said he hated the child he once was, the child who had lived in that house.

LYLE: I see. Go on, Mrs. Evans.

MRS. E: Then he said he was going inside . . . that he *had* to go inside the house . . . but that he was afraid.

LYLE: Of what?

MRS. E: He didn't say of what. He just told me to wait out there on the walk . . . Then he went up onto the small wooden porch . . . knocked on the door. No one answered. Then Frank tried the knob . . . The door was unlocked . . .

LYLE: House was deserted?

MRS. E: That's right. I guess no one had lived there for a long while . . . All the windows were boarded up . . . and the driveway was filled with weeds . . . I started to move toward the porch, but Frank waved me back. Then he kicked the door all the way open with his foot, took a half step inside, turned . . . and looked back at me . . . There was a . . . a terrible fear in his eyes. I got a cold, chilled feeling all through my body—and I started toward him again . . . but he suddenly turned his back and went inside . . . The door closed.

LYLE: What then?

MRS. E: Then I waited. For fifteen . . . twenty minutes . . . a half hour . . . Frank didn't come out. So I went up to the porch and opened the door . . . called to him . . .

LYLE: Any answer?

MRS. E: No. The house was like . . . a hollow cave . . . there were echoes . . . but no answer . . . I went inside . . . walked all through the place . . . into every room . . . but he wasn't there . . . Frank was gone.

LYLE: Out the back, maybe.

MRS. E: No. The back door was nailed shut. Rusted. It hadn't been opened for years.

LYLE: A window then.

MRS. E: They were all boarded over. With thick dust on the sills.

LYLE: Did you check the basement?

MRS. E: Yes, I checked the basement door leading down. It was locked, and the dust hadn't been disturbed around it.

LYLE: Then . . . just where the hell did he *go*?

MRS. E: I don't *know*, Lieutenant! . . . That's why I called you . . . why I came here . . . You've got to find Frank!

END FIRST TRANSCRIPT

> NOTE: Lieutenant Lyle did not find Franklin Evans. The case was turned over to Missing Persons—and, a week later, Mrs. Evans returned to her home in California. The first night back she had a dream, a nightmare. It disturbed her severely. She could not eat, could not sleep properly; her nerves were shattered. Mrs. Evans then sought psychiatric help. What follows is an excerpt from a taped session with Dr. Lawrence Redding, a licensed psychiatrist with offices in Beverly Hills, California.

Transcript is dated August 3, 1975, Beverly Hills.

REDDING: And where were you . . . ? In the *dream*, I mean.

MRS. E: My bedroom. In bed, at home. It was as if I'd just been awakened . . . I looked around me—and everything was normal . . . the room exactly as it always is . . . Except for *him* . . . the boy standing next to me.

REDDING: Did you recognize this boy?

MRS. E: No.

REDDING: Describe him to me.

MRS. E: He was . . . nine or ten . . . a *horrible* child . . . with a cold hate in his face, in his eyes . . . He had on a red sweater with holes in each elbow. And knickers . . . the kind that boys used to wear . . . and he had on black tennis shoes . . .

REDDING: Did he speak to you?

MRS. E: Not at first. He just . . . smiled at me . . . and that smile was so . . . so *evil!* . . . And then he said . . . that he wanted me to know he'd won at last . . .

REDDING: Won what?

MRS. E: That's what I asked him . . . calmly, in the dream . . . I asked him what he'd won. And he said . . . oh, my God . . . he said . . .

REDDING: Go on, Mrs. Evans.

MRS. E: . . . that he'd won Frank! . . . that my husband would *never* be coming back . . . that he, the boy, *had* him now . . . forever! . . . I screamed—and woke up. And, instantly, I remembered something.

REDDING: What did you remember?

MRS. E: Before she died . . . Frank's mother . . . sent us an album she'd saved . . . of his childhood . . . photos . . . old report cards . . . He never wanted to look at it, stuck the album away in a closet . . . After the dream, I . . . got it out, looked through it until I found . . .

REDDING: Yes . . . ?

MRS. E: A photo I'd remembered. Of Frank . . . at the age of ten . . . standing in the front yard on Forest . . . He was smiling . . . that same, awful smile . . . and . . . he wore a sweater with holes in each elbow . . . and knickers . . . black tennis shoes. It was . . . the *same* boy exactly—the younger self Frank had always hated . . . I *know* what happened in that house now.

REDDING: Then tell me.

MRS. E: The boy was . . . waiting there . . . inside that awful, rotting dead house . . . waiting for Frank to come back . . . all those years . . . waiting there to claim him— because . . . *he* hated the man that Frank had become as much as Frank hated the child he'd once been . . . and the boy was *right*.

REDDING: Right about what, Mrs. Evans?

MRS. E: About winning . . . It took all those years . . . but he won . . . and Frank lost.

END TRANSCRIPT

Hugh B. Cave was long just a name to me out of the famous history of Weird Tales. He graduated from that school of fiction to the more demanding and better-paying "slicks," and was out of our field for many, many years. His interest in fantasy and horror was recently rekindled by Karl Edward Wagner and David Drake's small press, Carcosa, which will be bringing out two volumes of his fiction (as illustrated by the talented Gothic artist, Lee Brown Coye). You can clearly see the influence of the "slicks" in this horror story concerning a young couple, a very strange house, and its even stranger inhabitants.

LADIES IN WAITING

by Hugh B. Cave

Halper, the village real-estate man, said with a squint, "You're the same people looked at that place in April, aren't you? Sure you are. The ones got caught in that freak snow storm and spent the night there. Mr. and Mrs. Wilkes, is it?"

"Wilkins," Norman corrected, frowning at a photograph on the wall of the old man's dingy office: a yellowed, fly-spotted picture of the house itself, in all its decay and drabness.

"And you want to look at it again?"

"Yes!" Linda exclaimed.

Both men looked at her sharply because of her vehemence. Norman, her husband, was alarmed anew by the eagerness that suddenly flamed in her lovely brown eyes and as suddenly was replaced by a look of guilt. Yes—unmistakably a look of guilt.

"I mean," she stammered, "we still want a big old house that we can do over, Mr. Halper. We've never stopped looking. And we keep thinking the Creighton place just might do."

You keep thinking it might do, Norman silently corrected. He himself had intensely disliked the place when Halper showed it to them four months ago. The sharp edge of his abhorrence was not even blunted, and time would never dull his remembrance of that shocking expression on Linda's face. When he stepped through that hundred-seventy-year-old doorway again, he would hate and fear the house as much as before, he was certain.

Would he again see that look on his wife's face? God forbid!

"Well," Halper said, "there's no need for me to go along with you this time, I guess. I'll just ask you to return the key when you're through, same as you did before."

Norman accepted the tagged key from him and walked unhappily out to the car.

It was four miles from the village to the house. One mile of narrow blacktop, three of a dirt road that seemed forlorn and forgotten even in this neglected part of New England. At three in the afternoon of an awesomely hot August day the car made the only sound in a deep green silence. The sun's heat had robbed even birds and insects of their voices.

Norman was silent too—with apprehension. Beside him his adored wife of less than two years leaned forward to peer through the windshield for the first glimpse of their destination, seeming to have forgotten he existed. Only the house now mattered.

And there it was.

Nothing had changed. It was big and ugly, with a sagging front piazza and too few windows. It was old. It was gray because almost all its white paint had weathered away. According to old Halper the Creightons had lived here for generations, having come here from Salem where one of their women in the days of witchcraft madness had been hanged for practicing demonolatry. A likely story.

As he stopped the car by the piazza steps, Norman glanced at the girl beside him. His beloved. His childhood sweetheart. Why in God's name was she eager to come here again? She had not been so in the beginning. For days after that harrowing ordeal she had been depressed, unwilling even to talk about it.

But then, weeks later, the change. Ah, yes, the change! So subtle at first, or at least as subtle as her unsophisticated nature could contrive. "Norm . . . do you remember that old house we were snowbound in? Do you suppose we might have liked it if things had been different? . . ."

Then not so subtle. "Norm, can we look at the Creighton place again? Please? Norm?"

As he fumbled the key into the lock, he reached for her hand. "Are you all right, hon?"

"Of course!" The same tone of voice she had used in Halper's shabby office. Impatient. Critical. *Don't ask silly questions.*

With a premonition of disaster he pushed the door open.

It was the same.

Furnished, Halper had called it, trying to be facetious. There were dusty ruins of furniture and carpets and—yes—someone or something was using them; that the house had *not* been empty for eight years, as Halper claimed. Now the feeling returned as Norman trailed his wife through the downstairs rooms and up the staircase to the bed chambers above. But the feeling was strong! He wanted desperately to seize her hand again and shout, "No, no, darling! Come out of here!"

Upstairs, when she halted in the big front bedroom, turning slowly to look about her, he said helplessly, "Hon, please—what is it? What do you *want*?"

No answer. He had ceased to exist. She even bumped into him as she went past to sit on the old four-poster with its mildewed mattress. And, seated there, she stared emptily into space as she had done before.

He went to her and took her hands. "Linda, for God's sake! What *is* it with this place?"

She looked up and smiled at him. "I'm all right. Don't worry, darling."

There had been an old blanket on the bed when they entered this room before. He had thought of wrapping her in it because she was shivering, the house was frigid, and with the car trapped in deepening snow they would have to spend the night here. But the blanket reeked with age and she had cringed from the touch of it.

Then—"Wait," he had said with a flash of inspiration. "Maybe if I could jam this under a tire! . . . Come on. It's at least worth a try."

"I'm cold, Norm. Let me stay here."

"You'll be all right? Not scared?"

"Better scared than frozen."

"Well . . . I won't be long."

How long was he gone? Ten minutes? Twenty? Twice the car had seemed about to pull free from the snow's mushy grip. Twice the wheel had spun the sodden blanket out from under and sent it flying through space like a huge yellow bird, and he'd been forced to go groping after it with the frigid wind lashing his half-frozen face. Say twenty minutes; certainly no longer. Then, giving it up as a bad job, he had trudged despondently back to the house and climbed the stairs again to that front bedroom.

And there she sat on the bed, as she was sitting now. White as the snow itself. Wide-eyed. Staring at or into something that only she could see.

"Linda! What's wrong?"

"Nothing. Nothing . . ."

He grasped her shoulders. "Look at me! Stop staring like that! What's happened?"

"I thought I heard something. Saw something."

"Saw *what*?"

"I don't know. I don't . . . remember."

Lifting her from the bed, he put his arms about her and glowered defiantly at the empty doorway. Strange. A paper-thin layer of mist or smoke moved along the floor there, drifting out into the hall. And there were floating shapes of the same darkish stuff trapped in the room's corners, as though left behind when the chamber emptied itself of a larger mass. Or was he imagining these things? One moment they seemed to be there; a moment later they were gone.

And was he also imagining the odor? It had not been present in the musty air of this room before; it certainly seemed to be now, unless his senses were playing tricks on him. A peculiarly robust smell, unquestionably male. But now it was fading.

Never mind. There *was* someone in this house, by God! He had felt an alien presence when Halper was here; even more so after the agent's departure. Someone, something, following them about, watching them.

The back of Linda's dress was unzipped, he realized then. His hands, pressing her to him, suddenly found themselves inside the garment, on her body. And her body was cold. Colder than the snow he had struggled with outside. Cold and clammy.

The zipper. He fumbled for it, found it drawn all the way down. What in God's name had she tried to do? This was his wife, who loved him. This was the girl who only a few weeks ago, at the club, had savagely slapped the face of the town's richest, handsomest playboy for daring to hint at a mate-swapping arrangement. Slowly he drew the zipper up again, then held her at arm's length and looked again at her face.

She seemed unaware he had touched her. Or that he even existed. She was entirely alone, still gazing into that secret world in which he had no place.

The rest of that night had seemed endless, Linda lying on the bed, he sitting beside her waiting for daylight. She seemed to sleep some of the time; at other times, though she said nothing even when spoken to, he sensed she was as wide awake as he. About four o'clock the wind died and the snow stopped its wet slapping of the windowpanes. No dawn had ever been more welcome, even though he was still unable to free the car and they both had to walk to the village to send a tow truck for it.

And now he had let her persuade him to come back here. He must be insane.

"Norman?"

She sat there on the bed, the same bed, but at least she was looking *at* him now, not through him into that secret world of hers. "Norman, you do like this house a little, don't you?"

"If you mean could I ever seriously think of living here—" Emphatically he shook his head. "My God, no! It gives me the horrors!"

"It's really a lovely old house, Norman. We could work on it little by little. Do you think I'm crazy?"

"If you can even imagine living in this mausoleum, I *know* you're crazy. My God, woman, you were nearly frightened out of your wits here. In this very room, too."

"Was I, Norman? Really?"

"Yes, you were! If I live to be a hundred, I'll never stop seeing that look on your face."

"What kind of look was it, Norman?"

"I don't know. That's just it—I don't know! What in heaven's name *were* you seeing when I walked back in here after my session with the car? What was that mist? That smell?"

Smiling, she reached for his hands. "I don't remember any mist or smell, Norman. I was just a little frightened. I told you—I thought I heard something."

"You *saw* something too, you said."

"Did I say that? I've forgotten." Still smiling, she looked around the room—at the garden of faded roses on shreds of time stained wallpaper; at the shabby bureau with its solitary broken cut-glass vase. "Old Mr. Halper was to blame for what happened, Norman. His talk of demons."

"Halper didn't do that much talking, Linda."

"Well, he told us about the woman who was hanged in Salem. I can see now, of course, that he threw that out as bait, because I had told him you write mystery novels. He probably pictured you sitting in some sort of Dracula cape, scratching out your books with a quill, by lamplight, and thought this would be a marvelous setting for it." Her soft laugh was a welcome sound, reminding Norman he loved this girl and she loved him—that their life together, except for her inexplicable interest in this house, was full of gentleness and caring.

But he could not let her win this debate. "Linda, listen. If this is such a fine old house, why has it been empty for eight years?"

"Well, Mr. Halper explained that, Norman."

"Did he? I don't seem to recall any explanation."

"He said that the last person to live here was a woman who died eight years ago at ninety-three. Her married name was Stanhope, I think he said, but she was a Creighton—she even had the same given name, Prudence, as the woman hanged in Salem for worshipping demons. And when she passed away there was some legal question about the property because her husband had died some years before in an asylum, leaving no will.''

Norman reluctantly nodded. The truth was, he hadn't paid much attention to the real-estate man's talk, but he did recall the remark that the last man of the house had been committed to an asylum for the insane. Probably from having lived in such a gloomy old house for so long, he had thought at the time.

Annoyed with himself for having lost the debate—at least, for not having won it—he turned from the bed and walked to a window, where he stood gazing down at the yard. Right down there, four months ago, was where he had struggled to free the car. Frowning at the spot now, he suddenly said aloud, ''Wait. That's damn queer.''

''What is, dear?'' Linda said from the bed.

''I've always thought we left the car in a low spot that night. A spot where the snow must have drifted extra deep, I mean. But we didn't. We were in the highest part of the yard.''

''Perhaps the ground is soft there.''

''Uh-uh. It's rocky.''

''Then it might have been slippery?''

''Well, I suppose—'' Suddenly he pressed closer to the window glass. ''Oh, damn! We've got a flat.''

''What, Norman?''

''A flat! Those are new tires, too. We must have picked up a nail on our way into this stupid place.'' Striding back to the bed, he caught her hand. ''Come on. I'm not leaving you here this time!''

She did not protest. Obediently she followed him downstairs and along the lower hall to the front door. On the piazza she hesitated briefly, glancing back in what seemed to be a moment of panic, but when he again grasped her hand, she meekly went with him down the steps and out to the car.

The left front tire was the flat one. Hunkering down beside it, he searched for the culprit nail but failed to find any. It was underneath, no doubt. Things like flat tires always annoyed him; in a properly organized world they wouldn't happen. Of course, in such a world there would not be the kind of road one had to travel to reach this place, nor would there be such an impossible house to begin with.

Muttering to himself, he opened the trunk, extracted jack, tools and spare, and went to work.

Strange. There was no nail in the offending tire. No cut or bruise, either. The tire must have been badly made. The thought did not improve his mood as, on his knees, he wrestled the spare into place.

Then when he lowered the jack, the spare gently flattened under the car's weight and he knelt there staring at it in disbelief. "What the hell . . ." Nothing like this had *ever* happened to him before.

He jacked the car up again, took the spare off and examined it. No nail, no break, no bruise. It was a new tire, like the others. Newer, because never yet used. He had a repair kit for tubeless tires in the trunk, he recalled—bought one day on an impulse. "Repair a puncture in minutes without even taking the tire off the car." But how could you repair a puncture that wasn't there?

"Linda, this is crazy. We'll have to walk back to town as we did before." He turned his head. "Linda?"

She was not there.

He lurched to his feet. "Linda! Where are you?" How long had she been gone? He must have been working on the car for fifteen or twenty minutes. She hadn't spoken in that time, he suddenly realized. Had she slipped back into the house the moment he became absorbed in his task? She knew well enough how intensely he concentrated on such things. How when he was writing, for instance, she could walk through the room without his even knowing it.

"Linda, for God's sake—no!" Hoarsely shouting her name, he stumbled toward the house. The door clattered open when he flung himself against it, and the sound filled his ears as he staggered down the hall. But now the hall was not just an ancient, dusty corridor; it was a dim tunnel filled with premature darkness and strange whisperings.

He knew where she must be. In that cursed room at the top of the stairs where he had seen the look on her face four months ago, and where she had tried so cunningly to conceal the truth from him this time. But the room was hard to reach now. A swirling mist choked the staircase, repeatedly causing him to stumble. Things resembling hands darted out of it to clutch at him and hold him back.

He stopped in confusion, and the hands nudged him for-

ward again. Their owner was playing a game with him, he
realized, mocking his frantic efforts to reach the bedroom yet
at the same time seductively urging him to try even harder.
And the whisperings made words, or seemed to. "Come
Norman . . . sweet Norman . . . come come come . . ."

In the upstairs hall, too, the swirling mist challenged him,
deepening into a moving mass that hid the door of the room.
But he needed no compass to find that door. Gasping and
cursing—"Damn you, leave me alone! Get out of my way!"
He struggled to it and found it open as Linda and he had left
it. Hands outthrust, he groped his way over the threshold.

The alien presence here was stronger. The sense of being
confronted by some unseen creature was all but overwhelm-
ing. Yet the assault upon him was less violent now that he
had reached the room. The hands groping for him in the eerie
darkness were even gentle, caressing. They clung with a
velvet softness that was strangely pleasurable, and there was
something voluptuously female about them, even to a faint
but pervasive female odor.

An *odor*, not a perfume. A body scent, drug-like in its
effect upon his senses. Bewildered, he ceased his struggle for
a moment to see what would happen. The whispering became
an invitation, a promise of incredible delights. But he allowed
himself only a moment of listening and then, shouting Linda's name, hurled himself at the bed again. This time he was
able to reach it.

But she was not now sitting there staring into that secret
world of hers, as he had expected. The bed was empty and
the seductive voice in the darkness softly laughed at his
dismay. "Come Norman . . . sweet Norman . . . come come
come . . ."

He felt himself taken from behind by the shoulders, turned
and ever so gently pushed. He fell floating onto the old
mattress, half-heartedly thrusting up his arms to keep the
advancing shadow-form from possessing him. But it flowed
down over him, onto him, into him, despite his feeble resis-
tance, and the female smell tantalized his senses again, de-
stroying his will to resist.

As he ceased struggling he heard a sound of rusty hinges
creaking in that part of the room's dimness where the door
was, and then a soft thud. The door had been closed. But he
did not cry out. He felt no alarm. It was good to be here on

the bed, luxuriating in this sensuous, caressing softness. As he became quiescent it flowed over him with unrestrained indulgence, touching and stroking him to heights of ecstacy.

Now the unseen hands, having opened his shirt, slowly and seductively glided down his body to his belt . . .

He heard a new sound then. For a moment it bewildered him because, though coming through the ancient wall behind him, from the adjoining bedroom, it placed him at once in his own bedroom at home. Linda and he had joked about it often, as true lovers could—the explosive little syllables to which she always gave voice when making love.

So she was content, too. Good. Everything was straightforward and aboveboard, then. After all, as that fellow at the club had suggested, mate-swapping was an in thing in this year of our Lord 1975 . . . wasn't it? All kinds of people did it.

He must buy this house, as Linda had insisted. Of course. She was absolutely right. With a sigh of happiness he closed his eyes and relaxed, no longer made reluctant by a feeling of guilt.

But—something was wrong. Distinctly, now, he felt not two hands caressing him, but more. And were they hands? They suddenly seemed cold, clammy, frighteningly eager.

Opening his eyes, he was startled to find that the misty darkness had dissolved and he could see. Perhaps the seeing came with total surrender, or with the final abandonment of his guilt feeling. He lay on his back, naked, with his nameless partner half beside him, half on him. He saw her scaly, misshapen breasts overflowing his chest and her monstrous, demonic face swaying in space above his own. And as he screamed, he saw that she did have more than two hands: she had a whole writhing mass of them at the ends of long, searching tentacles.

The last thing he saw before his scream became that of a madman was a row of three others like her squatting by the wall, their tentacles restlessly reaching toward him as they impatiently awaited their turn.

Dennis Etchison is a young Californian whose chilling
"Soft Wall" was featured in Whispers #4 and subse-
quently chosen for inclusion in Gahan Wilson's First World
Fantasy Awards anthology. Dennis's stories often deal
with the psychology of fear, and this new tale depicts a
college campus, where a chilling experiment in terror and
death slowly unfolds.

WHITE MOON RISING

by Dennis Etchison

It went like this: in her room at the top of the stairs in the
empty sorority house she lay warm and rumpled in her bed,
trying hard to sleep some more. It was now near noon and the
light streaming through the open curtains had forced her
awake again. She did not seem to care if she ever got up; she
had no classes, not for a week. Still she could not make
herself relax. The late morning flashed a granular red through
her eyelids. Then she heard the front door down below open
and close, the click echoing through the abandoned house like
a garbage can dropped in an alley at dawn. Probably it was
one of the few remaining girls returning from an overnight
date or to pick up books before leaving for vacation. Lissa
hoped so. Now she could hear footsteps treading up the stairs.

She tried to imagine who it was. The footsteps reached the top of the stairs and stopped. Firmly, deliberately the footfalls turned and came down to the hall, toward her room. Maybe it was Sharon. She wanted it to be Sharon. She kept her eyes tightly closed. The shoes thumped deep into the rug; the loose board in the middle of the hall creaked. Finally whoever it was reached her room—there, just on the other side of the door. Lissa felt ice crystals forming in her blood. She waited for the knock, for the clearing of the familiar throat, for the sound of her own name to come muffled through the door. But there was no sound. Still she waited. She held a breath. The blood pulsed coldly in her ears like a drum beaten underwater. She wanted to speak out. Then the sound of a hand on the loose doorknob. And the almost imperceptible wingbeat of the door gliding open. I know, she thought, I'll lie perfectly still, I won't let anything move in my body and I'll be safe, whoever it is won't see me and will go away. Yes, she thought, that's what I will have to do. Now she clearly felt a presence next to her bed. She was sure that someone was standing there in the doorway to her right, a hand probably still on the knob. She had not heard it rattle a second time. Time passed. She counted her heartbeats. At last she knew she could hold her breath no longer. She would have to do something very brave. With a rush that screamed adrenaline into her body she sat bolt upright, at the same instant snapping her head to the right and unsticking her eyes with a pop. There was no one there. The door was still closed and locked. The room was empty. Suddenly she realized that her kidneys were throbbing in dull pain. She knew what that was. It was fear.

The sunlight washed in through the window.

"Oh Joe," said his wife, "it makes me sick, just physically ill. And I know it gets to you, too."

Joe Mallory cleaned up the steak and eggs on his plate with a last swipe, then hesitated and let his fork mark a slow pattern through the smear of yolk that remained.

"No." He cleared his throat. "No, honey. Just a job." Gently he removed the newspaper from her side, poked it in half and tried to find something else to read.

"Joey," she said. She reached across the tablecloth suddenly and covered his hand. "I know you. And I know I shouldn't have let you take this job, not this one."

He looked up and was surprised and strangely moved to see her clear brown eyes glistening. As he forced his shoulders to shrug and his mouth to smile, she placed her other hand as well over his. From the open kitchen window sprang the sounds of bright chains of children on their way to the elementary school. He could almost see their black bowl haircuts and dirty feet. He wished he could help them, but it was already too late. He blinked, trying to concentrate.

"Babe," he said calmly, resurrecting a pet name they had abandoned before he went overseas. "One more semester and I'm finished with night classes. Look. You know the size of the government checks, and you know they aren't going to get any bigger. We both know Ray can't take me on without a degree—"

"You know he would, Joey, if you ask him again. What's a brother for?" Instantly she darkened, regretting the last. She held his hand, hoping that he would let it pass.

"Now let me finish," he said slowly. "I can't handle a position like that yet, not without leaning on someone half the time. I have to do it right. This damned uniform is just a job until I'm ready. Till then, well, what else do I know? Really, now?" He flipped her hands over and warmed them with his. "I have to make things right before I go ahead, to feel like I'm my own man. I thought you understood that."

"Oh, I know all that. I'm sorry. I know. It was just all the details, the whole horrible thing, these last few weeks. It sounds so awful."

She rested her forehead on her arm and cried for a few seconds. Then she pressed her nose and stood up, stacking the dishes. "Come on, you big jock. You'll be late."

He pushed away from the table and crossed the kitchen in three steps. He took his wife in his arms and held her close for a long minute, while the electric clock hummed high and white on the wall.

She rocked back and forth with his body. Finally she began to laugh.

"Get out of here," she said, trying hard.

"Meet me at work," he said. "I'll take you to Fernando's for dinner."

The tears settled diamond-bright in her eyes. She kissed him noisily and pushed him out the door.

She watched him through the window.

He came back in.

"Forgot something," he said. He walked briskly to the breakfast nook, picked up the morning paper and dropped it in the waste can. "Give my love to the ice cream man," he said before he shut the door again.

"Hey, I don't even know the . . ."

He was gone and she stopped laughing. She went to the can and picked out the paper. She spread it on the table and stared down at it.

"Shit," she said very seriously. "Oh shit, Joe. . . ."

The latest headline read:

> *Security Doubled*
> ANOTHER BRUTAL COED SLAYING

Lissa, now in tank top and embroidered Levi's, toed into her sandals and slipped down the stairs, her thin fingers playing lightly over the handrail.

"Sharon?" On the wall at the foot of the stairs she noticed the poster Sharon had brought with her from New York. It was one of those old *You Don't Have to Be Jewish to Love Levy's* advertisements, showing an Indian biting into a slice of rye bread; Sharon had replaced the Indian with the horribly burned face of an Asian child, and now she saw that someone had written across the face with a red marking pen the words *You Don't Have to Be a Unicorn to Enjoy the Tapestry* in an unmistakably feminine hand. She wondered what *that* meant. "Has anybody seen Sharon?" she called, tapping her nails on the railing. Then, "Is anybody here?"

She thought she heard voices and stepped off the stairs. But she saw only the bright, still day outside the open front door, and the two familiar Security guards at the edge of the dry lawn. They stood with their hands behind their backs and, Lissa thought, peculiar smiles on their faces; as they rocked on their heels their billy clubs swung tautly from wide, black belts.

Something about them gave her the creeps.

Her eyes listlessly scanned the living room, finding nothing to settle on.

She stepped away from the open front door. Sharon must have left it open. On the way out, probably to see Eliot.

She could call Eliot and find out, couldn't she?

She took two steps toward the phone. She stopped. The thought of the newly installed tap put her off again. Damn it, she thought. It irks me, just the idea of it. It really does.

She sighed. She stood in the middle of the rug, her left hand resting on the back of the sofa and her right hand fingering her left elbow. She took a breath, held it, let it out. Then she went over to the big front door and nudged it shut. With her back. She didn't particularly want to look outside.

Officer William W. Williams was doing push-ups on the grass.

"How many I got, John?"

"Uh, forty-seven by my count, Bill."

"You lyin'!"

"You're not going to break no record today, Williams," said Officer Hall around a lumpy chili dog from the food service machines.

"You shut up, Hal." Williams spat to one side and pumped three more times. The muscles on his shining arms inflated with each stroke.

"Fifty," said Joe matter-of-factly, "and still counting."

Williams quivered high on his corded arms for a beat, then dipped again.

"Mother," he breathed.

The sun, setting some kind of record for April, beat down in shimmering waves, now mercifully on the tin roof of the pergola so that the officers were able to remove their spongy hats, at least for half an hour. Joe felt not quite a breeze but at least a shift in the hovering air layers here in the shade; the sweat in his short black hair was beginning to evaporate, cooling and contracting his scalp. It was, he thought without knowing why, a day for ice cream. Williams, however, chose to remain under the sun, bridging again and again over the blanched grass.

"What did the Chief have to say this morning?" asked Joe. "Sorry I missed the briefing."

The men did not answer.

As far as Joe could see the campus was deserted, the gray buildings flat and silent, the sparsely sown trees moving not at all in the noonday heat. Though he knew better, Joe wondered idly if anyone other than Security was on the grounds today.

Old John, white-haired and better suited to a Santa Claus costume than a black uniform, folded his hands unsteadily.

"It was another one of his pep talks, Joe. You know Withers." Joe didn't very well, but it didn't matter. "I guess you didn't miss anything."

Hall resumed chewing.

Joe realized that Williams had suspended over the lawn. Finally he moved. *Down.*

"Well, I hope we get him," offered Joe, "and soon. A guy like that has got to be sick, and needs help."

Up. Williams stopped.

Hall stopped eating.

Joe felt odd. He repeated to himself what he had said, trying to figure why they were uptight. Something about Withers, maybe. Except for old John, they didn't seem to like the Chief. That must be it.

"Hell," said Hall, "this is the easiest job in the world. We don't have to do anything. A person commits a violation, he does himself in." He spoke carefully, as if laying out a scientific fact. "Because if he's human, he's ashamed of the act. That's all the lever we need." Barely changing his tone he said, "Look at that one, will you?"

They looked. A young girl, slender and poised, was crossing the parking lot in old Levi's, very tight, and a form-fitting top.

Down. "Hoo. That one is sweet and tough," said Williams. *Up.*

"You take girls like that," Hall went on. "They don't *have* any sense of shame. Man, somebody's got to teach her a lesson."

"I'm not sure I follow you," said Joe.

Down. Williams rolled over onto his back. "Gimme some of that Dr. Pepper."

Hall cackled and took the bottle over to Williams. He knelt and whispered something. Williams nodded, then drained the bottle and lay back, gazing dreamily through the low trees by the pergola. "Somebody gimme my shirt an' gun." He sang a few notes to himself. "You know what we need around here?" he asked. "Bows an' arrows. That's what we had in

'Nam. Pick a sentry out of a tree at a hundred yards. *Whoosh.* Simple as that. Don't make no noise.''

The girl was disappearing from sight.

''What time's it getting to be?'' asked Joe. He reached for his walkie-talkie. ''We'd better check in with the command post.''

''No reason to hurry,'' said Hall.

Williams rolled over onto his belly. *Up.* He started counting again. *Down.*

Up.

Down.

''Hey, you can knock it off,'' Hall said to him. ''She's gone.''

They all had a good laugh over that.

Lissa walking across the grass: what were they laughing about?

Beyond the glimmering parking lot she glanced over her shoulder at the pergola, blurry without her glasses, bouncing behind her with each step. She shrugged and went on.

She looked down. She slipped her shoes off and felt the warm grass, following her feet past the Library and the new Student Union, staying on the shade. At the far side of the campus she climbed the cool steps to the lab.

''Knock-knock?''

She slid around the open door.

The stink from the tiered cages was overpowering; she knew at once that it would be too much for her.

She heard someone clear his throat.

She held her breath, tucked in her top, and walked forward between the skittering enclosures.

''Oh!''

An electric buzz rattled the cages.

The rats scrambled over one another, hundreds and hundreds of rats. She almost screamed. The buzzing stopped. The rats subsided.

A hand, cold and clammy as sweating brass, touched her neck. She stiffened. It seemed to be trying to press her straight down into the floor.

''Ah, but you're not Sherrie, are you.'' It was a statement. ''Apologies.''

She was released. She turned. She saw a moist left hand

recently relieved of its rubber glove; as she faced it, an acrid fume sliced up her nostrils. Formaldehyde.

She stumbled back. "W'll, hi, Eliot. I was looking for Sharon." She rubbed at her watering eyes. "I was on my way to your apartment, but I thought I'd stop by here first." She looked up into his pallid, implacable face. And shuddered. "You haven't seen her?"

"Afraid not, Lissa."

He simply observed her, waiting.

She wanted out, but she said, "Well, what are you up to in here, anyway? I never saw all these—these *mice* the last time I was here."

He snapped off his right glove and moved to the sink, applied talc. He pocketed his pale hands in his white coat and leaned against a supply cabinet.

"A low voltage is discharged through the bottom of each cage," said Eliot, "every two minutes, twenty-four hours a day. At various stages I remove typical specimens and dissect the adrenal cortex, the thymus, the spleen, the lymph nodes and so forth, and of course the stomach. There is a definite syndrome, you know."

Are you for real? she wondered, drifting to the window. Below, a fat, greasy-looking mama's boy with horn-rimmed glasses gazed up at the window. She had seen him hanging around a number of times lately. Too many times. She stepped away from the window.

"The adrenal cortex," continued Eliot conversationally, "is always enlarged. All the lymphatic structures are shrunken. And there are deep ulcers, usually, in the stomach and upper gut."

He's not kidding, she thought. She looked outside again. The young man was gone. She felt relieved. "What do you call it?" she said, almost reflexly.

"A stress rig," said Eliot. Cheerfully, she thought. Then, "Sherrie's probably back at the House by now. Be careful going home, will you? I know I don't need to remind you." When she did not say anything, "About what happened to the others. It was a combination, a choke hold from behind, forearm across the throat, under the chin, one arm in a hammerlock. Fractures of the larynx, internal hemorrhaging. And this vertebra, this one right here, at the base of the neck.

That's what finished them. He had to lift them off their feet. Here.'' He reached out to show her.

Suddenly, jarringly, the cages buzzed.

Let me out of here! She felt sick.

''Well, I'll see you later, Eliot.'' She did not wait for an answer.

Outside and down the stairs, a breeze was coming in with the dusk. It's really summer, she thought. She wanted desperately to be at the beach. She could almost smell the Sea & Ski basting her skin. A bird sang high on a telephone wire. O let there always be summers, she thought. A hundred, a thousand of them. That was what she wanted. She wanted there to be a thousand summers.

Joe trod blankly along University Drive. Off duty at last, he was on his way back to the campus, where his wife would be waiting.

''How long has this been happening?'' he asked, a little dazed.

''Ed Withers's been paying off Hall to keep him quiet ever since, Lord, seven-eight months,'' said old John, strolling with his hands behind his back, his voice low as a moribund bulldog's. ''Anyway, Joey''—he had never called him that before—''I figured you ought to know. What I mean to get across is, try to keep to yourself as much as you can while you're here. They're a kind of—oh, they're a bunch of what you would call motivated young officers. Highly motivated.''

''What I can't understand,'' Joe persisted, ''is why everyone is keeping his mouth shut.''

Old John averted his eyes and took an unexpected number of steps to answer. He fingered his handcuffs nervously; they glinted in the day's dying rays of sunlight. ''Job's a job, you know what I mean,'' muttered old John.

Joe turned those words over and over as they came to Portola Place.

What in the world did that have to do with it? He stopped at the curb. ''What does that have to do with it?'' he asked.

But old John was trekking on down Portola Place. He continued to keep an eye on Joe, however. Joe saw him put a hand behind his ear.

''Nothing,'' Joe shouted. ''Nothing at all. See you Friday.''

He shook his head. Even here, he thought. He took a

too-deep breath of the lukewarm air, squinting as the setting
sun peeped its staring red eye from between the buildings. He
started walking again. He lowered his head and watched his
feet move, crossing the street at a fast clip.

So Hall's wife was getting pumped by the Chief of Security. And Chief Withers was being—was there a less melodramatic word for it?—blackmailed by Hall. With a promotion
thrown in. Joe throttled a bitter laugh. He wondered whether
Hall's wife knew that end of it. And whether she was smugly
enjoying the benefits with her husband. What the hell, what
the hell, what the hell, Joe thought aimlessly. And heard a
rustling in the bushes.

"Where's the cook?"

"She's not coming in again till after vacation."

"Well, where's the House Mother?" said Kathy. "I know,
I know, there's no House Mother here. Ooh, I wish I was still
with a PT!"

"Better not let Madam President hear you bitching," said
Sharon. "She'll kick you out on your lilywhite ass."

Kathy groaned and went upstairs.

Lissa laughed. She had seen the House Mother for the Pi
Taus; her face had more lines in it than *War and Peace,*
which she had been reading for English 260. Trying to read.
Part I had been on the Six O'Clock Movie Monday. Dutifully
she had watched it, but for some reason she had had to miss
Part II. Part III had been on for a few minutes now.

"Henry Fonda's the only one who acts like he read the
book," said Sharon, giving up on the color controls and
laying her legs over the arm of the couch again. The set,
which rendered everything the color of bile, did look, as
Sharon had once remarked, "like somebody took a whiz on
it." Lissa tried to follow the plot, but by now it made no
sense at all to her.

"Who's been leeching my Marlboros, anyway?" said
Sharon, digging under the cushions.

Lissa flipped over to Channel 11. "Hey, Chiller's on."

"Right arm," said Sharon.

"Is that *Frank*enstein?"

"Fuck yes," said Sharon. "I've seen this flick so many—"

"You know, I've never seen it all the way through," said
Lissa. "My folks would never let me."

"Ha!"

"No, really."

"Well, go ahead, knock yourself out."

Fascinated, Lissa watched the scene in which little Maria so innocently shared her flowers with the Monster on the riverbank. One by delicate one they cast daisies on the water. Then, very slowly, the Monster's expression began to change, as the child ran out of flowers, as the scene began to fade out.

"That's the part they always cut," said Sharon. "You should see his face right after this, before they find her with her neck broken. You know what I think? I don't believe he even meant to kill her at all. I think he just sort of, you know, crushed her to him. You know what I mean? I don't think there was anything evil about it. They were both innocents. Neither one of them knew anything about it."

A bald-headed used-car salesman appeared on the screen, his face a sneer of chartreuse.

Joe stood stock-still and waited for the next sound.

It did not come.

He stepped onto the blue-shadowed lawn. His hand steadied on his flashlight.

He heard footfalls on the other side of the hedge, close to a house.

He let himself into the foliage, deciding to follow it up. Leaves, small and shiny, tracked past him on either side, hard branches skidding off his head, almost knocking his hat to the ground.

Close to the other side, he saw a man's back moving quickly away from him along the side of the house, toward the front sidewalk. The house was dark, probably empty; he hoped so. He felt disoriented for a fraction of a second, almost as if he were not really here but somewhere else entirely. Then he saw the figure stand straight and slow to a normal gait, crossing under the street lamp. Then the figure returned to a crouch and headed into the trees on the other side. Peeping Tom? Or the one he had been hired to catch? Well, if this is the one, he must be one poor scared son of a bitch right now, even if he doesn't know he's being watched. In fact, Joe realized, his own heart hammering at the back of his badge, that part wouldn't really have anything to do with the feeling, not anything at all.

Joe pulled free of the hedge and backed up. He moved down behind the next four houses in line and then continued forward to the street and crossed at the end of the block. He cut into the alley just past the houses.

He stayed close to the wooden fence, navigating around trash barrels—empty, they would drum an alarm down the whole of Sorority Row.

He heard tennis shoes grinding into the gravel.

A young man crossed the alley not fifty feet in front of him.

They heard Kathy put a record on the turntable upstairs.

The TV screen receded into the deepening shadows of the living room. A cricket started up, sounding so close that Lissa glanced nervously about to see if it was in the house with them. Outside, an elderly officer paced past the hedge, hands behind his back.

"Look at that old codger." Sharon's ash flared and hissed before her face, then arced down. "I'll bet they still don't give them real bullets to use. Yeah, I saw his gun one time. The barrel was plugged up with wood or bubble gum or something. I wonder if they're going to do any good now that we need them? Somebody needs them. The only thing they've been good for so far is to *remind* us all. D'you see what I mean?" She sat forward. "God, I've got to get away from here for a while. I'm starting to vegetate. When's Eliot coming over?"

"He didn't say."

"He always takes his time. I don't know what he does on his way over here, wandering around jacking his brain off with some new pet theory."

"Sharon!"

"Well, it's the truth."

They sat with the sound turned down. The cricket synched with the record for a few bars, then continued on its own again.

"Can I have one of those, please?"

"I didn't know you were smoking now, Lees."

"I'm not. Not really."

The young man crossed the alley.
Joe froze.

Then he followed.

Passing between two houses, he stopped again and dropped to one knee.

He saw ahead to the next street. The young man had already crossed over and was now hesitating by one of the huts on the other side. Houses, he told himself. Now Joe looked between the trees and houses as down a tunnel: as the street lamp flicked on, the pavement mottled under the new light, his eyes focused through to a square of still-bright sky visible now above the long campus parking lot.

He waited.

Another figure, nearly a silhouette, appeared against the sky.

It was a woman.

He snapped to, aware that he had lost track of his prey. The young man was gone. He had slipped through, probably to the lot. But—*had* he gone through, or was he still somewhere on the block between, sidestepping from house to house?

He had blown it.

He started to move anyway.

Then it hit him. The woman. The woman waiting in the lot.

It had to be his wife.

"Eliot," said Sharon, "is very into it. And therefore out of it. If you know what I mean. There are moments with us. Not many, but there are. You were right, though. Sometimes I do wonder if it's worth it. God, I've been staring into this damn box too long. Now it's beginning to stare back." She clicked off the TV with her toes. "I don't need to turn on the tube to see rape, murder and perversion. I can get all that right here at school."

Lissa heard a record droning upstairs. It sounded like Dylan.

turn, turn, turn again

"Tell her to turn it over, will you?" said Sharon. "That song's bumming me out."

Lissa felt her way to the top of the first landing.

"Lis-sa? Bring down some munchies, will you? Um, Screaming Yellow Zonkers. Whatever she's got hidden up there. An-y-thing!"

Lissa smiled.
turn, turn to the rain and the wind
She walked on down the hall.

Joe had squatted so long that his gaze was fixed, almost as if the rectangle of light sky had somehow been looking back down into him instead. His eyes stung.

Fatigue. He hoped. Four days a week had seemed fine at first. Enough time to do some good, maybe, but not enough to—but it was late now, much later than he had thought, judging by the color of the sky. Marlene, he realized, blinking alert, had been waiting—how long? How long had he crouched here? And how long before, at the other village? Block, he reminded himself, block.

He crossed the street, his breath jangling in his ears like dog tags.

He shot a glance at the patch of sky and the dark figure of his wife.

His pace quickened.

As he headed over a lawn, a young man bolted out of the shrubs, a pair of horn-rimmed glasses clattering from his face.

With Ritz crackers and a five-pack of Hydrox cookies in one hand, she drew the knob toward her, cutting the sliver of light from Kathy's room, and made for the stairs.

There was a knock on the front door.

The stairway was an unknown in the dark. She waited.

Finally, "Sharon? Can you get that?"

The knock again.

She descended, pressing against the wall.

"Just a—" She felt a catch in her throat. Why?

The door swung open.

The kid was squirming on the lawn, his face jumping.

"Whatsa matter? I'm on my way home from a study date! Whatsa *matter?*"

Joe closed the cuffs, pressed the key into the notch and set the lock.

Something in the young man's face, swarming in a film of sweat, refused to let Joe relax. He shoved the glasses at him and pulled him to his feet.

He glanced ahead. The sky was dark, too dark to see her.

He whipped up the antenna on his walkie-talkie. It shook in his hands, waving back and forth in the night air.

She saw a woman, backlighted in the open doorway.

"I'm sorry," said the woman. "But I wonder if you've seen my husband. He was supposed to meet—"

"No, I—" stammered Lissa. "Do you mean he was outside?" *Where was Sharon? Where?* She left the doorway. "Just a minute, okay?"

She felt around the room. "Share?" she called. *I know, she thought. She said she was hungry. I'll check the kitchen. If I can only find the light!*

"Sha-ron!" she called, and wondered why her voice was breaking.

"We don't want to hurt you," Joe said. "Believe that."

He drew his prisoner through the shrubs, crushing twigs and unseen garden creatures in his path.

He turned up the gain and depressed the call button. He needed back-up. His throat was dry and the back of his tongue hurt.

A shrill electronic sound whined close by. Instantly he recognized it. It was feedback—his own signal being picked up on another receiver.

"I guess you wouldn't know who I mean," the woman said from the doorway. "But he's one of the Security . . ."

It's so dark, thought Lissa at the door to the kitchen. She forced herself across the chill linoleum, her arms outstretched like antennae.

She heard a sound—a low voice. It was singing:

> *some folks like t' talk about it*
> *some don't*

A wind from nowhere blew through her chest.

He pushed the kid ahead of him, following the sound. Louder. Joe was relieved. Reinforcements were near.

Then he noticed his prisoner's stare.

At the rear of the last house by the parking lot, dark shapes were moving.

• • •

She seemed to swim through darkness past the smooth pulsating refrigerator where there were always tooth marks in the cheese, to the drawer from which the tools had been quietly disappearing for weeks, clamoring for something, anything with which to protect herself. It was silly, she knew, but—there. A butcher knife.

Joe released his own wrist and locked the kid to the branch of what might have been a rubber tree.

"We'll be back for you, Charlie," he said.

She felt herself drawn down the short stone steps from the kitchen to the storage porch, to the low singing and other voices and what sounded like a scratching close to the screen door that opened into the back yard.

The officer plunges through the shrubbery. At that someone slams out the back door, sees dark forms and the girl held to the dirt and reflexly cocks back an arm, white moons rising on the nails that clench the knife. The officer sees the downed girl, uniforms, another figure lunging into it. There is no time to question, not now while there is still time to stop it before it happens again. He remembers them sitting there dumbly in their baggy pajamas, their wooden bowls empty of the ice cream a few minutes before it happened, and how he had gone away and done nothing, not even when he heard the laughter and the grunting and the automatic fire. And the screams. But not this time. He dodges and grabs the empty hand, wrenching it into a hammerlock as he encircles the waist with his left arm, releasing the wrist with his right and setting his forearm under the chin. The back arches and the legs kick madly, but the hand refuses to let go the knife. Faces turn up. One of the officers stays atop their victim. It is Williams who closes in from the front, spreading his milky palm across the distorted mouth, covering it. "Nice going, Joe." He grins. "Now you one of us, too." Joe does not yet understand. Now he feels a slip in the neck and the body swings like the clapper of a bell in his arms. Now he hears new footsteps behind him and a sudden skull-splitting screech. It is the scream of a woman. He thinks he recognizes it but it is too late, now it really is too late as the girl in his arms swings one last anguished time, as her knife slices at the dark with a flash and he sees a face reflected in the blade for an instant before it drops into the leaves. But he must know what he has seen. He has seen the face of a killer. It is the same face he has always seen.

The moonlight washes down on them all.

Richard Christian Matheson bears the cross of being the son of famed writer Richard Matheson. It is not easy to follow in the footsteps of a famous father, especially in his same field; however, Richard has many credits other than his genealogy. At seventeen he became the youngest advertising copywriter employed by the national advertising offices of J. C. Penney, then he taught creative writing for a while, attended Cornell University, and went into freelance advertising work. He (along with the son of the late Charles Beaumont) sold a script to TV's "M*A*S*H" and now has a potential TV-series idea on parapsychology under serious consideration by two major outlets. "Graduation" is a story that shows both the influence of the elder Matheson and the talents of this newcomer. It is a chilling story that could have been made right at home for an episode of "Twilight Zone," if that show was still around.

GRADUATION
by Richard Christian Matheson

January 15

Dear Mom and Dad:
    It has been an expectedly hectic first week; unpacking, organizing, getting scheduled in classes, and of course, frater-

nizing with the locals to secure promise of later aid should I need it. I don't think I will. My room is nice though it has a view which Robert Frost would scoff at; perhaps a transfer to a better location later this semester is possible. We'll see.

I had a little run-in with the administration when I arrived; a trivial technicality. Something about too much luggage. At least more than the other dormitory students brought with them. I cleared it up with a little glib knowhow. As always. Some of the guys on my floor look as if they might be enjoyable and if I'm lucky maybe one or two will be interesting to talk to as well. But I can't chase after "impossible rainbows." That should sound familiar, Dad, it's from your private collection and has been gone over a "few" times. A few. But maybe this time, it's true. Anyway, the dormitory looks as if it's going to work out well. Pass the word to you-know-who. I'm sure it will interest him.

The dinner tonight was an absolute abomination. It could easily have been some medieval mélange concocted by the college gardener utilizing lawn improver, machinist's oil, and ground-up old men. And I question even the quality of those ingredients. I may die tonight of poisoning. Maybe if I'm lucky it will strike quickly and leave no marks. Don't want Dad's old school to lose its accreditation after all. However, I'm a little concerned that the townspeople will be kept awake tonight by the sound of 247 "well-fed" freshmen looking at their reflections in the toilet bowl. Today while I was buying books an upper-classman called me green for not getting used ones. If he was in any way referring to the way my face looks right now, he should be hired by some psychic foundation. He can tell the future.

Anyway, Mom, I certainly do miss your cooking. Almost as much as I miss my stomach's equilibrium. Ugh.

The room gets cold early with the snow and all. But I have plenty of blankets (remember the excessive luggage? . . . you guessed it) so that poses no difficulty. I'll probably pick up a small heater next week, first free day I get. For now I'll manage with hot tea, the collected works of Charles Dickens, and warm memories of all of you back home. Until I write again, I send my love and an abundance of sneezes.

Here's looking achoo . . .

                                        Yours regurgitatively,

February 2

Dear Mom and Dad:

Greetings from Antarctica. It is unbelievably cold up here. If you can imagine your son as a hybrid between a popsicle and a slab of marble, you've got the right idea, just make it a little colder. In a word, freezing. In another word, numbing. In two other words, liquid oxygen. I may be picking up that heater sooner than I thought. I see no future in becoming a glacier.

I met my professors today, all of whom seem interested and dedicated. My Calculus class might be a trifle dreary, but, then, numbers put a damper on things any way you look at it. The other courses look promising so far. Tell you-know-who that he-knows-who is genuinely excited about something. I'm sure he'll be cheered by that forecast of future involvements.

Burping is very popular in my wing of the dormitory and some of the guys have been explaining its physical principles to me, complete with sonic demonstrations to validate their theories. One guy, Jim, who looks a little like a bull dog with slightly bigger eyes (and a much bigger stomach) apparently holds the record in two prestigious areas: he drinks the most and belches the loudest. For your own personal information files, he also seems to know the fewest words a person can possess and still communicate with. I estimate that the exact number of words is a high 1 digit counting number, but I could still be going too easily on him. His belches, however, are enormously awesome. He is able (he whispered to me when I bumped into his drunken body in the hallway last night) to make time stand still temporarily with one of his burps.

Furthermore (he said), that would be one of his lesser efforts. Were he to launch a truly prize-winning belch (he said) civilization as we know it would be obliterated and the earth's atmosphere rendered noxious for 2,000 years. Personally, I feel he exaggerates a bit. Maybe 1,500 years.

Jim doesn't stop burping until 1 or 2 in the morning, which makes studying a degree harder. It's like having a baby in the dorm, with Jim erupting and gurgling into the a.m. hours. Except that he weighs 300 pounds. But I'm learning to live with it. Occasionally, he gets to be more than a petty annoyance and I get upset, but it's really nothing to worry about.

So tell you-know-who to not put himself into a state. I'm fine.

If we could harness the secret of Jim's aberration and regulate it at timed intervals perhaps Yellowstone Park would be interested. Oh well, he'll probably quiet down soon. I miss you all a lot and send my fondest love. Until I thaw out again, bye for now.

Bundlingly yours . . .

P.S. Avoid telling you-know-who I'm "cold" up here. He has this thing about that word.

February 22

Dear Mom and Dad:

An enlivening new roommate has entered my monastic quarters. He is slight in frame and says very little; a simple kind of person with a dearth of affinities, except for cheese, which he loves. I call him Hannibal owing to his fearlessly exploratory nature. You see Hannibal, while not easy to detect, is very much present. He comes out to mingle only during the evening. The late evening. More precisely, that part of the evening when I like to try and catch some sleep. Hannibal is evidently on a different schedule than I.

In short, I have mouse trouble.

Hannibal, in all fairness, is but one of the offenders. He is joined each evening by a host of other raucous marauders who squeal and scratch until dawn, determined to disturb my rest. They're actually quite cute, but are, regardless of angelic appearances, a steadily unappreciated annoyance.

I mentioned my visitors to some of the other students in the dormitory and they said I wasn't the only victim of the whiskered nocturnal regime. They advised setting traps and, failing that, to use a poison which can be purchased from the student store. It is rumored to yield foolproof results. I know it sounds all together like a cross borrowing from Walt Disney and an Edgar Allan Poe story, but, regrettably, I must do something.

As an alternate plan, I thought of possibly speaking with a brainy flutist I know from orchestra class, who is quite talented. Whether or not he would care to revivify a gothic tale simply for the benefit of my slumbrous tranquility is something we will have to discuss. Also the question of playing and walking at the same time may come up. But I'll try to circumvent that aspect. It's a slightly off-beat gig but it seems an improvement on the other method. I'll speak with him.

My classes are going fairly well, with no serious laggings in any subject despite the effects of Jim and Hannibal's henchmen upon my alertness. Thanks for the letter and a very special thanks for those fantastic cookies, Mom. They were delicious. You really made my day. And the travelling scent of your generosity made me quite sought after for a "little sample" of what food can really taste like. Jim went ape over them and said he wouldn't mind taking the whole next box off my hands. Which is something like a man with no legs admitting that he, occasionally, limps. Good old Jim. He'll probably eat himself to death one day. Although it would take him at least two days to do it right.

In light of the popularity of your largess, I have determined that everybody else must have the same immense regard for the school cook I do. He is acquiring a definite reputation, the likes of which has been shared by a handful of historical figures. Like Lizzie Borden, Jack the Ripper, and endless other notables. The man has no regard for the human taste bud. All in all, I'm convinced that our chef will most assuredly go to hell.

Anyway, Mom, thanks again for the cookies. They were eaten with rapturous abandon. And you may have saved several students from ulcers. What better compliment? All my love to everyone back home. Including you-know-who.

> Thwarted by burps, squeaks,
> and bad food . . .

P.S. I think Jim (our resident sulphur spring) finally knows what it's like being kept up at night. He too has mouse trouble. (At least someone will visit him.)

March 9

Dear Mom and Dad:

Got in a small amount of trouble today as a result of being late to class and complicating matters by arguing with my professor over a dumb thing he said about me.

You see, in Philosophy I, as it is taught by Marshall B. Francis, you are not allowed an impregnable viewpoint. It must always be open to comment. And he says he likes to analyze. I told him he likes to shred and butcher. Whereupon he requested a "formal presentation of my personal philosophy of life's purpose."

Since, as you know, my philosophy responds unfavorably to direct assault, I refused. Mistake number one.

He told me if I didn't cooperate he'd have me leave the class and withdraw all credit from my participation thus far. I thought this unfair, so we started yelling at one another and in the clouded ferocity of our exchanges I accidentally slashed him on the cheek with my pen. It wasn't deep, but it scared him a lot. It wasn't at all like it may seem; I say that only because I know what you're probably thinking. Believe me, it was just a freak accident with one lost temper responding to another.

We talked in the infirmary later and he said he understood and would allow me a second chance. After that kindness, I volunteered my philosophy without hesitation (rather sheepishly), and he smiled at my completion of the apologies. He said that sometimes you have to be willing to fight for your beliefs and that he respected my actions in class, saving the accident, of course. I think we'll be great friends by the end of the year (if he doesn't get infected and die); however, philosophers consider life to be a danger so I guess it wouldn't surprise him too much.

It is still very cold with no trace of warmth. Jim continues to noisily burn (or is it burp) the midnight oil much to the chagrin of everyone in the dorm. If a sonic boom occurred during the evening, it would be completely overlooked. Buried.

Once again, my love to all of you back home, and I sure would like to hear from you, so please write. Better not tell you-know-who what happened to me today. He'll get the wrong impression. He has enough people to worry about as it is.

With new-found philosophy,

P.S. Hannibal is no longer with me. He and his men are squeaking across those great Alps in the sky. That poison really was foolproof.

March 18

Dear Mom and Dad:

My social horizons are expanding here in Isolation City. In one day, I met the remainder of my floormates (truly a rogues' gallery) at a party and also a very nice girl who works as my lab partner.

I met my across-the-hall neighbor quite by chance over a game of poker. I beat him over and over and he had to write me a few IOUs. When I asked him what room he was in (so I might stop by and "collect"), it turned out to be the room directly across from mine. It's weird how you can overlook someone who is right under your nose. Anyway, he's a nice guy, but is badly in need of tutoring in the finer points of the gentlemanly wager. He is absolutely the worst gambler I have ever encountered. I suspect that his brain has decomposed from excessive exposure to Jim, who is his favorite card player. They play to one another's caliber it seems. Two drunks leading each other home.

My neighbor's name is Marcum Standile, Jr. As a rather unusual point of insight into his personal life, we figured out tonight (in my room after the party) that Marcum owes roughly $40,000 to various other dormitory inhabitants with whom he has played poker. This sum is exceeded only by Jim's, whose debts accrued in two short months to a figure which is something akin of the annual budget for Red China. Perhaps my training in calculus is coming in handy for once.

I'll write more about Susie later. Everything is pretty good academically speaking and the sun is, even, occasionally making a token appearance. Miss you very much and send all my love.

With endless computation,

P.S. Got a letter from you-know-who. Guess he took the accident a little too seriously. Tell him to relax.

April 4

Dear Mom and Dad:

I'm rich! Marcum got his monthly allotment from his financially overstuffed folks and came through with over $40 for yours truly. So far, this much money has me in quite an influential position since word of my monetary windfall has spread like an epidemic. I am popular beyond belief. I've considered opening up a loan service (with determined interest) so as to make the entire endeavor worth my expended energy as well as expended funds. An idea which I took from a movie with George Segal, "King Rat." The entire prison camp where he was (also) being held captive by the enemy, had less money than George so he became the nucleus of all existing finance. The concept appeals to me. I'll probably just buy a heater and an electric blanket, though. Fancy dies so quickly in a young man's heart. Sniff.

I am referred to alternately as "Rockefeller" or "Pal," depending on the plight of who I'm speaking with. I never dreamed any one person could have so many "Pals." Last night someone pinned a sign to my door that says "Fort Knox North." It's only right. Being rich is such toil. Tell you-know-who I will use it wisely.

My lab partner and I have become even better friends in the past few weeks. I think I mentioned in the last letter that her name is Susie, actually Susan Johnson. What I failed to include in that brief description is that she is kind of like my girlfriend, is stunningly beautiful and intelligent and popular and maybe the first girl, since Beth's death, that I really care about. Without pouring forth excessives about Susie, I'll simply say that I know you'd love her. She is quite a unique person and around here that's a godsend, the prevailing ambience being composed of uptight females. I only hope that she feels the same about me. But that will come in time. I think it would crush me if she were just experiencing feelings of friendship. But I suspect that her eyes are the best spokesman for her affections and they tell me everything is going perfect. Tell you-know-who not to hold his breath. She isn't at all like Beth, so don't let him even attempt to connect things. Beth was just something that happened. I'm sorry about it, but it was, after all, an accident and I think I would resent you-know-who making more of this than there is. Or maybe making less of it. It feels right to me. Not like with Beth. So please keep you-know-who off the subject completely; it's not fair.

By the way, I think I might make the dean's list, so cross your fingers. Philosophy I is going very well and Marshall B. Francis and I are becoming friends of the close variety. As I predicted.

I miss you all very much and send my love. Please write.

With Krupp-like fortune,

P.S. Thanks for the latest batch of cookies, Mom. I'm not sure I can eat all of them myself. Plenty of willing mouths around here, though.

April 17

Dear Mom and Dad:

Terrible news. Remember Jim, the guy who belched and kept everybody up? He was found this morning, in his room, dead. The school won't issue any kind of statement, but everyone thinks it might have been suicide. I don't think there was a note or anything, and it could have just been an accident.

If it was suicide, it would have made a lot of sense, speaking strictly in terms of motivation. He wasn't a very happy person, his weight and all making him almost completely socially ostracized. He was only 20 years old. It's a shame things like this have to happen.

It certainly is going to be quiet around here without his belching and carryings-on; which is kind of a relief even if the circumstances are so tragic. Nobody has mentioned the funeral but I hear his parents are going to have him buried locally. That's the nicest thing they could do for him. He really liked the college and the town and everything, and although unhappy, was happier here than he would have been anywhere else. It's going to be abnormally quiet around here. Maybe with the improved conditions we'll get some new scholars out of this dorm. I know I'll sleep better. Still, I feel as if every death has a meaning; a reason for happening. I may bring that up in Philosophy I. Anyway, it's a damn shame about Jim. Marcum lost a great card partner.

On a slightly cheerier note, Susie and I are still seeing each other, but I have a difficult time figuring her out. Maybe she isn't the demonstrative type. If that is the case, I can understand her reticence, but if not, I can't help wondering what's wrong. We talk all the time but she doesn't seem to be able to let me know she cares. It's odd because Beth was similar in that way.

I'm sure time will make its own decision. Sound familiar, Dad? It's another one of your polished "classics." What would life be without my father's inimitable cracker-barreling? A bit more relaxing perhaps . . .

Incidentally, the loan business is beginning to take shape. I'll write more about it later. For now, it's looking quite hopeful. Monte Carlo, here I come.

Pass the word to you-know-who, about my business. It's

what he likes to hear. Former client makes good and all that
stuff. You know.

Miss you all very much and send my deepest love.

> Destined to be wealthy (but
> in semi-mourning),

P.S. My room is starting to bother me. Maybe a change!

April 25

Dear Mom and Dad:

You-know-who wrote me a letter I received today. He
wants me to come home. The onslaught of Jim's death along
with the isolating geography up here has him surprisingly
alarmed. He feels that the milieu is just too strenuous for me
to manage. I disagree with him completely and feel that I'm
taking Jim's death very well. I'm not overreacting beyond
what is reasonable. After all, Jim and I were almost complete
strangers. Maybe the ease of detachment comes because of
that.

I wrote you-know-who tonight after dinner, but I think a
word from you might help to quell his skepticism. I know you
told him about the death out of good conscience, but, as I
recommended, it may have been a bad idea. All in all, I
couldn't be happier and the thought of leaving depresses me
very much. I think my letter will stand on its own merit, but a
word from you would assist the cause enormously.

Business is in full swing here in Fort Knox North. I've
made over $15 in interest this week. Once again, I'm baffled
as to how to spend the newly mounting sums. Perhaps a place
where liquor and painted women are available to book-weary
students? However, I'll probably squander my gain away on
decent food. The indigenous delicacies are becoming as palat-
able as boiled sheet metal. (But nowhere near as tender.)
Really disgusting. I look forward to a meal by the greatest
cook in the known world. I hope you're listening, Mom.

Food can destroy all faculties but humor, I've discovered.
In fact, the worse the food the better the humor of those who
must eat it or so it seems. Next to maggots the students at this
school have the second best sense of humor. Maggots must be
uproarious. And they don't even have to knock 'em dead. It's
taken care of. Just the opposite here: the chef is trying to

knock us dead. Comparatively speaking, I would welcome the chance to become a maggot.

I talked to the dean of housing today about changing rooms and he told me (morbidly enough) that the only available room is Jim's. It seemed grisly at first, but I gave it serious thought and am going to move in tomorrow. It's been cleaned up (all but boiled out) so there is no trace of anything that indicated someone lived in it. Or died in it. For obvious reasons, I think you would agree, telling you-know-who would just fuel the flame. He can't expect everyone to react to death the same way. It doesn't spook me to be in Jim's room.

I wonder, though, if his spirit will inhabit my lungs and create zombie burps. All, no doubt, from your cookies, Mom. He was really hooked. Phantom gases are an interesting concept, but don't exactly arrest me esthetically. Quiet, I think I hear a cookie crumbling.

My studies are going exceptionally well. Something interesting happened in Philosophy I today. Remember I told you I was going to mention the point about Jim's death maybe being the happiest salvation he could have chosen? Well, I made the point today and nobody would talk about it. They all seemed disturbed about the personalized nature of the question since it wasn't just a hypothetical inquiry. Some people even made peculiar comments. People are unpredictable when it comes to death.

Things are "OK" with Susie. We're supposed to go to a concert tonight. Will tell you about that in next letter. Miss you all hugely and send my fondest love.

Sleeping better,

P.S. Susie may get my class ring tonight. Lucky girl.

April 26

Dear Mom and Dad:

Something ghastly has happened. It's hard to even write this letter as I am extremely upset.

Susie and I returned from the school auditorium sometime after midnight, following the concert, and sneaked into my dormitory room to listen to some music. I had planned to ask Susie how she felt about me after we settled down. The concert had been very stimulating and we were both being quite verbal, competing for each other's audience as many thoughts were occurring to both of us. We talked for several hours and were almost exhausted from the conversation before quieting down.

As we sat listening to the music, on my bed together, I bent over to her cheek and, kissing her gently, asked her how she felt about our relationship and where it was going. She was silent for what must have been minutes. Then she spoke. In almost a pale whisper she said that we would always be good friends and that her regard for me was quite sincere but that she couldn't feel romantically about me ever. She didn't explain why, even though I asked her over and over.

Maybe the fact that I was tired had something to do with it, but I began to cry and couldn't stop. Her admission had taken me entirely by surprise. I had thought things were just beginning to take shape.

I guess Susie sensed that my hurt was larger than even the tears revealed for she got up from the bed to walk to the other side of the room. Working things out in her mind, I guess. She walked to the window to let in some air. As she raised it I could feel the cold wind rush in, and I looked up to see Susie's hair blowing as she kneeled near the window, looking out over the fields. It was so quiet that the whole thing seemed like a dream; the cold air plunging in on us, the music playing with muted beauty for us alone, the near darkness making shadowy nothings of our separateness.

Susie leaned out the window, and I watched her, transfixed, thinking that what she had said was a story, that she was only playing. She only continued in her silence, staring into the night's blackness.

I guess she wanted more air or something because she raised the window, and as I rose to help her with it, a screaming cut the air.

She had fallen out the window.

She kept screaming until she hit the walkway below. Then there was silence again. She was taken to the hospital and operated on for a fractured skull, broken shoulder, and internal injuries.

She was pronounced dead at 6:30 this morning.

The police questioned me today about the accident but seemed satisfied that it was a tragic mishap. They could, I'm sure, see that my grief was genuine.

I am left with almost nothing now. Susie was everything I

worked for other than school, and without her here, that means nothing. I am thinking of coming home. You-know-who needn't say anything to you or me about what he thinks. He's wrong. And, at this point, I don't need advice. My treatment will be mine alone from now on. I don't want interference from him any more.

I am very seriously depressed. I keep thinking that, had Susie told me long ago that she cared we wouldn't have spent so long, last night, in my room. If only she had cared, everything might have been different. I think these thoughts must occur to anyone who loses someone cherished. I didn't think something like this could happen to me. I find it hard to go on without someone caring. If you don't care about someone who cares about you, why should you even exist? Without that there is no reason.

> In deepest hopelessness,

P.S. Maybe no letters from me until I feel better.

> April 28

Dear Mom and Dad:

Things are no better with me than my last letter reported. Since Susie's death I am unable to concentrate on studies and am falling seriously behind in my classes. I sit alone most of the time in my room, watching the fields as the wind's lickings and swirlings create giant patterns. Before today, I had thought it the most beautiful view in the dorm.

Speaking of the dorm, I now find myself unable to associate with any of the other dorm residents. They all remind me of Susie. I almost hate this building because it remembers everything that happened in it. It will not forget anything and each time I get inside it I feel subsumed by its creaking examinations of me. I am now easily given to imaginings about many things and question all things. I trust only myself now.

My loan business is being attended to assiduously with the scrutiny of a watchmaker fearing he has left out a part from a shipment of hundreds of timepieces. I am losing money now. The clientele is not paying me back punctually or with owed amounts adequately covered. Everybody on my floor and many people scattered throughout the building have taken out loans. Almost none have returned them. I am almost at my wit's end trying to get the money. But you can't torture people to get it. I'm really getting desperate. I have such contempt for those who borrow things and either refuse to return them or consciously allow themselves to let their obligation slide through negligence. Negligence should beget negligence. It's only fair that way.

I have been going to concerts the past two nights. They seem to help me relax. I despise returning to the dormitory more and more. Everytime I get inside I feel suffocated. I realize that I must try to adjust and get back into the swing of things, but it is not easy. I am trying. Tell you-know-who.

That's all I can tell you. I can't foresee much of anything now. My dearest love to both of you. Please write.

Confused with sickness,

April 30

Dear Mom and Dad:

Last night, almost as if the dormitory knew my hate for it (like a dog who senses its master's loathings), it took its own life along with the lives of many inside its cradling horror.

As I walked back from a 10:30 concert (Chopin) at the campus center, I came upon the dormitory burning bright orange in the black chill of the night. Firemen say it was caused by an electrical short circuiting or something. Nineteen students were eaten by flames, unable to escape the building. The remains were charred beyond recognition and teeth and dental records are being matched up to discern who the students were.

It doesn't seem to matter who someone is once he is dead. Only what he did while he lived. An honorable life will not tolerate an impure death. But the life that deceives and cloaks its meaning with artifice and insensitivity cannot die reasonably. Perhaps Marshall B. Francis would have something to say about that. All death seems to need is an attached philosophy to resolve its meaning. Otherwise it is just an end. I may talk to him.

There is nothing left for me now of course. I am numbed by the death which surrounds me here. My room and belongings were destroyed in the fire, and the purpose of my schooling has become inconsequential to both myself and what I want.

I will try another school, in another place. Things must be different elsewhere. Somewhere there must be a safe place. A place where things such as what I have seen haven't happened. If there is, I will find it.

I'm catching a plane tomorrow at noon and should arrive at about 5:30. My love to you until then.

Forward looking,

P.S. I got an *A* in philosophy.

Ray Russell was one of the prime reasons for the success of Playboy *during its youth and finally put in a total of seven years as one of its editors. After that, most of his time has been spent as a screen writer and many of his stories (including the classic ''Sardonicus'') have been sold for cinematic treatment. The fantasy and science fiction field has much to thank Mr. Russell for during his* Playboy *tenure since it was he who brought many of our people to the attention of its audience. Herein Ray tackles the classic deal-with-the-devil tale and shows Satan is still one heck of a businessman.*

MIRROR, MIRROR[*]

by Ray Russell

Alan sold himself to the Devil for a mirror.

The moment the contract was signed, Alan's front doorbell rang and the Devil slipped out the back. When Alan answered the ringing, two thick-thewed delivery men carried into his house a large flat oval shape wrapped in brown paper. Alan instructed them to bring it into his study and lean it against the south wall. After they had left, he locked himself into the study, drew the blinds, and tore the paper off his acquisition.

*Copyright © 1977 by Ray Russell.

The oval mirror was as tall as Alan, of good quality glass set in an ormolu frame. It was quite handsome. Alan was pleased.

But the image that stared back at him from the glass was obviously *dis*pleased. It was merely himself, dressed exactly as the real Alan, in shirt sleeves and pearl-gray slacks, but the expression on the face was angry and the writhing mouth spat three silent syllables, the last of which (Alan deduced from the placement of upper teeth on lower lip) began with an "f".

Alan grew furious and blurted out: "It's a fraud!"

The image in the glass turned its back to Alan and strode out of sight.

Alan, perplexed and vexed, turned away from the mirror and left the room.

Having carefully relocked the door to his study, Alan now paced the floor outside that room. His furrowed face hardened into a mask of bitterness as the truth became clear.

He had requested, for his private use, a magic glass in which he could see the future. The Devil had given him precisely that.

What Alan had *meant* was a glass that would foretell all future events, like the crystal ball of fable, magazine cartoon, and cliché.

Of what conceivable earthly or, for that matter, unearthly value was a mirror that did no more than reflect an image *five seconds* ahead of time?

If the reflection were twenty-four hours in the future, or even twelve, he could put it to some use; hold up newspapers to the mirror, read the next day's racing results and stock market listings. He could win wagers on elections, predict earthquakes and other disasters, beat Broadway critics to the punch, become famous as a prophet, make a lot of money, be praised and feared and sought after.

But five seconds?

Alan howled with rage. The stinking goat had tricked him!

He did not sleep all night. He paced, cursed, smoked cigarettes, drank whiskey, drank coffee, scribbled thoughts on paper, tore up the paper in frustration, pounded his head with his fists, formed and rejected a dozen ideas, two dozen, a hundred. None of them were any good. He could do *nothing* with those absurd five seconds. The mirror was utterly worthless.

As the dawn began to reach hesitantly into his house, he fell into a sleep of total exhaustion. Five hours later he awoke, much refreshed, with a new idea in his head. That evening, he would have cause to wonder who had put it there.

He made several telephone calls, inviting a variety of people to cocktails in the afternoon. He then phoned a modish caterer, to order liquor and exotic hors d'œuvres.

Next, he carried the mirror out of the study and into the living room, where he hung it in a conspicuous place.

Alan's idea was simple, if not brilliant. The mirror would be made useful to him, after all. Not as directly as he had hoped, but indirectly. It would become a conversation piece. It would fascinate all sorts of people. Among his invited guests were a nationally syndicated gossip columnist, several show people of all sexes, tattletales of all ages, beauteous if vacuous ladies of the beau monde, a nice sampling of that worthless world Alan despised and admired.

These creatures would be impressed and awed by his mirror. They would squeal and gibber and ask how the trick was done. They would question him about the mirror's origins; he would be deliciously cryptic, hinting at other dark, nameless forces at his beck and call. Word would spread, by mouth and print, about the mysterious Cagliostro in their midst. He would be lionized, fêted, adulated. His lightest statement would carry weight. He would be a frequent guest on television talk shows, entering the homes of millions of people. He would be written up in magazines of huge circulation. His photo would appear everywhere. Publishers would offer him gigantic sums for his ghost-written autobiography. He would be in great demand on the lecture circuit, at stunning fees. He would be considered a sage, and his advice on all matters would urgently be sought. He would be deemed delightfully dangerous, and women would fall at his presumably cloven feet, yearning to learn the arcane amatory techniques of which surely he was a master. He would become a legend in his own time, for in our epoch, Alan well knew, it is not necessary to be gifted or accomplished in order to attain legendary status. And perhaps, some distant day, when he was very old, he might sell the mirror for a vast amount of money.

It would not be a bad life, he told himself, as he showered and prepared for the cocktail party.

His guests began to arrive at about six, and everything

went as he'd wished. The mirror was a great success, and so was he. He saw the hot glitter in their eyes, heard their voices coarsen with a kind of lust, filled his grateful lungs with the acrid perfume of glamor (didn't "glamor" have a dazzling original meaning?—he'd have to look it up in the Unabridged in the morning).

All but a few of his guests were remarkably ugly, but it was a fashionable ugliness that passed for beauty in certain strata of society, and most of them were no longer young, although they strove to present the appearance of youth, aided by dyes, diets, corsets, injections, surgery, dentistry. One person of indeterminate age—Alan was fairly sure it was a woman—had hair bleached white as the well-known sepulcher and skin the texture of cold gravy. Several of the men wore hair not their own. Costly gems, throbbing with inner fire, pulsated on many a turkey neck and talon.

They cavorted before the glass like performing apes. They grinned, frowned, rolled their eyes, stuck out their tongues. Some made obscene gestures.

When the guests reluctantly left, one of them was persuaded to stay a little longer. She was beautiful, haughty, confident; her face was on the cover of every fashion magazine; she had starred in a chic movie—and yet Alan possessed her mere minutes after the last of the others had departed. It happened on the soft carpet in front of his marvelous, his glamorous mirror (an interesting experience, that: he told himself he might try placing the glass on the ceiling over his bed some time, just as an experiment).

He dismissed her somewhat later, after a cozy tête-à-tête supper, and only after solemnly promising he would call her the next day.

Alone, Alan stood in front of the mirror, intensely pleased with himself. His reflection appeared to be pleased too. Why not? The Alan of five seconds from now would be just as content as the Alan of now. He had won. In stories, the Devil always wins by cleverly wording the contract and then sticking literally and precisely to that wording—observing the letter of it, but violating the spirit, for the Devil has a brilliant mind, and is The Father of Lawyers. By such a device he had triumphed over Alan—temporarily. But Alan had turned the tables on him by making those five useless seconds useful. He had traded on human curiosity, cashed in on human

gullibility, much in the manner of the Devil himself. He had
beaten the Devil at his own game. He had bested him. Alan's
image smiled broadly and, five seconds later, Alan did likewise.

A few moments after that, however, there were *two* figures
in the mirror. The Devil's image appeared behind Alan's, and
tapped Alan's reflection on the shoulder.

The real Alan, though he'd felt nothing, quickly whirled
around—but it was all right, there was no One behind him, he
was alone.

He immediately turned back to the mirror. The images of
both the Devil *and Alan* had vanished from the glass. It
reflected an *empty room*.

Icy sweat covered him in an instant as he recalled a condition of the contract: the mirror was *"for his private use."* But
Alan had put it on display, shown it to many others. He had
violated the contract. The Devil was therefore entitled to . . .
foreclose.

Alan smelled a goat-stink. He felt somebody tap him on the
shoulder.

Brian Lumley is a sergeant in the British Royal Military
Police and a fine writer as well. His "Born of the Winds"
received a nomination for a 1976 World Fantasy Award
and was one of only a handful of stories in recent years
that have been successful additions to the Lovecraft-Der-
leth Cthulhu Mythos. This is another one and led off the
first issue of Whispers. It was selected for two Best-of-Year
anthologies and is, I believe, the first heroic-fantasy addition to the Mythos to appear professionally.

THE HOUSE OF CTHULHU

by Brian Lumley

Where weirdly angled ramparts loom,
Gaunt sentinels whose shadows gloom
Upon an undead hell-beast's tomb—
 And gods and mortals fear to tread;
Where gateways to forbidden spheres
And times are closed, but monstrous fears
Await the passing of strange years—
 When that will wake which is not dead . . .

"Arlyeh," a fragment from
Teh Atht's *Legends of the
Olden Runes*. As translated
by Thelred Gustau from the
Theem'hdra Manuscripts.

Now it happened aforetime that Zar-thule the Conqueror who is called Reaver of Reavers, Seeker of Treasures and Sacker of Cities, swam out of the East with his dragonships; aye, even beneath the snapping sails of his dragonships. The wind was but lately turned favorable, and now the weary rowers nodded over their shipped oars while sleepy steersmen held the course. And there Zar-thule descried him in the sea the island Arlyeh, whereon loomed tall and twisted towers builded of black stones whose tortuous twinings were of contorted angles all unknown and utterly beyond the ken of men. Aye, and this island was redly litten by the sun sinking down over its awesome black crags and burning behind the asymmetrical aeries and spires carved therefrom by other than human hands.

And though Zar-thule felt a great hunger and stood sore weary of the great sea's expanse behind the lolling dragon's tail of his ship *Redfire,* and even though he gazed with red and rapacious eyes upon the black island, still he held off his reavers, biding them that they ride at anchor well out to sea until the sun was deeply down and gone into the Realm of Cthon; aye, even unto Cthon, who sits in silence to snare the sun in his net beyond the Edge of the World. Indeed, such were Zar-thule's raiders as their deeds were best done by night, for then Gleeth the blind Moon God saw them not nor heard in his celestial deafness the horrible which ever attended unto such deeds.

For, notwithstanding his cruelty, which was beyond words, Zar-thule was no fool. He knew him that his wolves must rest before a whelming, that if the treasures of the House of Cthulhu were truly such as he imagined them in his mind's eye—then that they must likewise be well guarded by fighting men who would not give up easily. And his reavers were fatigued even as Zar-thule himself, so that he rested them all down behind the painted bucklers lining the decks and furled him up the great dragon-dyed sails and set a watch that in the middle of the night he might be roused and rousing in turn the men of his twenty ships in unto and sack the island of Arlyeh.

Far had Zar-thule's reavers rowed before the fair winds found them, aye, far from the rape of Yaht-Haal, the Silver City at the edge of the frostlands. Their provisions were all but eaten, their swords all oceanrot in rusting sheaths; but now they ate them all of their remaining regimen and drank them of the liquors thereof and cleansed and sharpened their dire blades before taking themselves into the arms of Shoosh, Goddess of the Still Slumbers. They well knew them one and all that soon they will be at the sack, each for himself and loot to that sword's wielder whose blade drank long and deep.

And Zar-thule had promised them great treasures, aye, even *great* treasures from the House of Cthulhu, for back there in the sacked and seared city at the edge of the frost-lands he had heard it from the bubbling and anguished lips of Voth Vehm the name of the so-called "forbidden" isle of Arlyeh. Voth Vehm, in the throes of terrible tortures, had called out the name of his brother-priest, Hath Vehm, who guarded the House of Cthulhu in Arlyeh. And too Voth Vehm had answered even in the hour of his dying to Zar-thule's additional tortures; crying out that Arlyeh was indeed forbidden and held in thrall by the sleeping but yet dark and terrible god Cthulhu, the gate to whose House his brother-priest guarded.

Then had Zar-thule reasoned that Arlyeh must contain riches indeed, for he knew it was not meet that brother-priests betray one another; and aye, surely had Voth Vehm spoken exceedingly fearfully of this dark and terrible god Cthulhu that he might thus divert Zar-thule's avarice from the ocean sanctuary of his brother-priest, Hath Vehm. Thus reckoned Zar-thule, even brooding on the dead and disfigured hierophant's words, until he bethought him to leave the sacked city. Then, with the flames leaping brightly and reflected in his red wake, Zar-thule put to sea in his dragonships; aye, even did he put himself to sea, all loaded down with the silver booty, in search of Arlyeh and the treasures of the House of Cthulhu. And thus came he to this place.

Shortly before this midnight hour, the watch roused Zar-thule up from the arms of Shoosh, aye, and all the freshened men of the dragonships; and then beneath Gleeth the blind Moon God's pitted silver face, seeing that the wind had fallen, they muffled their oars and dipped them deep and so closed in with the shoreline. A dozen fathoms from beaching, out rang Zar-thule's plunder cry, and his drummers took up a stern and steady beat by which the trained but yet rampageous reavers might advance to the sack.

Came the scrape of keel on grit, and down from his dragon's head leapt Zar-thule to the sullen shallow waters, and all his captains and men, to wade ashore and stride the night-black strand and wave their swords—and all for naught! Lo, the island stood quiet and still and seemingly untended . . .

Only now did the Sacker of Cities take note of this isle's truly awesome aspect. Black piles of tumbled masonry, festooned with weeds from the tides, rose up from the dark wet sand, and there seemed inherent in these gaunt and immemorial relics a foreboding not alone of bygone times; great crabs scuttled in and about the archaic ruins and gazed with stalked ruby eyes upon the intruders; even the small waves broke with an eerie *hush, hush, hush* upon the sand and pebbles and primordial exuviae of crumbled yet seemingly sentient towers and tabernacles. The drummers faltered and paused and silence reigned.

Now many of them among these reavers recognized rare gods and supported strange superstitions, and Zarthule knew this and had no liking for their silence. It was a silence that might yet yield mutiny!

"Hah!" quoth he, who worshipped neither god nor demon nor yet lent ears to the gaunts of night: "See—the guards have known of our coming and have fled to the far side of the island—or perhaps they gather rank at the House of Cthulhu." So saying he formed him up his men into a body and advanced into the island.

And as they marched they passed him by the paleolithic piles not yet ocean-sundered, striding through silent streets whose fantastic facades gave back the beat of the drummers in a strangely muted monotone.

And lo, mummied faces of coeval antiquity seemed to leer from the empty and oddly-angled towers and craggy spires; fleet ghouls that flitted from shadow to shadow apace with the marching men, until some of those hardened grew sore afraid and begged them of Zar-thule: "Master, let us get us gone from here, for it appears that there is no treasure, and this place is like unto no other; and that it stinks of death, aye even of death and of them that walk the shadowlands."

But Zar-thule rounded on one who stood close to him muttering thus, crying: "Coward!—out on you!" Whereupon he lifted up his sword and cleft the trembling reaver in two parts, so that the sundered man screamed once before falling with twin thuds to the black earth. But now Zar-thule perceived that indeed that many of his men were sore afraid, and so he had him torches lighted and brought up and they pressed on into the island.

There, beyond low dark hills, they came to a great gathering of queerly carved and monolithic edifices, all of the same strange design comprising confused angles and surfaces and all with the stench of the pit, aye, even the fetor of the very pit about them. And in the center of these malodorous megaliths there stood the greatest tower of them all, a massive menhir that loomed and leaned windowless to a great height and about which at its base squat pedestals bore likenesses of blackly carven krackens of terrifying aspect.

"Hah!" quoth Zar-thule. "Plainly is this the House of Cthulhu; and see its guards and priests have fled them all before us to escape the reaving!"

But a tremulous voice, old and mazed, answered from the shadows at the base of one great pedestal saying, "No one has fled, O reaver, for there are none here to flee, save me—and I cannot flee for I guard the gate against those who may utter The Words."

At the sound of this old voice in the stillness, all the reavers started and peered nervously about at the leaping torch-cast shadows, but one stout captain stepped forward to drag from out of the dark an old, old man—and lo, all and all they fell back at once seeing the mien of this mage. For he bore upon his face and hands, aye, and upon all visible parts of him, a gray and furry lichen that seemed to crawl upon him even as he stood crooked and trembled in his great age.

"Who are you?" demanded Zar-thule, aghast at the sight of so hideous a spectacle of afflicted infirmity; even Zar-thule, aghast . . .

"I am Hath Vehm, brother-priest of Veth Vehm who serves the gods in the temples of Yaht-Haal the Silver City. I am Hath Vehm, Keeper of the Gate at the House of Cthulhu, and I warn you that it is forbidden to touch me." He gloomed with rheumy eyes at the captain who held him until that raider took away his hands.

"And I am Zar-thule the Conqueror," quoth Zar-thule, less in awe now, "Reaver of Reavers, Seeker of Treasures and Sacker of Cities. I have plundered Yaht-Haal, aye, plundered the Silver City and burned it low. And I have tortured Veth Vehm unto death. But in his dying he cried out a name, aye, even with hot coals eating at his belly. And it was your name he spake. And he was truly a brother unto you, Hath Vehm, for he warned me of the terrible god Cthulhu and of this 'forbidden' isle Arlyeh. But I knew he spake not truly that he sought him only to protect a great and holy treasure and to protect his brother-priest who guards that treasure, doubtless with strange runes to frighten away the superstitious reavers! But Zar-thule is neither afraid nor credulous, old one. Here I stand and I say to you on your life that I'll know the way into this treasure house within the hour!''

And now Zar-thule's captains and men had taken heart. Hearing their chief speak thus to the ancient priest of the island, and noting the old one's trembling infirmity and hideous disfigurement, they had gone about and about the beetling tower of obscure angles until one of them had found him a door. Now this door was great, tall, solid, and wide and nowise hidden to the beholder; and yet at times it seemed narrow at its top and indistinct at its edges. It stood straight up in the wall of the House of Cthulhu, and yet looked as if to lean to one side . . . and then in one and the same moment lean to the other! It bore leering inhuman faces carven of its surface and horrid hieroglyphics, and these unknown characters seemed to writhe about the gorgon faces, and aye, those faces, too, moved and grimaced in the light of the flickering flambeaux.

The ancient Hath Vehm came to them where they gathered in wonder of the great door and spake thus: "Aye, that is the gate of the House of Cthulhu; I am its guardian."

"So," spake Zar-thule, who was also come there, "and is there a key to this gate? I see no means of entry."

"Aye, there is a key, but none such as you might readily imagine; for it is not of metal but of words!"

"Magic?" asked Zar-thule, undaunted, he had heard aforetimes of similar thaumaturgies.

"Aye, magic!" agreed the Guardian of the Gate.

Zar-thule put the point of his sword to the old man's throat, observing as he did so the furry gray growth moving upon the elder's face and scrawny neck saying: "Then say those words now and let's have done!"

"Nay, I cannot say The Words—I am sworn to guard the gate that The Words are *never* spoken, neither by myself nor by any other who would foolishly or mistakenly open the House of Cthulhu. You may kill me—aye, even take my life

with that very blade you now hold to my throat—but I will
not utter The Words . . .''

"And I say that you will—*eventually!*'' quoth Zar-thule in
an exceedingly cold voice . . . in a voice even as cold as the
northern sleet. Whereupon he put down his sword and ordered two of his men to come forward, commanding that they
take the ancient and tie him down to thonged pegs made fast
in the ground, one thong to each arm and one to each leg, so
that he was spread out flat upon his back not far from the
great and oddly fashioned door in the wall of the House of
Cthulhu.

Then a fire was lighted of the sparse shrubs of the low hills
and of driftwood fetched from the shore; and others of Zar-
thule's reavers went out and trapped certain great nocturnal
birds that knew not the power of flight; and yet others found a
spring of brackish water and filled them up the water-skins.
And soon tasteless but satisfying meat turned on spits above a
fire, and in the same fire swordpoints glowed red, then white;
Until Zar-thule and the captains and men had eaten their fill,
whereupon the Reaver of Reavers motioned to his torturers
that they should attend to their task. And the torturers came
forward to retrieve their swords; aye, for of course those
swords that had their tips in the fire were theirs. And Zar-
thule had trained these torturers himself, so that they excelled
in the arts of the pincer and hot irons.

But here there came a diversion. For some little time a
certain captain—his name was Cush-had; he who first found
the old priest in the shadows of the great pedestal and dragged
him forth—had been peering most strangely at his hands in
the firelight and rubbing them upon the hide of his jacket. Of a
sudden he cursed and leapt to his feet, springing up from the
remnants of his meal. He danced about in a frightened manner,
beating wildly at the tumbled flat stones about with his hands.
Then of a sudden he stopped and cast sharp glances at his
naked forearms. In the same seconds his eyes stood out in his
face and he screamed as if he were pierced through and
through with a keen blade; and he rushed to the fire and thrust
his hands in its heart, even to his elbows. Then he drew his
arms from out the flames, staggering and moaning and calling
upon certain trusted gods, and tottered away into the night,
his arms steaming and dripping bubbly liquid upon the ground.

Amazed, Zar-thule sent a man after him with a torch, who

soon returned trembling with a very pale face in the firelight to tell how the madman had fallen—or leapt—to his death in a deep crevice, but that before he fell there had been visible upon his face a creeping, furry grayness! And as he had fallen, aye, even as he crashed down to his death, he had screamed: "Unclean, unclean, unclean!"

Then, all and all when they heard this, they remembered the old priest's words of warning when Cush-had dragged him out of hiding, and the way he had gloomed upon the unfortunate captain, and they looked at the ancient where he lay held fast to the earth. The two reavers whose task it had been to tie him down looked them one to the other with very wide eyes, their faces whitening perceptibly in the firelight, and they took up a quiet and secret examination of their persons; aye, even a *minute* examination . . .

Zar-thule felt fear rising in the reavers like the east wind when it rises up fast and wild in the desert of Sheb. He spat at the ground and lifted up his sword, crying: "Listen to me! You are all superstitious cowards, all and all of you, with your old wives' fears and mumbo-jumbo. What's there here to be frightened of; an old man, alone, on a black rock in the sea?"

"But I saw upon Cush-had's face—" began the man who had followed the demented captain.

"You only *thought* you saw something," Zar-thule cut him off. "It was only the flickering of your torch-fire and nothing more. Cush-had was a madman!"

"But—"

"Cush-had was a madman!" Zar-thule said again, and his voice turned very cold. "Are you, too, insane? Is there room for you, too, at the bottom of that crevice?" But the man shrank back and said no more, and yet again did Zar-thule call his torturers that they should be about their work.

The hours passed . . .

Blind and coldly deaf Gleeth the old Moon God may have been, and yet perhaps he had sensed something of the agonized screams and the stench of roasting human flesh drifting up from Arlyeh that night, for certainly he seemed to sink down in the sky very quickly.

Now, however, the tattered and blackened figure stretched out upon the ground before the door in the wall of the House of Cthulhu was no longer strong enough to cry out loudly, and Zar-thule despaired for he had perceived that soon the priest of the island would sink into the last and longest of slumbers; and still The Words were not spoken. Too, the reaver king was perplexed by the ancient's stubborn refusal to admit that the door in the looming menhir concealed treasure; but in the end he put down this effect of certain vows Hath Vehm had no doubt taken in his inauguration to the priesthood.

The torturers had not done their work well. They had been loath to touch the elder with anything but their hot swords; they would *not*—not even when threatened most direly—lay hands upon him or approach him more closely than absolutely necessary to the application of their agonizing art. The two reavers responsible for tying the ancient down were dead, slain by former comrades upon whom they had inadvertently lain hands of friendship; and those they had touched, their slayers, they too were shunned by their companions and sat apart from the other reavers.

As the first gray light of dawn began to show behind the eastern sea, Zar-thule finally lost all patience and turned upon the dying priest in a veritable fury. He took up his sword, raising it over his head in two hands—and then Hath Vehm spoke:

"Wait," he whispered, his voice a low, tortured croak, "wait, O reaver—I will say The Words."

"What?" cried Zar-thule, lowering his blade. "You will open the door?"

"Aye," the cracked whisper came, "I will open the Gate—but, first, tell me: did you truly sack Yaht-Haal the Silver City and raze it with fire and torture my brother-priest to death?"

"I did all that," Zar-thule callously nodded.

"Then come you close." Hath Vehm's voice sank low. "Closer, O reaver king, that you may hear me in my final hour."

Eagerly the Seeker of Treasures bent him down his ear to the lips of the ancient, kneeling down beside him where he lay—and Hath Vehm immediately lifted up his head from the earth and spat upon Zar-thule!

Then, before the Sacker of Cities could think or make a move to wipe the slimy spittle from his brow, Hath Vehm said The Words; aye even in a loud and clear voice he said them—words of terrible import and alien cadence that only an adept might repeat—and at once there came a great rumble from the door in the beetling wall of weird angles.

Forgetting for the moment the tainted insult of the ancient priest, Zar-thule turned to see the huge and evilly carven door tremble and waver and then by some unknown power move or slide away until only a great black hole opened where it had been. And lo, in the early dawn light, the reaver horde pressed forward to seek them out the treasure with their eyes; aye, even to seek out the treasure beyond the open door. And Zar-thule too made to enter the House of Cthulhu, but again the dying hierophant cried out to him:

"Hold! There are more Words, O reaver king!"

"More Words?" Zar-thule turned and the priest, his life ebbing quickly, smiled mirthlessly at the sight of the furry gray blemish that crawled upon the barbarian's forehead over his left eye.

"Aye, more Words! Listen: long and long ago, when the world was very young, before Arlyeh and the House of Cthulhu were first sunken into the sea, wise elder gods devised a rune that should Cthulhu's House ever rise and be opened by foolish men, it might be sent down again—aye, and even Arlyeh itself sunken deep once more beneath the salt waters. *Now I say those other Words!*"

Swiftly the king reaver leapt, his sword lifting, but ere that blade could fall Hath Vehm cried out those other strange and dreadful Words; and lo, the whole island shook in the grip of a great earthquake. Now in awful anger and fear Zar-thule's sword fell and hacked off the ancient's whistling and spurting head from his ravened body; but even as the head rolled free, so the island shook itself again, and the ground rumbled and began to break open.

From the open door in the House of Cthulhu, whereinto the host of greedy reavers had rushed to the treasure, there now came loud and singularly hideous cries of fear and torment . . . and of a sudden and even more hideous stench. And now Zar-thule knew truly and truly indeed there was no treasure.

Great ebony clouds gathered swiftly and livid lightning crashed; winds rose up that blew Zar-thule's long black hair over his face as he crouched in horror before the open door of the House of Cthulhu. Wide and wide were his eyes as he tried to peer beyond the reeking blackness of that namelessly ancient aperture—but a moment later he dropped his great sword to the ground and screamed; aye, even the Reaver of Reavers screamed. For two of his wolves had appeared from out of the darkness, more in the manner of whipped puppies than true wolves, shrieking and babbling and scrambling frantically over the queer angles of the orifice's mouth . . . but they had emerged only to be snatched up and squashed like grapes by titantic tentacles that lashed after them from the dark depths beyond! And these rubbery appendages drew the crushed bodies back into the inky blackness, from which there instantly issued forth the most monstrously nauseating slobberings and suckings before the writhing members once more snaked forth into the dawn light. This time they caught at the edges of the opening, and from behind them pushed forward—*a face!*

Zar-thule gazed upon the enormously bloated visage of Cthulhu, and screamed again as that terrible Being's awful eyes found him where he crouched—found him and lit with an hideous light!

The reaver king paused, frozen, for but a moment—and yet long enough so that the ultimate horror of the thing framed in the titan threshold seared itself upon his brain—before his legs found their strength. Then he turned and fled; speeding away and over the low black hills and down to the shore and into his ship which he somehow managed, even single-handed and in his frantic terror, to cast off; and always in his mind's eye there burned that fearful sight, the awful *Visage* and *Being* of Lord Cthulhu.

There had been the tentacles, springing from a green pulpy head about which they sprouted like lethiferous petals about the heart of an obscenely hybrid orchid; a scaled and amorphously elastic body of immense proportions, with clawed feet fore and hind; long narrow wings ill-fitting the horror that bore them in that it seemed patently impossible for *any* wings to lift so fantastic a bulk—and then there had been the eyes! Never before had Zar-thule seen such evil rampancy expressed in the ultimately leering malignancy of Cthulhu's eyes!

And Cthulhu was not finished with Zar-thule, for even as the king reaver struggled madly with his sail, the monster came across the low hills in the dawn light, slobbering and groping down to the very water's edge. Then, when Zar-thule saw against the morning the mountain that was Cthulhu, he went mad for a period; flinging himself from side to side of his ship so that he was like to fall into the sea, frothing at the mouth and babbling horribly in pitiful prayer—aye, even Zar-thule whose lips never before uttered prayers—to certain benevolent gods of which he had heard. And it seems that these kind gods, if indeed they exist, must have heard him!

With a roar and a blast greater than any before, there came the final shattering that saved Zar-thule's mind, body, and soul, and the entire island split asunder; even the bulk of Arlyeh breaking into many parts and settling into the sea. And with a piercing scream of frustrated rage and lust—a scream which Zar-thule heard with his mind as well as his ears—the monster Cthulhu sank Him down also with the island and his House beneath the frothing waves.

A great storm raged then such that might attend the End of the World; banshee winds howled and demon waves crashed over and about Zar-thule's dragonship, and for two days he gibbered and moaned in the rolling, shuddering scuppers of crippled *Redfire* before the mighty storm wore itself out.

Eventually, close to starvation, the one-time Reaver of Reavers was discovered becalmed upon a flat sea not far from the fair strands of bright Theem'hdra; and then, in the spicy hold of a rich merchant's ship, he was borne in unto the wharves of the city of Klühn, Theem'hdra's capital.

With long oars he was prodded ashore, stumbling and weak and crying out in his horror of living—for he had gazed upon Cthulhu! The use of the oars had much to do with his *appearance*, for now Zar-thule was changed indeed, into something that in less tolerant parts of the world might certainly have expected to be burned! But the people of Klühn were kindly folk; they burned him not but lowered him in a basket into a deep dungeon cell with torches to light the place and daily bread and water that he might live until his life was rightly done. And when he was recovered to partial health and sanity, learned men and physicians went to talk with him from above and ask him of his strange affliction, of which all in all stood in awe.

I, Teh Atht, was one of them that went to him, and that was how I came to hear of this tale. And I know it to be true for oft again over the years I have heard of this Loathly Lord Cthulhu that seeped down from the stars when the world was an inchoate infant. There are legends and legends, aye, and one of them is that when times have passed and the stars are right Cthulhu shall slobber forth from His House in Arlyeh again, and the world shall tremble to His tread and erupt in madness at His touch.

I leave this record for men as yet unborn, a record and a warning: leave well enough alone, for that is not dead which deeply dreams, and while perhaps the submarine tides have removed forever the alien taint which touched Arlyeh—that symptom of Cthulhu which loathsome familiar grew upon Hath Vehm and transferred itself upon certain reavers of Zar-thule—Cthulhu himself yet lives and waits upon those who would set him free. I know it. In dreams . . . I myself have heard His call!

And when dreams such as these come in the night to sour the sweet embrace of Shoosh, I wake and tremble and pace the crystal-paved floors of my rooms above the Bay of Klühn, until Cthon releases the sun from his net to rise again, and ever and ever I recall the aspect of Zar-thule as last I saw him in the flickering torchlight of his deep dungeon cell; a fumbling gray mushroom thing that moved not of its own volition but by reason of the parasite growth which lives upon and within it . . .

John Crowley's first book, The Deep, *received much critical acclaim, and his second novel, titled* Beasts, *is following well in its footsteps. "Antiquities" was the first short story of his I had ever seen, and it is a member of the story saga known as the traveller's tale, a cycle brought to its zenith by the late Lord Dunsany's Mr. Joseph Jorkens. While not exactly taking the name of the Lord in vain, John does take a gentle look at those traveller's reminiscences. This is a story of ancient Egypt, succubi, and much more . . .*

ANTIQUITIES

by John Crowley

"There was, of course," Sir Jeffrey said, "the Inconstancy Plague in Cheshire. Short-lived, but a phenomenon I don't think we can quite discount."

It was quite late at the Travellers' Club, and Sir Jeffrey and I had been discussing (as we seemed often to do in those years of the Empire's greatest, yet somehow most tenuous, extent) some anomalous irruptions of the foreign and the odd into the home island's quiet life—small, unlooked-for effects which those centuries of adventure and acquisition had had on an essentially stay-at-home race. At least that was my thought. I was quite young.

"It's no good your saying 'of course' in that offhand tone," I said, attempting to catch the eye of Barnett, whom I felt as much as saw passing through the crepuscular haze of the smoking room. "I've no idea what the Inconstancy Plague was."

From within his evening dress Sir Jeffrey drew out a cigar case, which faintly resembled a row of cigars, as a mummy case resembles the human form within. He offered me one, and we lit them without haste. Sir Jeffrey started a small vortex in his brandy glass. I understood that these rituals were introductory—that, in other words, I would have my tale.

"It was in the latter eighties," Sir Jeffrey said. "I've no idea now how I first came to hear of it, though I shouldn't be surprised if it was some flippant note in *Punch*. I paid no attention at first; the 'popular delusions and madness of crowds' sort of thing. I'd returned not long before from Ceylon, and was utterly, blankly oppressed by the weather. It was just starting autumn when I came ashore, and I spent the next four months more or less behind closed doors. The rain! The fog! How could I have forgotten? And the oddest thing was that no one else seemed to pay the slightest attention. My man used to draw the drapes every morning and say in the most cheerful voice, 'Another dismal wet one, eh, sir?' and I would positively turn my face to the wall."

He seemed to sense that he had been diverted by personal memories, and drew on his cigar as though it were the font of recall.

"What brought it to notice was a seemingly ordinary murder case. A farmer's wife in Winsford, married some decades, came one night into the Sheaf of Wheat, a public house, where her husband was lingering over a pint. From under her skirts she drew an old fowling-piece. She made a remark which was later reported quite variously by the onlookers, and gave him both barrels. One misfired, but the other was quite sufficient. We learn that the husband, on seeing this about to happen, seemed to show neither surprise nor anguish, merely looking up and—well, awaiting his fate.

"At the inquest, the witnesses reported the murderess to have said, before she fired, 'I'm doing this in the name of all the others.' Or perhaps it was 'I'm doing this, Sam (his name), to save the others.' Or possibly, 'I've got to do this, Sam, to save you from that other.' The woman seemed to have gone quite mad. She gave the investigators an elaborate and scarifying story which they, unfortunately, didn't take down, being able to make no sense of it. The rational gist of it was that she had shot her husband for flagrant infidelities which she could bear no longer. When the magistrate asked witnesses if they knew of such infidelities—these things, in a small community, being notoriously difficult to hide—the men, as a body, claimed that they did not. After the trial, however, the women had dark and unspecific hints to make, how they could say much if they would, and so on. The murderess was adjudged unfit to stand trial, and hanged herself in Bedlam not long after.

"I don't know how familiar you are with that oppressive part of the world. In those years farming was a difficult enterprise at best, isolating, stultifyingly boring, unremunerative. Hired men were heavy drinkers. Prices were depressed. The women aged quickly, what with continual childbirth added to a load of work at least equal to their menfolk's. What I'm getting at is that it is, or was, a society the least of any conducive to adultery, amours, romance. And yet for some reason it appeared, after this murder pointed it up, so to speak, dramatically, that there was a veritable plague of inconstant husbands in northern Cheshire."

"It's difficult to imagine," I said, "what evidence there could be of such a thing."

"I had occasion to go to the county that autumn, just at the height of it all," Sir Jeffrey went on, caressing an ashtray with the tip of his cigar. "I'd at last got a grip on myself and begun to accept invitations again. A fellow I'd known in Alexandria, a commercial agent who'd done spectacularly well for himself, asked me up for the shooting."

"Odd place to go shooting."

"Odd fellow. *Arriviste,* to speak frankly. The hospitality was lavish; the house was a red-brick Cheshire *faux*-Gothic affair, if you know what I mean, and the impression it gave of desolation and melancholy was remarkable. And there was no shooting; poured rain all weekend. One sat about leafing through novels or playing Cairo whist—which is what we called bridge in those days—and staring out the windows. One evening, at a loss for entertainment, our host—Watt was his name, and . . ."

"What was his name?" I asked.

"Exactly. He'd become a student of mesmerism, or hypnotism as he preferred to call it, and suggested we might have a bit of fun probing our dark underminds. We all declined, but Watt was insistent, and at last suborned a hearty local type, old squirearchical family, and—this is important—an inveterate, dirt-under-the-nails farmer. His conversation revolved, chiefly, around turnips."

"Even his dark undermind's?"

"Ah. Here we come to it. This gentleman's wife was present at the gathering as well, and one couldn't help noticing the hangdog air he maintained around her, the shifty eyes, the nervous start he gave when she spoke to him from behind; and also a certain dreaminess, an abstraction, that would fall on him at odd moments."

"Worrying about his turnips, perhaps."

Sir Jeffrey quashed his cigar, rather reproachfully, as though it were my own flippancy. "The point is that this ruddy-faced, absolutely ordinary fellow *was cheating on his wife*. One read it as though it were written on his shirt front. His wife seemed quite as aware of it as any; her face was drawn tight as her reticule. She blanched when he agreed to go under, and tried to lead him away, but Watt insisted he be a sport, and at last she retired with a headache. I don't know what the man was thinking of when he agreed; had a bit too much brandy, I expect. At any rate, the lamps were lowered and the usual apparatus got out, the spinning disc and so on. The squire, to Watt's surprise, went under as though slain. We thought at first he had merely succumbed to the grape, but then Watt began to question him, and he to answer, languidly but clearly, name, age, and so on. I've no doubt Watt intended to have the man stand on his head, or turn his waistcoat back-to-front, or that sort of thing, but before any of that could begin, the man began to speak. To address someone. Someone female. Most extraordinary, the way he was transformed."

Sir Jeffrey, in the proper mood, shows a talent for mimicry, and now he seemed to transform himself into the hypnotized squire. His eyes glazed and half-closed, his mouth went slack (though his moustache remained upright) and one hand was raised as though to ward off an importunate spirit.

" 'No,' says he. 'Leave me alone. Close those eyes—those eyes. Why? Why? Dress yourself, oh God . . .' And here he seemed quite in torment. Watt should of course have awakened the poor fellow immediately, but he was fascinated, as I confess we all were.

" 'Who is it you speak to?' Watt asked.

" 'She,' says the squire. 'The foreign woman. The clawed woman. The cat.'

" 'What is her name?'

" 'Bastet.'

" 'How did she come here?'

"At this question the squire seemed to pause. Then he gave three answers: 'Through the earth. By default. On the *John Deering*.' This last answer astonished Watt, since, as he told me later, the *John Deering* was a cargo ship he had often dealt with, which made a regular Alexandria–Liverpool run.

" 'Where do you see her?' Watt asked.

" 'In the sheaves of wheat.' "

"He meant the pub, I suppose," I put in.

"I think not," Sir Jeffrey said darkly. "He went on about the sheaves of wheat. He grew more animated, though it was more difficult to understand his words. He began to make sounds—well, how shall I put it? His breathing became stertorous, his movements . . ."

"I think I see."

"Well, you can't, quite. Because it was one of the more remarkable things I have ever witnessed. The man was making physical love to someone he described as a cat, or a sheaf of wheat."

"The name he spoke," I said, "is an Egyptian one. A goddess associated with the cat."

"Precisely. It was midway through this ritual that Watt at last found himself, and gave an awakening command. The fellow seemed dazed, and was quite drenched with sweat; his hand shook when he took out his pocket-handkerchief to mop his face. He looked at once guilty and pleased, like—like—"

"The cat who ate the canary."

"You have a talent for simile. He looked around at the company, and asked shyly if he had embarrassed himself. I tell you, old boy, we were hard-pressed to reassure him."

Unsummoned, Barnett materialized beside us with the air of one about to speak tragic and ineluctable prophecies. It is his usual face. He said only that it had begun to rain. I asked for a whisky and soda. Sir Jeffrey seemed lost in thought during these transactions, and when he spoke again it was to muse: "Odd, isn't it," he said, "how naturally one thinks of cats as female, though we know quite well that they are distributed between two sexes. As far as I know, it is the same the world over. Whenever, for instance, a cat in a tale is transformed into a human, it is invariably a woman."

"The eyes," I said. "The movements—that certain sinuosity."

"The air of independence," Sir Jeffrey said. "False, of course. One's cat is quite dependent on one, though he seems not to think so."

"The capacity for ease."

"And spite."

"To return to our plague," I said, "I don't see how a single madwoman and a hypnotized squire amount to one."

"Oh, that was by no means the end of it. Throughout that autumn there was, relatively speaking, a flurry of divorce actions and breach-of-promise suits. A suicide left a note: 'I can't have her, and I can't live without her.' More than one farmer's wife, after years of dedication and many offspring, packed herself off to aged parents in Chester. And so on.

"Monday morning after the squire's humiliation I returned to town. As it happened, Monday was market day in the village and I was able to observe at first hand some effects of the plague. I saw husbands and wives sitting at far ends of wagon seats, unable to meet each other's eyes. Sudden arguments flaring without reason over the vegetables. I saw tears. I saw over and over the same hangdog, evasive, guilty look I described in our squire."

"Hardly conclusive."

"There is one further piece of evidence. The Roman Church has never quite eased its grip in that part of the world. It seems that about this time a number of R.C. wives clubbed together and sent a petition to their bishop, saying that the region was in need of an exorcism. Specifically, that their husbands were being tormented by a succubus. Or succubi— whether it was one or many was impossible to tell."

"I shouldn't wonder."

"What specially intrigued me," Sir Jeffrey went on, removing his eyeglass from between cheek and brow and polishing it absently, "is that in all this inconstancy only the men seemed to be accused; the women seemed solely aggrieved, rather than guilty, parties. Now if we take the squire's words as evidence, and not merely 'the stuff that dreams are made on,' we have the picture of a foreign, apparently Egyptian, woman—or possibly women—embarking at Liverpool and moving unnoticed amid Cheshire, seeking whom she may devour and seducing yeomen in their barns amid the fruits of the harvest. The notion was so striking that I got in touch with a chap at Lloyd's, and asked him about passenger lists for the *John Deering* over the last few years.''

''And?''

''There were none. The ship had been in dry dock for two or three years previous. It had made one run, that spring, and then been moth-balled. On that one run there were no passengers. The cargo from Alex consisted of the usual oil, dates, sago, rice, tobacco—and something called 'antiquities.' Since the nature of these was unspecified, the matter ended there. The Inconstancy Plague was short-lived; a letter from Watt the next spring made no mention of it, though he'd been avid for details—most of what I know comes from him and his gleanings of the Winsford *Trumpet,* or whatever it calls itself. I might never have come to any conclusion at all about the matter had it not been for a chance encounter in Cairo a year or so later.

''I was *en route* to the Sudan in the wake of the Khartoum disaster and was bracing myself, so to speak, in the bar of Shepheard's. I struck up a conversation with an archaeologist fellow just off a dig around Memphis, and the talk turned, naturally, to Egyptian mysteries. The thing that continually astonished him, he said, was the absolute *thoroughness* of the ancient Egyptian mind. Once having decided a thing was ritualistically necessary, they admitted of no deviation in carrying it out.

''He instanced cats. We know in what high esteem the Egyptians held cats. If held in high esteem, they must be mummified after death; and so they were. All of them, or nearly all. Carried to their tombs with the bereaved family weeping behind, put away with favorite toys and food for the afterlife journey. Not long ago, he said, some *three hundred thousand* mummified cats were uncovered at Beni Hassan. An entire cat necropolis, unviolated for centuries.

''And then he told me something which gave me pause. More than pause. He said that, once uncovered, all those cats were disinterred and shipped to England. Every last one.''

"Good Lord. Why?"

"I have no idea. They were not, after all, the Elgin Marbles. This seemed to have been the response when they arrived at Liverpool, because not a single museum or collector of antiquities displayed the slightest interest. The whole lot had to be sold off to pay a rather large shipping bill."

"Sold off? To whom, in God's name?"

"To a Cheshire agricultural firm. Who proceeded to chop up the lot and resell it. To the local farmers, my dear boy. To use as fertilizer."

Sir Jeffrey stared deeply into his nearly untouched brandy, watching the legs it made on the side of the glass, as though he read secrets there. "Now the scientific mind may be able to believe," he said at last, "that three hundred thousand cats, aeons old, wrapped lovingly in winding cloths and put to rest with spices and with spells, may be exhumed from a distant land—and from a distant past as well—and minced into the loam of Cheshire, and it will all have no result but grain. I am not certain. Not certain at all."

The smoking room of the Travellers' Club was deserted now, except for the weary, unlaid ghost of Barnett. Above us on the wall the mounted heads of exotic animals were shadowed and nearly unnameable; one felt that they had just then thrust their coal-smoked and glass-eyed heads through the wall, seeking something, and that just the other side of the wall stood their vast and unimaginable bodies. Seeking what? The members, long dead as well, who had slain them and brought them to this?

"You've been in Egypt," Sir Jeffrey said.

"Briefly."

"I have always thought that Egyptian women were among the world's most beautiful."

"Certainly their eyes are stunning. With the veil, of course, one sees little else."

"I spoke specifically of those circumstances when they are without the veil. In all senses."

"Yes."

"Depilated, many of them." He spoke in a small, dreamy voice, as though he observed long-past scenes. "A thing I have always found—intriguing. To say the least." He sighed deeply; he tugged down his waistcoat, preparatory to rising; he replaced his eyeglass. He was himself again. "Do you suppose,'' he said, ''that such a thing as a cab could be found at this hour? Well, let us see.''

''By the way,'' I asked when we parted, ''whatever came of the wives' petition for an exorcism?''

''I believe the bishop sent it on to Rome for consideration. The Vatican, you know, does not move hastily on these things. For all I know, it may still be pending.''

One of my most rewarding associations from my work in the fantasy and science fiction field is that with Gahan Wilson, famed macabre cartoonist for Playboy, *the* Magazine of Fantasy and Science Fiction, National Lampoon, *and many other areas. His talents are Brobdingnagian and do not limit themselves only to artwork. You can well imagine my delight to publish a story by the noted James Sallis and David Lunde that was based on one of his best macabre cartoons, and dedicated to him. I greatly enjoyed the tale even though I was nagged by a slight misgiving about its ending. After the story's publication, Gahan voiced to me that same misgiving, and I thought that Jim and David should make an effort to rewrite the story from that other viewpoint. They did so, reluctantly, with David writing to me a most-convincing letter in support of their original version. Since the altered portion of the story was only over the last hundred or so words of the tale, Doubleday's Sharon Jarvis and I thought it would be interesting to present both versions of the story with the associated letters and let the reader decide what version satisfies him the most.*

A WEATHER REPORT
FROM THE TOP OF THE STAIRS
(for Gahan Wilson)

by James Sallis and David Lunde

Darkness is streaming down the bare branches of elms, blackening their trunks against the snow.

The boy's feet scuff going upstairs to bed as he fits them into the worn half-moons of the wooden steps, trying to avoid the creaky ones.

The darkness mingles with smoke from the chimney, intricate open-lace patterns, blue behind gray. It seeps into the pond behind the house and turns it, beneath the willow, to mush, the mush to bluewhite slate. Cars like colored appendages of the clouds move silently at the ends of long umbilicals of exhaust. The pale sun closes its petals on the horizon: blue deepening, the sky turns the color of plums.

Like one of those fragile, tableau nativities built of colored sugar, soft pastels in half an eggshell, Mr. Wilson and his wife sit on a nubby couch in the old wooden house. The couch is gently yellow, the room done in burnished golds and blue, the rug a ripe wheat. Now the colors change and flicker, shifting with the light of the fire, with the firefly lights of the Christmas tree in the corner beside it, with the triumphant trumpeting of the angel at the top. Around them in dimness, corners are softened, angles bundled in shadow. Light flushes from a phone booth across the street.

(In silence: the wet hiss of cars passing, a clatter of trelliswork on the back porch, the sigh and creak of an old house walking through itself, an old house that dreams of snow, a cool white bed for sleeping.)

The uneven tideheat of the fire before them, washing up in waves, reddening, receding. From the bare white kitchen, mixing with the resinous tang of evergreen, comes the sweet nutmeg smell of eggnog, of coffee done and warm, waiting. Fire crackles like cellophane, wood shifts on a slope of embers.

(His arm around her shoulder.)

And outside, a face passing the window. A man trudging slowly home from pushing dirt across floors, warm pipe steaming, smoke eddying white against the darker gray. Streetlights shelled in rainbow. And other lights (rouge, ochre, pale soft blue) blinking open in windows, in stiff green limbs. Angels regarding the street.

(A feeling told without words, told by an arm around a shoulder, by being together now, by a shared brandy.

"Last year . . ."

"Yes . . ."

By a smile.)

And outside, gently, quietly, it begins to snow. First a flourish, then small flakes, then larger and quicker, till the sky is boiling with whiteness, till it is like a fine dust of flour filling the air, falling. Falling.

(His arm around her shoulder.

Talking now. About the morning.

"Will he like it?"

"Of course. For a while, at least . . ."

Country music on the radio.

Nostalgia. Reminiscence of things done, of those not done, a life. Images of a child growing, so young yet, so much before him, but so much of the shaping done already. Looking back, looking forward.)

Snow stipples flat gray air, slurs the streets, shuts people into their rooms behind their windows. And suddenly with the bright snow it is:

Night . . .

"What will it be this time?" said a voice from one of the shelves.

"Not a firetruck. Not a cherry-red, shiny-metal firetruck," said another. "That was last year."

"Not roller skates with two keys."

"Nor a stuffed brown Koala."

And there in the attic it echoed among them, all the things it wouldn't, couldn't be.

"A train with a caboose the color of red fire."

"A steamshovel for backyard digging."

"A service station with pumps that pump."

"A terrycloth clown."

"A machine to make flavored, bright icicles."

"A candy bank."

"A box that moos when you turn it over."

"A popcorn machine like the ones at movies."

"A tiny man with rivets for joints."

"A purple cow with a balloon udder you can fill and milk."

"A whistle made of milkwhite glass."

"A disintegrator ray gun that shoots colored sparks."

"A scale model cannon."

"A toy soldier all scarlet and blue."

They were quiet then; the house was calm. His footsteps faded out of memory and the boy slept. The fire died low, the radio faded, talking moved through the house and upstairs to the bedroom. Softened, softened, hushed. (Listen closely: snow brushes against the roof, nothing more.) Now, softly, quietly, while they're sleeping . . .

"They're giving him a gun this year." It was a voice sawdust might have, the sound sawdust would make if wind blew across it.

"Gun?" Rust popping off an iron bar. The toy soldier.

"A small one. Pellets."

"So he can hunt with his father; so his father can teach him to hunt."

The snow went on, came on, snow like puffy eiderdowns wrapping the houses like German grandmothers bundling children . . .

"No. That was two years ago."

"He still has it downstairs."

"Imagine. Two years . . ." That was the stuffed, cinnamon-colored Koala, the teddy, "Theodore Bear" (blind now, his black button eyes gone).

The rockinghorse reared creakily, paint peeling in strips like tatters of last summer's circus signs.

"What will it be this time?"

"What . . ."

"This time . . ."

"This year . . ."

Outside, the snow began to smack as it hit, then while they listened grew soft again and drifted, drifted. Breezes made a game of the flakes, scattering them from one another. A million white fireflies all floating, all flitting to the ground . . .

"You know what we'll do?" It was the sawdust voice, the toy with peeling paint. "Someday when it's raining, someday this summer, he'll want one of us and come up here. Or he'll be all full of sadness, and he won't know what it is, and he'll come up here, to us, to find out." Phrases galloped as once upon a time long ago the toy had itself, a cockhorse on its way to Banbury Cross. "Then! Then we'll gang up on him, we'll get him!"

VERSION I

Horns tooted. Whistles shrilled, trilled. Music boxes strummed across their cylinders, producing impromptu ensembles of triumph, victory. Animals brayed and cheered. The clown laughed and laughter rolled among them, rippling, ringing waves of laughter. A small box tipped off into the air, turning top over bottom, top over bottom, top over bottom. It moved twice before it struck the floor.

"No!" The tiny man with rivets for joints, stiff, rusting. He waited for them to listen. Snow whispered around the roof, a few flakes slipping through cracks to splash on the attic floor. "No. We've got to give him another chance, just one more. We have to wait, have to be patient. He hasn't forgotten completely. I know. That's why we're being kept here. Another chance . . ."

Snow for a moment sifted down sideways, sweeping angels in itself. Frost painted grins on the windowpane.

"No! Don't listen to him." The toy soldier. "We can't wait any longer, we can't! Soon we won't be able to move any more. Look at him; he's so stiff he can't walk. Teddy can't see. And me, my arm is gone, my bayonet is dull now, before it's too late. Tomorrow morning, tomorrow! We'll all march down the steps, we'll take sticks and guns, we'll march right into his room. Catch him by surprise! Demand our rights! Fight for them if we have to!" Scarlet and blue. "Drive him down to bloody ruin . . ."

"Tear his head off!"

"Kick him!"

"Rip off an arm!"

"Pull out his eyes!"

"See how he works!"

The music boxes struck up martial airs: "The Star-Spangled Banner," "Dixie," "Marching Through Georgia."

"We'll teach him." The soldier again. "It's the only way. The only thing he understands is force. We'll make him surrender!"

Snow outside went Shhhhhh and a hush settled on the toys. They listened to the snow, the million crystals, ring down in the night. Listened on shelves in the attic at the top of the stairs.

"Tomorrow, do you hear!"

Soft, soft broom sweeping at the house.

"Tomorrow!"

But the others were asleep, all the ghosts of Christmas past.

And below them the boy slept, and his dream rode a prancing cockhorse at the head of candy-bright armies crashing and clashing, guns and drums and blood black as licorice in the soldiering snow.

Gahan Wilson's comments on this first version were: "I enjoyed the Salis-Lunde piece. Very nice Bradburian feel to it, although the implication that the toys won't 'get him' after all on account of their decay is contrary to what I believe will happen. In *my* world, Stuart, they get him, and they get him good—Yessir."

And, thus, this second, slightly altered version was born.

VERSION II

Horns tooted. Whistles shrilled, trilled. Music boxes strummed across their cylinders, producing impromptu ensembles of triumph, victory. Animals brayed and cheered. The clown laughed, and laughter rolled among them, furious, frenzied waves of laughter. A small box tipped off into the air, turning top over bottom, top over botom, top over bottom. It moved harshly before it struck the floor.

"No!" The tiny man with rivets for joints, stiff, rusting. He waited for them to listen. Snow whispered around the roof, a few flakes slipping through cracks to splash on the attic floor and vanish. "No, we can't. We've got to give him another chance, just one more. We have to wait, have to be patient. He can't have forgotten us, he loved us once, we made him happy!''

Hoots and catcalls drowned his tiny voice.

"You're a fool!" The toy soldier. "What made him happy was tormenting us. How long did you lie out in the rain and dirt before his mother brought you here, how many months of rain and pain? Look what he did to Teddy's eyes! And he broke my arm and Horse's leg! You know how he is. We can't wait any longer, we can't! Soon we won't be able to move any more. You're already so stiff you can't walk. No, he's had his chance. We have to strike now, before it's too late. In an hour or two when they're all asleep. We'll all march down the steps, we'll take sticks and guns, we'll march right into his room. Take him by surprise! We'll teach him!" Scarlet and blue. "Drive him down to bloody ruin . . ."

"Tear his head off!"

"Kick him!"

"Rip off an arm!"

"Pull out his eyes!"

"See how he works!"

The music boxes struck up martial airs: "The Star-Spangled Banner," "Dixie," "Marching Through Georgia."

"He'll be sorry!" The soldier again. "It's the only way. The only thing he understands is force. We'll show him how it feels. We'll make him suffer."

Outside the wind laid a shroud of snow across the blackened earth. They listened to it wail and keen, alert as sentries as they waited in the dark. Waited on shelves in the attic at the top of the stairs.

"Soon, do you hear!"

Snow blowing hopelessly back and forth.

"Soon . . ."

And they waited, silent, motionless, more alive than they had ever been.

And below them the boy slept, and his dream rode a prancing cockhorse at the head of candy-bright armies crashing and clashing, guns and drums and blood black as licorice in the soldiering snow.

Accompanying this rewritten version, was the following letter:

Dear Stuart,

I am enclosing the revision of A WEATHER REPORT FROM THE TOP OF THE STAIRS that you asked for. I think that it does what you and Gahan felt the original version did not do: that it makes quite clear the fact that the toys are going to "get" the boy. However, Jim and I both feel that in doing so, the story has become much more one-dimensional and much less interesting, and simply a much worse story. We would like to persuade you to use the original version in the anthology & we hope that when you compare the two you will agree with us.

When we wrote the story, we were not simply trying to explain Gahan's cartoon. Rather, we used it as a starting point for a story which included both Jim's and my slightly different conceptions. Jim really felt that it was too late for the toys, they had only words left, they were a collection of shattered dreams. I wanted the story to say something about human nature and nurture in the area of violence. The boy's violence is evident in what he has done to the toys & in the violence which has rubbed off on them and now causes them to desire revenge & in the fact that his gun is the toy which has lasted longer than any other. On page three, the parents, nostalgic, think to themselves "so much of the shaping done already." That and the boy's dream that ends the story are meant to suggest a wider context in which to apply the story's idea. But we did not want the story to be heavily didactic; we wanted it to be slightly ambiguous at the end. It does not really matter whether the toys get their revenge or not, because that is not really the focus of the story. As I see it, the boy is evidence that people are inherently violent *and* that violence is encouraged by our upbringing, here by his loving parents, who really do love him but don't know what they're doing.

Please let me know what you think about the two versions. I hope you will agree that the first is better.

Well, dear reader, good luck with your decision.

The late Canon B. A. Smith was the author of Dean
Church *(Oxford University Press); he was a very interesting clergyman, a collector of ghostly tales, and himself
living for years in a rectory (Holy Trinity, Micklegate,
York) where monks' bones were forever poking up from
the front lawn. (The janitor then burnt them.) Through the
efforts of noted author Russell Kirk* (The Conservative Mind),
*the horror stories this man had written for his own enter-
tainment were retrieved from oblivion and shown to me. I
found them an impressive grouping of tales in the M. R.
James tradition, and Whispers Press will be publishing
them all in a hardcover collection that will be illustrated
by Steve Fabian. Meanwhile, whet your appetite with
this haunting account of demons, saints, and the Scallion
Stone . . .*

THE SCALLION STONE

by Basil A. Smith

"So you're on your way to Northumberland and the Farne
Islands, are you?" said Aitchison, and added with genial
irony, "I suppose if it hadn't been for my having Prideaux
Selby's catalogue, you'd never have broken your journey here
at all!"

"Well, I did want to check up on one or two species,"

laughed the ornithologist. "And I don't dislike sleepy little Durham, you know. For a night's lodging, within hearing of the cathedral chimes, I can even put up with a cantankerous old sinner like you!"

With such good-natured banter and amid the comfortable surroundings of Aitchison's library, a stranger—had there been one there, hidden for some melodramatic reason, behind an armchair—would have had no difficulty in guessing that Drury was an old academic friend with a good claim to familiarity with his aged host.

"Ah!" reflected Aitchison a few minutes later as the pair of them, like good bachelors, sat watching the fire go out, "it's a long time since I did more than peep at Holy Island. Let's see; it's fifty years since the St. Cuthbert centenary. I remember crossing to the Farne about then."

"Is there much archaeological stuff there?" asked Drury. "Any Cuthbert relics still?"

"Fourteenth-century chapel and site of the old boy's hermitage. But unless you're keen there's nothing very exciting," said Aitchison.

"It's the birds I'm after chiefly, of course," said Drury, "but while I'm there I might as well kill two birds with one stone!"

"Talking of stones," responded the antiquary quite seriously, "you really ought to see the Scallion Stone."

"What's that then?" asked the other. "Some ancient carved work?"

"No," said Aitchison, "it's more of a geological curio—in shape, something between an oblong block and a wedge— about five feet in length and nearly two in breadth at its widest, I should say—surface pretty smooth, with five elongated shapes like fossils standing out. The name comes from these, I suppose, for they look like spring onions, or scallions as they call them in these parts. The whole thing's very curious."

"And you say this is still to be seen on the island?" asked Drury.

"I should be surprised if anyone's disturbed it," rejoined Aitchison. "In fact I doubt whether many people know of its existence, and with the amount of seaweed there is, they are not likely to come across it by accident."

Drury was quite intrigued, and very soon the two had

forgotten their wine, while Aitchison was drawing sketches and setting down directions which would help his guest to locate the phenomenon which seemed so well worth searching for.

Drury enjoyed his expedition, and a few days later he was back in Durham loaded with notes and photos of his beloved seabirds. Aitchison had urged him to stay the night, and talk soon turned upon the Scallion Stone once more.

"Yes, I did manage to get at it after tearing up a load or two of Channeled Wrack," said Drury. "In fact, I took a photo, too. I got a print out from it last night. You can have it if you like."

Aitchison was most interested when Drury brought down the photo for him. He scrutinized it for a minute, then put it down with knitted brow.

"That's strange," he murmured, "it must have changed."

"How do you mean?" asked Drury with some astonishment.

"Well," said Aitchison reflectively, "your photo here shows five 'scallions' all pretty much the same. Actually, when I saw this stone, four were complete and the fifth was what I should call disfigured, almost as if wrenched and depleted at the end."

"You're probably mistaken," said Drury half-amused. "Anyway it seems a trivial point to keep in mind for all these years. Archaeology has made you mighty keen and observant, my boy."

"Oh, it's not that," repudiated Aitchison, "it's the legend that fixes it in my mind. I ought to have told you. It comes from Bede. You remember he tells us St. Cuthbert used to go from Lindisfarne into solitary retreat over on the Farne. There, with the sea to shut him off from the rest of the world, he spent his time in prayer and fasting. He was so engaged at the last period of his life, and when his monks came—fearing for his life—to look after him, they found the good man dying. All he had by him were five onions—or at least four, and a fifth which looked to be partly eaten."

"So, so," said Drury with mild enthusiasm, "and now my photo here just fails to tally with the tale by making the five complete. Are you sure it wasn't the same, and this bit of detail from Bede has put a twist on your memory? It's no great matter anyhow."

Aitchison was rummaging in a receptacle at his desk. Presently he handed to his friend another photo, old and discolored but accurate enough in detail.

"There," he said, "I took that myself when I was there. Now compare it with yours."

Certainly there was a difference. It was as Aitchison had said: the recent likeness showed five scallions, plump and alike, the old one showed four complete and one quite mutilated and apparently hollow and dank at the lower end.

"Very queer," admitted Drury, "how could it come about?"

"Broken fossils do not heal themselves," declared the serious Aitchison. "That's not a natural thing."

"By the look of you, one would think it boded something supernatural," teased Drury gaily.

Aitchison turned sharply on him then.

"That's what I mean exactly," he said with smart decisiveness.

"You surprise me, Aitchison," replied the friend, somewhat askance.

"I know. You're still a skeptic about such things. So was I, and should be still but for a nasty experience. And, indeed, the whole thing hangs round this stone, and a certain man called Calladine."

"You'd better tell me about this," said Drury quite animated now.

"I will," said Aitchison, "if you'll first poke that fire."

It was in the Christmas vacation of 1886 that I came across Calladine. I had long promised myself a thorough survey of the castle at Bamburgh and the better to do so I was staying in the village at—the "Penda" I think it was called then—a little inn kept by old Colin Gray and his wife. I was scarcely more than an undergraduate in those days, and it was a real pleasure to me when I found another guest there capable of providing some good company and conversation. I was at first puzzled to think why a young doctor—he would be in his early thirties—was secreting himself in such an outlandish place as the Northumberland coast, which as you know is uncommonly bleak and melancholy in the winter months. He told me at first he was "spying out the land" with a view to setting up a country practice in those parts, having had to leave London through a nervous breakdown. As I afterwards learned, he was there for a double reason: on the advice of a criminal psychologist he was seeking both to recuperate his health and to avoid public attention. (You may have heard of the Crewe-Delton case which gave the police such trouble but ended in a complete acquittal for Delton in the trial. Well, "Calladine" was none other than Delton, but he shall always be Calladine for me, poor devil.)

We got on well, the short time I was there. He was a man of cultured interests, especially in your line of Natural Philosophy, as we used to call it. Our talks together when we strolled on the seashore were often interrupted by little excursions on his part into the field of marine botany and zoology. He was also an uncommonly fine photographer, and I well remember how proud he was to have designed his own camera, which had a remarkable flashlight device for use in semi-darkness. This, together with his own skill, he most generously put at my service for making records of various architectural features at the castle. Indeed, it was one afternoon at the end of such operations that I first noticed something queer about him.

I had turned back to fetch my pipe, which I suddenly remembered was on the ledge of one of the upper windows, and I left Calladine down in the inner bailey waiting for me. Now it so happened that as I picked up the pipe I caught a glimpse of him through the window. He was gazing out to sea and I should have thought that natural enough but for an open-mouthed attitude of fascination that seemed to have taken hold of him. Whatever he was looking at, I could not from my position see, but as I watched I suddenly saw him shudder as if something revolting had been enacted before his eyes. When I rejoined him he looked pale and said nothing. Somewhat inquisitive, I made excuse to look out seawards myself but detected nothing unusual.

"There is something haunting about the twilight on the coast, isn't there?" I observed.

"How do you mean?" asked Calladine eagerly, then added, "I suppose if you're of a poetic turn you can imagine some fantastic things at times."

There is a sense of restraint which prevents a man from making pointed intrusions into another's thoughts on certain occasions, and my curiosity had to go unsatisfied. I felt that if Calladine had some sort of secret fear it was probably due to his illness, and the best motto for a friend in such a case seemed to be *Quieta non movere*.

You will understand this the more when I tell you Calladine could, on occasion, be very violent and scornful, especially about matters of superstition. An instance will show what I mean. Gray, like most fisherfolk, had quite a mental museum (as I should call it) of local tales and beliefs. One evening in the bar his talk had been running on these lines when I came in. The topic, whatever it was, had evidently ended and I was only in time to catch something about "sea blood." Pricking up my ears, I asked what the mystery was about. Gray, to satisfy me, was going to take up the thread again when Calladine, who had been sitting pensively in the corner, sprang up with an oath and broke the whole gathering up with a stormy tirade against "such credulous nonsense." After this he flung out of the room and I followed him in some anxiety, for it was obvious that the poor fellow's nerves were playing the devil with him again.

Actually, however, he seemed to come round very cheerfully out of these fits. For days he was serenity itself, rambling along the shore in the mornings with his camera and often meeting me at the castle later.

Only once was this harmony broken. It was in November when we were looking forward to some duck-shooting. The weather had been very hard, and Gray—who was an expert in such matters—thought we might expect a flight or two of inland birds coming seawards from the frozen ponds. Now in this sport, as you know, a good deal depends upon your getting well hidden from sight, usually in a shelter pit dug in the sands. And so we found ourselves with spades "howking a hole," as Colin called it, in readiness for the flights. The old man was choosing for himself a strategic point some yards away while Calladine and I got to work with our shoveling. We had been at it silently for a time, and a goodish oblong cavity was beginning to take shape, when Calladine drew in his breath with a gasp and suddenly stopped work.

I had my back to him at the time, but turning round I saw him staring into the sand and trembling from head to foot.

"Did you see that?" he said, pointing down. But I could see nothing remarkable.

"It's gone now, of course," he added, with relief, "but it gave me a queer turn."

"Why, what did you see?" I asked in some bewilderment.

"Oh, I know," said he, despairingly. "It's my crazy nerves again. I suppose you think I'm mad."

And there he sat with his handkerchief to his brow looking very sick and tired, I thought, while Gray came up and looked silently on. We rallied him a bit but he had no more appetite for sport that evening, so we got him back home and into a warm bed.

I felt sure at the time that these hallucinations would be serious for Calladine sooner or later. Next day, however, he came down to breakfast much refreshed, and the matter was scarcely referred to at all. A few days later I had to be back in Newcastle, and when I left him he seemed as sane as any man could he.

Weeks passed without any news. Then one morning I got a letter from Gray—one of those clumsy, countrified epistles which only appear at times of domestic crisis—begging me to return to Bamburgh at once to settle whether "the Doctor is quite Wise in his head."

It was a sorry tale the old man had to tell as we drove along in the dogcart after he had met me at the train. To cut a long story short, suffice it to say he had let Calladine persuade him (no hard matter with an old sportsman!) to get the guns out and have another try at the ducks, despite the lateness of the season. Gray had an idea of the flight lines, and so the pair of them were lying in wait one evening some distance apart among the hollows, watching the sky. Then what should happen, but Calladine gives a cry of terror, just as the birds could be heard coming overhead. Of course, off they veered out of shot and left the old man cursing with disgust. But he ran to his companion none the less, and found him lying dazed and shuddering. His plight was worse than ever before.

Indeed, the upshot was that Calladine had been little better than a nervous invalid since. He became more than usually morose and developed such frightening symptoms that Gray and his wife began to watch him closely. They had heard him in his room at nights get out of bed, strike a light, and groan time and again. He sounded to be always washing at the bowl. Then one morning he apologized to Mrs. Gray for leaving bloodstains on the sheets.

"I meant to mention it before," he said. "My hands—I mean my nose—sometimes bleeds in the night."

The strange thing is, there was no trace of blood about, but she dare not tell him so for he was an awkward man to contradict at any time. She talked the matter over anxiously with her husband, and that day Colin wrote for me to come.

When I arrived at the inn Mrs. Gray was very thankful to see me, and I was equally relieved to learn that Calladine was upstairs sound asleep. I could not help reflecting, as we sat at tea, upon the difficulties of my position. After what I had heard, it seemed plainly my duty to get Calladine away at all costs, but it was not a pleasant thing to realize that I had practically come to certify the wretched man as insane. On such an errand one is not sanguine about the sort of reception that is in store. I had a delicate task before me, and one thing I wanted to do first was to talk matters over more fully with Gray. During our conversation in the dogcart I thought I had detected in him a note of understanding toward Calladine, as if the old man believed there was really "something in" these delusions. Moreover, my curiosity about that interrupted episode over "sea blood" was again demanding satisfaction. All told, I determined to probe the mystery at its most mysterious.

As soon as Mrs. Gray had retired (after a weary day and several sleepless nights) to an early bed, I plied old Colin with an extra drink or two, then got him to draw up to the fire and unburden his mind.

And a fine tale I got, to be sure. First, about "sea blood." To say in local parlance that a person had "got the sea blood" meant, I found, that he was contaminated by an insidious disease resulting from a sort of curse. Local people—"St. Cuthbert's ain," as Gray would call them— were thought to be immune from this scourge because the ancient spirits of the coast had no power against those born within the pale of the saint's domain. Even strangers were not susceptible except at certain times, like anniversaries, and then only in winter months; so very rarely was a case expected. But tradition still held the day of St. Cuthbert's death to be an evil time each year. The last quite clear eruption of this curse fell, as I now learnt, upon a little French girl, a refugee and orphan of one of the prisoners at Berwick when

Gray was a small boy. (The end of the Napoleonic wars it would be, for he was a good age in '87 when he told me all this.)

I asked him what the symptoms were. All he remembered was that she could not sleep at all at nights for fear, but would cry out most pitifully about some ghastly vision. It was in these spasms that her feet were noticed to exude a sickly, blood-like sweat. The village folk then put it down to her going barefoot in the sands—a thing she did, it seems, quite often despite the cold. Rumors spread that the girl had trodden on some evil creature of the sea. Then one old fishwife gravely recalled that this could be none other than the half-forgotten "sea blood" curse. There was no cure, she said, except the victim should go across to Farne to "touch the Scallion" in St. Cuthbert's name. (And that was how I first came to hear about this Stone of ours.) Most folks, Gray said, were loath to make resort to such unearthly charms, but yet all felt a growing pity for the child.

At last one day, in spite of some fear of "what parson would say," they wrapped her up in shawls, and six men took out a boat for the island, so that they could at least try the power of this reputed spell and see if Mother Blackett was right about it after all.

Alas, they never reached the island. Winds or currents tossed them back out of their course, and finally the boat capsized not far from where they started. Some of the crew always swore it was sucked down by supernatural forces claiming the child. At any rate, despite all care and effort, she alone was drowned. The poor thing never even rose, and—search as they would—no trace of her was found. The wrecked boat, however, was at rare intervals partly visible some distance out beyond low tide.

"It's an ill place," remarked Gray in conclusion, "and folks that's canny will give it a wide berth."

We sat for a while with no sound but the fire flames and the ticking of the clock in all the house, and the distant rustle of the eternal sea outside. I was trying to think out the bearing of this sinister tradition upon Calladine and his troubles, when—all at once—we were both startled by the clicking of the latch on the stair door and turned round to find Calladine himself, disheveled and half-dressed, coming toward us. There

was an awful smile of desperation on his face which, coupled
with a false sort of calmness in his manner, made him seem
almost a different person from the steady companion I had
first known.

"Sit down, the pair of you," he ordered, "I've overheard
the whole delightful story. And now I suppose, Mr. Aitchison,
you're going to call it 'very interesting' and say 'how pictur-
esque these old fancies are.' Very pretty superstition, isn't it,
my friend?"

There was a leering hostility about the man which scared
me for his sanity, but I answered with some warmth, "Look
here, Calladine, don't be a fool. No one believes in evil
spirits nowadays. Queer things may have happened, but all
this is heightened by subjective coloring, as any man knows."

"Oh yes!" he said, with mocking scorn. "What are you
doing here, anyhow? You think I'm off my head. And you've
come to tell me to pull myself together, and haul me off to
some genteel madhouse 'for the good of all concerned.' Very
kind of you, I'm sure, but I'll have you know my reason is as
sound as yours."

"Of course it is," I put in as patiently as I could. And then
he snapped at me.

"None of your soothing nonsense, either. My reason's
sound, I tell you, but that does not save me from being under
this hellish curse that Gray's been telling you about. I'm
hounded to my grave by something devilish, and all your
talking will not alter it."

He sobbed and wept in pitiful hysteria, so I motioned Gray
to bring some whisky in, and tried to steady the poor chap.

"It's no good coddling me," he raved, "I used to tell
myself it was a case of nerves and I was only seeing things.
But now I know the affair is real. When Gray picked me up
that night I knew it was not fancy. As I'm alive, there was
something both visible and—yes, good God—and tangible. I
touched the brute, Aitchison, like a snake there in the sand.
And every night I wake to feel that horrid slime and find my
hands all bleeding with it again. Yet, because I cannot prove
it to you, you think I'm just a ramping lunatic, eh?"

His voice was rising again. I could not answer him and
dared not ask for details from him in such a state. Moreover,
as I looked at Gray, I knew the old man too believed the
reality of Calladine's account. Then, on the spur of the

moment, a way occurred to me that might, I thought, bring reason into play.

"Now listen," I said, "you've had your say. Both you and Gray believe all this. But I tell you plainly I'm convinced there is no unearthly monster in the case. I'm convinced this 'sea blood' is a delusion. I'm also convinced, Colin, there is no such thing as your Scallion Stone, or any other shred of fact behind this stuff. You can't prove anything."

"And there you're wrong, sir," answered Gray quietly. "I've not seen the 'blood' on Mr. Calladine, but there's them as did see it on that bairn. And I have seen queerish sights around the shore, times past."

"What things have you seen then?" I demanded.

"Well," said he uncomfortably, "they're hard to talk about. Movements in the sand, I'd say, and sometimes lights and shapes—uncanny things, sir, particular near-in at sea."

"Until I see something myself," said I impatiently, "I cannot help thinking the pair of you are deluded. You can't show me anything 'tangible.' "

"I think I could take you to the Stone, if need be, Mr. Aitchison," said Gray. "Would you believe us then? It was about the time I took Mr. Nettleby, our other Vicar, to it that I saw those lights very plain at night. If I could get Mr. Calladine there, and him to touch the Stone, I am sure, sir, he might be saved."

I noticed Calladine prick up his ears a bit but he said nothing. I too was hesitant, but a moment's thought showed me my opportunity.

"You really can find us the Stone?" I said slowly, like one prepared to be convinced. "If you do prove right, I'm with you both. After all, I suppose, it's not unreasonable: when there's a curse, there's a way of breaking it. If natural powers are really beaten, I'll join you to get this supernatural charm. I meet you with an open mind.

"So cheer up, Calladine," I added. "We'll fathom this and have your mind freed from the beastly scourge somehow. And when can we see this Stone to start with, Colin? The sooner the better—but not a word to Mrs. Gray."

The old man thought we could manage it next day and promised he would have a boat ready straight after breakfast if we wished. And so it was agreed. We drank up more cheerfully than we had done with Calladine since first I knew him. When I saw him up to bed again I felt I could congratulate myself on having humored him at least some way toward recovery.

I did not myself intend going to bed just then, despite the departure of Calladine and Gray, for it was not yet ten o'clock. In all probability I should have sat with a book for a while. But my inclinations were overruled by the importunate looks and antics of Gray's young terrier, Rap. It seemed a pity on such a fine night to refuse giving the poor little fellow a stroll, so I took up my hat and stick, and off we went.

While Rap was pursuing his own particular investigations here and there, I too was trying to sniff out a trail of sense and satisfaction in the dark corners of my mind. I began of course to seek justification for my rôle of benevolent hypocrite. These old wives' tales of Gray's were too fantastic for my serious credence, but this I thought might well be a case where—psychologically speaking—Beelzebub might cast out Beelzebub. And for Calladine's sake it seemed worth trying: to cure a deluded sufferer it could certainly not be very wrong for me to pretend to share the delusion. So I thought.

Then, for some unknown reason, I began to toy with the matter in a reflective rather than a practical mood. Perhaps it was the struggling moonlight softening the atmosphere and my common sense at the same time. I tried in vain to dismiss the significance of Gray's having seen something as well as Calladine's. It must be superstitious imagination, I told myself, but who had started the process? Had Calladine influenced Gray, or had the gossip and attitude of Gray and his neighbors borne in upon Calladine? Superstition is curiously infectious. Would anyone ever have seen a ghost if he had not first heard of someone else's seeing one?

By this time our walk had taken us almost to the castle. My steps, or Rap's, being on familiar ground, decided their own route, and I soon found myself looking out to sea from the inner bailey. It was the spot where Calladine had stood when I glanced at him from the window and first noticed him with that queer, fascinated stare. And now I was looking out where he had looked, toward the Longstone light. It was about high tide, and I was taking a drowsy interest in the rhythm of the rollers, crumbling to whiteness in the dim moonlight, when something made me strangely alert.

A little beyond what would be low-water mark when the tide ebbed, there seemed to be a patch of submerged light, like a pool of phosphorescent green, shimmering on the sea bed. From it there came, straggling limply in all directions, a number of short rootlike lines. But one line, like a huge proboscis, thicker than the rest, was pointed shorewards. To all appearance it was anchored there, for not only did it heave and waver in the water, but I caught glimpses of it shining here and there across the sands. But my eye was mainly on that central ganglion in the sea, with its floating, nervous threads.

Now, as I looked, the color changed and the whole shape shone magically transfused with crimson, like some colossal lobster seen through the thick, distorting medium of a bull's-eye windowpane. Then suddenly up shot those cruel feelers; a seabird shrieked; I saw an eddy of dispersing wings above the bloody spot, and all was gone. In a twinkling the glowing light had died and every mark of the apparition vanished.

I waited, staring, to assure my wits but nothing further happened. Yet Rap was back, cowering at my side, no doubt disturbed—as I was—by that harrowing scream. Back to the inn we went and I had strange thoughts to ponder on the way. If superstition fools the senses to such a pitch, then who is sane? All my earlier self-assurance had deserted me, and when I got to bed it was to find but intermittent sleep. A haunting spirit of misgiving brooded over me and cast a shadow on the outcome of the morrow's doings.

Events moved rapidly that day. First, when we woke, our plans had gone awry. Calladine was ill and haggard beyond description—after some extra-hellish dream, he said, some nightmare on the fate of that dead girl. He was completely demoralized once more, and in no mood to keep our bargain of the previous night.

"I saw her beckoning to me, poor little wretch, as the boat sank and the waters were drowning her cries," he muttered. "I know this is an evil day for me out there. That sea moan is sounding in my head like a ghost call. Let's all stay here till it goes off. After today I know I shall be all right again."

Poor Calladine! I never shall forget those words of his, and that imploring look. What devil drove me to make light of such an appeal? Oh, yes, I soothed and sympathized all right.

I coaxed him off to rest again. I even fetched tobacco for him from the shop. But in my heart I secretly determined I was going to see that Stone myself: Gray had the boat all ready and it might be many a day before the sea was again suitable to cross; and then I must be back to town next day at least, I argued to myself. My own experiences had wrought in me a fascination close on frenzy to see and know the most that could be known. And soon, so deadly soon, I knew it!

Within an hour I left him dozing—God forgive me—and we went. I need not tell you of that little voyage in the morning sun. You've been yourself. Nor need I tell you of the Stone and of my childish wonderment at seeing it in fact as Gray had said. There were the four completed bulbs—and the fatal fifth so dank and gaping: I well remember that. And then, of course, I took my fill of satisfaction by photographing it as well.

But was I satisfied? I wondered. What was there yet in store? I felt as one who hears a prelude played and waits the fall of chords that mark the onset of the major theme.

"We should have brought *him* with us, sir," I heard Gray murmur in reproach. And then at once I saw the lines of fate converging on him—my poor friend, Calladine. A sudden guilty fear welled up inside me now. Old Colin's thought was doubtless of the man's being cured by touching the Stone, but in my mind I saw a thousand chances of some untoward act he might be led to by his crazy brain while we were dallying there.

Into the boat we tumbled, and as we rowed I heard anew those ominous words, *"I know this is an evil day for me out there."* The afternoon sky was darkening noticeably as we rowed. A yellow dullness lowering in the air boded the rising of an unseasonable storm. No rain, however, had fallen when we got to land, but Mrs. Gray came running out to meet us from the house.

"Mr. Calladine's gone out," she panted. "Can't you find him, Colin, afore this storm comes on? If he's caught I'm sure he'll get his death."

We took the coat she gave us and hurried down the beach, and as we ran I felt it was a race against a darker foe than rain. At last Gray spotted him. Indeed, but for a surface mist, we should have seen him earlier from our boat.

"Good Lord!" cried Gray, "the man's stark mad. Look there! He's at the wreck."

In the distance we could see the black hulk of that fatal boat in which the girl had drowned. An exceptionally low tide—due to the equinox, no doubt—had brought about one of those rare occasions when the sea exposed this melancholy hulk. And that small figure moving about was surely Calladine, clambering on the half-buried vessel.

"Dang the fool! What's he tampering with?" groaned Colin with a curse. "He knows to keep away. I told him there's something wicked there. And now the tide'll cut him off."

As we approached I noticed Calladine had got his camera in his hand, and now we heard him call.

"By Jove! I've made a choice discovery, Aitchison. Queer sort of sea plant with abnormal features, and quite huge. Seems to be growing through the timbers down here."

"Yes, all right, but come on, man! You look like being caught," I cried. "The tide's already here."

Gray had dropped back somewhat and was scanning the blackening clouds.

"There'll be a clap just now, sir," he bawled.

But neither of us could get quite to the boat because of a shore pool engulfing it on our side. The first fringe of the approaching tide was now lapping also on the seaward side, whence Calladine apparently had come upon his prize. Nor had we any view into the boat as it was shored up on its side, facing away from us. All we could see in that livid daylight were the rotting timbers, and Calladine slithering round the gunwale and fumbling with a flashlight pan.

"I must just get one exposure of it somehow," he yelled, strapping the camera to a withered rowlock.

A moment's silence followed, then—

"Good God! It's . . ."

One agonizing scream, a blinding flash, and I felt myself thrown headlong in the wet, quaking sand, with the mortal crack and roar of thunder in my ears.

The next I knew was being dragged to my feet by Gray amid the drenching torrents of a cloudburst. Giddily I pulled myself together, and joined with him in calling, "Calladine! Hey, Calladine," and wading about in the swirling sea. All

our cries were in vain. Nothing could we find save bits of
wreckage floating here and there. From one I snatched the
fatal camera still strapped to it.

In haste I went for help while Colin stayed to search. Even
when men and lanterns and a boat arrived it was a fruitless
task. Splinters of wood and fragments of what seemed like
bloody seaweed—all beefy red and gristly—and that was all.
There was no sign of unhappy Calladine. With the lanterns
flickering we took our last look across the evening sea and I
could not help but muse upon my vision of the previous night
when

> The water, like a witch's oils,
> Burnt green, and blue and white.

"Death by misadventure" was all that could be safely said
of my poor friend's fate. The only evidence was a fresh-
stripped skeleton found three days later. But the fisherfolk put
the whole tragedy down to malevolent powers. Talk turned
on spiritual forces, incarnate in some carnivorous sea plant of
monstrous dimensions. Folklore was rife about "St. Cuthbert's
fiends," and "sea blood" and the like.

The sexton, too, who had been digging a grave that tragic
afternoon, soon had a tale to tell. I got it from the parson
later, when no doubt it had gathered details by transmission
several times. This fellow had, so Mr. Ainsley said, often
noticed a reddish slime in the ground when he was excavat-
ing. Beetles and worms seemed greatly drawn to this stuff
from all directions, and he could not make out where it oozed
from. He had never liked the look of it himself and so had
kept pretty clear. Besides, it had a most obnoxious stench, he
said. Now, on the afternoon of Calladine's death, this man
was in the graveyard at his work when the ground began to
quake and he saw a subsidence, not in the old quarter where
you might expect it among the vaults, but where the recent
burials had been. He rushed to where the soil was broken
most and was in time to see a curious sight.

There were his beetles and other insects by the hundred
making, through a ruddy patch of soil, toward a writhing
length of something like an elephant's trunk. It gleamed with
a phosphorescent light, he said, and seemed to have tough
veins pulsating along it, but it lashed out so violently that in a

moment it was gone. He saw what looked like tawny-colored bristles twitching on the thing, with insects being impaled upon them and sucked into scaly apertures within the trunk. But what horrified the fellow most were tentacles stuck piercing through a newly buried coffin for purposes so obvious and evil.

It must have been a gruesome sight, and it always sets me wondering about that rootlike line I saw, the night before the tragedy, running from the sea across and under the sands, and also about what Calladine must certainly have seen and touched when out with Gray the other time.

I should think less of this but for a startling thing that came from that camera of his. One of the demonstrators at the laboratory—for amusement, it seems—betook himself to develop the plates when it arrived, along with Calladine's other things, in Newcastle. Anyway, what should Dr. Angus bring me one morning but a photograph of the very sight that Calladine beheld at the moment of his death!

If you will kindly reach down that large book—that old one in faded leather—on my cabinet, you will find this same photograph inside.

Drury had soon seen enough. Even after a glass of brandy and soda he was still shivery for some time at the thought of those countless layers of rank, concentric lobes and the unfolding bunch of antennae, just glimpsed there in the very instant of disclosing that inane and meager "face" within the vortex.

"Poor devil!" he shuddered. "What did he take it for at first? Some monstrous species of *Drosera?* That stuff like fungus reminds me of those ghastly frilled lizards they have in Australia. But then these writhing tubes? If you think of an ultra-ghoulish octopus as well, you've still not sized this nightmare up. There's something horrible beyond—"

"Yes," mused Aitchison solemnly, " 'something *beyond*.' "

"I almost feel that you are right," said Drury reluctantly, "but I don't quite grasp your supernatural basis for all this."

"Well," answered Aitchison, "even in the modern texts we have Bede's word for it that Farne Island was haunted in St. Cuthbert's time. But I confess it was a reference in this antiquated folio here that first made me read between the lines. Look at it yourself."

Here he passed his friend the book in which that ugly
photograph had long been kept. After glancing with some
curiosity at the title page *(A Discreet Inquirie into the
Spiritual Topographie of the Northern parts of Englande*, by
the Revd. Dr. Wm. Danby, 1579), Drury turned to the place
inside, which Aitchison had found, and read:

Evil report was knowen of this same islande of Farne in
old time. Baeda well notyth it, spirituum malignorum
frequentia humanae habitationi minus accommodus. HIST.
ECC. iv, 28.

Again wher he writyth of the sojourn of the holie
Cuthbert therupon he bearyth witnes how that, afore this
Servant of the Lorde, no man was ther ever so bold to
dwell on this islande alone by reson of the foul fiends
ther resident. VITA CUTHB. 17.

Truely, as he saith, No phantasie so grievous but this
good man by spiritual stryving might put to flyte. How-
beit the faithfull Herefrid, when he comyth to him on the
Farne, findyth his dyeing master sore pressed. That holie
man had ther but five onions beneath the truckle bed, the
which he bringyth forth as token of meate enogh to keep
him lively. Therat, quoth Herefrid, methoght one of
them to be a little gnawed yet certeinly not more than
half bitten upon. Then spake the sainte, Never in all
my sojourn in this islande did mine enimyes so hardlie
plague me as uppon these last five dayes. Nor yett, saith
Herefrid, was I bold enogh to ask him what manner
persecucions he thus endured. VITA CUTHB. 37.

"Ah! I begin to see it now," murmured Drury in reverie,
as his host rose and put both book and photograph away.
"That's where your Scallion Stone comes in. So, Demon
Number Five, that gave old Cuthbert the slip, has now done
his damnedest and been put to rest. But what a sinister thing
to know when you stood that morning looking at the last
fossil, clammy and vacant, that Thing was still at large!"

"Aye," said Aitchison, "and what of Calladine who knew
it? He asked me once what sort of hell hag an 'amphibian
vampire' would be to dream about."

Robin Smyth is a Britisher whose "The Inglorious Rise of the Catsmeat Man" is a superior effort in black humor, and the reader response to its appearance in Whispers *made it one of the most popular tales I published. I have read this story well over a dozen times, and it still tickles the Ambrose Bierce within me. I trust it will yours as well.*

THE INGLORIOUS RISE
OF THE CATSMEAT MAN

by Robin Smyth

Back in nineteen thirty-five it was. Year of the Silver Jubilee. That's when it all started. Thirty-five was a year of ups and downs for most people. It was a year of ups for dear old King George the Five because he'd lived it up for twenty-five years as Fid. Def. Ind. Imp. and it was a year of downs for my old man, downs and outs you might as well say, as this was the year he fell in the giant mixer at Bleeson's Cement Works, which annoyed the Bleeson board of directors no end because dad's blood and bones messed up a ten-ton consignment of cement and cost the Bleeson mob somewhere in the neighborhood of ninety quid gross profit. Not that I missed me old man much mind you (well, old I call him, he was only just forty when he toppled overboard) even though I was only a boy of fourteen at the time of the mishap. Fourteen being the start of crucial times in a boy's life, or so all the headshrinkers say. Well, he was a violent, drunken old pig, see, used to thump Huckleberry out of my dear, beautiful mother and she used to cry real tears and sometimes the salt tears were red-running with blood from cuts he inflicted on her pale face. And I hated him.

I love my dear mother, see. Really, I do. Some blokes think you're a bit mad when you say things like that. Girls do too. Especially girls. Girls get jealous, see. Why, when I tell girls I can actually remember my moment of birth, they look at me all peculiar, like . . . but, it's true. I do remember! Beautiful it was. Like plunging out of a dark, silent tunnel into the light of life. Love my mother, I do. Yes.

That's why I was a bit choked when dear mother married again. So quick, too. Only just three months and a day after father's messy passing. Not that I was worried about the old rat's memory, it was just . . . well . . . I liked being alone in the house with dear mother. Liked her just being with me. Near me. Close. Didn't really want anybody else sort of intruding.

Actually, though, the bloke she married, he wasn't too bad when I really recollect it. Used to call me "mister" instead of "sonny" or "boy" and during the first months of the marriage he bought me a cricket bat and a Hornby clockwork train set and often he would take me to see a circus or the latest Marx Brothers picture. Mind you, he had bundles of money. Hundreds! So he could afford these luxuries, really. He was in the catsmeat business, see. That's what he was called: Hollins the Catsmeat Man. Big bloke he was, all red-faced and black, brilliantined hair and he used to wear a brown warehouse overall down to his ankles and a great pair of brown, polished boots and a brown bowler hat with a dent in the middle and round the town he would go with his great tray of meat on his head and a big bell, swinging and clanging at his side and all the time he'd holler: "Ceeeee . . . aaaaaaaaaats meat for seeeee . . . aaaaaaale! Beeeeee . . . eeeeeeest ceeeeee . . . aaaaaaaaaaats meat!" And people would come from all over to buy his stringy red meat at sixpence a pound for their pet moggies if they was well-off clients and for their own consumption if they weren't.

I used to work in the shop. Well, it wasn't a shop really

. . . it was the front room of Hollins's little terraced down Mafeking Avenue, which was where me and dear mother moved soon after she was wed. The house was one of them two up-two down efforts with a lavatory out back and a yard the size of a fourpenny postage stamp. This front room was my bedroom too. I mean, I had to sleep somewhere. Hollins put the tin hat on me sharing with dear mother and him. First of all it was a bit uncomfortable having your bed set up amongst a stack of horseflesh and mutton . . . especially during the summer months when the old bluebottles used to come sucking and buzzing about, crawling all over your face and hands, bloated with butcher's blood and, cor! The stink was enough to putrefy a graveyard. But I got used to it and I even started a lucrative sideline . . . breeding maggots . . . which I used to sell, a farthing a pokey bag to all the fishing kids around. Always had a cunning business brain, I did . . . suppose it's that what took me where I am today. Any old rate, to cut the boasting and get back to the originals, Hollins the Catsmeat Man, also being a shrewd nut where business was concerned, told my mum that I would keep the front room rent free, plus grub and six bob a week pin money if she and me would run the "shop." Dear mother, being as dumb as she was beautiful, agreed, not realizing that foxy old Hollins had a bounden duty to succor and provide for his stepson during his formative, early-work years and, indeed, should not have been seeking profit from the sweat and labor of one so young. Still! That's life! And every morning come the dawn, I'd thrust up me window and slap a few trays of catsmeat on the sill and by eight, darling mum'd come and join me and whilst Hollins was out on his rounds, swinging his bell and bawling his head off, mum and me'd sit chopping up great chunks of meat into slices and slabs, all friendly and cosy together, like a couple of surgeons in the window, and folks would come from ours and the neighboring streets and buy from us and the men would say that it was a treat to be served their catsmeat by such a lovely gal as my mum . . . and they'd wink and crack little jokes and that . . . and as the months went by, Hollins's trade perked up no end, but Hollins, instead of getting grateful and being pleased with dear mother and me, grew sullen and churlish and started calling my mum horrible names like: slut! and, tramp! and, Jezebel! . . . and I just couldn't understand the change in the man. Sort of just like my old feller used to be.

"I wish 'e was dead, Boysie," she said to me one hot August morning as we sat slicing up a horse steak.

"Dead, mother? Who?"

"Hollins!"

"Why, mother?"

"Cos 'e's cruel, Boysie!" She lifted one fragile white hand and pushed back the hair which framed her face. "Look! He did that to me last night with a fag."

I felt a sudden hatred for Hollins as I looked at the four neatly placed burn marks on my mother's cheek. "Why'd he do that, mother?"

"Cos I wouldn't kiss him. Well 'e stunk someink terrible, he did. Bin on the rum half the day, he had." She shivered. "I hate 'im more than I ever hated your father, I'll tell yer."

"I'll kill 'im if you like, mother." I slashed at the meat. "I'll slit his throat and chop his head off if you want me to."

She let the hair flop about her face. She looked at me with a tenderness I'd never before witnessed. "I couldn't let yer do that, Boysie. That'd be murder. Young as you are, they'd 'ang you for it."

"Not if they never find out." I selected a cube of meat and sliced it neatly. "And I know a way that I could get rid of him for sure. No one'd never discover what happened to 'im, and we could have a business and everything. Just me and you, mother. We'd be laughing. We'd be rich."

There was a silence. I chopped more meat. Slowly. "But if I done him, mother, you'd have to make me a very special promise."

"And what's that, darling Boysie?" she cooed.

"You've got to promise never no more to go with other blokes. No kissin' and cuddlin', like. No more getting married."

She smiled, leaned forward and kissed me gently on the forehead. "Of course, I promise. There's only one man I need and that's you . . . my darling little Boysie."

I loved it.

Well, mother and me we worked it together. I done Hollins with a specially sharpened carver when he was totaling up his week's takings in the upstairs back bedroom, then between us mother and me chopped him up into little lumps and mixed best part of him with the catsmeat on the window trays. Went down a treat with the clients, he did and old Mrs. Sollicutts from the buildings, a regular catsmeat eater, came back a-drooling, begging for more of that "real, lovely liver, what was the best she'd ever tasted!"

In fact, before Mr. Hollins was exhausted, mother and me were showered with flattering compliments.

"Delicious, braised!" said Beattie Flower, the barmaid from the Sailors' Haven.

"Sure and I wouldn't be after wasting choice cuts like that on my moggie," enthused Old Man Murphy the Irish street fiddler.

"Nicest meat pie me mummy ever made," commented little Timmy Brown, the postman's son.

Course, it didn't take long for mother and me to realize the potential. If we could get a regular supply of Hollinsmeat . . . well . . . we could bump our prices and make a fortune. Naturally, even though he was a big bloke, Hollins didn't go far once he was diced up . . . and, I mean, there was a hell of a lot of wastage, like bones, teeth, hair . . . things like that (which we just buried in the yard) and it began to look, by the end of the week, that mother and me were going to be stuck with the regular line in catsmeat.

Any old rate, one night, mother and me were sitting in the cosy little parlor, downstairs back, she combing and brushing her long, golden hair and me just sitting back in this old rocker, gaping at her and marveling at her beauty when all of a sudden she looks at me with those green-gray gorgeous eyes of hers and says:

"Y'know, Boysie, mother's been thinking."

"Yes, mother. And what have you been thinking about?"

"Our future, darling."

She tossed back her head and her soft hair seemed to float about that china-doll face.

"We could make a lot of money, y'know, if we . . . well, darling Boysie . . . if we could obtain another consignment of meat same as Mister Hollins."

"But Mister Hollins has all run out, mother . . .'cept for that pound of rump we've been saving for ourselves."

She gave me a very fond smile and my heart went boomp, boomp, boomp! She said: "There are other gentlemen like Mister Hollins."

I frowned: "You're not thinking of goin' a-courting again, are you, mother?"

She pouted her luscious lips: "Mmmmm . . . well . . . sort of!"

A sudden sort of evil-hate feeling came over me. "But you promised, mother," I said. "No more chaps. No more kissing and cuddling. No more . . ."

"There'll be no kissing, darling. No cuddling. I'll just go parading around the bars and backstreets where the big men gather . . . and I'll entice them with me looks."

"Entice?" I felt this dark rage welling up. "Sounds dirty. What's it mean, mother?"

She put her finger to her lips and thought for a moment. "Entice means . . . lure!"

"Lure?"

"Well . . . seduce!"

"Sounds dirty too," I said. I frowned. "You promised."

Like the tinkling of bells was her laughter. "Silly, darling Boysie," she trilled. "Mother loves you. All mother's suggesting is that she brings," she wagged a finger, "just brings, mind you, these gentlemen home."

I whined. "But why, mother?"

"So that you, my darling, can dispatch them, same way as you dispatched the late Mr. Hollins!"

The evil-hatred feeling flew away from me like a passing dark raven. I felt love now. Love for this mother of genius.

"Then we chops 'em up," I enthused, "just like we chops up the late Mr. Hollins . . . and we sells 'em at twice the normal catsmeat price per pound and it's all profit and within a year or so we'll be livin' in style . . . wahoooo!"

She came over and draped her arms about me, pulling my face to her springy bosom, till I almost sweetly stifled in that tender flesh. "Oh, my lovely Boysie," she cooed. "Won't it be wonderful?"

During the next year a brigade of gentlemen passed through our street door. Mr. Hargreaves, Mr. Johnson, Mr. Squires, Mr. McCauley, Mr. Hartwell, Mr. Smith, Mr. O'Grady, Mr. O'Toole, O'Hara and O'Dee. Mr. Wallington-Smith, and D'Arcy-Jones, Mr. Ivor D. Evans from somewhere in Wales . . . by the dozen they came and went. Mother enticing 'em, me dispatching 'em and all of 'em, rich and poor, holy and unholy, young and middle-aged ending up as slices and cubes on the catsmeat trays in the window. It was a marvelous arrangement and with our bank balance swelling like a fat man's belly, mother and me were seriously considering bigger and classier premises . . . and all the while the fame of our tasty catsmeat spread wider abroad, people coming from as far afield as Hammersmith Broadway and Kings Cross to buy.

Yes, it was all very wonderful for that glorious year, then mother had to go and entice Graham Gunterstone from the lounge bar of a Chelsea pub and all our plans and hopes and dreams from that fateful moment were doomed to be as useless as an overcoat for a Teddy bear.

Graham Gunterstone was young and handsome with blond, wavy hair, blue-blue eyes, a tiny nose, even teeth, an Oxford accent and manners so perfect they made me heave. From the moment he swaggered into our cosy little house, I was itching to lay about me with the meat cleaver . . . to part that pansy hair with a neat, bloody channel across the scalp . . . to slice off that teeny nose, to hack out those sparkling blue eyes, to chop off the tongue and silence forever his irritating whine.

But dear mother had other plans for Graham and in a most devious way, she dissuaded me from slicing him up immediately, saying he needed fattening up. I fell for her lies, as well. Well, if a chap can't trust his mother, who can he trust? I mean, I didn't credit for a moment that she would retract her promise to me.

I didn't know that she would be spending her evenings cuddling and kissing Graham Gunterstone: fondling his ears and stroking his face and telling him how much she loved him. I didn't know . . . oh, and it makes me sick just thinking of it . . . my beautiful mother! I didn't know she'd actually go to bed with Graham. But I caught them at it. Up in the back bedroom what she used to share with Mr. Hollins . . . this sacred room which I had never been allowed to enter. It was disgusting.

Here was me worrying my eyeballs out in the front room, running short of catsmeat while my trusted mother is upstairs back, gasping and puffing, giggling and kissing, playing with the most unhealthy games with our immediate meat supply.

Well, I got the bang needle, I can tell you. I crept downstairs, picked up the cleaver and tiptoed again to the bedroom door. I could hear dear mother, talking and giggiing and that pansy-boy Graham, tittering and breathing heavy and from the general gist of the overheard chatter, I realized that dear mother didn't love me at all and had broken her faithful promise to me by kissing and cuddling with every bloke she'd enticed since we took over from Mister Hollins. Unable to contain myself longer, I burst into that darkened, filthy room and yelling blue murder I let the pair of 'em have it, fast as I could.

There was a lot of sensation when I gave myself up. You know what papers are. Things like: "Cannibals in S.W.6." and "Frenzied Ghoul Axes Mother and Lover!" and "The Inglorious Rise of the Catsmeat Man!" But, as you will appreciate, that was all paper claptrap. Facts are, mother and me were in business and would have stayed in business if she had kept her word. I was faithful. She wasn't. Simple as that.

Anyway, I wound up in Broadmoor where I've now re-sided for thirty-four years. There is some talk of letting me out on a short parole . . . sort of to prepare me for my eventual release. Trouble is, as I explained to Sir Georgie Ringle, our chief head-shrinker . . . where would I get employment?

There's not much call for catsmeat men nowadays.
Is there?

Charles E. Fritch was the editor of Gamma, *a short-lived but fine science fiction magazine of the early 1960s. His fiction appeared frequently in the science fiction journals of the 1950–56 era, but after that his primary output was aimed toward crime and adventure writing. He, though, did find time to break that habit long enough to write a biography of Kim Novak. William Nolan was kind enough to put me in touch with Charles, and I am pleased to present you with one of his all-too-infrequent stories. It is a deal-with-the-devil tale wherein that fine gentleman gives our hero a fighting chance, or does he? . . .*

THE PAWNSHOP

by Charles E. Fritch

"It's not that I have anything against you personally, Davis," the old man said. "But I simply must kill you."

"But why, Mr. Carver?" the young man wanted to know. He'd stopped straining at his bonds, realizing at last the futility of that. "I've been your faithful employee for the past two years. If I'm going to die, at least tell me why."

"Because I'm old," Jonathan Carver said wearily, "and ready to die myself, and my soul is in hock."

"I don't understand," James Davis said.

Carver grunted. "Of course you don't. You're young,

happily married, with children. You have your whole life ahead of you. Or you would have," he amended, matter-of-factly, "if I weren't going to kill you."

The old man glanced around the soundproof basement. The two of them were alone, of course. The door was locked and bolted from the inside. Davis's young body was securely manacled to the wall, and there was no danger of his escaping.

"I suppose I do owe you an explanation," he admitted.

I was a very young man (Jonathan Carver said) and I needed a thousand dollars. I had this idea for a new kind of radio component that would replace vacuum tubes. With a little money I could set myself up in business. But as I say, I was very young, very inexperienced, I was afraid someone would steal my ideas. I was also desperate.

I had this ring my mother had given me—a diamond, not very large, probably not worth very much, I thought, but I had to raise money somehow, so on impulse one day I stopped in a pawnshop to see what I could get for it. It was a dark, dusty old shop cluttered with the usual junk one finds in such a place. The proprietor was a middle-aged man of medium height and average appearance who didn't even look at the ring I thrust under his nose.

"I'll give you a thousand dollars cash for something else," the man said; "something you don't even know you have."

A thousand dollars! Exactly the amount I needed. "Yes," I agreed quickly. "Anything. I'd give my soul for a thousand dollars."

The man smiled, and with good reason, for that's precisely what he had in mind.

You laugh at that. Well, I don't blame you. I laughed too, because of course I thought he was jesting; or else he was a madman. But then he went to his cashbox and brought out a thousand dollars in one-hundred-dollar bills and placed them on the counter. Madman or not, his money was sane enough for my purpose.

I reached for the money, but he stopped me. "First," he said, placing a small card on the counter before me, "you must put your thumbprint in the blank space. That makes it legal."

I believed it to be nonsense, but for a thousand dollars I desperately needed, I'd be willing to humor the devil himself.

I placed my finger in the blank space on the card and was surprised to find it was very warm. When I took my thumb away, the imprint was imbedded in the formerly blank area.

He didn't stop me as I gathered up the ten one-hundred-dollar bills. I said, "I suppose you'll want this back with interest?"

He said, "Of course not. Read the fine print on back of the card. You don't repay us with money, but with bad deeds."

He turned away and disappeared amid the clutter in the back of the store. I was going to call to him for an explanation, but I decided not to. After all, I had my money, and what good would it do me to argue ridiculous points with someone so obviously addled? I glanced at the card again. It held my thumbprint, as big as life, my name, and the amount borrowed: $1,000.00. The reverse side of the card held a library of small print, which I'd read later, if I had the time.

I had no patience with it now, for I was eager to get started on my new project. My mind was filled with a multitude of things I had to do—rent an old shack to be used as my first workshop, buy machinery, tools, and raw materials, perhaps even hire some part-time labor. So it was quite by accident that as I was rushing from the pawnshop, the card in one hand, counting my money, that I ran into the path of a speeding car.

For an instant, a horrible thought flashed across my mind: the devil was about to collect my soul before I had a chance to pay him off!

But then the car swerved to miss me, skidded, and went up onto the sidewalk and crashed into the porch of a tenement building. Gasoline flooded from the vehicle's tank and caught fire. The apartment dwellings were old and dry, and they went up like tinderwood. Before the fire department could do anything, the entire block was destroyed. There were a few injuries, but miraculously no one was killed.

That night in my hotel room I happened to glance at the pawnshop ticket. The number had changed. Instead of the original $1,000.00, the figure was $999.00. I recalled what the pawnbroker had told me: *"You don't repay us with money, but with bad deeds."*

I was astonished, not so much at the magical change in the number on the ticket, but that destruction of so many buildings, coupled with the various injuries sustained by several

persons, was worth a mere one dollar. At that rate, I'd have
to set fire to nine hundred ninety-nine more buildings in order
to pay my debt.

That was nonsense, I decided, and immediately dismissed
the thought. When I had a thousand dollars in profit from my
venture, I'd pay off the loan, adding whatever interest was
due.

I rented the shack, bought what tools I needed, invested
money in raw materials, and worked night and day to build
up my little business. Within six months, I had to move to a
larger location. I'd hired three full-time employees. I was
making a good living, and I had several thousand dollars in
my bank account. I withdrew twelve hundred of the savings
and returned to the pawnshop where I'd "hocked my soul."

Or I tried to. I went back to the same location. Still across
the street were the charred ruins of the tenements which had
not been replaced. But there was no pawnshop. According to
neighbors, there never had been one there. It was my imagination, they said. The pawn ticket, however, was very real,
and on it I read the statement that I would not be allowed to
redeem my soul under any circumstances except those speci-
fied. That's when I decided to read the fine print in the
contract.

There was just no getting around it. I *had* to do bad deeds,
if I wanted to get my soul back. Actually, assuming there was
such a thing as a soul and a person as the devil and a place
called Hell, it seemed logical that Satan would want such
things written into a contract. It was his purpose on Earth to
do evil deeds, or to have them done, and according to the fine
print every little bit helped. For example, if once a day I
kicked a dog on the street, it might not register right away on
the card, but it would all add up over the years.

To tell the truth, I wasn't totally convinced just then to take
all this at face value. During six months, the number had
remained at the $999.00 figure, not budging. Of course, I'd
been too busy at honest labor to do anything bad, even
accidentally. At the rate I was going, I'd never do enough
evil to pay off my debt before I died—and then it would be
too late.

I put the thought from my mind. After all, I was a young
man, and death seemed so distant as to be nonexistent. I

threw myself wholeheartedly into my work, hardly bothering even with the simple pleasures of life.

Except for Mary, that is.

She was a pretty thing, with soft brown hair, liquid eyes, a pert nose, rich red lips. She was quite innocent when she came to work for me at the plant because I needed some office help. Would you believe she had to support a sick mother? Oh, it was a marvelous set-up. I think she genuinely liked me, but even then she might not have done what I wanted if I hadn't intimated she might be fired otherwise. The poor girl needed the money, even the modest stipend I gave her every week. Besides, I told her I loved her and that we'd get married some day when the factory was built up enough.

And the silly goose had to go and get pregnant! She came to me in tears, saying she couldn't have an illegitimate child and I'd have to marry her. I told her I didn't have to do any such thing. I said she was probably fooling around with dozens of other fellows. I told her to go find the true father and not to bother me any more. To make doubly sure she kept away, I fired her.

I learned later that she took her life, and shortly thereafter her mother grew worse and also died. I didn't think it was my fault, but apparently my friends in the pawnshop did, for they gave me a credit of one hundred dollars for the two lives.

I began to take the ticket and the contract more seriously after that. I mean, just on the off chance there was something to this devil and soul business. I read the fine print on back of the card carefully. It didn't spell out all the credits available, but it made it clear that human life was at a premium, and the more I could make that human suffer, the more credit I got.

Which, by the way, Davis, is why I intend torturing you before I kill you. I'm sure you can see my logic in that.

Anyway, I realized happily that it wouldn't really be going out of my way to do bad deeds. It was common in the business world then just as it is now. In fact, I suspect many big businessmen have sold their souls to the devil and are now doing bad deeds in the name of industry in order to redeem their pledges. And along the way, I could do a few things when the opportunities presented themselves.

For example, I went to church. That surprises you, does it? Well, you won't be surprised when you hear the reason. When they passed the plate, instead of putting something in it,

I always took something out. Stealing was worth a few points, but stealing from the devil's opposition was even better. Not enough, perhaps, to register immediately as a credit on my pawn ticket, but it all added up, as the fine print insisted.

If only I'd been in munitions, I could've had my debt wiped out long ago. Or even if I'd been in the service, maybe I could've tossed a few grenades in the right spots to pile up some credits; unfortunately, the head-shrinkers decided I was unfit for military duty, whatever that meant. So I had to do it the hard way, a little at a time.

I kicked dogs whenever they came within booting range, littered places that had do-not-litter signs, laid off my employees just before Christmas, broke windows when no one was looking, let the air out of tires—and so on. It got so I never let an opportunity pass without taking advantage of it, no matter how small it might be. Compared to me, Ebenezer Scrooge was a fairy godmother.

And every once in a while, the figure on the ticket would change, sometimes only a penny at a time. But then, I was a young man, and I had plenty of time. At least, that's what I thought. But the years went by so swiftly. My bank balance built up into the millions. I own five factories turning out electronic equipment for the government and private industry. I have a big home and several cars.

And now, I'm very close to dying, and I still owe the devil fifty dollars and seventy-three cents.

"So you see," Jonathan Carver said to the manacled young man, "why I must kill you. I must torture you seventy-three cents' worth and then destroy your fifty-dollar body. Perhaps, because you have a wife and children who will be distraught and penniless, I have some leeway, but I can't afford to take any chances. It's nothing personal, Davis, I want you to understand that."

James Davis wet his lips. "Wait. You're making a mistake. You wouldn't be doing a bad deed killing me."

"Please," Jonathan Carver said wearily. "Don't waste my time with nonsense."

"It's not nonsense," Davis rushed on desperately. "You see, I've got a pawn ticket myself."

Jonathan Carver paused to stare at the young man.

Davis nodded. "My wife, Beth. You've never met her, but

she's beautiful. When I first met her, she didn't love me. I remember I was walking along the street thinking I'd sell my soul if I could only have her for my wife. Suddenly I looked up to see this pawnshop where none had been before. On impulse I went in. The man said he'd loan me one thousand dollars to buy roses for the girl I loved. He said an eloquent gesture like that would make her love me. I thought he was mad, but he counted out the money and said if it didn't work, I owed him nothing. If it did—''

''Your soul,'' the old man said.

''Right. I didn't see what I had to lose, and I was crazy enough myself to try it. And of course it worked. Beth was so impressed with the nut who loved her enough to fill half her house with red roses on a whim, she started taking a new interest in me. We were married a month later.'' James Davis paused. ''So you see, I'm working to pay off my own debt, just like you. I've got a lifetime of bad deeds ahead of me. If you kill me now, you'll be doing the world a favor—but not yourself.''

Jonathan Carver stared thoughtfully at the man. ''I don't believe you,'' he said finally.

''The pawn ticket is in my wallet,'' the young man said. ''See for yourself.''

Cautiously the old man extricated Davis's wallet from a rear pocket and fumbled through the cards until he came to a familiar one that held a thumbprint, the name James Davis, and the number $997.46.

''You've got a long way to go,'' Carver grunted.

''I just started,'' Davis said, almost apologetically. ''You'd be surprised at some of the things I had to do to get the loan down that far. Anyway, as you can see, we're both working for the same employer.''

The old man sighed. ''All right.'' He shuffled forward to release the man from his manacles. ''Perhaps,'' he added hopefully, ''we can even work together—for our mutual benefit.''

James Davis rubbed circulation into his unbound ankles and wrists. ''I'm afraid not.'' He smiled and said pleasantly, ''One of the things I've been doing during my two-year employment as your bookkeeper is embezzling funds from you.''

Jonathan Carver's face turned livid. ''What?''

"That's right." The young man's strong hands leaped out to grasp the old man by the throat. "And here's where I earn a fifty-dollar credit for myself."

Carver's puny hands scrabbled at the fingers tightening into his windpipe. He gasped and wheezed, and his face changed color.

"But you mustn't kill me," he muttered hoarsely. "You said killing an evil person is not a bad deed."

"I lied," James Davis said simply. "Lying is worth a few points too, you know. Besides, you don't really think the devil is going to let you redeem your soul, do you?"

Suddenly the old man laughed. "Nor yours," he said.

James Davis's fingers cut off the old man's words forever, but years later the young man growing old remembered them and knew the beginnings of fear.

Robert Aickman is an English author whose stories of eerie and supernatural occurrences are strange mixtures of allegory, poetry, and style. They create exceptional moods and often conclude in a less-than-explicit manner, something his detractors frequently point out; however, his stories are written exactly as he wants them to be. His subtle hints tease from you feelings and fears you would rather not know existed, and you are free to let your mind determine just what has happened and to accept or reject a supernatural explanation. Aickman's "Pages from a Young Girl's Journal" was the recipient of the first World Fantasy Award for short fiction and his recent collection, Cold Hand in Mine, *collects that gem with seven other "strange stories." Here is an original from the pages of* Whispers *that shows us that minds and mirrors can play very bizarre games, very bizarre . . .*

LE MIROIR

by Robert Aickman

Celia's father was old enough to be her grandfather, perhaps her great-grandfather. Notoriously, it is one of the advantages that men have over women.

He had beautiful, silvery hair, and a voice like a distant bell of indeterminate note; but, unfortunately, he could move only very slowly, and, even then, aided by a shiny black staff, with a most handsomely jeweled knob. Celia had never known her mother, and that lady's portrait was always turned to the wall, from which position, in accordance with her father's adjuration, she had never cared to drag it, or to set about dragging it, for it looked very heavy.

The old house was crumbling now, and something beautiful was lost to it with every year that ended: even the drawing of an unknown, smiling woman by Raphael; even the tiny box found in the Prince of the Moskowa's fob, and soaked in his blood. In the end, one would have thought that there remained only the mirrors; the looking glasses, if you insist. The mirrors or looking glasses, and the bare utilities for the bare living which had to substitute for life.

All the looking glasses were, of course, mercury-silvered, so that, as well as reflecting, they embellished and discriminated. In each of the state rooms were three or four of the objects; on the walls, on floor stands, on bureaux and escritoires. In the state bedrooms the looking glasses were even more subtly placed and more ingeniously set, in that long ago they had been offered more curious topics to touch upon. It is unnecessary to select from the lists of past guests, because the lists included everyone.

Day by day, Celia's father would toil round the rooms, struggling up the grand staircases, crawling perilously down them; in every room, on every landing, at every dark corner, gazing in the looking glasses, outstaring time. Sometimes, at a respectful distance, he was followed for much of the way by his old Nurse, though more commonly Nurse was confined by neuritis and weakheadedness to her bed in the little apartment under the flaking tiles that she had occupied since first she came. How old Nurse could be was a subject sedulously eschewed.

Right from the cradle (and Celia's cradle had aforetime cradled both the shapely John Dryden and the unproportioned Alexander Pope), Celia had vouchsafed her frail, dreamlike drawings; in pencil, even in chalk; and, later, with water color finely touched in. She had studied every urn in the park, and every ancient tree, by every condition of light: the Elizabethan oaks, the Capability Brown beeches, the single exotics planted with ceremony by Mr. Palgrave, by Bishop Wilberforce, by the Prince Imperial. The tenant farmer's herds served well as artistic auxiliaries; and, sometimes at dusk, the Mad Hunt, which all at these times could hear but only those with the Sight could behold. It was natural that when at length Celia had arrived at her sixteenth birthday, she should wish to go to Paris in order to increase her power and widen her range.

Still in a dream, she found herself enrolled at a long-established and old-fashioned private atelier: Étien's it had been familiarly named by many generations of students, some of them always British. One felt that Watteau and Greuze must have been among the more recent pupils; Claude, among the earlier professors. But now, as is often found with aging institutions, seven eighths of the attendants were excessively youthful; too young to be taken quite seriously as yet by anyone. The remaining one eighth was composed of shaky eccentrics and inadequates who had been attending (and, of course, contributing) since the year Dot. The professors were wayward, though one or two were geniuses, and merely at cross purposes with the times in which they found themselves. Genius, however, comes normally in inverse measure with capacity to impart. The two things are strongly opposed. One of the pupils, a very old, very tough American woman brought a sackful of cakes and pastries for consumption by all during the two breaks each day.

Celia, aged sixteen years and eleven days ("Give me back my eleven days," she cried out in a brief moment of melancholy), was escorted to France by Mr. Burphy, the Chief Clerk in Totlands, her father's solicitors, and of course her own too. They even consumed an evening meal of a sort in the restaurant at the Gare de Lyon, the most gorgeous in Europe. But all the arrangements had really been made by Celia's distant cousin, Rolf, who lived with two other men of the same generation in a beautiful house up the hill at Meudon, and who knew all the ins and outs. Cousin Rolf fixed Celia up at Étien's and he even found her a nearby apartment: very high up, but with two rooms, though small ones, and with what amounted to a private staircase down to the sanitary facilities on the floor immediately below. Celia had no occasion ever to encounter in person her remote, though helpful Cousin Rolf. It was unexpected that a girl of Celia's age and background should be deposited on her own in Paris, and among artists; but she had requested it, she had always spoken quantities of French, and she could not see that there was anyone to make a fuss, as all her aunts were in Ireland, about 150 miles from Dublin, and in no position to go anywhere else, even had they wished to. Fortunately, Celia could depend upon an adequate allowance. This was mainly because her father did not understand the value of money, and, throughout his long life, had made a point of refusing all advice about it, or about anything else.

The first things that Celia bought (apart from a few dresses, pairs of shoes and stockings, lovely lingerie, and even one or two hats, either very small or very large) were additional chattels for her miniature rooms, which, upon entry, she was surprised to find almost unfurnished, as if she had been living still in the days of Mimi, Musetta, Colline, and all those well-known people. In particular, there was not one single mirror or looking glass, not one; not even a cracked fragment in the downstairs cabinet, with, perhaps, MILTON at one corner, or, possibly, JEYES. such as one found in bathing machines.

So Celia went out and purchased four or five looking glasses immediately. All but one would be merely for use each day and were backed with nitrate, though certainly not mass-produced or in any way commonplace; but the last of her acquisitions might have stood in any bedroom at home.

Celia had spotted it in one of the low, dark, hopelessly untidy shops, and its capture had been an impulse of the instant, as is everything that is in any way real. Elements of nostalgia, even of plain homesickness, no doubt entered in.

The shop had proved to be run not by the usual very old man, but by an even older woman, though spryer and more grasping than Nurse at home. The aged tricoteuse had driven a terribly hard bargain, but Celia had to possess the glass; first, for the obvious reason that she could not live without it; second because it bore extremely faded traces of mysterious male and female figures round the upper part of the frame; third, because the face that had just looked back at her from its shallows and depths had not been her own.

The short distance along which the glass had to be borne presented an even worse problem than the haggling, and the need for lugging it up so many narrow, winding, and decrepit stairs a worse one still.

But the most complex of ordeals sometimes finds its own resolution, and now Celia sat before the beautiful mirror or looking glass, now in one new dress, now in another, and intermittently without troubling to put on a dress at all. She had to seat herself for these transactions, because the looking glass was so short in the frame. She had heard that our ancestors were more stunted than we are, though even this (she knew) had been contested by a woman who owned an immense collection of very old clothes, all of which she had measured anew, giving years to the work. Possibly the beautiful looking glass had been designed for the Gonzaga dwarfs, men and women even as the faded figures gamboling round the top of the frame? Celia wondered if she would ever visit their tiny suites at Mantua; of which her father had shown her small yellow photographs taken years before with early flashlights. In the meantime, she would have to find a chaise longue that was stumpier in the shanks. Her own limbs were as long as they were lovely.

So life continued, for Celia could not quite say how long, as her father wrote letters of any kind only on formal occasions, and Totlands really had no business to transact with her beyond paying out her allowance, with her usual precise punctuality. She had been well aware that Mr. Burphy had been more frightened of her than anything else. How long ago it began to seem! Time flies when we watch it, but has no need to fly when we ignore it.

One morning, Celia felt quite certain of something that of late she had more and more suspected: she was not merely looking older, but looking much older; older, more grained, more perceptibly skinny. The first bright light of spring must have wrought the trick.

At least, Celia presumed it was the spring; which she had always distrusted, even artistically. She knew that spring is the season of maximum self-slaughter; and who could wonder? It was the season when doubt was no longer possible. Momentarily, she clutched at the neckline of her dress, and managed to inflict an actual rent. Even the fabric of her garments seemed to have weakened slightly; and this had been an expensive garment, once.

Celia did not care to look very often in any of the glasses after that, but crept past and around them, her eyes on the jade or turquoise carpet.

All the same, life has in some sense to go forward, as long as it bears with us at all; and Celia, despite her tendency to melancholy, was perfectly courageous. Moreover, she was finding more and more of herself in her art, and had been assured that soon she might quite easily win a medal of some kind. Of course, that had been said to her privately, in order not to upset the others.

She bought many new dresses to replace the one she had torn. She even bought six fancy dresses, or costumes that were all but that; with a view to meeting life from time to time in different and selected disguises. She bought a silk tie and two pairs of silk socks for a man she knew; all in excitingly aggressive colors and patterns. Sometimes she dwelt upon what it would be like to nurture eight or nine children, the fruit of her womb; upon their complex teething and schooling; upon some brusque, shadowy figure to pay for it all and act as head of the household.

How long could it have been for Celia, despite her precautions, caught her own eye in the glass and realized that she must be middle-aged and beyond all chance of concealment? And, needless to say, it had happened at that same dreadful morning hour, when the brightness of the sun is equaled only by the blackness of the heart.

Other faces had continued glinting back at her from time to time, but now she recognized that a stranger had intruded for ever.

She opened a letter that morning from David Skelt, the senior partner in Totlands. He had never before been under any necessity to write to her personally, but had been able to leave the task to his staff, or at least to a partner who was greatly his junior.

Mr. Skelt informed her that her father had become so frail that Nurse would have to be supplemented by at least one other nurse; and that her own allowance would have henceforth to be halved at the least, in consequence. He referred to these new nurses as "trained nurses." Presumably, that might make a big difference in some way.

Prices in Paris were said to be rising and the people to be changing in character; but Celia knew that she still had her art, as well as her beautiful looking glass. She realized that her art must mean more to her with every day that sped past. Whether strangers cared for her art or not, the other pupils could be counted upon for loyalty without flaw. Moreover, most of the pupils were nowadays little more than children, so that all could not sensibly be described as lost. There could always be a completely new generation. The future was an open question yet.

Celia even felt that she could hold her own with the looking glass by a continuous act of will: unremitting, resolute, robust. Long ago, Nurse had upheld virtues of that kind, and now the time was come to practice them. One never knew what one could do until one tried. If one tried hard enough, one could be any age one chose. In the library at home, she had come upon St. Thomas Aquinas's promise to that effect, even though in Latin, and in Gothic type that grew faint and gray as one watched, and never had much shape to the letters at the best of times.

Alas, there were crab-sized holes in Celia's petticoat, and, up and down the staircase, rats on the rampage for food, however moldy and mottled. Cousin Rolf could not have known. Their delicate paws were like swift kisses on one's face and arms. It was just as in the attics at home.

Celia took to attending each year the service at the Chapelle Expiatoire, and to painting pictures entitled "Son of St. Louis, Ascend to Heaven!" At these times, she could feel the divine benediction cloaking her shoulders, like a soft stole.

The other pupils at the art school were either complete babies, feeding from bottles containing corn flour; or, in certain cases, motionless skeletons, also fed with corn flour, though not from bottles, because they could not suck.

It did not take long by any standard for the point to be reached where Celia's ever smaller allowance was intersected by the ever larger cost of everything. Sometimes the watchful could see her white hair and white face at the edge of the rotting curtain as she looked out at the march past for social justice. Through hunting glasses and telescopes they could see plainly that her eyes were at once animated and frightened by the coarse thumping of the drums, the amateur screaming of the brass, the bellowing of the inebriated.

She began cutting away the gangrene from her limbs, or what she assumed to be gangrene. She was too scared to use the sharpest knife she had, as no doubt she should have done. She preferred the small, elegant fruit knives, precisely because they were rather blunt; and because they were silver, though not hallmarked with a lion, as had been so many of the knives at home. A trained surgeon would have acted upon other values, though it is hard to see that they would have made much difference in the end.

The times had become so harsh, and the people so indifferent, that the art school, after all those years, was in real danger of shutting.

Celia reflected that one's art is strictly one's own, and that never should it mean more to her than it meant now, or shudderingly seldom.

Faces she took to belong to Raphael, Luca Giordano, and Frederick Leighton now looked upon her, exaltedly and exhortingly, from within the beautiful looking glass. When she was not at art school, or trying to buy simple things with almost no money (a dressing jacket, a pair of gloves, a flask of flowery liqueur), Celia spent most of her time gazing, as she would hardly have been able to deny. Only in that way could she be true to herself. But never until now had she seen faces or forms to which she could attach names. Too often of late she had seen shapes for which no name was possible. On occasion, they had emerged, and had had to be driven back with implements she had found on sale second-hand at very low prices near Les Halles and presumably intended for the meat trade in one of its aspects. Sometimes she was horrified by the spectacle she was compelled to make of herself, and her father might have had an asthmatic attack, had he seen it.

Celia knew perfectly well that if she was to stand any chance of making a permanent mark, as the faces expected of her, then she should practice much more, as ballerinas have to do, and ladies and gentlemen who master enormous pianofortes. She should be plucky, confident, and indefatigable, like Rosa Bonheur. She should probably look like Rosa Bonheur also, though she had enough difficulty already in hanging on to looks of any kind. Still, there it was. The demands of art are notoriously boundless; nor are they subject to appeal.

"Oh, let me join you!" cried Celia, stretching out her arms to the real Celia within the beautiful mirror's mysterious depths. The real Celia stretched voluptuously in a patterned dress on the chaise longue she had bought with such innocent ardor, and on which the beseeching Celia lay among the decayed wreckage, virtually upon the sloping floor, gazed upon by a hundred expectant eyes. The colored figures at the top of the frame had entirely faded long ago.

Celia thought that the real Celia slightly moved one pale

hand and even opened her eyes a little wider. She could not remember whether the patterned dress was a silk dress for parties or a cotton dress for shopping. The pattern was known as Capet.

In any case, there would be no actual harm done if she continued to supplicate, to beseech.

Once, about this time, Celia actually heard from Mr. Burphy. It was the very first letter she had ever received from him, and Celia was quite glad that she had opened it, even though the address on the envelope had merely been typewritten. Mr. Burphy said that he had often thought of their romantic trip to Paris together, that he fancied there might be no harm in his recalling it now, that her father unfortunately needed more trained nurses all the time, that there was almost no money left from which to pay for anything, and that he, Mr. Burphy, was about to retire after generations of service with the firm, and was writing to everyone he knew and could remember, for that reason. The rest of the staff had subscribed to buy him a small electric clock, which had taken him completely by surprise, and particularly when Mr. Daniel himself had found a few moments to participate in the presentation!

Celia thought for a long, long time about the elms, and urns, and tiny bubbling springs in her father's park; and about the tenant farmer's comely, contented cows, and occasional frisky bulls. She thought about the forty-seven catalogued likenesses of her ancestors and collaterals; many of them in large familiar groups; one of them turned to the wall. She thought about the schoolroom with a dozen desks and only one occupant. She thought of the withered feathered fans in the conservatory, the property of ladies who, for her, had been dead always. She listened in memory to the Mad Hunt at twilight, and saw it take form. She smelt the rotting grapes, with the German name; and the ullaged wine, with no name at all. She felt the wet camel-hair bristles on the back of her slender hand, as she painted the world and herself into a certain transcendence.

Celia had all along been required to pay the rent in advance, especially as she was a foreigner; and she became anxious if she did not meet all demands in cash, and with punctuality to say the least of it. Often her purse, however

slim, was considerably more than punctual, and most of all
with the rent.

These rigors may have combined to reverse the effect
intended, as so often in life; because somehow the payment
due from Celia, after that last payment she was able to make
and had made more prematurely than ever, came to be overlooked altogether. It is not such an uncommon event in Paris
as is generally supposed.

Quite unfairly, there was a small scandal when Celia was
certified to have been dead for something like four or five
months before any part of her was actually found by a visitor
from the outside world.

After various alarums had been raised, some of them by
observers on the other side of the street, the elderly married
couple who lived far below Celia, and looked after the place
as best they could, sent their burly young nephew, Armand,
to beat upon the door, and, if necessary, to beat it down.
Armand admitted that he had not cared for the job from the
first.

Not much difficulty was encountered, or effort required.
Even the noise was minimal, or at least the disturbance;
largely because the elderly couple had prudently selected a
time which was well after dark, but well before most people
had taken to their beds—in fact, when most people are likely
to be most preoccupied, with one distraction or another.

In no time, Armand came hurtling all the way down again,
nearly doing himself an injury in the feeble light. What he
had to say was that he had quite clearly seen Madame lying
there in the mirror, but no Madame in the room itself.

However, this summary proved possibly erroneous on at
least two counts. The figure seen in the mirror proved, upon
Armand's cross-examination by his adoring aunt and all the
community, to be not Madame at all but Mademoiselle perhaps, and therefore beside the present point. And Madame
was in the room herself, though as to what had happened to
her, the pathologist ultimately declined to make a declaration.
The press thought it might have been rats, and it was mainly
that hypothesis which caused the scandal, such as it was.

Joseph Payne Brennan's "Slime" and "Green Parrot"
are two of my favorite horror stories. Mr. Brennan's work
has appeared in Weird Tales, Alfred Hitchcock's Mystery
Magazine, Magazine of Horror, Macabre, *and, of course,*
Whispers. *"The Willow Platform" closed out* Whispers #1
and has since appeared in a British Best-of-Year anthol-
ogy. It is a Lovecraftian tale of forbidden books and
dimensions best left unopened . . .

THE WILLOW PLATFORM
by Joseph Payne Brennan

Thirty years ago Juniper Hill was an isolated township, with a
small village, dirt roads and high hilly tracts of evergreen
forest—pine, hemlock, tamarack and spruce. Scattered along
the fringes of wood were boulder-strewn pastures, hay fields
and glacially formed, lichen-covered knolls.

Ordinarily I stayed in Juniper Hill from early June until late
September. As I returned year after year, I came to be
accepted almost as a native—many notches above the few
transient "summer people" who stayed for a month or so and
then hurried back to the world of traffic, tension and tedium.

I wrote when I felt like it. The rest of the time I walked the
dirt roads, explored the woods and chatted with the natives.

Within a few years I got to know everyone in town, with

the exception of a hermit or two and one irascible landowner who refused to converse even with his own neighbors.

To me, however, a certain Henry Crotell was the most intriguing person in Juniper Hill. He was sometimes referred to as "the village idiot," "that loafer," "that good-for-nothing," etc., but I came to believe that these epithets arose more from envy than from conviction.

Somehow, Henry managed to subsist and enjoy life without doing any work—or at least hardly any. At a time when this has become a permanent way of life for several million persons, I must quickly add that Henry did not receive one dime from the township of Juniper Hill, either in cash or goods.

He lived in a one-room shack on stony land which nobody claimed and he fed himself. He fished, hunted, picked berries and raised a few potatoes among the rocks behind his shack. If his hunting included a bit of poaching, nobody seemed to mind.

Since Henry used neither alcohol nor tobacco, his needs were minimal. Occasionally, if he needed a new shirt, or shoes, he would split wood, dig potatoes or fill in as an extra hay-field hand for a few days. He established a standard charge which never varied: one dollar a day plus meals. He would never accept any more cash. You might prevail upon him to take along a sack of turnips, but if you handed him a dollar and a quarter for the day, he'd smilingly return the quarter.

Henry was in his early thirties, slab-sided, snuff-brown, with a quick loose grin and rather inscrutable, faded-looking blue eyes. His ginger-colored hair was getting a trifle thin. When he smiled, strangers assumed he was wearing false teeth because his own were so white and even. I once asked him how often he brushed his teeth. He doubled up with silent laughter. "Nary brush! Nary toothpaste!" I didn't press the point, but I often wondered what his secret was—if he had one.

Henry should have lived out his quiet days at Juniper Hill and died at ninety on the cot in his shack. But it was not to be.

Henry found the book.

Four or five miles from Henry's shack lay the crumbling ruins of the old Trobish house. It was little more than a cellar hole filled with rotted boards and fallen beams. Lilac bushes had forced their roots between the old foundation stones; maple saplings filled the dooryard. Old Hannibal Trobish, dead for fifty years, had been an eccentric hermit who drove off intruders with a shotgun. When he died, leaving no heirs and owing ten years' taxes, the town had taken over the property. But the town had no need for it, nor use for it, and so the house had been allowed to decay until finally the whole structure, board by board, had dropped away into the cellar hole. There were hundreds of such collapsed and neglected houses throughout New England. Nobody paid much attention to them.

Henry Crotell, however, seemed fascinated by the moldering remains of the Trobish house. He prowled the area, poked about in the cellar hole and even lifted out some of the mildewed beams. Once, reaching in among the sagging foundation stones, he was nearly bitten by a copperhead.

Old Dave Baines admonished Henry when he heard about it. "That's an omen, Henry! You'd better stay away from that cellar hole!"

Henry pushed out his upper lip and looked at his shoes. "Ain't 'fraid of no old snake! Seen bigger. Last summer I rec'lect. Big tom rattler twice as big!"

Not long after the copperhead incident, Henry found the book. It was contained in a small battered tin box which was jammed far in between two of the foundation stones in the Trobish cellar.

It was a small, vellum-bound book, measuring about four by six inches. The title page and table of contents page had either disintegrated or been removed, and mold was working on the rest of the papers, but it was still possible to read most of the print—that is, if you knew Latin.

Henry didn't, of course, but, no matter, he was entranced by his find. He carried the book everywhere. Sometimes you'd see him sitting in the spruce woods, frowning over the volume, baffled but still intrigued.

We underestimated Henry. He was determined to read the book. Eventually he prevailed upon Miss Winnie, the local teacher, to lend him a second-hand Latin grammar and vocabulary.

Since Henry's formal schooling had been limited to two or three years, and since his knowledge of English was, at best, rudimentary, it must have been a fearful task for him to tackle Latin.

But he persisted. Whenever he wasn't prowling the woods, fishing, or filling in for an ailing hired hand, he'd sit puzzling over his find. He'd trace out the Latin words with one finger, frown, shake his head and pick up the textbook. Then, stubbornly, he'd go back to the vellum-bound volume again.

He ran into many snags. Finally he returned to Miss Winnie with a formidable list of words and names which he couldn't find in the grammar.

Miss Winnie did the best she could with the list. Shortly afterwards she went to see Dave Baines. Although, in his later years, Baines held no official position, he was the patriarch of the town. Nearly everyone went to him for counsel and advice.

Not long after Miss Winnie's visit, he stopped in to see me. After sipping a little wine, he came to the point.

"I wish," he said abruptly, "you'd try to get that damned book away from Henry."

I looked up with surprise. "Why should I, Dave? It keeps him amused apparently."

Baines removed his steel-rimmed spectacles and rubbed his eyes. "That list Henry brought Miss Winnie contains some very strange words—including the names of at least four different devils. And several names which must refer to—entities—maybe worse than devils!"

I poured more wine. "I'll see what I can do. But I really can't imagine what harm could come of it. That book is just a new toy to Henry. He'll tire of it eventually."

Dave replaced his spectacles. "Well, maybe. But the other day Giles Cowdry heard his funny high-pitched voice coming out of the woods. Said it gave him the creeps. He slipped into investigate and there was Henry standing in a clearing among the pines reading out of that moldy book. I suppose his Latin pronunciation was pretty terrible, but Giles said a strange feeling came over him as Henry went on reading. He backed away and I guess he was glad enough to get out of earshot."

I promised Dave I'd see what I could do. About a week later while I was taking a walk through the woods in the vicinity of Henry's shack I heard a kind of chant emanating from nearby.

Pushing through a stand of pines, I spotted Henry standing

in a small open area among the trees. He held a book in one hand and mouthed a kind of gibberish which, to me at least, only faintly resembled Latin.

Unobtrusively, I edged into sight. A fallen branch cracked as I stepped on it and Henry looked up.

He stopped reading immediately.

I nodded. "Mornin', Henry. Just taking a stroll and I couldn't help hearing you. Must be a mighty interesting little book you've got there. Can I take a look at it?"

Ordinarily, Henry would greet me with an easy grin. This time he scowled. "Ain't givin' my book to nobody!" he exclaimed, stuffing the volume into a pocket.

I was annoyed and I suppose I showed it. "I didn't ask to *keep* the book, Henry. I merely wanted to look at it." Actually this wasn't entirely true; I had hoped to persuade him to give me the book.

He shrugged, hesitated and then, turning, started off through the woods. "I got chores. No time for talk," he muttered over his shoulder.

The next day I reported my failure to Dave Baines.

"Too bad," he commented, "but I suppose we'd better just forget about it. If he won't give that infernal book to you, he won't give it to anybody. Let's just hope he loses interest in it after a time."

But Henry didn't lose interest in the vellum-bound book. On the contrary, he developed an obsession about it. He went hunting or fishing only when driven by acute hunger. He neglected his potato patch. His shack, never very sturdy, began to disintegrate.

Less often during the day now, but more often at night, his high-pitched voice would be heard arising from one of the dense groves of pines or hemlocks which bordered the dusty country roads. Scarcely anyone in Juniper Hills knew Latin, but everyone who heard Henry's chant drifting from the dark woods agreed that it was an eerie and disturbing experience. One farmer's wife averred that Henry's nocturnal readings had given her nightmares.

Somebody asked how Henry could see to read in the dark, since nobody ever had seen a light in the woods from whence the sounds emanated.

It was, as is said, "a good question." We never found out for sure. It was possible that Henry had finally memorized the contents of the book, or part of it. This, however, I personally found difficult to believe.

Henry's explanation, when it came, was even more difficult to accept.

One hot summer morning he turned up at the village general store. He looked emaciated and his clothes were in tatters, but he seemed imbued with a kind of suppressed animation. Perhaps exhilaration might be the better word.

He bought a two-dollar work shirt and three tins of corned beef. He did not appear chagrined that these purchases very obviously emptied his tattered wallet.

Loungers at the store noticed that he was wearing a ring. Some commented on it.

Surprisingly, Henry held it out for inspection. He was visibly proud of it. Everyone agreed later that they had never seen a ring like it before. The band might have been shaped out of silver, but worked into it were tiny veins of blue which appeared to glow faintly. The stone was disappointing: black, flat-cut and dull in luster.

Unusually voluble, Henry volunteered some information on the stone. "Ain't no good in daylight. Nighttime it comes alive. Throws out light, it do!"

He gathered up his purchases and started for the door. He paused at the threshold, chuckling, and turned his head. "Light a-plenty," he added, " 'nuff light to read by!"

Still chuckling to himself, he walked out into the hot sunlight and off down the road.

The only other information we received about the ring came from Walter Frawley, the town constable, who met Henry in the woods one day. Frawley reported that he had asked Henry where he had acquired the ring.

Henry insisted that he found it, purely by chance, tangled up among the roots of a huge pine tree which formerly grew near the ruins of the old Trobish house. The great pine had toppled in a severe windstorm several years before. Natives estimated the tree was at least one hundred years old.

Nobody could satisfactorily explain how the ring had become entangled in the roots of a century-old pine tree. It was possible, of course, that old Hannibal Trobish had buried it there many decades ago—either to hide it, or to get rid of it.

As the hot summer advanced, Henry went on chanting in the woods at night, giving late travellers "a case of the nerves'' and causing some of the farm watch dogs to howl dismally.

One day I met Miss Winnie in the village and asked for her opinion of Henry's book, based on the list of words and names which he had brought to her for translation or clarification.

"The book is medieval in origin," she told me. "And I think it was written by someone who pretended to be a wizard or sorcerer. Poor Henry is out there in the woods at night chanting invocations to nonexistent devils dreamed up by some medieval charlatan who was quite possibly burned at the stake!"

I frowned. "Why do you say 'nonexistent devils,' Miss Winnie?"

"I don't *believe* in such things," she replied a bit stiffly. "I went to Dave Baines about the book because I thought it was having a bad effect on Henry. Heaven knows I'd be delighted if he learned Latin, but I don't think he's going about it properly. And he's neglecting everything. People tell me his little hut is falling apart and that he doesn't eat anymore."

I thanked her and went my way, even more concerned than I had been before, but totally unable to see how I could help. I felt that Henry still liked me, but I knew his stubbornness was monumental.

Not long after my talk with Miss Winnie, I heard rumors that Henry was building some kind of stage or platform on a small knoll adjacent to one of the deeper stands of hemlock. The knoll was about a mile from one of the less-traveled country roads. It was quite high, almost level with the tops of the hemlocks. I had been on it a few times and recalled that on a clear day it overlooked a huge expanse of forest and field.

One afternoon when the summer heat had subsided somewhat, I went to have a look at Henry's platform. After nearly becoming lost in the dark hemlock woods, I slipped into the sunlight and climbed the side of the knoll, a small hill made up of glacial stones and gravel.

It was barren except for a few stunted shrubs, ground creepers and dried lichen patches. Centered on the exact top was a twenty-foot structure built primarily out of willow saplings. A few stakes of heavier wood had been driven in around the base to strengthen the whole. The top of the bizarre lookout tapered to a tiny wooden platform, just large enough for one person. A crude hand-ladder had been attached to one side and a kind of rail ran around the perimeter of the platform.

It was, altogether, shaky and perilous-looking. Henry was no heavyweight, and he would probably survive a twenty-foot drop onto the slippery side of a knoll, but I felt, nevertheless, that he was risking serious injury.

I circled the little structure and sat down nearby for a time, but Henry did not appear. At length, as the afternoon sun beat down on the knoll, I got up and made my way uneventfully through the hemlocks and back to the road.

Dave Baines shook his head when he learned of the willow platform. "That Latin book is drivin' Henry loco. I expect he'll fall off that thing, break a leg, or maybe his spine, and end up in the county hospital."

I suggested condemning the willow tower since it was obviously hazardous and was, moreover, built on land to which Henry had no title.

Dave shrugged. "What good would it do? He'd be madder than a hundred wet hens, and he'd likely just go out and rig up another somewhere else."

I let it go at that. I wasn't a native of the town and I certainly wasn't going to spearhead any "movement" to demolish Henry's willow platform.

Not long after my talk with Dave, the stories started circulating. At night, it was rumored, Henry's chanting could be heard all over town. It was becoming louder all the time.

Frank Kenmore came in with a story about Henry screeching from the top of the willow tower while it swayed wildly in the wind and "tongues of fire" floated over the hemlock trees.

John Pendle complained that his old mare had bolted and thrown him from his buggy into the ditch one night when Henry started his "crazy yellin'."

Young Charlie Foxmire swore that he had crept through the woods at midnight and seen Henry on his tower "laughin'" like a madman and talkin' to somebody in the trees."

I determined to find out for myself what actually was taking place. Late one evening I went out to the front veranda and listened. Sure enough, when the wind was right, I could hear Henry's steady chanting.

I turned off my lights and started out for the willow tower.

It was tough going through the hemlocks, but Henry's high-pitched chant kept me on my course. When I reached the knoll, I circled around until I was directly at Henry's back. I advanced only a few feet up the side of the knoll, crouched down and then very cautiously lifted my head.

Henry, book in hand, was standing on the tiny platform. The flimsy structure was swaying slightly in the wind. A bluish glow, whose source I could not at first locate, illuminated the book and part of Henry's face. His chant rose and fell eerily. He kept glancing from the book out over the top of the black hemlock forest, almost as if he were addressing a huge unseen audience which listened among the trees. In spite of the relative warmth of the summer night, I found myself shuddering.

His chant seemed to go on endlessly, as he turned the pages of the book. His voice became stronger as he continued. The wind rose and the platform swayed a little more.

I crouched motionless until my muscles ached, but there was no response from the depths of the hemlock woods. I was shocked when I realized that I had been *waiting* for a response!

I saw clearly at last that the strange blue glow emanated from the ring on Henry's finger. I experienced the weird conviction that the glow strengthened as Henry's chant grew stronger.

At length, the tension, plus the uncomfortable position in which I remained crouched, began to tire me. I had intended to stay until Henry finished his nocturnal incantations, but on second thought I decided to leave before he descended. I was convinced that he would be furious if he found me spying on him when he came down.

Moving carefully, I slipped backwards into the trees. A carpet of hemlock needles, inches deep, effectively muffled my footsteps. I groped my way to the road and walked home. I was too exhausted to assess the full implications of what I had seen. In spite of my fatigue, I did not sleep well. Unpleasant dreams, bordering on nightmare, harried me until morning.

I reported to Dave Baines. He appeared deeply concerned.

"Henry's going to destroy himself—or be destroyed by something, if we don't get him away from there."

I nodded. "That's the way I feel—but what can we do?"

Dave began polishing his spectacles. "I'll think of something."

Three days later as I was returning from the village store early one morning, I met Henry. He was shuffling along dispiritedly. I inquired, casually, where he was heading.

He stopped, eyes on the ground, and began kicking at the dirt road with one foot.

"Dave Baines," he told me, "got me on over ta Miller's place. Extry hay hand. Says they be hard up fer help. Wants me to go—sort of a favor to *him!*"

He shook his head and scowled. "Wouldn't go fer nobody else. Nobody! But Dave done me favors. Lots of favors. So I got to go."

"That's fine, Henry!" I said. "You'll be well fed and earn a few dollars! The almanac's predicting a long winter!"

He looked at me scornfully. "Ain't worried about winter. You know what I think?"

"What's that, Henry?"

He hesitated. "Well, I trust Dave, I reckon. But it could be somebody put him to it—so's they could get in my shack and take my book!"

His faded blue eyes took on an unfamiliar glint. He continued before I could comment.

"It won't do nobody no good! Because I got my book right here!" He tapped his overall pocket. "Right here!" he repeated triumphantly.

I assured him that Dave was undoubtedly acting in good faith and that nobody I knew in Juniper Hills would trespass in his absence.

Somewhat mollified, but still dispirited, he shuffled off. I noticed that he was still wearing his unusual ring with the flat black stone.

Kent Miller's place was at the far northern end of Juniper Hill. And Miller possessed several huge hay fields. If I judged correctly, Henry would not be back for several days.

That evening I decided to pay another visit to Henry's willow platform. As I started through the hemlock woods toward the knoll, I felt a bit like an intruder. But then I reminded myself that the knoll did not belong to Henry. And perhaps I might stumble on some clue which would be the key to Henry's obsession.

The thick hemlock woods were like a dark and aromatic tomb. I reached the knoll with a feeling of relief. At least I was in the open; I could see sky and feel a breeze on my face.

As I glanced up at the willow tower, I almost laughed aloud. How absurd it looked! Poorly constructed, fragile, swaying in the slight wind—how foolish I was to have been so impressed by a country loafer's childish obsession!

I scrambled up the shaky ladder nailed to one side of the tower and cautiously edged out onto the flimsy platform. The moon had not yet risen and there was not much to see—the dark continuing mass of hemlocks, a few fireflies and, far off, the twinkling light in a farmhouse window.

I was both relieved and disappointed. I told myself that I was a fool. What *had* I expected to see?

As I was about to start down the ladder, I thought I heard a faint chant somewhere in the deep distance. It was like an echo, almost inaudible—yet I paused with my hand on the platform railing and listened.

As I waited, it grew stronger, but only by a small degree. I looked out over the hemlocks and frowned. The contour of the woods seemed to have changed; the outlines of the trees seemed different.

I strained my eyes into the darkness, unable to comprehend what I thought I was witnessing. The wind rose, and the chant grew louder.

Henry was returning, I told myself, and I must hurry away before he reached the knoll with his infernal book and the ring that glowed in the dark.

Two things happened then almost simultaneously. As I started to let myself over the side to go down the ladder, I glanced once more toward the black mass of hemlocks. Only they weren't hemlocks. They were immense, towering trees, tropical in outline, which resembled giant ferns against the sky.

And as I stared in amazement and disbelief, a figure faced me on the platform—a figure with distorted features and glittering eyes which looked like an evil caricature of Henry Crotell!

With a rush of horror, I realized that I could see *through* the figure to the night sky beyond.

After a frozen moment of immobility, I went over the side of the platform. I slid partway down the apology for a ladder and fell the rest of the way.

As soon as my feet touched earth, they were racing for the trees. And when I entered them, they were the dark sweet hemlocks which I knew.

I rushed through them, gouging and scratching myself on projecting branches. Henry's chant, somewhat weak but still persistent, followed me.

I could hear it, far off in the night, when I stumbled onto my porch and opened the door.

I sat up for hours drinking coffee and at last fell asleep in my chair. I was slumped there, red-eyed and unshaven, when someone knocked.

I got up with a start, noticing that sunlight was pouring through a nearby window, and opened the door.

Dave Baines looked at me keenly, both abashed and a bit amused. "Sorry I woke you up. I'll come back—"

I shook my head. "No, no! Sit down. You're the very person I want to see!"

He heard me out in silence. After he had polished his glasses for five minutes, he spoke.

"I'm not sure, but I'd be willing to venture the opinion that the figure you saw on the platform was what some folks call an 'astral projection.' Henry's still at the Miller place; I called this morning to find out. One of the field hands came in after midnight and saw him fast asleep—he never would have had time to come down here, rant on that crazy tower of his and walk back again. Henry, consciously or unconsciously, projected part of himself back here to the knoll. A kind of intense wish fulfillment, I guess. Chances are he doesn't even remember it this morning."

I shook my head in disbelief. "But what did I *hear?*"

Dave replaced his spectacles. "You heard his chanting all right, but not with your ears. You heard it inside your head, with your mind only. No reason telepathy, or projection, can't be audible as well as visual. It's all the result of a mind's—or a psyche's—fierce desire to be in another place. The desire is so strong that part of that person—call it 'ecto-plasm' or what you will—actually does return."

"But what about the trees?" I interjected. "What made the wood and the hemlocks change? Why did I seem to be looking out over a great forest of tropical fern trees—or whatever they were?''

Dave got up, rather wearily. "That I can't explain, at least not now." He sighed. "I wish the whole business was over with. I just have a feelin' Henry's going to come a cropper."

Henry did "come a cropper" the very next night. Just before dusk, as we learned later, when the haying crews at Miller's were leaving the fields for supper, Henry, scorning both a meal and the pay due him, slipped over a fence and set out on the main road for Juniper Hill.

It was after eleven, and I was about to get ready for bed, when Henry's familiar chant, clear and strong, came to me on the night breeze.

I told myself that he had "projected" himself again and that only an ectoplasmic caricature of him was chanting on the willow platform.

But I could not convince myself that such was the case. His voice was too high-pitched and powerful. There was none of the weak, tentative quality of the night before.

I set out for the knoll with my misgivings. I suppose I felt a kind of obligation to see the business through. Perhaps a sense of responsibility moved me. In addition, I will admit to a degree of curiosity.

As I started through the hemlock woods, however, I experienced a feeling of acute apprehension. Henry's garbled chant, this night, was louder than I had ever heard it before. It flooded the wood. And I detected in his voice an edge of excitement bordering on hysteria.

I reached the knoll without incident and paused within the shadows cast by the surrounding hemlocks. Something seemed to warn me to keep well out of sight.

Henry, book in hand, stood on the willow platform, chanting rapidly in a shrill voice. His ring glowed more brightly than ever, bathing the book and his own face in an eerie blue light. There was a moderate wind; the tower swayed gently from side to side.

I studied the figure on the platform carefully; there was no doubt in my mind that it was Henry in the flesh. What I saw was not the projection, or apparition, of the previous night.

As he moved his head to read from the book, or to look over the black expanse of the hemlock woods, I noticed that his expression mirrored intense agitation and expectancy.

His chant rose and fell in the night, and again I sensed a frightening transformation in the contour and general appearance of the surrounding forest. Massive trees which did not resemble hemlocks seemed to loom against the darkened sky.

Once again I felt that a vast unseen audience waited among these alien trees—and that Henry was aware of their presence.

His chant swiftly became an incoherent shriek. His eyes appeared to protrude from his head; his face became so contorted it was scarcely recognizable.

I quickly became convinced that while formerly he was chanting to invoke someone or something—he was suddenly chanting frantically in an attempt to forestall the advent of whatever he had been trying to conjure.

Too late. The thing came slowly prancing and gliding over the tops of the huge fern-like trees. It was black even against the darkness of the night sky, but it seemed to contain within itself a kind of lambent flame. An aura of cold blue fire flickered about it.

If it had a definite shape, that shape was not easily apparent, because it continually flowed in upon itself, contorting and writhing in a manner which I found intensely repellent.

In size, it was enormous. If you can imagine a team of six or eight black horses, somehow joined together and all attempting to gallop off in different directions at once, you might have some faint conception of the appalling thing's appearance.

Henry saw it. His shrill chanting ceased and his mouth fell open. He was frozen into immobility. His face became wooden. Only his eyes remained alive—two bulging points of blue light which glazed with ultimate horror even before the monstrous entity came over the knoll.

I wanted desperately to intervene, but I was nearly as terrified as poor Henry. And I sensed that, in any case, I would be completely helpless if I did attempt to interfere.

Deliberately and inexorably, the prancing nightmare made for the knoll. Once overhead, it paused. The blue fires which animated it intensified.

It descended slowly, straight for Henry. It seemed to tread on air, very carefully, as it came down above him. I could detect neither eyes nor mouth in the fearful creature, but I knew that it must be equipped with a sensory apparatus—quite probably superior to my own.

Its convulsions almost ceased as it dropped toward the willow platform. When it was within a few feet of that upward-staring white face, its legs—or whatever kind of appendages they were—snaked down and wrapped themselves tightly around the doomed man.

At last he was able to scream. His shriek of agony transfixed me. It was heard all over the township of Juniper Hill—and beyond. It would be useless for me to attempt to convey the torment and terror which that cry contained. I cannot. The writhing thing ascended slowly. As it rose, Henry almost disappeared within the hideous seething tangle of the creature. But as it glided off, away from the knoll, out over the tops of those enormous trees, that terrible shriek rang on and on.

The fearful intruder, flickering with fire, finally vanished in the night, its progress marked by a tiny bit of blue flame.

I have no recollection of how I groped my way out of the woods and reached home. When Dave Baines stopped in the next morning, I was still sitting in the chair, staring at the wall. He told me later that he feared I was in shock.

At length, however, I was able to relate the events I had witnessed just a few hours before.

Dave listened without comment, interrupting only once to tell me that Henry's final scream had awakened people all over the town.

I finished weakly, grateful for the flask of whiskey which Dave had produced.

He removed his glasses and polished them very carefully. "We'll never see Henry alive again—and maybe not dead either!"

I set down my glass. "But, Dave, what *was* it? I was sober and in my right mind—and yet my brain refuses to accept what it tells me I saw."

Dave helped himself to the whiskey. "Henry was tampering with malign forces, entities which probably existed when the earth was young. Nature, you know, was an experimenter with many life forms—and not all of those life forms were necessarily on the physical plane, or at least not as we know it. Some of them probably existed and passed away, and the tenuous elements of which they were composed left no traces—certainly nothing like heavy skulls and body bones which could survive physically for millions of years.

"I think Henry summoned up, as it were, an early form which we now vaguely refer to as an 'elemental.' In a sense, it still exists—but in another time, you might say another dimension. From what you've described, it was quite probably looked on as a god to be worshipped by earlier inhabitants of this planet. What those inhabitants were—or who they were—I can't say. Perhaps the present location of the knoll and the hemlock wood was the place of worship. And quite possibly those early worshippers offered up sacrifices to the thing which they venerated and feared."

Dave shook his head. "I don't know—it's speculation. But that's all that I can offer. I believe that old Hannibal Trobish was somehow involved in the business. I think both that Latin book and Henry's ring belonged to him. He may have invoked that damnable entity and survived. Probably he knew how to keep out of its clutches once it appeared. Poor Henry learned just enough Latin to chant those incantations and summon up the thing, but, obviously, he had no idea how to escape it, or dismiss it, once it was evoked.

"That ring *may* have been a protective talisman. But chances are the ring itself was of no help unless the intruder was placated or its powers nullified by various sacrifices and/or specific formulas. I imagine these formulas were contained somewhere in the book, but that Henry had not learned enough Latin to avail himself of them.

"The great fern-tree forest you thought you saw—well, I don't know. It may have been a sort of telepathic image projected from the past—possibly, even, from the organ which served that creature as a brain. Even if the thing existed in another plane or time continuum, Henry's chants undoubtedly enabled it to slip through—temporarily at least—to the present."

Old Dave got up and moved toward the door. "If you'd ever lived in the far north—as I did at one time—you'd know the legend of the wendigo. A lot of people today think it is sheer nonsense. But they haven't sat around a campfire at midnight and heard the best guide in Canada swear by all the saints that he had glimpsed such a thing! I don't say that Henry's nightmare, necessarily, was just that—but it appears to have been a related entity."

A week later, in a cornfield more than twenty miles from the northern edge of the township of Juniper Hill, a farmer found a bundle of bones which appeared to have passed through a blast furnace. The bones were burned to the marrow. The ghastly skeleton might have remained forever unidentifiable save for one thing—on the brittle finger bone of one hand a peculiar-looking ring was found. In spite of the condition of the skeleton, the ring was undamaged by the fire. The shining band was shaped out of a metal which resembled silver, fretted with tiny veins of blue which glowed faintly. The ring's stone was black, flat-cut and dull in luster.

The burned remains of Henry Crotell were borne back to Juniper Hill and buried. The ring was left on the finger bone.

A few weeks later, on orders of Dave Baines, the cellar hole of the old Trobish house was filled in and leveled off.

The willow tower went down under high winds during the winter. In the spring, as improved highways were planned in Juniper Hill, a track was cut through the hemlock woods and the entire knoll which held the willow platform was bulldozed away in order to secure its stone and gravel for the new roadbeds.

The Latin book which led Henry to his doom was never located. I think it safe to assume that it was reduced to ashes by the same terrible fire which consumed him.

*Manly Wade Wellman's nonfiction has earned him a Pu-
litzer Prize nomination and his fantasy work a World
Fantasy Award. His tales of John, the wandering ballad
singer of the Southern mountains, were collected by Arkham House under the title of* Who Fears the Devil *(which
served as a basis for a movie that did not succeed in
capturing the flavor and meaning of Manly's John). Others of his stories have seen translation to television on
such shows as "Twilight Zone" and "Night Gallery."
Manly's fiction deals with authentic folklore and the real
people from our Southern mountain heritage. He, as he is
wont to say, was invited to the firesides and tables of these
people and from them learned their ways and legends.
They are a noble people and Manly always gives them a
place of honor in his tales, one they had earned. This story
is based on authentic legend of the Cherokee Indians. The
books mentioned really exist and are, to the author's
knowledge, the only published considerations of the Dakwa,
until this tale . . .*

THE DAKWA
by Manly Wade Wellman

Night had fallen two hours ago in these mountains, but Lee
Cobbett remembered the trail up from Markum's Fork over
Dogged Mountain and beyond. Too, he had the full moon and

208

a blazing skyful of stars to help him. Finally he reached the place where Long Soak Hollow had been, where now lay a broad stretch of water among the heights, water struck to quivering radiance by the moonlight.

Shaggy trees made the last of the trail dark and uneasy under his boot soles. He half-groped his way to the grassy brink and looked across to something he recognized. On an island that once had been the top of a broad rise in the hollow stood a square cabin in a tuft of trees. Light from the open door beat upon a raftlike dock and a boat tied up there.

Dropping his pack and bedroll, Cobbett cupped his big hands into a trumpet at his mouth.

"Hello!" he shouted. "Hello, the house, hello, Mr. Luns Lamar, I'm here! Come over and get me!"

A shadow slid into the doorway. A man tramped down to where that dock was visible. He held a lantern high.

"Who's that a-bellowing?" came back a call across the water.

"Lee Cobbett—come get me!"

"No, sir," echoed to his ears. "Can't do it tonight."

"But—"

"Not tonight!" The words were sharp, they meant that thing. "No way. You wait there for me till sunup."

The figure plodded back to the doorway and sat down on the threshold with the lantern beside it.

Cobbett cursed to himself, there on the night shore. He was a blocky man in denim jacket and slacks, with a square, seamed face and a mane of dark hair. Scowling, he estimated the distance across. Fifty yards? Not much more than that. If Luns Lamar wouldn't come, Lee Cobbett would go.

He put the pack and roll together next to a laurel bush and sat on them to drag off his boots and socks. He stripped away slacks, jacket, blue shirt, underwear, and stood up naked. Walking to the edge of the lake, he tested it with his toe. Chill, like most mountain water. He set his whole foot in, found bottom, and waded forward to his knees. Two more steps, and he was waist deep. He shivered as he moved out along the clay bottom until he could wade no longer. He struck out for the light of the cabin door.

The coldness of the water bit him, and he swam more strongly to fight against it. Music seemed to be playing somewhere, a song he had never heard, like a muted woodwind. A hum in his head—no, it came from somewhere away from the cabin and the island, somewhere on the moonbright water. It grew stronger, more audible.

On he swam with powerful strokes. His body glided swiftly, but a current sprang up around him, more of a current than he had thought possible. And the melody heightened in his ears, still nothing he could remember, but tuneful, haunting.

Then a sudden shuddering impact, a blow like a club against his side and shoulder.

He almost whirled under. He kicked at whatever it was, shouting aloud as he did so. Next moment he was at the poles that supported the dock, grabbing at them with both hands. Luns Lamar stooped above him and caught his thick wrists.

"You damned fool," grumbled Lamar, heaving away.

Cobbett scrambled up on the split slabs, kneeling.

"Whatever in hell made you swim over here?" Lamar scolded him.

"What else was there for me to do?" Cobbett found breath to say. "You said you wouldn't come and fetch me, even when you'd written that letter wanting me to bring you those books. I don't know why I should have moped over there until tomorrow, not when I can swim."

"I wouldn't go out on this lake tonight, even in the boat." Lamar helped Cobbett to his feet. "Hey, you're scraped. Bleeding."

It was true. Cobbett's sinewy shoulder looked red and raw.

"There's a log or snag right out from the dock," he said, heading for the cabin's open door.

"No," said Lamar. "That wasn't any log or snag."

They went inside together. The front half of the cabin was a single room, raftered overhead. Cobbett knew its rawhide-seated chairs, the plank table, the oil stove, tall shelves of books, a fireplace with a strew of winking coals and a glowing kerosene lamp on the mantel board. Against the wall, an ancient army cot with brown blankets. In a rear corner, a tool chest, and upon that a scuffed banjo case. Lamar brought him a big, frayed towel. Cobbett winced as he rubbed himself down.

"That's a real rough raking you got," said Lamar, peering.

He, too, was known to Cobbett, old and small but sure of movement, with spectacles closely set on his shrewd face. He wore a dark blue pullover, khaki pants, and scuffed house slippers.

"We'd better do something about that," he said and went to a shelf by the stove. He took down a big, square bottle and worried out the cork, then came back. "Just hold still."

He filled his palm with dark, oily liquid from the bottle and spread it over the torn skin of Cobbett's ribs and shoulder.

"What's in that stuff?" Cobbett asked.

"There's some sap of three different trees in it," replied Lamar. "And boiled tea of three different flowers, and some crushed seeds, and the juice of what some folks call a weed, but the Indians used to prize it."

He brought an old blue bathrobe with GOLDEN GLOVES in faded yellow letters across the back. "Put this on till we can go over tomorrow and get your clothes," he said.

"Thanks." Cobbett drew the robe around him and sat down in the chair. "Now," he said, "if that wasn't a log or snag, what was it?"

Lamar wiped his spectacles. "You won't believe it."

"Not without hearing it."

"I asked you to fetch me some books," Lamar reminded.

"Mooney's study for the Bureau of Anthology, *Myths of the Cherokee*," said Cobbett. "And Skinner's *Myths and Legends of Our Own Land*. And *The Kingdom of Madison*. All right, they're over yonder in my pack. If you hadn't flooded Long Soak Hollow, I could have brought them right into his cabin without even wetting my feet. If you'd come with the boat, they'd be here now. Why don't you get to telling me what this is all about?"

Lamar studied him. "Lee, did you ever hear about the Dakwa?"

"Dakwa," Cobbett said after him. "Sounds like Dracula."

"It's not Dracula, but it happens to be terrible in its own way. It's what rubbed up against you while you were out there swimming." Lamar scowled. "Look here, let's have a drink. I reckon maybe we both need one."

He sought the shelf again and opened a fruit jar of clear, white liquid and poured generous portions into two glasses. "This is good blockade whiskey," he said, handing a glass to Cobbett. The liquid tingled sharply on Cobbett's tongue and warmed him all the way down.

Lamar sipped in turn. "It's hard to explain, even though we've known each other nearly all our lives."

"You've known me nearly all my life," said Cobbett, "but I haven't known you nearly all yours. I've heard that you studied law, then you taught in a country school, then you edited a little weekly paper. After that, I don't know why, you quit everything and built this cabin. You don't ever come out of it except to listen to mountain songs and mountain tales, and sometimes you write about them for folklore journals." Cobbett studied his friend. "Why not start by telling me what you've done, drowning Long Soak Hollow like this?"

"It wasn't my doing," growled Lamar. "Some resort company did it, to make a lake amongst the summer cottages they're building for visitors. You remember how this place of mine was set—high above the little creek down in the hollow, safe from any flood. I wouldn't sell out, but that company bought up all the land round about and put in a dam, and here it is, filled in. I'm like Robinson Crusoe on my island, but I'm not studying to go ashore till tomorrow."

Cobbett drank again. "Because of what?"

"Because of one of those same old tales that makes a noise like the truth." Lamar showed his gold-wried teeth. "The Dakwa," he said again. "It's in those books I asked you to fetch along with you."

"And I said they're across the water that scares you," said Cobbett. "What," he asked patiently, "is the Dakwa?"

"It's what tried to grab you just now," Lamar flung out. "It used to be penned up in the little creek they called Long Soak, penned up there for centuries. And now, by God, it's out again in this lake they've damned up, a-looking for what it may devour." His face clamped desperately. "Devour it whole," he said.

"You say it's out again," said Cobbett. "What do you mean by again? How long has this been going on?"

"Centuries, I told you," said Lamar. "The tale was here with the Cherokee Indians when the first settlers came, before the Revolutionary War. And the Dakwa's hungry. Two men and a boy—Del Hungant and Steve Biggins and a teenager from somewhere in the lowlands named McIlhenny—they just sort of went out of sight along this new lake. Folks came up from town and dragged for them, and nothing whatever dragged up.''

"Not even the Dakwa," suggested Cobbett.

"Especially not the Dakwa. It's too smart to be hooked.''

"And you believe in it," said Cobbett.

"Sure enough I believe in it. I've seen it again and again, just an ugly hunch of it in the water out there. I've heard it humming.''

"So that's what I heard," said Cobbett.

"Yes, that's what. And once, the last time I've ever been out in the boat at night, it shoved against the boat and damn near turned it over with me. You'd better believe in it yourself, the way it rasped your skin like that.''

Cobbett went over to the bookshelf and studied the titles. He took down Thompson's *Mysteries and Secrets of Magic* and leafed through the index pages.

"You won't read about it in there," Lamar told him sourly. "That's only about old-world witches and devils, with amulets and charms against them, and all the names of God to defeat them. The Dakwa doesn't believe in God. It's an Indian thing—Cherokee. Something else has to go to work against it. That's why I wanted those books, hoping to find something in them. They're the only published notices of the Dakwa.''

Cobbett slid Thompson's volume back into place and went to the door and opened it.

"You fixing to do something foolish?" grumbled Lamar.

"No, nothing foolish if I can help it," Cobbett assured him. "I just thought I'd go and look at the stars before bedtime.''

He stepped across the threshold log into grass. Dew splashed his bare feet. He paced to the dock and gazed up at the moon, a great pallid blotch of radiance. Gazing, he heard something again.

Music, that was all it could be. Perhaps it had words, but words so soft that they were like a faint memory.

Out upon the dock he stepped. Ripples broke against its supporting poles. Something made a dark rush in the water, close up almost to the boat. Whatever it was glinted shinily beneath the surface. Cobbett stared down at it, trying to make out its shape. It vanished. He turned and paced back to the cabin door, that faint sense of the music still around him.

"All right, what did you find out there?" Lamar demanded.

"Nothing to speak of," said Cobbett. "Now then, I had a long uphill trudge getting here. How about showing me where I'll sleep?"

"Over yonder, as usual." Lamar nodded toward the cot.

"And we'll get up early tomorrow morning and go get my gear and those books of yours."

"Not until the sun's up," insisted Lamar.

"Okay," grinned Cobbett. "Not until the sun's up."

When Cobbett woke, Lamar was at the oil stove, cooking breakfast. Cobbett got into the robe, washed his face and hands and teeth and unclasped the banjo case. He took out Lamar's old banjo, tuned it briefly and softly began to pick a tune, the tune he had heard the night before.

"You cut that right out!" Lamar yelled at him. "You want to call that thing out of the water, right up to the door?"

Cobbett put the banjo away and came to the table. Breakfast was hearty and good—flapjacks drenched in molasses, eggs and home-cured bacon, and black coffee so strong you'd expect a hatchet to float in it. Cobbett had two helpings of everything. Afterward, he washed the dishes while Lamar wiped.

"And now the sun's up," Cobbett said, peering at it through the window. "It's above those trees on the mountain. What do you say we get me back into my clothes?"

Wearing the GOLDEN GLOVES bathrobe, he walked out to the dock with Lamar. He had his first good look at the boat. It was well made of calked planks, canoe style, pointed fore and aft, with two seats and two paddles. It was painted a deep brown.

"I built that thing," said Lamar. "Built it when they started in to fill up the hollow. Can you paddle? Bow or stern?"

"Let me take stern."

Getting in, they pushed off. Lamar, dipping his paddle, gazed at something far out toward the middle of the lake. Cobbett gazed too. Whatever it was hung there on the water, something dark and domed. It might have been a sort of head. As Cobbett looked, the thing slipped under water. The light of the rising sun twinkled on a bit of foam.

Lamar's mouth opened as if to speak, but closed again on

silence. A score of determined strokes took them across to a shallow place. Cobbett hopped ashore, picked up his clothes and pack and blanket roll, and came back to stow everything in the waist of the boat. Around they swung and headed back toward the island. Out there across the gentle stir of the water's surface, the dark, domed object was visible again.

"Whatever it is, it's watching us," ventured Cobbett. "It doesn't seem to want to come close."

"That's because there's a couple of us," grunted Lamar, paddling. "I don't expect it would tackle two people at a time, by daylight."

That seemed to put a stop to the conversation. They nosed in against the dock. Tying up, Lamar helped Cobbett carry his things into the cabin. Cobbett rummaged in the pack.

"All right, here are those books of yours," he said. "Now I'll get dressed."

While he did so, Lamar leafed through Mooney's book about Cherokee myths.

"Sure enough, here we are," he said. "Dakwa—it's a water spirit, and it used to drag Cherokee hunters down and eat them. It's said to have been in several streams."

"Including Long Soak," supplied Cobbett.

"Mooney doesn't mention Long Soak but, yes, here too." Lamar turned pages. "It's still here, and well you know that's a fact." He took up two smaller volumes. "Now, look in this number two book of Skinner's *Myths and Legends of Our Own Land*. Hmmm," he crooned.

"More Dakwa?" asked Cobbett, picking up the other book he had brought.

"Skinner titles it, 'The Siren of the French Broad.' This time it's not as grotesque as in Mooney. It's supposed to be a beautiful naked woman rising up to sing to you. So, if you're a red-blooded American he-man, you stoop close to see and hear better and it quits being beautiful, it suddenly has a skull and two bony arms to drag you down." He snapped the book shut. "I judge the white settlers prettied the tale up to sound like the Lorelei. But not much in any of these books to tell how to fight it. What are you reading there in *The Kingdom of Madison?*"

"I'm looking at page thirteen, which I hope isn't unlucky," replied Cobbett. "Here's what it says about a deep place on the French Broad River: 'There, the Cherokees said, lurked the *dakwa*, the gigantic fish-monster that caught men at the riverside and dragged them down, swallowed them whole.' And it has that other account, too: 'The story would seem to inspire another fable, this time of a lovely water-nymph, who smiled to lure the unwary wanderer, reached up her arms to him, and dragged him down to be seen no more.' ''

"Not much help, either. That's about what Mooney and Skinner say, and it's no fable, no legend.'' Lamar studied his guest. "How do you feel today, after that gouging it gave you in the water last night?''

"I feel fine.'' Cobbett buttoned up his shirt. "Completely healed. It didn't hurt me too much for you to cure me.''

"Maybe if it had been able to get you into its mouth, swallow you up—''

"Didn't you say that was an old Indian preparation you sloshed on me?''

"It's something I got from a Cherokee medicine man,'' said Lamar. "A valued old friend of mine. He has a degree in philosophy from the University of North Carolina, but he worships his people's old gods, is afraid of their evil spirits, carries out their old formulas and rituals, and I admire him for it.''

"So do I,'' said Cobbett. "But you mentioned certain plants in the mixture.''

"Well, for the most part there were smashed-up seeds of viper's bugloss and some juice of campion, what the country folks call rattlesnake plant.''

Both of those growths had snake names to them, reflected Cobbett. "I think you might have mentioned to me why you wanted these books,'' he said.

"Why mention it?'' groaned Lamar, adjusting his spectacles. "You wouldn't have believed me then. Anyway, I don't see how this extra information will help. It doesn't do more than prove things, more or less. Well, I've got errands to do.''

He walked out to the dock. Cobbett followed him.

"I'm paddling across and going down the trail to meet old Snave Dalbom,'' Lamar announced. "This is his day to drive down to the county seat to wag back a week's supplies. He lets me go with him to do my shopping.''

He got into the boat and began to cast off.

"Let me paddle you over," offered Cobbett, but Lamar shook his head violently.

"I'll paddle myself over and tie up the boat yonder," he declared. "I'm not a-going to have you out on this lake, maybe getting yourself yanked overboard and down there where they can't drag for you, like those three others who never came up."

"How do you know I won't go swimming?" Cobbett teased him.

"Because I don't reckon your mother raised any such fool. Listen, just sit around here and take it easy. Snave and I will probably get a bite in town, so fix your own noon dinner and look for me back sometime before sundown. There's some pretty good canned stuff in the house—help yourself. And maybe you can read the whole tariff on the Dakwa, figure out something to help us. But I'm leaving you here so you'll stay here."

He shoved out from the dock and paddled for the shore opposite.

Cobbett strolled back to the cabin, and around it. Clumps of cedar brush stood at the corner, and locusts hung above the old tin roof. The island itself was perhaps an acre in extent, with cleared ground behind the cabin. A well had been dug there. Lamar's well-kept garden showed two rows of bright green cornstalks, the tops of potatoes and tomatoes and onions. Cobbett inspected the corn. At noon he might pick a couple of ears and boil them to eat with butter and salt and pepper. On the far side of the garden was the shore of the island, dropping abruptly to the water. Kneeling, Cobbett peered. He could see that the bottom was far down there, a depth of many feet. Below the clear surface he saw a shadowy patch, a drowned tree that once had grown there, that had been overwhelmed by the lake.

That crooning music, or the sense of it, seemed to hang over the gentle ripples.

He returned to the cabin and sat down with Mooney's book. The index gave him several page references to the Dakwa and he looked them up, one by one. The Dakwa had been reported where the creek called Toco, and before that called the Dakwai, flowed into the Little Tennessee River. Again, it was supposed to lurk in a low-churned stretch of the French Broad River, six miles upstream from Hot Springs.

There were legends. A hunter, said one, had been swallowed whole by a Dakwa and had fought his way out to safety, but his hair had been scalded from his head. Mooney's notes referred to Jonah in the Bible, to the swallowing of an Ojibwa hero named Mawabosho. That reminded Cobbett of Longfellow's poem, where the King of Fishes had swallowed Hiawatha.

But Hiawatha had escaped, and Jonah and Mawabosho had escaped. The devouring monster of the deep, whatever it might be, was not inescapable.

Again he studied the index. He could not find any references to the plants Lamar had mentioned, but there was a section called "Plant Lore." He read it carefully:

> . . . the cedar is held sacred above all other trees . . . the small green twigs are thrown upon the fire in certain ceremonies . . . as it is believed that the anisgina or malevolent ghosts cannot endure the smell . . .

Below that, a printed name jumped to his eye:

> . . . the white seeds of the viper's bugloss *(Echium vulgara)* were formerly used in many important ceremonies . . .

And, a paragraph or so beyond:

> The campion *(silene stellata)* . . . the juice is held to be a sovereign remedy for snake bites . . .

He shut up the book with a snap and began to take off his clothes.

He searched a pair of bathing trunks out of his pack and put them on. Next, he explored Lamar's tool chest. Among the things at the bottom he found a great cross-hilted hunting knife and drew it from its riveted sheath. The blade was fully a foot long, whetted sharp on both edges. Then he went out to the woodpile and chose a stafflike length of hickory, about five feet in length. There was plenty of fishing line in the cabin, and he lashed the knife to the end of the pole like a spearhead. From the shelf he took the bottle of ointment that had healed him so well and rubbed palmsful on himself from head to foot. Remembering the Indian warrior who had been swallowed and came out bald, he lathered the mixture into his dark, shaggy hair. He smeared more on the blade and the pole. When he was done, the bottle was two-thirds empty.

Finally he walked out with his makeshift spear. He paused at the corner of the cabin, gazing at what grew there.

Those cedar bushes. *The anisgina or malevolent ghosts cannot endure the smell,* Mooney had written, and Mooney, the scholarly friend of the Cherokees, must have known. Cobbett found a match and gathered a sheaf of dry twigs to make a fire. Then he plucked bunches of the dark green cedar leaves and heaped them on top of the blaze. Up rose a dull, vapory smoke. He stood in it, eyes and nose tingling from the fumes, until the fire burned down and the smoke thinned away.

Spear in hand, he paced around the cabin and past the garden and to the place where the margin shelved steeply down into the lake.

He gazed at the sunken tree, then across the lake. No motion there. He looked again at the tree. He could see enough of it to remember it, from times before Long Soak was dammed up. It was a squat oak, thick-stemmed, with sprawling roots driven in among rocks, twenty feet below him.

Yet again he looked out over the water. Still no sign upon it. He began to hum the tune he had heard before, the tune Lamar had forbidden him to pick on the banjo.

Humming, he heard the song outside himself, faint as a song in a dream. It made his skin creep.

From the deep shadowy bottom something came floating upward, straight toward where he knelt.

A woman, thought Cobbett at once, certainly a woman, certainly what the myth in Skinner's book said, not terrible at all. He saw her streaming banner of dark hair, saw her round, lithe arms, her oval, wide-eyed face, and her plump breasts, her skin as smooth and as richly brown as some tropical fruit. Her eyes sought him, her red lips moved as though they sang. Closer she came. Her head with its soaking hair broke clear of the water. Her hand reached to him, both her hands. Those beautiful arms spread wide for him.

He felt light-headed. He almost leaned within the reach of the arms when she drew back and away, still on the surface. His homemade spear had drooped between them. Her short, straight nose twitched as though she would sneeze.

A moment, and then back she came, to the very brink. And changed suddenly. Her eyes spread into shadowed caverns, her mouth opened to show stockades of long, stale teeth. Her arms, round and lithe no longer, drove a taloned clutch at him.

He thrust with the spear, and again she slid swiftly back and away. Off balance, Cobbett fell floundering into the water.

He plunged deep with the force of his fall. In the shimmering blur above him he saw a vast, winnowing shape, far larger than the woman had seemed. It was dark and somehow ribbed, something like a parachute fluttering in a gale. He rose under it, trying to stab and failing again. He could not dart a swift thrust under that impeding water. He clamped the hickory shaft so that it lay tight along his forearm and made a pushing prod with it. The point struck something, seemed to pierce. The broad shape slid away with a flutter that churned the lake all around. Cobbett rose to the surface, gratefully gulping a mighty lungful of breath.

The Dakwa, whatever it was, whatever it truly looked like, had dived out of sight as he came up. Cobbett swam for the shore, one-handed, as another surging wave struck him. He dived deeply, as deeply as he could swim without letting go of his spear.

There it was, stretched overhead again. The dimness of the water, the hampering slowness put upon his movements, seemed like a struggling nightmare. He turned over as he swam. The dark blotch extended itself and came settling down upon him, like a seine dropped to secure a prey. Clamping his spear to his right arm from elbow to wrist, he stabbed, not swiftly but powerfully. Again he felt something at the point. He slid clear and swam upward until his head broke the surface and he could breathe.

He thought no longer of winning to shore. He was here in the lake, he had to fight the Dakwa, do something to it somehow. Underwater was best, where he could see his adversary beneath the surface. Huckleberry Finn had counted on a whole minute to swim without breath under a steamboat. He, Lee Cobbett, ought to do better than that.

But before he went under, ripples and waves. His charging enemy broke into sight, making a veering turn. He saw the slanting spread of it, suddenly rising high, like the murky sail of a scudding catboat. At waterline skimmed the jut of a woman's semblance, a sort of grotesque figurehead, hair in a whirl, teeth bare and big.

Cobbett dived, as straight down as he could manage. The cavern-eyed head was almost at him as he dipped under. Groping talons touched his legs and he felt the stab of them, but he twitched clear. As he swam strivingly down, headfirst, he saw the shape of the water-whelmed oak there, standing where the lake had swallowed it. Its trunk looked bigger than arms could clasp, its roots clutched crookedly at rocks. He slid toward it and went behind as that sprawling shape descended to engulf him. It did not want him there below, poking and stabbing. Cobbett's left hand found and seized a stubby branch of the oak. He rose a trifle. As the Dakwa came gliding toward him and just beneath him, he drove down hard with the spear.

The force of the blow would have pushed him upward if he had not held the branch. That solid anchor helped him bring weight and power into his stab as it went home.

All around him the water suddenly rippled and pulsed, as though with an explosion. Darkness flooded out around him, like sepia expelled by a great cuttlefish, but he clung to the branch and forced the spear grindingly into what it had found, and through and beyond into something as hard and tough as wood. As oak wood. He had spiked the Dakwa to the root of the tree.

The spear lodged there as though clamped in a vise. He let go of it and swam upward. It seemed miles to the surface, to air. He knew he was very tired. He came up at the grassy shag that fringed the island's shore.

With both hands he caught the edge. It began to crumble, but he heaved himself out with almost the last of his strength. Sprawling on the grass, he squirmed dully around and looked down to see what he had done.

No seeing it. Just bubbles and ripples, in water gone poisonously dark, as with some dull infusion. Cobbett panted and moaned for air. At last he got to his hands and knees, and finally stood shakily upright.

His thigh was gashed and the skin on his arm and chest looked rasped, although he could not remember how that last contact had come. He almost fell in as he stooped and tried to see into the lake. If he could not see, he could sense. The

Dakwa was down there and it was not coming up. Strength began to return to his muscles. He scowled to himself as he summoned his nerve. Drawing a deep breath into himself, he dived again. Down he swam, determinedly down.

There it was, writhed around the roots of the oak like a blown tarpaulin. It stirred and trembled. He could make out that forward part, the part shaped with head and arms and breasts to lure its prey. There was where his spear had struck. The knife that had been lashed on for a point was driven in, clear to the cross hilt, at the very region of the spine, if the Dakwa had a spine. It was solidly nailed down there, the Dakwa, like some gigantic, loathsome specimen on a collector's pin. It could not get away and come after him. He hoped not.

Slowly, laboriously, he swam up again, and dragged himself out as before. Getting to his feet, he half-staggered to the cabin and inside. Blood from his wounded leg dripped to the floor. He found the fruit jar full of blockade whiskey, screwed off the lid, put it to his mouth and drank and drank. After that, he took the bottle of ointment and spread it on the places where the Dakwa had gashed and scraped him.

He felt better by the moment. Picking up the robe Lamar had lent him, he put it on. More strongly he walked out and to the place where he had gone in to fight the Dakwa.

The water was calm now, and clearer. He could even make out what was prisoned down there at the root of the oak; you could see it if you knew what you were looking for. It was still there. It would stay there.

Midway through the afternoon, Lamar tied up at the dock again. He came with heavy steps to the cabin door, loaded down with a huge can of kerosene and a gunny-sack crammed with provisions. Cobbett was inside, wearing the GOLDEN GLOVES robe, busy at the stove.

"Welcome back," he greeted Lamar over his shoulder. "I've been fixing a pot of beans for supper. I've put in a few smoked spare ribs you had, and some ketchup and sliced onions, and a sprinkle of garlic salt I happened to bring with me."

Lamar dropped his burden and stared. "What are you a-doing in my bathrobe again? Did you manage to get chopped up the way you did last night, you damned fool?"

"A little, but not as badly chopped up as something else."

"What are you blathering about? Listen, though. In town, I found out that these resort folks can be made to drain out their lake. If I bring the proper kind of lawsuit in court—"

"Don't do it," said Cobbett emphatically. "Without the water in there, something ugly will come in sight. Right at the foot of the steep drop behind the garden."

"The Dakwa?" quavered Lamar. "You trying to say you killed it?"

"Not exactly. I have a theory it can't be killed. But I went in all doped over with your sacred Cherokee ointment and smoked up with cedar, and I was able to stand it off. Finally, I spiked it to the roots of the tree down there."

Lamar crinkled his face. He was beginning to believe, to be aware of implications.

"What about when it comes up again?" he asked.

"I doubt if it can come up until the oak rots away," said Cobbett. "That will take years. Meanwhile, we can study the matter of how to cope with it. I'd like to talk to your friend, that Cherokee medicine man. He might figure how to build on the Indian knowledge we already have."

"We might do something with dynamite," Lamar began to suggest. "The way some people blow fish up."

Cobbett shook his head. "The Dakwa might not be affected. And a charge let off would break up that tree, tear down some of the bank, even wreck your cabin."

"We can get scientists," said Lamar, gesturing eagerly. "I know some marine scientists, a couple of fellows who could go down there with diving gear."

"No," said Cobbett, turning from the stove. "You don't want them to have bad dreams all their lives, do you?"

GOAT

by David Campton

Goat Kemp knew more than was good for anybody. There
wasn't a soul in the village, except Slow Harry, who didn't
feel unease lest the old devil should blurt out something better
left unsaid. If I worried less than most, it was because I had
less to hide—merely certain books outside a schoolmaster's
required reading. But Goat knew about them. He whispered a
title to me one evening after I had disregarded his cigarette
cadging: after which he loped away with a packet of twenty. I
should have stood firm—after all what could Ashbee's porno-
graphic bibliography have meant to my neighbors? But my
poise had been shaken. How could he have known? When not
in my hands, the book is kept locked in a desk. Where I
shivered, though, others quaked.

It was Goat Kemp who had Sam Fernie before the magis-
trates over a few brace of pheasants. Sam swore revenge, but

he had been a fool not to share those birds with Goat: better part with one than lose them all.

It was Goat Kemp who drove little Miss Mellat to desperation. As she waited her turn in the village shop he bleated, "What about the child?" Later, on the church porch after the service, "Where is it buried?" Then across the listening street, "Is coltsfoot-rock poison?" How all those details might have added up we never learned because Miss Mellat took her secret into the river with her. All because she once remarked that Goat Kemp needed a bath.

Which was only true. His filth had medieval quality, peeling in tiny flakes. His nickname, though, came from more than his personal hygiene. His triangular face, trailing cobweb of a beard, and slanting, red-rimmed eyes all suggested a father of either sub- or super-human origin. The villagers accepted that Kemp had been either sired by a goat or by the Devil.

No one knew how he came by his uncanny knowledge, but we all knew how he used it. "Nice to see you, Goat," we greeted him as he shuffled up to the bar. "What are you having, Goat?" Even if we paid for every glass, it amounted to a modest tribute. He never stayed long in The Ox—particularly if Slow Harry should be there.

"Turnip!" he would spit at Harry. "Great slobbering turnip."

Nothing worried Harry. He was content, sitting in the inglenook of The Ox, grinning, nodding, and occasionally shouting a joyful, obscene, monosyllable at the climax of someone's joke. He did not slobber much, and anyway wiped his chin from time to time on his sleeve. Goat hated him because he had no vices. With his big hands and big head he lacked opportunities for falling into temptation. Goat could not blackmail a man without fear and beyond reproach.

In a way our two oddities canceled each other out. Goat took: Harry gave. We liked Harry and feared Goat.

Then a new fear began to haunt the district. I believe Sam Fernie's children started it, calling after Goat in the street. They only repeated expressions learned at their father's knee, but Goat turned on them, his slant eyes glowing like coals.

"I saw what you did to Mrs. Bugle's catmint," he spat. "She thought it was the cats, but I know who."

"Tell if you like," retorted Young Sam. His behind had smarted from his father's belt often enough; he knew the price and was resigned to paying. His sister, Kate, stuck out her tongue.

"Who tipped ink into the teacher's desk?" hissed Goat.

"I did," said Young Sam, protecting his sister while calculating that he might as well be strapped for two misdemeanors as one.

Two tongues stuck out at Goat. Two thumbs pressed against two snub noses.

"We're not afraid," defied Young Sam.

"You will be," snarled Goat.

"He does frighten me," whispered Kate.

"Don't let him," ordered Young Sam.

Anticipating Goat he confessed to the crimes, and was sent early to bed, where he lay face downward for comfort. No doubt Kate was thinking of Goat's threat when she made her last call that night at the lavatory at the end of the garden.

Her cries brought Fernie and his wife running from the cottage. Young Sam watched from the bedroom window, and told me about it afterward. Kate leaned against the rough, wooden door, her face a white blob in the moonlight. She screamed and screamed, and could not be calmed.

"What had she seen?" "Was it a rat?"

She pointed to something lying by the path. It was a crude doll, about the height of a nine-year-old girl. Its head was a mangold, and its limbs bundles of twigs.

"Is this all that scared you?" Fernie tried to laugh the terror away. "Just this old thing?"

"It walked behind me," sobbed the girl. "It put out its arms and touched me."

"Look. No arms. No legs. Nothing but dry sticks."

"It touched me," screamed Kate. "It touched me."

They coaxed the child into the cottage, and when kitchen-cupboard remedies failed, sent for the doctor. After sedation Kate slept, but for years afterward needed a night light in her room.

Fernie accepted her story of the turnip head, but it stood to reason that a bundle of sticks could not move under its own accord. Someone had attacked his daughter; however when he searched the garden for signs of an intruder, he found nothing in the way of footprints or trampled plants. Oddly enough by next morning the mannikin, too, had disappeared.

Fernie was a sound man with a snare, and could produce a

rabbit for the asking, but he always took time to add two and two together, and several days passed before he began to suspect Goat Kemp. The children talked about slanging Goat in the street; in Goat's garden stood such a scarecrow; and in the bar of The Ox, Goat himself sneered at Kate's nerves.

Suddenly Fernie was standing in front of Goat, and silence like a blanket had fallen.

"You know something." Beer and the firelight reddened his face.

Goat bleated. The noise was meant for a laugh. We, like fools, instead of calling for another round, or starting a game of darts, we sat waiting for the next move, as though these were actors instead of men with blood to spill.

"If I believed you harmed my girl, I'd beat that smirk into the back of your neck," said Fernie.

"Talk," sneered Goat, and took another swig of bitter.

A flat-handed swipe knocked the glass from his hand, and smashed it against the far wall. Goat dabbed at the bruised corner of his mouth.

"That'll cost you the price of another drink," he said.

A gaping seam tore further as Fernie seized a handful of Goat's coat. "What do you know?" he roared.

"She frightens easy, don't she?" grinned Goat. "A scrap of kindling and an old root. As long as she meets nothing worse . . ."

After which he took Fernie's fist full in his mouth, and hurtled across the room after his glass.

"Witch spawn," thundered Fernie.

Blood trickled from the corner of Goat's mouth, leaving a red streak on his dust-colored beard. We waited for the threats. Instead Goat's crooked, yellow, animal teeth were bared in the caricature of a smile, which was worse.

"Any more questions?" he creaked.

"You did it," shouted Fernie. "You scared my girl into screaming hysterics. You and that damned scarecrow."

"You saw me, did you?" smiled Goat. "Or perhaps she saw me. Climbing over the wall, maybe. Hiding under a gooseberry bush. Next time . . ."

The old creature's head banged against the paneling as Fernie hit him again.

"Come near her, and I'll kill you," roared Fernie. "I'll— I'll . . ."

As words failed, he picked up Goat and hurled him against the wall again and again. It was Slow Harry who stopped the beating, laying a big hand on Fernie's arm.

"Uh-huh," said Slow Harry, shaking his head.

"You all heard him," shouted Fernie, backing to the door. "Next time, he said. That was a threat. A threat."

No one spoke until the street door slammed behind him. Then we heard Goat moaning like the wind in a chimney.

"Killing, is it?" whined Goat. "Killing." He struggled to his hands and knees, and was sick.

An old man's bruises take time to heal, and it was days before Goat limped into the street again. For that time he lay untended in his darkened cottage. The village hated Goat; Goat hated the village. On Goat's part, during those groaning days, the hate strengthened, sharpened, and finally struck.

Sam Fernie had been troubled since Goat Kemp took to his bed. None of us wondered at that. We had learned the hard way that it did not pay to cross Goat; and Fernie's fists had dealt more than a crossing. Indeed, remembering how we had failed to protect Goat from the beating, most of us were concocting alibis against uncomfortable revelations—though personally I had no more to worry about than an illustrated edition of *The Age of Perversion*.

Fernie developed a nervous tic. His head would jerk as though he were trying to catch someone peering over his shoulder. He muttered about black spots, and we advised him to have his eyes tested, even though he could still hit a fly at a hundred yards.

At the end it was a feather—a wisp of white that he swore had floated round his head all day. Some of us saw it, nestling on his coat collar. He made occasional attempts to grab it, but it always eluded him, suddenly swirling away. We chased it along the bar. As we scrambled after it, the door opened, and the feather escaped into the night.

Slow Harry blinked on the doorstep.

"Feather," we laughed, as though that explained everything.

"Feather," said Harry, nodding.

Fernie sat easier that night than I had seen him for some time. Toward closing time he even joined in a couple of choruses. Harry sat in the inglenook as usual, nodding, wiping his chin. Occasionally he would repeat "Feather" as though it was important.

Last drinks finished, we ambled to the door. I can remember distinctly what happened, and my observations were clarified by repeating them again and again in the face of official disbelief.

Five of us crowded the doorway. Bert Huggins and the doctor's son were on the pub side of the door. Charlie Wells and myself were in the street. The village lighting is not brilliant, but as I swore on oath, the street was deserted. Sam Fernie was between us, crossing the threshold.

He stopped with a grunt, his mouth wide open, and he made a noise as though gathering breath for a sneeze.

"Bless you," I said in anticipation.

At least he died with a blessing. He crossed his hands over his chest, then crumpled. For a few moments we joked. "Take more water with it." "Put him to bed, mother." But when we turned him over his blue eyes were lifeless.

His hands fell away from his chest, revealing a metal ring shining against his shirt. It seemed to be a badge of sorts. It was in fact a butcher's skewer, and the rest of its length was buried in Fernie's heart.

"Feather," said Slow Harry.

Later I tried to explain to him that the lethal instrument had been a steel spike, driven in with remarkable force. But Slow Harry repeated, "Feather."

In certain matters I trusted Harry. If he said "Rain," sure enough a downpour would be on its way. "Wind," he says, and a gale sweeps in. His mother had a reputation with salves and brews; and the pair of them lived closer to nature than most of us. They recognized a sign when they saw one. I should not have tried to contradict Harry when he said "Feather."

However I had little time for pedantry. It is not pleasant to be suspected of murder. Although the four of us had no motive and little opportunity, the doctor insisted that the wound could not have been self-inflicted. According to the facts no one could have killed Sam Fernie. Yet he was dead.

A collection was taken for his widow and children. Everybody contributed—except Goat, who was not asked; however he came to the funeral. As the coffin was lowered into the ground, he made a strange grunting sound. "Heh-heh-heh." Some said he was sobbing, others thought he was laughing; but everyone felt his presence to be an intrusion and the noise a provocation. "Heh-heh-heh." Like an old goat coughing.

Sam Fernie's niece, Sue, voiced what we were thinking.

"Shut up and get out," she called to him. "A pity you're not in the hole instead of Sam."

Sue was a no-nonsense nineteen-year-old. She had the Fernie build, and the Fernie coloring. Given time the one would run to fat and the other to her late uncle's boiled complexion; but now she had blooming cheeks, a figure the boys fought over, and a voice that could be heard on the other side of the churchyard.

"What's yon bundle of stinking rags doing at a decent man's funeral?"

"What were you doing last night at Piggott's Alley?" countered Goat. Sue's cheeks flamed a deeper red as he pursued his advantage. "Are you counting on the doctor's son to get rid of the inconvenience you're expecting?"

He ended with a shriek as Sue's fingernails raked four bloody streaks across his cheek.

Everyone agreed later that it was a disgraceful thing to have happened at a respectable funeral; but sympathies lay with Sue, and we were relieved to see Goat slouch away. The rest of the ceremony passed without incident, and the ham sandwiches were excellent.

Sue's body was found by her mother next morning. She lay strangled on her bed with the marks of a rope around her neck. The police found her death even more baffling than her uncle's. The pantry window had been left ajar, but no more than would have admitted a reasonably plump clothesline. All the other doors and windows had been made fast.

Probably I could have helped the police, but I had already been connected with one killing and was not inclined to sharpen their suspicions. Besides, they would never have believed me.

Just after ten on the night of Sue's murder I was ambling from The Ox toward my bachelor bed and *Teach Them to Love,* when I noticed a movement by the wall of Piggott's Alley. A snake was wiggling across the pavement. It knew where it was going, and it moved as fast as I could walk. Having a layman's conviction that no British snake can be poisonous, I investigated.

The creature was about three feet long, the color and texture of old rope. It forged ahead, determinedly thrusting aside a crumpled newspaper, and eventually reached the end of the wall. There it paused before emerging into the light of the street lamp. Satisfied that all was clear, it dashed across the road, and I could see it quite clearly. It *was* a piece of old rope.

One end was frayed and the other end knotted. It was not a reptile taking on protective covering; it was exactly what it seemed to be. Yet it moved with intelligence. The night air was still, and the discarded newspaper lay inert in the gutter. Whatever propelled that yard of twisted fibers, it was not the wind.

Bolder by several pints of bitter, and untroubled by the thought that such lengths of hemp have choked the lives from countless men, I quickened my pace and followed the rope.

It seemed to sense discovery, because it reared up, the knot like a head swaying from side to side. After a few seconds it set rigid; it had seen me. Instead of being afraid I felt irritated—sure that I was being made a fool of. Beyond that piece of rope would be a length of thread, and beyond that someone laughing. Even a mediocre schoolmaster develops an eye for japes.

The thing turned and fled. I followed. I began to run, but still it eluded me. Some snakes can move faster than a galloping horse, but this was not a snake. Some boys can move faster than a beer-filled teacher, but slowly I managed to gain on it. At last it was just ahead of me. One spurt, and I stamped on it.

I felt it squirming underneath my feet, struggling to free itself. I had the impression of powerful muscles working furiously; however I am grossly overweight, and the thing was pinned down. For a few seconds I enjoyed the victory.

Then agony like a hot iron lashed across his shins as the rope struck with the force of a flying whip. I stumbled back with a yelp as the thing struck again. Unprepared and off-balance I crashed to the pavement. The rope came down across my back. If I had not been wearing my best Donegal tweed, that last blow would have torn a furrow across my shoulders. The air was knocked from my lungs, and the next breath I took was spent in a wail of pain. I curled into a foetal position waiting for further chastisement. It did not come, but I lay until I felt a hand on my shoulder.

Slow Harry lifted me to my feet.

"Bad," he said, shaking the saliva from his chin.

"The rope," I gasped, waving to where it should have been. There was, of course, no rope; but Harry seemed to understand.

"Rope," he repeated, as though it was an everyday occurrence—like finding a schoolmaster rolling in the gutter.

He assisted me, limping, to my front door. I thanked him—brusquely, but I was anxious to cosset my wounds. He seemed reluctant to leave my doorstep. His face, usually a blank fleshy mask, showed unusual signs of agitation. His mouth twitched, and there was a light in his eyes: not exactly intelligence, but as though he was trying to express thoughts for which words did not exist.

"Rope," he said at last. He put his hands to his throat and shook his head.

He wiped his chin and went away. I busied myself with warm water and ointment. When the news about Sue reached me next day, the only effective medicine was a large brandy.

The entire village seemed crushed by the second killing. If two such healthy beings could be struck down, where could anyone find safety? Mindful of our mortality, we all attended Sue's funeral. No one could remember such a mass of flowers. No one could remember the church so full.

Goat was in the graveyard as before, coughing, giggling, or bleating, while the vicar intoned the last words, and the coffin was lowered. As dirt hit the wooden lid, Goat fingered his cheek. The marks left by Sue's nails showed dimly under the grime. Then I understood.

Fernie struck Goat, and died. Sue struck Goat, and died. Kate Fernie had seen a bundle of twigs walking, and I had seen what I had seen.

"Heh-heh-heh," went Goat.

I looked across the grave into those slanting, yellow eyes. They were defying me to speak. Goat had powers, but I could no more accuse him than I could accuse the Archbishop. I drank, didn't I? I knew the old blackmailer's secret, and knew that he held my life in the palm of his filthy hand. Harry saved me from toppling into the hole.

The momentary faint left me light-headed. Why else would I address Goat across the newly-dug grave?

"What did you do with the rope, Goat?"

Faces turned to look at me; heads shook; tongues clucked; there were several loud sniffs, reminders of my pre-ceremony brandy.

"Did you burn the rope?" I mumbled.

Goat said nothing, but his lurid eyes seemed ringed with fire. I was aware of a freezing hollow inside me. I, too, was going to die. Unnaturally.

Goat slipped away ahead of the crowd. I watched them all leave until Harry and the sexton were with me, waiting to fill in the grave. The sexton spat on his hands—while others enjoyed the funeral's baked meats, there was still work to be done. Harry nodded to me.

"Feather," he said. It was a warning.

In point of fact it was not a feather, but a scrap of this-tledown. From time to time I tried to catch it, but inevitably I clutched at nothing. The class treated the episode as a comic turn until rapped heads and randomly distributed detentions reminded everyone where they were. I believe I gave a passable imitation of a schoolteacher at work, without revealing the panic fermenting inside of me.

After school I hurried to Harry's cottage. I had no idea how Slow Harry might give aid or comfort, but I believed he knew something of the terror which clawed at my heart. Harry knew things.

He was expecting me, offering me an inch-thick slice of bread and dripping, and a mug of black tea. Then he made the door fast—the first time in years that it had been locked and barred. I noticed that the bolts were freshly greased. Harry lifted into the fireplace the great iron pot that had been constantly on the boil in his mother's day. Even he grunted as he heaved it up, and weights that would have flattened me were toys to him. He winked and nodded at the pot.

"Iron," he laughed. "Iron." I could not see the joke.

Then we waited. A trying time because Harry was no conversationalist, and I gradually became tongue-tied with the fear which possessed me. I was not even allowed to leave, even though it was past opening time at The Ox. When I tried to open the door Harry lifted me bodily away.

"No," said Harry.

I fell to thinking that I might be in greater danger here than anywhere. What if Harry should be in league with Goat?

"No," said Harry. "Not Goat."

After which I tried to keep my thoughts under control; but they turned again and again to death—quick death, slow death, easy death, agonizing death, but always death. Harry patted my shoulder: this was as reassuring as a medieval executioner's formal request for pardon.

The day faded, and Harry brought out candles. We sat pale-faced in the flickering light. The windows were fastened, the clock was stopped, and there was no sound except the rumbling from my belly.

Suddenly the window was shattered, and one of the candles fell, cut in half. Something whistled past my face, and hit the wall behind my head.

I dropped to the floor. The object that had shot by me had returned, scored my left buttock, and drilled the table top. I could see the candle light through the hole. I screamed, shut my eyes, and lay still.

I heard sounds like ricocheting bullets. Things were broken—a teapot, a pudding bowl, a picture of Queen Victoria's coronation. Whatever the thing was, it intended to get Harry too. I heard him skipping about the room, and was amazed that a man of his bulk could move with such agility. Moreover he had the knack of knowing just where the object would strike next, and of arranging to be elsewhere when it did.

A moving target has more chance of survival than one lying prone, so I decided to join the dance. As I rose, everything seemed to freeze. Even the candle flame forgot to flicker. Harry was standing by the fireplace holding the cooking pot in one hand, and its massive lid in the other. In the center of the table lay a thimble, pointing straight at my chest.

I felt Harry's great boot kick me sprawling, while simultaneously I heard a clang. A bullet hitting an iron pot would make such a noise.

By the time I had struggled to my knees again, Harry had set the pot upside down on the stone floor. Whatever was inside clattered incessantly like an alarm bell. A covering of peg rugs eventually helped dull the sound.

I was panting like an old hound, but Harry stood as stolid

as ever, without even a hint of sweat on his face. He rubbed his sleeve across his chin.

"Goat," he said.

There was no answer when we called at Goat's cottage. Harry would have broken down the door, but I persuaded him to fetch the constable first. We found Goat on his bug-infested mattress, glassy eyes staring at the ceiling.

In due course the doctor wrote the death certificate, and the village turned out for the funeral. Perhaps everyone wanted to be sure that the old sinner was set down deep enough.

Until after the interment, each day and all day long, the thing in Harry's cottage kept up its clatter in the iron pot. After Harry had filled in the grave, I returned with him to his cottage. He took the pot into the garden, tipped it onto its side, and lifted the lid. Something streaked away like a flash of light in the direction of the graveyard.

Later I picked up a thimble lying by old Goat's grave. One thimble is very like another, but it could have been the one that pockmarked Slow Harry's woodwork. I argued with myself what should be done. If the force that animated the rope and the thimble had returned to Goat, he would be alive down there, clawing at the coffin lid. I could imagine the bloody fingers, the air wasted in unheard screams. Could I let another human being, even Goat, die in such terror?

I am not a sympathetic character. I tossed the thimble away, and limped toward The Ox. My wound was still sore, and besides, it was past opening time.

Ramsey Campbell's writings scare the heck out of me. He takes the real world, our world, and exploits our fears. Many readers find such familiarity uncomfortable, but that is exactly what Ramsey wants. "The Chimney" may just be the best "real" story Ramsey has ever written. At first there may appear to be some extraneous material, but Mr. Campbell has everything well in hand and acts as the hangman's noose, drawing everything together as the trap door opens . . .

THE CHIMNEY
by Ramsey Campbell

Maybe most of it was only fear. But not the last thing, not that. To blame my fear for that would be worst of all.

I was twelve years old and beginning to conquer my fears. I even went upstairs to do my homework, and managed to ignore the chimney. I had to be brave, because of my parents—because of my mother.

She had always been afraid of me. The very first day I had gone to school I'd seen her watching. Her expression had reminded me of a face of a girl I'd glimpsed on television, watching men lock her husband behind bars; I was frightened all that first day. And when children had hysterics or began to bully me, or the teacher lost her temper, these things only confirmed my fears—and my mother's, when I told her what had happened each day.

Now I was at grammar school. I had been there for much of a year. I'd felt awkward in my new uniform and old shoes; the building seemed enormous, crowded with too many strange children and teachers. I'd felt I was an outsider; friendly approaches made me nervous and sullen, when people laughed and I didn't know why I was sure they were laughing at me. After a while the other boys treated me as I seemed to want to be treated: the lads from the poorer districts mocked my suburban accent, the suburban boys sneered at my old shoes.

Often I'd sat praying that the teacher wouldn't ask me a question I couldn't answer, sat paralyzed by my dread of having to stand up in the waiting watchful silence. If a teacher shouted at someone my heart jumped painfully; once I'd felt the stain of my shock creeping insidiously down my thigh. Yet I did well in the end-of-term examinations, because I was terrified of failing; for nights afterward they were another reason why I couldn't sleep.

My mother read the signs of all this on my face. More and more, once I'd told her what was wrong. I had to persuade her there was nothing worse that I'd kept back. Some mornings as I lay in bed, trying to hold back half-past seven, I'd be sick; I would grope miserably downstairs, white-faced, and my mother would keep me home. Once or twice, when my fear wasn't quite enough, I made myself sick. "Look at him. You can't expect him to go like that"—but my father would only shake his head and grunt, dismissing us both.

I knew my father found me embarrassing. This year he'd had less time for me than usual; his shop—The Anything Shop, nearby in the suburbanized village—was failing to compete with the new supermarket. But before that trouble I'd often seen him staring up at my mother and me: both of us taller than him, his eyes said, yet both scared of our own shadows. At those times I glimpsed his despair.

So my parents weren't reassuring. Yet at night I tried to stay with them as long as I could—for my worst fears were upstairs, in my room.

It was a large room, two rooms knocked into one by the previous owner. It overlooked the small back gardens. The smaller of the fireplaces had been bricked up; in winter, the larger held a fire, which my mother always feared would set fire to the room—but she let it alone, for I'd screamed when I thought she was going to take that light away: even though the firelight only added to the terrors of the room.

The shadows moved things. The mesh of the fireguard fluttered enlarged on the wall; sometimes, at the edge of sleep, it became a swaying web, and its spinner came sidling down from a corner of the ceiling. Everything was unstable; walls shifted, my clothes crawled on the back of the chair. Once, when I'd left my jacket slumped over the chair, the collar's dark upturned lack of a face began to nod forward stealthily; the holes at the ends of the sleeves worked like mouths, and I didn't dare get up to hang the jacket properly. The room grew in the dark: sounds outside, footsteps and laughter, dogs encouraging each other to bark, only emphasized the size of my trap of darkness, how distant everything else was. And there was a dimmer room, in the mirror of the wardrobe beyond the foot of the bed. There was a bed in that room, and beside it a dim nightlight in a plastic lantern. Once I'd awaked to see a face staring dimly at me from the mirror; a figure had sat up when I had, and I'd almost cried out. Often I'd stared at the dim staring face, until I'd had to hide beneath the sheets.

Of course this couldn't go on for the rest of my life. On my twelfth birthday I set about the conquest of my room.

I was happy amid my presents. I had a jigsaw, a box of colored pencils, a book of space stories. They had come from my father's shop, but they were mine now. Because I was relaxed, no doubt because she wished I could always be so, my mother said, "Would you be happier if you went to another school?"

It was Saturday; I wanted to forget Monday. Besides, I imagined all schools were as frightening. "No, I'm all right," I said.

"Are you happy at school now?" she said incredulously.

"Yes, it's all right."

"Are you sure?"

"Yes, really, it's all right. I mean, I'm happy now."

The snap of the letter slot saved me from further lying. Three birthday cards: two from neighbors who talked to me when I served them in the shop—an old lady who always carried a poodle, our next-door neighbor Dr. Flynn—and a card from my parents. I'd seen all three cards in the shop, which spoilt them somehow.

As I stood in the hall I heard my father. "You've got to control yourself," he was saying. "You only upset the child. If you didn't go on at him he wouldn't be half so bad."

It infuriated me to be called a child. "But I worry so," my mother said brokenly. "He can't look after himself."

"You don't let him try. You'll have him afraid to go up to bed next."

But I already was. Was that my mother's fault? I remembered her putting the nightlight by my bed when I was very young, checking the flex and the bulb each night—I'd taken to lying awake, dreading that one or the other would fail. Standing in the hall, I saw dimly that my mother and I encouraged each other's fears. One of us had to stop. I had to stop. Even when I was frightened, I mustn't let her see. It wouldn't be the first time I'd hidden my feelings from her. In the living room I said, "I'm going upstairs to play."

Sometimes in the summer I didn't mind playing there—but this was March, and a dark day. Still, I could switch the light on. And my room contained the only table I could have to myself and my jigsaw.

I spilled the jigsaw onto the table. The chair sat with its back to the dark yawn of the fireplace; I moved it hastily to the foot of the bed, facing the door. I spread the jigsaw. There was a piece of the edge, another. By lunchtime I'd assembled the edge. "You look pleased with yourself," my father said.

I didn't notice the approach of night. I was fitting together my own blue sky, above fragmented cottages. After dinner I hurried to put in the pieces I'd placed mentally while eating. I hesitated outside my room. I should have to reach into the dark for the light switch. When I did, the wallpaper filled with bright multiplied airplanes and engines. I wished we could afford to redecorate my room, it seemed childish now.

The fireplace gaped. I retrieved the fireguard from the cupboard under the stairs, where my father had stored it now the nights were a little warmer. It covered the soot-encrusted yawn. The room felt comfortable now. I'd never seen before how much space it gave me for play.

I even felt safe in bed. I switched out the nightlight—but that was too much; I grabbed the light. I didn't mind its glow

on its own, without the jagged lurid jig of the shadows. And
the fireguard was comforting. It made me feel that nothing
could emerge from the chimney.

On Monday I took my space stories to school. People
asked to look at them; eventually they lent me books. In the
following weeks some of my fears began to fade. Questions
darting from desk to desk still made me uneasy, but if I had
to stand up without the answer at least I knew the other boys
weren't sneering at me, not all of them; I was beginning to
have friends. I started to sympathize with their own ignorant
silences. In the July examinations I was more relaxed, and
scored more marks. I was even sorry to leave my friends for
the summer; I invited some of them home.

I felt triumphant. I'd calmed my mother and my room all
by myself, just by realizing what had to be done. I suppose
that sense of triumph helped me. It must have given me a
little strength with which to face the real terror.

It was early August, the week before our holiday. My
mother was worrying over the luggage, my father was trying
to calculate his accounts; they were beginning to chafe against
each other. I went to my room, to stay out of their way.

I was halfway through a jigsaw, which one of my friends
had swapped for mine. People sat in back gardens, letting the
evening settle on them; between the houses the sky was pale
yellow. I inserted pieces easily, relaxed by the nearness of
our holiday. I listened to the slowing of the city, a radio
fluttering along a street, something moving behind the fireguard, in the chimney.

No. It was my mother in the next room, moving luggage. It
was someone dragging, dragging something, anything, outside. But I couldn't deceive my ears. In the chimney something large had moved.

It might have been a bird, stunned or dying, struggling
feebly—except that a bird would have sounded wilder. It
could have been a mouse, even a rat, if such things are found
in chimneys. But it sounded like a large body, groping stealthily in the dark: something large that didn't want me to hear it.
It sounded like the worst terror of my infancy.

I'd almost forgotten that. When I was three years old my
mother had let me watch television; it was bad for my eyes,
but just this once, near Christmas—I'd seen two children
asleep in bed, an enormous crimson man emerging from the

fireplace, creeping toward them. They weren't going to wake up! "Burglar! Burglar!" I'd screamed, beginning to cry. "No, dear, it's Father Christmas," my mother said, hastily switching off the television. "He always comes out of the chimney."

Perhaps if she'd said "down" rather than "out of" . . . For months after that, and in the weeks before several Christmases, I lay awake listening fearfully for movement in the chimney: I was sure a fat grinning figure would creep upon me if I slept. My mother had told me the presents that appeared at the end of my bed were left by Father Christmas, but now the mysterious visitor had a face and a huge body, squeezed into the dark chimney among the soot. When I heard the wind breathing in the chimney I had to trap my screams between my lips.

Of course at last I began to suspect there was no Father Christmas: how did he manage to steal into my father's shop for my presents? He was a childish idea, I was almost sure—but I was too embarrassed to ask my parents or my friends. But I wanted not to believe in him, that silent lurker in the chimney; and now I didn't, not really. Except that something large was moving softly behind the fireguard.

It had stopped. I stared at the wire mesh, half-expecting a fat pale face to stare out of the grate. There was nothing but the fenced dark. Cats were moaning in a garden, an ice-cream van wandered brightly. After a while I forced myself to pull the fireguard away.

I was taller than the fireplace now. But I had to stoop to peer up the dark, soot-ridged throat, and then it loomed over me, darkness full of menace, of the threat of a huge figure bursting out at me, its red mouth crammed with sparkling teeth. As I peered up, trembling a little, and tried to persuade myself that what I'd heard had flown away or scurried back into its hole, soot came trickling down from the dark—and I heard the sound of a huge body squeezed into the sooty passage, settling itself carefully, more comfortably in its burrow.

I slammed the guard into place, and fled. I had to gulp to breathe. I ran onto the landing, trying to catch my breath so as to cry for help. Downstairs my mother was nervously asking whether she should pack another of my father's shirts. "Yes, if you like," he said irritably.

No, I mustn't cry out. I'd vowed not to upset her. But how

could I go back into my room? Suddenly I had a thought that seemed to help. At school we'd learned how sweeps had used to send small boys up chimneys. There had hardly been room for the boys to climb. How could a large man fit in there?

He couldn't. Gradually I managed to persuade myself. At last I opened the door of my room. The chimney was silent; there was no wind. I tried not to think that he was holding himself still, waiting to squeeze out stealthily, waiting for the dark. Later, lying in the steady glow from my plastic lantern, I tried to hold onto the silence, tried to believe there was nothing near me to shatter it. There was nothing except, eventually, sleep.

Perhaps if I'd cried out on the landing I would have been saved from my fear. But I was happy with my rationality. Only once, nearly asleep, I wished the fire were lit, because it would burn anything that might be hiding in the chimney; that had never occurred to me before. But it didn't matter, for the next day we went on holiday.

My parents liked to sleep in the sunlight, beneath newspaper masks; in the evenings they liked to stroll along the wide sandy streets. I didn't, and befriended Nigel, the son of another family who were staying in the boardinghouse. My mother encouraged the friendship: such a nice boy, two years older than me; he'd look after me. He had money, and the hope of a moustache shadowing his pimply upper lip. One evening he took me to the fairground, where we met two girls; he and the older girl went to buy ice cream while her young friend and I stared at each other timidly. I couldn't believe the young girl didn't like jigsaws. Later, while I was contradicting her, Nigel and his companion disappeared behind the Ghost Train—but Nigel reappeared almost at once, red-faced, his left cheek redder. "Where's Rose?" I asked, bewildered.

"She had to go." He seemed furious that I'd asked.

"Isn't she coming back?"

"No." He was glancing irritably about for a change of subject. "What a super bike," he said, pointing as it glided between the stalls. "Have you got a bike?"

"No," I said. "I keep asking Father Christmas, but—" I wished that hadn't got past me, for he was staring at me, winking at the young girl.

"Do you still believe in him?" he demanded scornfully.

"No, of course I don't. I was only kidding." Did he believe me? He was edging toward the young girl now, putting his arm around her; soon she excused herself, and didn't come back—I never knew her name. I was annoyed he'd made her run away. "Where did Rose go?" I said persistently.

He didn't tell me. But perhaps he resented my insistence, for as the family left the boardinghouse I heard him say loudly to his mother: "He still believes in Father Christmas." My mother heard that too, and glanced anxiously at me.

Well, I didn't. There was nobody in the chimney, waiting for me to come home. I didn't care that we were going home the next day. That night I pulled away the fireguard and saw a fat pale face hanging down into the fireplace, like an underbelly, upside-down and smiling. But I managed to wake, and eventually the sea lulled me back to sleep.

As soon as we reached home I ran upstairs. I uncovered the fireplace and stood staring, to discover what I felt. Gradually I filled with the scorn Nigel would have felt, had he known of my fear. How could I have been so childish? The chimney was only a passage for smoke, a hole into which the wind wandered sometimes. That night, exhausted by the journey home, I slept at once.

The nights darkened into October; the darkness behind the mesh grew thicker. I'd used to feel, as summer waned, that the chimney was insinuating its darkness into my room. Now the sight only reminded me I'd have a fire soon. The fire would be comforting.

It was October when my father's Christmas cards arrived, on a Saturday; I was working in the shop. It annoyed him to have to anticipate Christmas so much, to compete with the supermarket. I hardly noticed the cards: my head felt muffled, my body cold—perhaps it was the weather's sudden hint of winter.

My mother came to the shop that afternoon. I watched her pretend not to have seen the cards. When I looked away she began to pick them up timidly, as if they were unfaithful letters, glancing anxiously at me. I didn't know what was in her mind. My head was throbbing. I wasn't going home sick. I earned pocket money in the shop. Besides, I didn't want my father to think I was still weak.

Nor did I want my mother to worry. That night I lay

slumped in a chair, pretending to read. Words trickled down the page; I felt like dirty clothes someone had thrown on the chair. My father was at the shop taking stock. My mother sat gazing at me. I pretended harder; the words waltzed slowly. At last she said, "Are you listening?"

I was now, though I didn't look up. "Yes," I said hoarsely, unplugging my throat with a roar.

"Do you remember when you were a baby? There was a film you saw, of Father Christmas coming out of the chimney." Her voice sounded bravely careless, falsely light, as if she were determined to make some awful revelation. I couldn't look up. "Yes," I said.

Her silence made me glance up. She looked as she had on my first day of school: full of loss, of despair. Perhaps she was realizing I had to grow up, but to my throbbing head her look suggested only terror—as if she were about to deliver me up as a sacrifice. "I couldn't tell you the truth then," she said. "You were too young."

The truth was terror; her expression promised that. "Father Christmas isn't really like that," she said.

My illness must have shown by then. She gazed at me; her lips trembled. "I can't," she said, turning her face away. "Your father must tell you."

But that left me poised on the edge of terror. I felt unnerved, rustily tense. I wanted very much to lie down. "I'm going to my room," I said. I stumbled upstairs, hardly aware of doing so. As much as anything I was fleeing her unease. The stairs swayed a little, they felt unnaturally soft underfoot. I hurried dully into my room. I slapped the light switch and missed. I was walking controllably forward into blinding dark. A figure came to meet me, soft and huge in the dark of my room.

I cried out. I managed to stagger back onto the landing, grabbing the light switch as I went. The lighted room was empty. My mother came running upstairs, almost falling. "What is it, what is it?" she cried.

I mustn't say. "I'm ill. I feel sick." I did, and a minute later I was. She patted my back as I knelt by the toilet. When she'd put me to bed she made to go next door, for the doctor. "Don't leave me," I pleaded. The walls of the room swayed as if tugged by firelight, the fireplace was huge and very dark. As soon as my father opened the front door she ran downstairs, crying, "He's ill, he's ill! Go for the doctor!"

The doctor came and prescribed for my fever. My mother sat up beside me. Eventually my father came to suggest it was time she went to bed. They were going to leave me alone in my room. "Make a fire," I pleaded.

My mother touched my forehead. "But you're burning," she said.

"No, I'm cold! I want a fire! Please!" So she made one, tired as she was. I saw my father's disgust as he watched me use her worry against her to get what I wanted, his disgust with her for letting herself be used.

I didn't care. My mother's halting words had overgrown my mind. What had she been unable to tell me? Had it to do with the sounds I'd heard in the chimney? The room lolled around me; nothing was sure. But the fire would make sure for me. Nothing in the chimney could survive it.

I made my mother stay until the fire was blazing. Suppose a huge shape burst forth from the hearth, dripping fire? When at last I let her go I lay lapped by the firelight and meshy shadows, which seemed lulling now, in my warm room.

I felt feverish, but not unpleasantly. I was content to voyage on my rocking bed; the ceiling swayed past above me. While I slept the fire went out. My fever kept me warm; I slid out of bed and, pulling away the fireguard, reached up the chimney. At the length of my arms I touched something heavy, hanging down in the dark; it yielded, then soft fat fingers groped down and closed on my wrist. My mother was holding my wrist as she washed my hands. "You mustn't get out of bed," she said when she realized I was awake.

I stared stupidly at her. "You'd got out of bed. You were sleepwalking," she explained. "You had your hands right up the chimney." I saw now that she was washing caked soot from my hands; tracks of ash led toward the bed.

It had been only a dream. One moment the fat hand had been gripping my wrist, the next it was my mother's cool slim fingers. My mother played word games and timid chess with me while I stayed in bed, that day and the next.

The third night I felt better. The fire fluttered gently; I felt comfortably warm. Tomorrow I'd get up. I should have to go back to school soon, but I didn't mind that unduly. I lay and listened to the breathing of the wind in the chimney.

When I awoke the fire had gone out. The room was full of darkness. The wind still breathed, but it seemed somehow closer. It was above me. Someone was standing over me. It couldn't be either of my parents, not in the sightless darkness.

I lay rigid. Most of all I wished that I hadn't let Nigel's imagined contempt persuade me to do without a nightlight. The breathing was slow, irregular; it sounded clogged and feeble. As I tried to inch silently toward the far side of the bed, the source of the breathing stooped toward me. I felt its breath waver on my face, and the breath sprinkled me with something like dry rain.

When I had lain paralyzed for what felt like blind hours, the breathing went away. It was in the chimney, dislodging soot; it might be the wind. But I knew it had come out to let me know that whatever the fire had done to it, it hadn't been killed. It had emerged to tell me it would come for me on Christmas Eve. I began to scream.

I wouldn't tell my mother why. She washed my face, which was freckled with soot. "You've been sleepwalking again," she tried to reassure me, but I wouldn't let her leave me until daylight. When she'd gone I saw the ashy tracks leading from the chimney to the bed.

Perhaps I had been sleepwalking and dreaming. I searched vainly for my nightlight. I would have been ashamed to ask for a new one, and that helped me to feel I could do without. At dinner I felt secure enough to say I didn't know why I had screamed.

"But you must remember. You sounded so frightened. You upset me."

My father was folding the evening paper into a thick wad the size of a pocketbook, which he could read beside his plate. "Leave the boy alone," he said. "You imagine all sorts of things when you're feverish. I did when I was his age."

It was the first time he'd admitted anything like weakness to me. If he'd managed to survive his nightmares, why should mine disturb me more? Tired out by the demands of my fever, I slept soundly that night. The chimney was silent except for the flapping of flames.

But my father didn't help me again. One November afternoon I was standing behind the counter, hoping for customers. My father pottered, grumpily fingering packets of nylons, tins of pet food, Dinky toys, a baby's rattles, cards, searching for signs of theft. Suddenly he snatched a Christmas card and strode to the counter. "Sit down," he said grimly.

He was waving the card at me, like evidence. I sat down on a shelf, but then a lady came into the shop; the bell thumped. I stood up to sell her nylons. When she'd gone I gazed at my father, anxious to hear the worst. "Just sit down," he said.

He couldn't stand my being taller than he was. His size embarrassed him, but he wouldn't let me see that; he pretended I had to sit down out of respect. "Your mother says she tried to tell you about Father Christmas," he said.

She must have told him that weeks earlier. He'd put off talking to me—because we'd never been close, and now we were growing further apart. "I don't know why she couldn't tell you," he said.

But he wasn't telling me either. He was looking at me as if I were a stranger he had to chat to. I felt uneasy, unsure now that I wanted to hear what he had to say. A man was approaching the shop. I stood up, hoping he'd interrupt.

He did, and I served him. Then, to delay my father's revelation, I adjusted stacks of tins. My father stared at me in disgust. "If you don't watch out you'll be as bad as your mother."

I found the idea of being like my mother strange, indefinably disturbing. But he wouldn't let me be like him, wouldn't let me near. All right, I'd be brave, I'd listen to what he had to say. But he said, "Oh, it's not worth me trying to tell you. You'll find out."

He meant I must find out for myself that Father Christmas was a childish fantasy. He didn't mean he wanted the thing from the chimney to come for me, the disgust in his eyes didn't mean that, it didn't. He meant that I had to behave like a man.

And I could. I'd show him. The chimney was silent. I needn't worry until Christmas Eve. Nor then. There was nothing to come out.

One evening as I walked home I saw Dr. Flynn in his front room. He was standing before a mirror, gazing at his red fur-trimmed hooded suit; he stooped to pick up his beard. My mother told me that he was going to act Father Christmas at the children's hospital. She seemed on the whole glad that I'd seen. So was I: it proved the pretense was only for children.

Except that the glimpse reminded me how near Christmas was. As the nights closed on the days, and the days rushed by—the end-of-term party, the turkey, decorations in the house—I grew tense, trying to prepare myself. For what? For nothing, nothing at all. Well, I would know soon—for suddenly it was Christmas Eve.

I was busy all day. I washed up as my mother prepared Christmas dinner. I brought her ingredients, and hurried to buy some she'd used up. I stuck the day's cards to tapes above the mantelpiece. I carried home a tinsel tree which nobody had bought. But being busy only made the day move faster. Before I knew it the windows were full of night.

Christmas Eve. Well, it didn't worry me. I was too old for that sort of thing. The tinsel tree rustled when anyone passed it, light rolled in tinsel globes, streamers flinched back when doors opened. Swinging restlessly on tapes above the mantelpiece, I saw half a dozen red-cheeked, smiling bearded faces.

The night piled against the windows. I chattered to my mother about her shouting father, her elder sisters, the time her sisters had locked her in a cellar. My father grunted occasionally—even when I'd run out of subjects to discuss with my mother, and tried to talk to him about the shop. At least he hadn't noticed how late I was staying up. But he had. "It's about time everyone was in bed," he said with a kind of suppressed fury.

"Can I have some more coal?" My mother would never let me have a coal scuttle in the bedroom—she didn't want me going near the fire. "To put on now," I said. Surely she must say yes. "It'll be cold in the morning," I said.

"Yes, you take some. You don't want to be cold when you're looking at what Father—at your presents."

I hurried upstairs with the scuttle. Over its clatter I heard my father say, "Are you still at that? Can't you let him grow up?"

I almost emptied the scuttle into the fire, which rose roaring and crackling. My father's voice was an angry mumble, seeping through the floor. When I carried the scuttle down my mother's eyes were red, my father looked furiously determined. I'd always found their arguments frightening; I was glad to hurry to my room.

It seemed welcoming. The fire was bright within the mesh. I heard my mother come upstairs. That was comforting too: she was nearer now. I heard my father go next door—to wish the doctor Happy Christmas, I supposed. I didn't mind the reminder. There was nothing of Christmas Eve in my room, except the pillowcase on the floor at the foot of the bed. I pushed it aside with one foot, the better to ignore it.

I slid into bed. My father came upstairs; I heard further mumblings of argument through the bedroom wall. At last they stopped, and I tried to relax. I lay, glad of the silence.

A wind was rushing the house. It puffed down the chimney; smoke trickled through the fireguard. Now the wind was breathing brokenly. It was only the wind. It didn't bother me.

Perhaps I'd put too much coal on the fire. The room was hot; I was sweating. I felt almost feverish. The huge mesh flicked over the wall repeatedly, nervously, like a rapid net. Within the mirror the dimmer room danced.

Suddenly I was a little afraid. Not that something would come out of the chimney, that was stupid: afraid that my feelings of fever would make me delirious again. It seemed years since I'd been disturbed by the sight of the room in the mirror, but I was disturbed now. There was something wrong with that dim jerking room.

The wind breathed. Only the wind, I couldn't hear it changing. A fat billow of smoke squeezed through the mesh. The room seemed more oppressive now, and smelled of smoke. It didn't smell entirely like coal smoke, but I couldn't tell what else was burning. I didn't want to get up to find out.

I must lie still. Otherwise I'd be writhing about trying to clutch at sleep, as I had the second night of my fever, and sometimes in summer. I must sleep before the room grew too hot. I must keep my eyes shut. I mustn't be distracted by the faint trickling of soot, nor the panting of the wind, nor the shadows and orange light that snatched at my eyes through my eyelids.

I woke in darkness. The fire had gone out. No, it was still there when I opened my eyes: subdued orange crawled on embers, a few weak flames leaped repetitively. The room was moving more slowly now. The dim room in the mirror, the face peering out at me, jerked faintly, as if almost dead.

I couldn't look at that. I slid farther down the bed, dragging the pillow into my nest. I was too hot, but at least beneath the sheets I felt safe. I began to relax. Then I realized what I'd seen. The light had been dim, but I was almost sure the fireguard was standing away from the hearth.

I must have mistaken that, in the dim light. I wasn't feverish, I couldn't have sleepwalked again. There was no need for me to look, I was comfortable. But I was beginning to admit that I had better look when I heard the slithering in the chimney.

Something large was coming down. A fall of soot: I could hear the scattering pats of soot in the grate, thrown down by the harsh halting wind. But the wind was emerging from the fireplace, into the room. It was above me, panting through its obstructed throat.

I lay staring up at the mask of my sheets. I trembled from holding myself immobile. My held breath filled me painfully as lumps of rock. I had only to lie there until whatever was above me went away. I couldn't touch me.

The clogged breath bent nearer; I could hear its dry rattling. Then something began to fumble at the sheets over my face. It plucked feebly at them, trying to grasp them, as if it had hardly anything to grasp with. My own hands clutched at the sheets from within, but couldn't hold them down entirely. The sheets were being tugged from me, a fraction at a time. Soon I would be face to face with my visitor.

I was lying there with my eyes squeezed tight when it let go of the sheets and went away. My throbbing lungs had forced me to take shallow breaths; now I breathed silently open-mouthed, though that filled my mouth with fluff. The tolling of my ears subsided, and I realized the thing had not returned to the chimney. It was still in the room.

I couldn't hear its breathing; it couldn't be near me. Only that thought allowed me to look—that, and the desperate hope that I might escape, since it moved so slowly. I peeled the sheets down from my face slowly, stealthily, until my eyes were bare. My heartbeats shook me. In the sluggishly shifting light I saw a figure at the foot of the bed.

Its red costume was thickly furred with soot. It had its back to me; its breathing was muffled by the hood. What shocked me most was its size. It occurred to me, somewhere amid my engulfing terror, that burning shrivels things. The figure stood in the mirror as well, in the dim twitching room. A face peered out of the hood in the mirror, like a charred turnip carved with a rigid grin.

The stunted figure was still moving painfully. It edged round the foot of the bed and stooped to my pillowcase. I saw it draw the pillowcase up over itself and sink down. As it sank its hood fell back, and I saw the charred turnip roll about in the hood, as if there was almost nothing left to support it.

I should have had to pass the pillowcase to reach the door. I couldn't move. The room seemed enormous, and was growing darker; my parents were far away. At last I managed to drag the sheets over my face, and pulled the pillow, like muffs, around my ears.

I had lain sleeplessly for hours when I heard movement at the foot of the bed. The thing had got out of its sack again. It was coming toward me. It was tugging at the sheets, more strongly now. Before I could catch hold of the sheets I glimpsed a red fur-trimmed sleeve, and was screaming.

"Let go, will you," my father said irritably. "Good God, it's only me."

He was wearing Dr. Flynn's disguise, which flapped about him—the jacket, at least; his pajama cuffs peeked beneath it. I stopped screaming and began to giggle hysterically. I think he would have struck me, but my mother ran in. "It's all right. All right," she reassured me, and explained to him, "It's the shock."

He was making angrily for the door when she said, "Oh, don't go yet, Albert. Stay while he opens his presents," and, lifting the bulging pillowcase from the floor, dumped it beside me.

I couldn't push it away, I couldn't let her see my terror. I made myself pull out my presents into the daylight, books, sweets, ballpoints; as I groped deeper I wondered whether the charred face would crumble when I touched it. Sweat pricked my hands; they shook with horror—they could, because my mother couldn't see them.

The pillowcase contained nothing but presents and a pinch of soot. When I was sure it was empty I slumped against the headboard, panting. "He's tired," my mother said, in defense of my ingratitude. "He was up very late last night."

Later I managed an accident, dropping the pillowcase on

the fire downstairs. I managed to eat Christmas dinner, and to go to bed that night. I lay awake, even though I was sure nothing would come out of the chimney now. Later I realized why my father had come to my room in the morning dressed like that; he'd intended me to catch him, to cure me of the pretense. But it was many years before I enjoyed Christmas very much.

When I left school I went to work in libraries. Ten years later I married. My wife and I crossed town weekly to visit my parents. My mother chattered, my father was taciturn. I don't think he ever quite forgave me for laughing at him.

One winter night our telephone rang. I answered it, hoping it wasn't the police. My library was then suffering from robberies. All I wanted was to sit before the fire and imagine the glittering cold outside. But it was Dr. Flynn.

"Your parents' house is on fire," he told me. "Your father's trapped in there. Your mother needs you."

They'd had a friend to stay. My mother had lit the fire in the guest room, my old bedroom. A spark had eluded the fireguard; the carpet had caught fire. Impatient for the fire engine, my father had run back into the house to put the fire out, but had been overcome. All this I learned later. Now I drove coldly across town, toward the glow in the sky.

The glow was doused by the time I arrived. Smoke scrolled over the roof. But my mother had found a coal sack and was struggling still to run into the house, to beat out the fire; her friend and Dr. Flynn held her back. She dropped the sack and ran to me. "Oh, it's your father. It's Albert," she repeated through her weeping.

The firemen withdrew their hose. The ambulance stood winking. I saw the front door open, and a stretcher carried out. The path was wet and frosty. One stretcher-bearer slipped, and the contents of the stretcher spilled over the path.

I saw Dr. Flynn glance at my mother. Only the fear that she might turn caused him to act. He grabbed the sack and, running to the path, scooped up what lay scattered there. I saw the charred head roll on the lip of the sack before it dropped within. I had seen that already, years ago.

My mother came to live with us, but we could see she was

pining; my parents must have loved each other, in their way. She died a year later. Perhaps I killed them both. I know that what emerged from the chimney was in some sense my father. But surely that was a premonition. Surely my fear could never have reached out to make him die that way.

DEAN R. KOONTZ

A master of
spine-chilling terror!

With more than 3 million copies of his books in
Berkley print, Dean R. Koontz is one of today's
most popular horror writers. His chilling tales
catch you by the throat, grip the pit of your
stomach, and dare you to turn the page. The terror
is just beginning...

__	09217-8	Strangers	$4.50
__	09760-9	Whispers	$4.50
__	09864-8	Night Chills	$3.95
__	09501-0	Phantoms	$3.95
__	09502-9	Shattered	$3.50
__	09278-X	Darkfall	$3.95
__	09931-8	The Face of Fear	$3.50
__	09860-5	The Vision	$3.95

Prices may be slightly higher in Canada.